EXOM

THE YOUNG KING

C.C.Davison

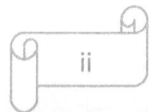

For my daughters

Contents

Contents

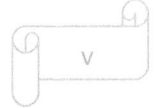

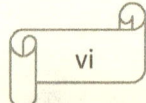

EXOM

THE YOUNG KING

PROLOGUE

Exom, a dense but isolated constellation within the galaxy. Comprising of ninety-six solar systems, Exom is surrounded by an extremely large, seemingly endless area of empty space, known simply as "The Void". Located in the Mid System, at the heart of Exom, is a very large planet called Aymyn. The native species of Aymyn, also called Aymyn, are the most predominant species throughout Exom. Human in appearance, their eyes have the most vibrant red iris. The Aymyn have spread out and colonised many planets in almost every system of Exom.

Exom is at war, and has been for a very long time, being invaded by an almost unstoppable species called the Skurj. An incredibly large, wingless, dragonesque type of creature that can survive in any environment, even open space. For the most part the Skurj seem completely indestructible. No one knew where the Skurj originated from, though there are a few theories, the most common one being from The Void itself. What is known is that the Skurj only seem to do one thing; travel from planet to planet, eating all organic life and regurgitating a blue-grey vile called "mazzie". A substance just as indestructible as the Skurj themselves, mazzie would slowly dissolve anything it encountered; rock, metal, even the core of the planet itself eventually.

While the Skurj have not reached the inner systems of Exom yet, they are slowly making their way through the outer rim systems, devouring all organic life, soon followed by the planets themselves. Exom's only hope of defeating the Skurj lies in the Zazar Corp. A military division under the command of the Royal Alliance, it comprises of a limited number of extremely skilled soldiers, almost all of whom are Morn. The Zazas are armed with the only weapon known to be able to pierce the Skurj's seemingly impenetrable skin, the Tription Flame.

EXOM

THE YOUNG KING

CHAPTER ONE

-------------------------- The Fall of Crom --------------------------

Sygra Steel, the strongest metal in all Exom, and of which many strengthened structures and tools are made from, is found only on the mining planet, Crom. Unfortunately, Crom is located in an outer rim system of Exom. Once protected by a Morn Zazar called Misharn, Crom became an unprotected planet when Misharn was killed while fighting in another Skurj battle on another protected planet alongside several other Zazars.

Due to the importance of Sygra Steel to Exom, the Royal Alliance petitioned the Free Zazars for one to select Crom to be their protectorate. Unfortunately, no other Zazar elected to select Crom. Before the Council could work on trying to change their minds, Crom was attacked by a small party of Skurj. Unable to send any Zazars to assist Crom, the Royal Alliance requested the assistance of the Troin Army, possibly the second most effective army in Exom but still unable to defeat the Skurj, to render assistance.

The Troin army, loyal to the Royal Alliance and the Troin Princess, Illyana, who serves on the Royal Alliance Council, immediately dispatched an armada of battle freighters. Under the Command of Commander Turrin, while staying in constant contact with the Royal Alliance Council via Holoprojection Communication, a technology used widely throughout Exom, the Troin fleet sped towards Crom.

Other than the large mining quarries, Crom is mostly a luscious green and nature filled planet. Large land masses of rolling hills and mountains.

A young Lygon, the native dwarven species of Crom, Fallon, has made his way to the top of a large hill in quite a hurry. As he looks down over the other side, the hillside stretches into a mountainside that lowers into a large quarry filled with industrial factories and mining equipment. Factories and mining equipment that ordinarily would be used to mine Sygra Steel. However, at this moment the workers are scurrying towards a reinforced bunker, those that are not already crammed inside, as the Crom military fight fiercely against three Skurj reeking death and devastation throughout the entire area.

Usually travelling in small numbers, for that is all that is really needed, three Skurj are currently tearing through buildings and structures in the Crom mine like they are made of paper. Seeking out and devouring the population.

Small makeshift buildings blown apart. Large machinery collapsing and smashing into the ground as the foundations are destroyed underneath. Not all of this a result of the Skurj's actions. Some, indeed, a lot, caused by the heavy artillery fire of the Crom army, with their large arsenal of land and air vehicles raining down heavily hundreds, maybe even more, missiles, lasers, and torpedos upon the Skurj. None of their weapons having any effect on the Skurj, however, inadvertently well and truly adding to the destruction and devastation that is taking place.

Multiple torpedoes making a direct impact and exploding on a single Skurj, barely shaking it, and leaving not so much as a scratch on the Skurj itself while completely decimating the area around it.

One Skurj leaps from the Flames of exploding missiles, completely unscathed, and launches itself at one of the airships hovering high above it. Before the airship can move out of the way, the Skurj is clung to the bottom of it, ripping and tearing the airship apart. The airship fires back with a constant barrage of laser fire from its hull mounted cannons, all of which is completely futile and ineffective as the Skurj continues to destroy the airship, sending it crashing into the middle of the warzone. The explosion levelling another nearby building.

Hundreds of Lygons have now huddled inside the bunker and have only just secured the large, reinforced doors. It's dark and silent, the walls and doors of the structure thick enough to block out the sounds of the active warzone just outside. That silence is short lived. There is a thunderous, earthshaking crash, as the bunker doors are torn apart like parchment and a single Skurj peers inside. The Lygons stare back in terror, but not for long, as the Skurj barges inside and devours each and every one of them.

Two Lygons race across the mine sight, trying to avoid all the explosions and, of course, the Skurj. They take shelter under a now destroyed piece of mining machinery. They look at each other, panting, and then look around wondering if it is safe to continue. They decide to take a chance. One of them steps out from under the mining machine, looks around, looks back at his friend and nods, right before a Skurj dives in and eats him.

His friend, shocked and terrified, places his hand over his own mouth to stop himself from screaming. It's no use. The Skurj looks over and sees him anyway, then dives under the mining machinery and eats him as well.

Another Lygon runs out in the mine holding a large laser rifle. He shoots frantically at the Skurj. Rapid continuous fire. The lasers bounce off the Skurj's body like a mirror, not leaving a scratch. The Skurj turns and looks at the Lygon as another Lygon jumps out to join him brandishing a large rocket launcher. He aims and fires the rocket directly into the face of the Skurj. The rocket explodes with an incredible force, the air sending the two Lygons flying back onto the ground. The Skurj, however, does not move. Just like the lasers, the rocket and explosion bounce right off it without leaving so much as a mark. The Skurj then pounces onto the two Lygons, tearing them apart before eating them.

A nearby land-based cannon fires a projectile into the air. As the projectile comes back down it breaks apart into many different missiles of different sizes, all guided and homing in on another single Skurj. Before it hits, the Skurj quickly darts away and the missiles impact with the ground creating even more explosions and destroying the area.

Multiple cascading exploding infernos ensue, desolating the area, flattening everything in their path. Everything except for the Skurj, which continue their rampage completely unaffected. The Skurj charge back and forth through the battlefield, attacking vehicles, devouring Lygons. Stopping only to regurgitate and forcefully expel mazzie into the air, showering down on everything and slowly dissolving whatever it touches.

In the distance, a castle stands partially built into the mountainside. Primitive but strong looking, and in a location that unfortunately is giving the occupants a great view of the unstoppable devastation that is occurring.

Fallon runs into the castle and straight to the throne room. Prince Shelk, the Prince of Crom, is seated on one of the smaller thrones that are placed at each side of a larger throne that overlooks the room. The main throne and other smaller throne remain empty. Standing beside the prince are several ambassadorial dressed advisory looking Lygons. Though the Prince and his advisors appear very worried, they are not running around in a panic throughout the throne room like many other Lygons are.

As Fallon runs up to the throne, he is immediately intercepted by another fellow Lygon, Musta. Musta grabs Fallon by the shoulders to have his entire attention. *"Zazars?"*, Musta asks, wanting to know if any Zazars are coming to protect them and their planet from this Skurj attack. Fallon looks back at Musta, shaking his head and looking devastated to be bringing such bad news. *"No Zazars are coming"*, Fallon replies.

Listening in, Prince Shelk's face changes from one of fear to despair. His despair sounding through his words as he turns and speaks to his advisors, *"We are now unprotected. We are alone"*.

Fallon anxiously turns to speak to the prince, *"What about the Troin?"*. The prince looks at Fallon, with the same look of despair, and can only shake his head. *"Too far away"*, the prince replies, his voice soft and breathy with hopelessness.

Another Lygon, Trim, runs into the throne room holding something in his hands wrapped in a cloth. He heads straight to a table beside the empty smaller throne and places the cloth wrapped item down on it. As the prince, Fallon and the Advisors watch on, Trim removes the cloth to reveal a metallic looking handle. A Tription Handle. A Zazar weapon used to summon the Tription Flame. Once belonging to their Zazar protector, Misharn, it was sent back to Crom following his death.

Trim picks up the Tription Handle and turns to address all his fellow Lygons in the throne room, whose attention he now has. *"Someone needs to make the Flame. Try!"*, Trim says to everyone as they stare back at him silently. An impossible request. It takes a certain mindset and focus to be able to summon the Flame. A skill that Zazar's are taught, and hardly any non-Zazars have mastered. Trim desperately looks around the room at all the other Lygons, hoping that at least one or more would volunteer. None do. They all just look helplessly back at him.

Trim holds out the Tription Handle to everyone, anyone, in the room. Still, no one steps forward, and all still looking full of fear and gloom. Fallon walks up and stands beside Trim. Trim turns to face him, curiously hopeful. His hope fades as he reads the expression on Fallon's face. *"We have no one trained to make the Flame"*, Fallon says. Trim desperately tries to hand the Tription Handle to Fallon as Fallon stands there, not taking it from him, only shaking his head and looking at him with helplessly sad eyes. Still, Trim continues to try to give the Tription Handle to Fallon. *"Try!"*, Trim demands.

More out of desperation, another Lygon runs up to Trim and takes the handle from him. Both Trim and Fallon, along with the rest of the Lygons in the room, including the prince, watch on with anticipation as this Lygon holds the handle, stares at it intensely and concentrates on it as hard as he can. His face squeezed up from the intensity of his concentration. Nothing happens. He relaxes and sighs, staring helplessly at the handle. He tries one more time, clearing his mind and focussing his thoughts. Still nothing happens. Feeling everyone's attention on him, he looks again very despondent at the Tription Handle. He stands there, silently, staring at the Tription Handle before handing it back to Trim. Trim takes it back, also feeling helpless and lost, not knowing what else to do.

The prince stands up from his throne and addresses the room. *"We fight how we always fight"*, the prince says, then looks over at the guards positioned around the throne room, *"Guards Ready!"*. The Guards, distinguishable from the rest of the Lygons with their dark burgundy body armour and dark blue capes, hold back and hide their fear and feeling of futility, and unsheathe their fighting sticks, knowing full well how ineffective they will be against the Skurj.

Unable to accept what he is seeing, Trim turns and looks disbelievingly at the prince and shakes his head. *"We can't fight without the Flame. Without the Zazar"*.

"Yet we must", the prince replies as he looks down despondently at Trim.

Unwilling to give up, Trim walks up and approaches another Lygon and tries to shove the Tription Handle upon him. *"Try"*, Trim once again demands. His effort is futile as his comrade does not attempt to accept it. Instead, he just looks back at Trim with a horrified and futile expression before turning away and running out of the throne room.

With no other option available, Trim now holds and squeezes the handle as he begins taking deep breaths and concentrates intensely. Again, nothing is happening. Trim does not give up and immediately tries again, refusing to let anything interrupt his focus and concentration. However, his focus and concentration are most certainly interrupted when the throne room doors burst open with a deafening crash and, standing in the doorway, is a single Skurj.

The throne room instantly goes silent, all the Lygons standing frozen just staring at the Skurj and too terrified for their voice boxes to emit a sound. The Skurj looks back at the terrified Lygons long enough for one of them to manage to scream. The scream soon added by more screams. Followed by panic and lots of chaotic aimless running.

Without any hesitation, the Skurj charges into the room, lunging at the nearest Lygon and devouring him instantly. All the other Lygons, including the prince and his advisors, try in vain to run away from the Skurj as the Skurj zips around the room at a blurring speed, biting down and swallowing each and every last one.

From outside the castle, the final Lygon screams can be heard and eventually fade to silence. In fact, everything is silent, including the mining site. There are no more explosions. No more gun or laser fire.

EXOM - THE YOUNG KING

No sounds of any people or airships. This is because there aren't any more. There is no one left. No army, no workers. The Skurj battle on Crom is over, and the Lygons have lost.

A single Lygon runs out from the castle, making it only a small distance before, out of nowhere, a Skurj jumps on him and eats him. The Skurj looks around, stands up on its back legs and then expels mazzie into the air. The mazzie flies up high, fans out and sprinkles back down to the surface. Beyond the Planet's atmosphere, looking back at the planet from space, Crom looks the same as it always has. From space you would never know that the Skurj were there. Not now anyway. In time there will be no organic life on the planet, consumed by the Skurj. Eventually there will be no planet, dissolved by the mazzie.

EXOM

THE YOUNG KING

CHAPTER TWO

The Aymyn are a very traditional race of people. So traditional, in fact, that it could be said that it has stunted their development over the millennia, though the Aymyn see it very differently. To put it simply, the Aymyn don't believe in change. Not that they don't believe that changes can occur, they just don't believe that change is good. They do concede, however reluctantly in most cases, that some change, when outside of their control, may have been necessary. And yes, all that is putting it simply.

The Aymyn's underlying tradition, religion, philosophy, and entire way of life, comes from a confirmed actuality named by the Aymyn as "Signs". An essence filling an individual Aymyn and shaping them into the person they are. The original and most powerful Sign, called "Sorell", sometimes referred to as "The Spark" or "Lightning Sign", created from it two more Signs, being "Light" and "Dark". From these two Signs, four more Signs were born, named by the Aymyn as "Parandrae", "Arandae", "Parkendal", and "Wendral". It is these last four Signs, known as the "Outer Signs", or "Main Signs" that contain the essence available to the Aymyn. An Aymyn can only contain the essence of one of these signs, and it is not something that they get to choose. The Sign will clearly present itself in the nature and personality of the individual Aymyn.

The Aymyn describe the Signs as follows; ***Parandrae, "the sign of the ground and which holds us together". Arandae, "the sign of*** *the Air and which gives us wings". Parkendal, "the Flame that gives us passion". And Wendral, "the sign of the calm and refreshing spring which joins and is friendly to all".*

An Aymyn of the Parandrae Sign will be someone who, for the most part, is a very grounded and accepting individual. They tend to make very good Leaders, Teachers, and Nurturers.

An Aymyn of the Arandae Sign is, by contrast, almost the complete opposite. Arandae Signs tend to be very fast paced, adventurous, impulsive and generally hard to tie down.

An Aymyn of the Parkendal Sign can be described as a little "hot headed", but in general are very passionate and determined in what they do. They are rarely impulsive, and if anything, could be described as stubborn.

An Aymyn of the Wendral Sign will always be a standout. They tend to be the friendliest, compassionate, empathetic, happy peacekeepers. It is rare that you will come across a Wendral Sign that you do not like. They will make you like them.

These four signs make up almost the entire Aymyn population. It is incredibly rare that you will come across an Aymyn who is not one of these signs.

The two signs, Light and Dark, known as the "Inner Signs" or "Power Signs", and for good reason, also have very strong properties and traits. And because it was these two signs that created the four outer signs, all Aymyn will have traits of Light and Dark, though to varying degrees, known as persuasions.

The Aymyn describe these two Signs as; *Light, "A power sign of constancy and security in what we know". And Dark, "The opposing power sign of Change and uncertainty".* Those with a strong persuasion towards the Light, which is the traditional and only accepted Aymyn way, will have a strong nature of not wanting things to change. Amongst other things, they will be opposed to technological advances outside of the Aymyn allowed innovations.

Those of a Dark persuasion are all for change, discovery, invention, and advancement. However, since Aymyn's strong underlying principle leans entirely towards the "Light", any "Dark" way of thinking was quickly shunned and outlawed. The principal and belief in the "Light" is so strong for the Aymyn that those that had any persuasion towards the "Dark", and questioning or challenging the status quo, were not only despised but also feared. You might think that those who had a persuasion towards the Dark would keep it a secret. However, just like the four main signs, an individual could not control their power sign persuasions any more than they could control their main sign's traits. Again, to put simply, an Aymyn's persuasion was just as strong a part of their personality as their main sign.

In the early days of Aymyn history, at least once in every generation or two, there would be someone born who was not one of the four Main Signs. A pure Light Sign Aymyn. An individual, whole and purely the sign of light, deeply committed to their core to stamp out and stop anything that brings about change. With their connection to this Power Sign, they were far superior in intelligence to those of the regular four signs, with the strongest of this sign even possessing the ability to see the signs of others, it literally appearing to them as a kind of aura surrounding the individual.

Due to Aymyn's strong Light foundation, those of a Pure Light Sign became leaders in the community. Eventually the Council of Light was formed to govern and lead the Aymyn people. The ruling monarch of Aymyn was also given the additional title of Guardian of the Light, and it was their responsibility to make decisions that favoured the Light principles.

Being that there has been proof of the existence of Pure Light Signs, it is also thought by many that there must also be those born who are pure Dark, though none have ever been seen. It is believed that a pure Dark sign would be equally as powerful and intelligent as those pure of Light. Perhaps even more so. However, given Aymyn's stand on the Dark Sign, it is speculated that if a Pure Dark sign had existed, or even still exists, that they would never disclose themselves to avoid their persecution and certain execution.

With all Signs, the strength of the traits that came with them were not always the same. Aymyns of the Arandae Sign would all be very active and adventurous, but not all equally so. Some would be a lot flightier, referred to as "Airy", while others you may need to look into them a bit harder to see those traits. The same was true with those of a Pure Power Sign. All Pure Light Aymyn were extremely intelligent, but not necessarily equally so. Likewise, only the strongest possessed the ability to see the Signs in others.

Which brings us, finally, to the extremely rare individuals who were not any of the four Main Signs and also neither of the Power Signs. They were not Parandrae, Arandae, Parkendal, Wendral, Light or Dark. These incredibly rare individuals, who only appeared once or twice in a lifetime during the early days of Aymyn, and then never again, were born of the Purest and Most Powerful Sign, the Sign that started it all. Sorell. The Spark or Lightning Sign.

Sorell, *"The sign of the seer. The most powerful sign of them all. Neither Light nor Dark, but with the traits and abilities of both, amplified".*

Those born of the Pure Sorell Sign had no favouritism towards either Light or Dark. They possessed superior intelligence and the ability to see the Signs in others. Theorone, a young Aymyn man living on Aymyn 20,000 years ago and considered the Strongest Lightning Sign to have ever existed, also the last Lightning Sign to have ever existed, also possessed the ability to see the future.

The Pure Sorell, or Lightning Sign Aymyn were called "Seers" and were always very respected in the community, even treated like celebrities. Since all Seers could see the individual auras around all Aymyn, so clearly able to identify their sign, amongst other things, it became the Seers duty to identify and announce to the community the Signs of others. This took place at a "Revealing Ceremony" during the Aymyn's adolescence, a very prestigious and special occasion. As almost every other Aymyn, except for the occasional Pure Light Sign, could not see the Sign Aura that surrounded each individual, most could only surmise and speculate as to their sign, or the sign of others, based on character and personality traits. It was not until an Aymyn's

Revealing Ceremony that their Sign would be officially disclosed and announced to them, as well as the community by a Seer.

The Seers, though very respected, were not privileged members of Aymyn society. They lived like regular Aymyn and were bound to the same strict Aymyn laws. Though they themselves were neutral when it came to Light and Dark persuasions, they were not allowed to encourage Dark thinking. Nor were they, no matter how intelligent they were or how much they could see and know, allowed to be involved with any developments outside of the allowed innovations.

The Aymyn's allowed innovations, called "The Golden Tiers", originally consisted of Agriculture, Medicine, and Defence. Though never progressing all that far with medicine and defence, the Aymyn reached such a level with their development of agriculture that they were able to terraform most landscapes, no matter how barren, into fertile farmland. This came in handy eons later when the Aymyn started to colonise other planets, after being forced to accept the technology of space and interstellar travel by a species called the Pizians during "The Assembly", a time when all intelligent life in Exom was united. Already being Masters of Agriculture and Terraforming, after the Assembly the Aymyn changed the Golden Tier of Agriculture to Trade instead.

------------------------------ The Pizians ------------------------------

The Pizians are the oldest and most advanced race in Exom. Not a very social or active species, interested only in research, at first glance they appear almost humanoid. The top half of them has a head, torso, and arms. However, the bottom half is that of an upright slug with millions of tiny, almost invisible hair-like follicles at the base of their tail. These follicles enable them to move around freely, and relatively quickly, while giving them the appearance of hovering above the ground.

The Pizians brought about "The Assembly" to Exom, the name given to the unifying of all planets with intelligent life. Sharing with these planets the technology to develop further as well as interstellar travel. However, their motives were not entirely selfless. The Pizian's, aware of the Skurj invasion of Exom, needed allies, resources, and above all new innovative ideas with which to try and fight them.

Even with the Pizian's advanced technology, they could not develop any kind of weapon that could defeat the Skurj. In fact, they could not even develop anything that could harm the Skurj in any way.

-------------------------------- The Troin --------------------------------

One more noticeable race throughout Exom is the Troin. Originally Aymyn, they left Aymyn, colonising the planet Liass, and called themselves Liassians. Over the centuries their biology began to change, and no one knew why. It could have been through the centuries of being exposed to something within the planet of Liass, or even possibly the Liassian's main food source, a plant that grew abundantly all throughout the planet. However, to this day it still remains a mystery as to what changed them.

The changes that happened to their biology were only on the inside of their bodies, not the outside, and not in a good way. It was like a disease. They all started to get sick, with the main symptom being a burning fever that affected both mind and body, eventually burning so hot that it literally burnt the inflicted Liassian up and killed them.

Though the Aymyn prided themselves on their medical knowledge, it being one of their Golden Tiers, no cure for the disease that plagued the inhabitants of Liass was ever found. Eventually a device known as a Tal, a simple bracelet filled with trillions of nanoparticles that extended into a lattice style armband when placed on the Liassian, was developed that kept the disease under control. The Tal was never a cure. The device only worked on the Liassians and no other Aymyn. The nanoparticles regulated the Liasian's body and stopped them from burning up. With the Liassian's biological change, they also quickly learnt to mentally control and use the nanoparticles within the Tal to do other things other than just regulate their bodies. They could also use the nanoparticles to create clothing over their bodies, even armour and weaponry. Though the Tal minimized the effects of the fever, it did not rid the Liassians of it completely. The Liassians, who had now changed their name to Troin, still ran quite hot. They were the perfect partner to cuddle up to on a cold night, but in general, because of this heat that their bodies generated, they wore very little in the way of clothing. Usually just enough to provide the barest of modesty and hardly much else. The Troin being a very confident race of people, also one of the effects the Tal had over the fever, had no issue with wearing very little in public and it soon became customary.

---------------------------------- **Assistance** ----------------------------------

Deeper in space, far beyond Crom, even beyond Crom's solar system, in an empty region of space with no other planets or asteroids nearby, four very large Troin battle freighters sit motionless in formation. Colloquially called "Starships", not because they travel amongst the stars, but rather due to their shape, resembling a kind of six-pointed star. Three points, larger than the remaining three that are in between these larger points, contain very powerful propulsion engines which enable the Starships to easily manoeuvre and change direction without the need to turn around. One engine would be powerful enough to move the Starships, however, all three are required to operate the Starship effectively.

These four Troin Starships, part of the Troin Armada, are on a rescue mission to Crom. A rescue mission that they are yet to discover that they are too late for. Their mission hindered by an unknown saboteur who has been shooting at them, as well as systematically destroying the Navigation and Detection Satellites (NADS) necessary for them to be able to plot a course safely to Crom.

In the distance a smaller Troin vessel, smaller only by comparison as the Starships are enormous, speeds towards them. It's flightpath seeming unsteady, as though whoever is flying the vessel does not have complete control over it.

Standing on the bridge of the leading Starship is Commander Turrin. A fully decorated and highly respected officer of the Troin Army. He is dressed in only what appears to be a simple grey singlet, shorts, and shoes, as too are the rest of his crew. Their minimal clothing created from the nanoparticles in their Tals, and quite normal attire for the Troin Army considering they are, after all, Troin.

A holoprojector is projecting an energy field that appears like a large pool of water hovering in the air above a small, fixed communications table at the front of the bridge. Inside this rippling pool of energy, the live streaming image of the Troin Princess, Princess Illyana, and fellow Royal Alliance Council member, Prince Niyan, can be clearly seen. They are looking at and speaking to Commander Turrin through a similar device back at the Royal Alliance Council Chambers on Aymyn.

"We are no closer to Crom, Your Highnesses", Commander Turrin says. *"We have taken enemy fire"*.

"Drones, Commander?", the Troin Princess asks, referring to the Jaimin Drone's, a large faction of bread, controlled and full body armoured, modified Aymyn. The Drone Army is very rampant throughout Exom, having seized control of many planets and outposts. Called Drones, because the individual Aymyn inside these thin but strong suits of armour were artificially bread for this very purpose. Mindless soldiers, their skeletal structure synthetically strengthened during their development process and their every thought and action controlled by a computer chip placed in the back of their head upon their "birth", without which they would not survive. Easily identifiable by their jet-black skin, gold eyes, bald heads and gold operation scarring all over their bodies. The Drones are strong and large in numbers, but not the most effective battle soldiers, due to their rudimentary battle programming.

Commander Turrin has his doubts. *"Appears too random and scattered to be the Drone Army, Your Highness"*, Turrin replies. *"Sharlon perhaps. May even be Dakari raiders in this system. We just don't know and have not caught sight of them. It's nothing we can't handle, and whoever or whatever it was appears to have gone now. But now someone is taking out the NADS in the area and we are flying blind"*. Turrin looks down at a display console built into the Communications Table and reads a brief update. *"Two more have just gone down while I am speaking to you"*.

Prince Niyan, a Trynian, a humanoid-ish amphibian race from the planet Trynan appears a little frustrated with Commander Turrin's report. Not frustrated at Turrin himself, but rather the lack of available information. *"What can you tell us, Commander?"*, Niyan asks.

"I am not able to confirm anything yet", Turrin replies. *"We can't see anything. I have sent my Vice out in a scout ship ahead of us as an escort before any of this happened, and we have not heard back from him either. Starting to fear the worst. If there is an enemy out there systematically taking out the NADS, then they are using some sort of technology that we are not equipped to detect because nothing other than our own ships are showing up on our scans".*

Niyan stares back at Turrin with a look of intriguing concern. *"Shadow Tech?"*, Niyan asks. An alarming thought. Shadow Tech is an outlawed cloaking technology, rendering small objects like doors, entrances and even faces invisible to detection, and appearing "blacked out" to the naked eye. The only ones suspected of using Shadow Tech these days are the Sharlon, a very organised and secretive group of Anti-Alliance Rebels whose motives seems to be to bring Chaos to Exom. Under the command of a mysterious woman known only as "Dark", the Sharlon are responsible for obstructing many Zazar and Troin rescue missions to planets under attack by the Skurj. Through their interference, they have been responsible for the destruction of many planets and the deaths of billions of beings. To anyone's knowledge, Shadow Tech has never been used to conceal entire ships, so Commander Turrin has his doubts as to it being used in this situation, and just simply shrugs as a response to Niyan's question.

Lieutenant Bries, one of the flight crew seated at the monitoring station on the bridge and keeping a close eye on both the activity within and outside of the Starship, has been watching the small vessel flying unsteadily towards them. The Vessel is being piloted by the Commander Turrin's second in command, Vice Commander Ardok. Lieutenant Bries is now concerned with the erratic flight of Ardok's vessel, and calls out to Commander Turrin, interrupting his conversation with the Councillors.

EXOM - THE YOUNG KING

"Commander", Bries calls out. *"We now have the Vice's scout ship on radar. He's on approach"*. Turrin does not respond more than a slight sigh of relief and nods to Bries, acknowledging him. Bries turns in his chair to face Turrin, looking a little alarmed. *"He's coming in too fast"*, he adds.

Now also more than just a little concerned, Turrin moves away from the Communications table and rushes over to Lieutenant Bries's monitoring station. He looks past Bries and focusses his attention on the display on the monitoring station in front of him. He notices the Vice Commanders erratic flying, and the speed at which he is approaching them, and then states out loud what everyone is now thinking, *"He's in trouble"*.

Turrin looks back at the communications table, still clearly seeing the Councillors in the energy projection field. *"Your Highnesses, got to cut this short"*. Not knowing or understanding what the situation is, but realising that something urgently needs the Commander's attention, both Princess Illyana and Prince Niyan respond back with a nod. *"Understood, Commander"*, Princess Illyana replies just before the holographic projector switches off and the energy field hovering over the communications table disappears. Turrin turns his attention again back to Lieutenant Bries's monitoring station. *"Have we got the Vice?"*, Turrin asks. Bries flicks through screens on his workstation display, then presses a couple of the buttons on the same display screen. *"Putting him through now, sir"*, Bries replies.

The holographic projector activates again, creating a new energy field hovering over the communications table. Turrin quickly walks over to it as the live streaming image of Vice Commander Ardok standing at the helm of his ship appears within the energy field. Ardok is dressed the same as the rest of the crew, simple shorts and singlet created from his Tal. All around Ardok, panels and consoles are sparking from small internal explosions. The sounds of the explosions and sparks can be clearly heard through the projection. Smoke is also starting to surround Ardok as he is seen still struggling to control his ship. His attention is not on the holographic energy field also created inside his bridge and hovering over a similar communications table to that in the Troin

Starship, though he is aware that it's there. Instead, he is concentrating on trying to fly his ship, while also stomping out small fires with his fist as they explode around him.

He jumps out of his seat, hurdles over a workstation behind him and opens a panel on one of the walls. Inside the panel, all the wires and components are on fire. He reaches in, pulls a cord and the inside of the panel floods with a kind of grey foam, smothering out the fire as he pulls his arm back out. He waves his arm and wipes off the excess foam that got on his arm, then runs over to his communications table and looks back at Turrin. *"Commander"*, he says, acknowledging Turrin's projected communication. He then quickly looks away at another panel on the wall that has just blown open, revealing another fire inside that as well. Again, he reaches in, but is unable to reach the cord as the fire burns his arm. He pulls his arm back in pain.

Then while still watching the fire inside the panel, a stream of nanoparticles, the same colour as his Tal, flow out of his Tal and cover his hand and arm, solidifying into a Troin armour glove and sleeve. Ardok reaches back inside the panel, pulls the cord releasing the foam, then kicks the panel closed with his foot. He runs back to the projected energy field, as his Troin armoured glove and sleeve reverts into nanoparticles and flows back into his Tal. He looks back at Turrin, smiling awkwardly.

"You're coming in too fast", Turrin says to him calmly. Ardok nods back as a small panel cover on the communications table flies off almost hitting him. *"In trouble here, Commander"*, Ardok replies.

"I can see that", Turrin says as he studies what is going on in the background behind and around Ardok. *"Can you slow it down?"*, he asks Ardok as he looks back at him. Ardok jumps back over another workstation and takes a seat back at the helm controls. He activates a screen on his panel and slides a slide switch displayed on that screen. *"Trying to"*, Ardok replies. Nothing changes. The ship's speed does not decrease. Another explosion, this time at the helm controls in front of Ardok, blowing out his control panel and display. Ardok quickly sits back in his seat and throws his arms back to avoid being hit by the explosion. He then reaches down and starts patting out the fires and

sparks on the control panel. The display screen is all burnt out. The helm control is now dead. Ardok slams his fist on the control panel, in a vain attempt to make it work again. Of course, it has no affect at fixing it. *"Helm controls gone"*, Ardok yells out. He sits back again in his chair and shrugs as he takes a deep breath, realising that he now has absolutely no control over his ship. He leaps out of his chair, back over the workstation behind him and rests his hands on the communications table. *"Sorry Commander"*, he says to Turrin again through the projection field. *"This is now a rescue call"*.

Turrin quickly walks away from the communications table and approaches two of his crewmen who are seated at another workstation along the wall of the bridge. *"Evacuate your ship"*, he yells back at Ardok. *"We'll pick you up"*, Turrin adds as he places his hands on the shoulders of his two crewmen. *"Arm up for coldvac"*, he tells them. "Coldvac", short for "Cold Vacuum" and a term used when meaning someone is about to take a spacewalk, exiting the ship and entering open space in only a protected spacesuit.

The two crewmen immediately stand up, walk away from their workstation and head towards the main door to the bridge. As they walk, a stream of nanoparticles pours out of their Tals and starts to cover the crewmen's entire body. The nanoparticles instantly solidify along the way to form a full Troin Space Suit, complete with helmet, breathing apparatus and small jets on the underside of their forearms. The process happens very quickly and is completed before they reach the main doors to the bridge.

As Ardok's ship now speeds out of control towards the area where the Troin Starships sit still motionless, Ardok leaves the bridge and runs towards an emergency escaped hatch located off one of the ships corridors. He stops at the doorway to the hatch and looks out through the window to the inside of the escape hatch. He presses a console near the hatch door and the inner door to the hatch opens. He quickly steps inside and presses a console on the other side of the door to close the door again. The console sparks and then blows up in front of him as he looks on. Now, not at all surprised, he just shrugs, then like the Troin crewmen on the battle freighter, nanoparticles stream out of his

Tal, covering his entire body, and form a Troin Space Suit identical to the ones formed on the other crewmen. He turns and presses a console located next to the escape hatch's outer door. The door does not open, detecting that the inner door is still open. He presses it again. Still nothing. He looks back at the inner door and realises that this is the issue. Not knowing how, or having any time to fix it, he looks back at the outer door console. He reaches out his hand and more nanoparticles start to build up on and in front of his hand, quickly forming a large Troin laser weapon. He blasts the outer door console, and the outer door immediately opens, sucking him and everything else nearby in the ship out the door and into open space.

Commander Turrin paces around the bridge, looking uneasy and peering over the shoulders of his crewmen at their various workstations, as he waits for a report on the Vice Commanders situation. He looks over at Lieutenant Bries, who is studying the images and information on his display, looking quite concerned. *"Is he clear?"*, Turrin asks him.

"The Vice is", Bries replies not looking up from his display. He then peers over at Turrin, still looking very concerned. *"We're not"*, he adds.

Alarmed by Bries's words and expression, Turrin moves quickly over to Bries's workstation and examines his display screen. *"What do you mean?"*, he asks, an urgent tone in his voice. Bries leans back in his chair, giving his Commander an easier view of his display. *"It looks like when the Vice opened the escape hatch, it has altered his ship's trajectory"*, Bries explains. *"It's inbound, on a collision course - with us"*.

Turrin quickly walks over to the helmsman piloting the Battle Freighter. *"Move us away"*, he commands. The helmsman did not need to be told twice. In fact, he did not need to be told once. He had already started firing up the Starships large main thruster engines the moment he heard the news from Lieutenant Bries. *"Already on it"*, the Helmsman replies.

The large main thruster engines light up within the large points of the leading Starship, which is still sitting idle in space with the rest of the armada, as the Vice Commander's ship hurtles out of control directly at it. The Starship starts to surge forward, but not quick or far enough to get completely out of the way. Ardok's ship collides with one of the Starship's larger points. The main thruster engine contained within that large point of the Starship, along with Ardok's ship are completely obliterated. The rest of the Starship remains intact.

Red lights flash all throughout the bridge and on several of the workstations of the Starship. Turrin is hurriedly walking around reading each and every display on every workstation throughout the bridge. Looking over the shoulders of his crew as they also intensely study their display consoles for information on the ship's condition. *"Damage report"*, he yells back at Lieutenant Bries.

"We've lost a main engine, Commander", Bries replies. *"No casualties, but we are not going anywhere for a while"*.

"Sealing breaches", another crewman yells out. Which gets Turrin's attention.

"Hull?", Turrin asks.

"Intact", the crewman replies. Turrin looks relieved. Things have definitely not gone to plan, but they could certainly have turned out a lot worse.

The two crewmen in their Tal created Coldvac suits glide through open space, using the small propulsion jets on their arms to reach Vice Commander Ardok. Ardok is hunched up in the foetal position while in an uncontrolled spin, caused by the sudden exit and suction from his scout ship. The Two crewmen reach him and each grab onto one of his arms as he spins past them. They get pulled along with him for a while but use their jets to stabilize and steady the Vice Commander and themselves.

Turrin continues to pace back and forth through the bridge, observing the display screens of his crew. His thoughts now return to his mission. A rescue mission that is becoming more and more difficult to complete. First was the issue with the satellites. Now, the lead Starship is out of action. He walks back to the communications table and leans on it for a moment as he considers the situation. He needs to update the Council on the latest situation. He looks over at Lieutenant Bries. *"Can we get the council back?"*, he asks.

"Trying now, Commander", Bries replies. The holoprojector activates once more, again creating a shimmering pool of energy floating above the communications table. As Turrin looks into it, waiting to see the image of the council members he was speaking to earlier, the image of another person starts to form instead. Queen Aura, the Queen of Aymyn and Head of the Royal Alliance Council.

Turrin is a little surprised, not expecting to see her, though it should not have been all that surprising. He is quickly put at ease by Queen Aura's calming disposition and soft expression. *"Is everything alright, Commander?"*, Aura asks calmly but with serious interest and concern in her eyes.

Turrin stops leaning on the communications table and stands up straight as he addresses Queen Aura. *"Your Highness, we've lost one of our main point engines"*, he tells her. *"The mission has ended for this particular ship, I'm afraid"*.

Queen Aura looks back understandingly at him, but also obviously saddened as she nods her head. *"Understandable, Commander"*, she replies, not asking any other questions of Turrin or what has led to this conclusion. *"As it happens"*, she adds, *"it seems that now your pursuit to Crom would be a futile one I'm afraid"*. Turrin at first looks shocked but then quickly disheartened by the Queen's statement. He knows what the Aymyn Queen means by this. Crom and the Lygons are now beyond rescuing. Another planet and its inhabitants lost to the Skurj. *"Oh"*, Turrin replies, as he looks away, taking this news and situation personally, feeling as though he, as Commander of this mission, is responsible for this failure.

Queen Aura does not know what Turrin is thinking but can see his dispirited demeanour. She is not sure what she can say to change the way he is feeling. There is nothing anyone can say. This is a very sad situation to say the least. She turns the topic to the Troin crew. *"Are your people safe?"*, she asks.

The Commander recomposes himself and looks back at Queen Aura. *"No casualties"*, he replies. As he says that, the door to the bridge opens and Vice Commander Ardok walks in, followed by his two Troin crew rescuers, all still wearing their Troin Coldvac suits. Ardok's helmet starts to dissolve back into nanoparticles and is absorbed back into the rest of his suit. He walks up and stands beside Turrin and looks at Queen Aura through the energy field. *"Almost had one"*, Ardok says to her. Queen Aura looks back at him and watches as the rest of his Coldvac suit breaks down into nanoparticles and flows back into his Tal, leaving him once again wearing just his shorts, singlet, and shoes.

Aura glances at the Vice Commander and looks as though she is about to smile, but refrains. *"Good to see that you made it back safely, Vice Commander"*, she says warmly. Ardok smiles back as Aura again turns her attention to Turrin. *"Commander"*, she says, *"when you have completed your repairs, are you able to make your way to Aymyn? We have another matter that we would appreciate the assistance of your crew with"*.

The Commander, as always, is happy to oblige Queen Aura, but does not want to understate the condition of the Starship. *"It will take more than a repair"*, he explains. *"Looks like an entire section Rebuild, which we are currently working on. When we are moving again our first stop will be to meet up with you on Aymyn"*.

This time Queen Aura does smile. *"I appreciate that, Commander"*, she says. She looks back at Ardok, still smiling, and nods. *"Vice Commander"*, she adds. Ardok smiles and nods politely back at her as the holoprojector switches off and the energy field once again disappears. Commander Turrin remains staring at where the holo-energy field had been hovering above the communications table, wondering what new task Queen Aura had for them. He looks at Ardok, who looks back at him, no longer holding his "happy to be alive" appearance, and now starting to display the same disappointment that Turrin and the rest of the crew are showing as they reflect on the outcome of their mission.

Turrin steps away from the communications table and turns to address his crewmen. *"How long till we are moving?"*, he asks them.

"The rebuild is underway, Commander", Lieutenant Bries answers as he continues to study the screens on his display console. *"Shouldn't be too long now".*

While remaining motionless in space, the lead Starship's point appears to be less damaged now than it was after the collision with Ardok's ship. A result of one of the more common technologies used throughout Exom. The kind of technology that repairs, or in this case rebuilds, entire structures autonomously. A different kind of technology than that used by the Troin in their Tals, though to the naked eye looks very similar. This building technology does not use nanoparticles but rather small, harmless energy fields that build, or rebuild, almost any structure using resources and raw materials stored in storage bays. The same technology can also be used to revert structures to their raw material and placed back into storage. A very handy development when it comes to repairing ships and large structures. However, surprisingly, is more commonly used throughout Exom for furnishing. Building furniture like beds, chairs and tables as needed, then deconstructing them again when not required. It makes moving very easy. Or if you just want to convert your bedroom into a clear dance floor for a short while and then back into a fully furnished bedroom once you have finished dancing.

In this case this technology is being used to rebuild and repair the Starship's damaged point and engine. Destroyed sections now become like new again. The process is not quite as fast as the nanoparticles in the Troin's Tals, but is still surprisingly fast, and already most of the point and engine has been rebuilt with amazing speed. Once rebuilt, the entire Troin Armada will set course for Aymyn.

EXOM

THE YOUNG KING

CHAPTER THREE

------------------------- The Royal Alliance -------------------------

During The Assembly, the populated planets were understandably filled with fear after hearing of the Skurj. The Kingdom of Aymyn created and homed an interplanetary council called "The Royal Alliance". The Royal Alliance was open to an individual representative from each planet which had a "One World Government". These representatives, usually, but not limited to, a member of that planet's royal family or ruling empire, could speak on behalf of their entire planet.

Incredibly strict rules were imposed on all members of the Royal Alliance Council to facilitate and allow the sharing of any and all information, no matter how confidential or controversial. These rules were also in place to safeguard and protect that information.

One of the most known rules was regarding relationships. Members of the Royal Alliance Council could only be in a romantic relationship with another member of the Royal Alliance Council. While there were not that many relationships within the Royal Alliance Council, most choosing to refrain instead, any breach of this rule was punishable by death. It was also due to these strict rules that not every planet that had a One World Government would elect to even join the Royal Alliance Council.

------------------------ Zazars and the Flame ------------------------

Hope came to Exom in the form of a kind of metal, that was found on the planet Garggsl, called "Tription". It was a rare and thought to be completely useless metal, especially by the native species of Garggsl, the Cribbles, a civilized race that resembled a man-sized humanoid-bat-like species. When the Tription Metal was melted and rolled a particular way, it developed an incredibly unique and powerful property. When held by a species that was not native to Garggsl, with the right kind of mental training, focus and concentration, the metal would emit a gaseous red Flame. A Flame that was later referred to as Tription Flame, or simply "The Flame". The Cribbles, being native to Garggsl, were not able to produce The Flame, however, so the discovery was quite accidental after the Assembly. The right mindset, focus and concentration to produce the Flame was also not easily obtained and often required gruelling, and even painful training. Though there were a very rare few to whom it came naturally.

What made the Flame so special was that it could penetrate and cut through almost anything - even the Skurj. Almost anything, as it could not cut through Tription Metal itself , nor could it harm the native species of Garggsl, who seemed to be completely immune to it.

The Tription Metal was forged into a cylindrical handle shape, with the inner core made of the rolled Tription Metal capable of producing the Flame and the outer surface coating made of regular Tription Metal. At one end of the "Tription Handle" the rolled Tription core was exposed allowing the Flame to come out of the handle.

A gaseous Flame, though a start, was not an effective weapon on its own and in this form. Through further mind control, the summoner of the Flame could also shape the Flame into a solid object, such as a sword or a whip. In this form the Tription Flame was a very valuable handheld weapon. Unfortunately, it could only be used as a handheld weapon. Once the summoner ceased contact with the Tription metal the Flame would disappear. So, for any kind of Tription Flame, Sword or Whip to be sustained, the summoner would need to remain in contact with the Tription Handle at all times.

EXOM - THE YOUNG KING

For the Tription Flame to be an effective weapon in battle, the Summoner would need to be an exceptional soldier. One possessing not only extraordinary combat ability, but also being able to maintain the necessary mindset required while fighting to keep the Flame burning and the Sword or Whip formed. As this was no small feat, in fact for most an impossible task, and being that the Tription Flame was the only weapon that Exom had with which to fight the Skurj, a project was undertaken on Aymyn to form an elite group of soldiers, highly trained and skilled enough to specifically engage the Skurj in battle as well as maintain the Flame while doing so. The project was called "The Team of Lords" and saw the formation of the "Zazar Corp". The members of the Zazar Corp, themselves called "Zazars", an old Aymyn word for "Lord", had to undergo an almost impossible selection test. The test involved simulated extreme combat scenarios without any kind of safety. The survival numbers of those tested was less than 1%. The successful test completion rate of those tested was even lower.

It seemed the only species that was capable of completing the Zazar Testing were the Morn. A towering and incredibly muscular species, well over three meters tall, with four arms, from the planet Morntra. Unfortunately, the survival and success rate for the Morn undergoing the Zazar Test was also extremely low.

The Morn did not look human, their appearance almost beastly, hairless with very strong barbaric features. They also did not tend to speak a lot and maintained an unsocial demeanour. Meeting one, or even looking at them, one could mistakenly think of them as primitive and not overly intelligent. One would be wrong. The Morn are actually very intelligent, at least as intelligent as any Aymyn. And when it came to battle, the Morn were an incredible force to be reckoned with.

Surprisingly, the Morn on Morntra did not have an actual army of their own. The population of Morntra, though quite low in numbers, lived very simply and peacefully. Their size and manner tended to keep other races away, which suited them fine. The only Morn combatants were those in the Zazar Corp.

Due to the extreme criteria and low success rate of the Zazar Test, the Zazar Corp was not a very large army. It was the requirement, expectation, and purpose of the Zazar Testing, for an individual Zazar to be able to fight off a Skurj attack on an individual planet on their own. Though this hardly ever happened as the Zazars would often fight together.

A special entitlement bestowed on all Zazars was the privilege of selecting an individual planet, and only one, to be called their "Protectorate". The Protectorate, also more commonly referred to as "A Protected Planet", formed part of the Zazar Initiative established by the Royal Alliance Council, the only body in command of the Zazar Corp. The Zazar Initiative and Protectorate, though had the appearance of a privilege, was actually the only way the Royal Alliance could control the limited resources and manpower of the Zazar Corp. Any Protected Planet, if subject to a Skurj attack, had the protection of the entire Zazar Corp. Not only the individual Zazar that selected that planet as their Protectorate would fight to defend it, but also any and all Zazars in the Zazar Corp would come to their aid.

Any planet that was not selected by a Zazar to be their Protectorate unfortunately was given no assistance by any Zazar. In fact, for a Zazar to do so, would result in their expulsion from the Corp, which in turn would revert their Protectorate back to an Unprotected Planet. Obviously, due to the low number of Zazars and the large number of inhabited planets in Exom, this left a greater number of planets without any protection from a Skurj attack. A pain and issue felt all throughout Exom.

Each Zazar was free to choose any planet to be their Protectorate. The choice was completely theirs and could be made at any time. Once made, however, it could never be changed. A Zazar and their protectorate were joined together until one was no more. If a Zazar fell in battle, then their planet would become unprotected, just like it happened with Crom when their Zazar protector, Misharn, was killed while assisting other Zazars fight the Skurj on another protected planet. Likewise, in the unlikely event that a protected planet was devoured by the Skurj, that planet's Zazar Protector was free to choose a new planet. Strangely, there were Zazars who had never selected a planet to be their protectorate. This was completely their right and, though they were very strongly encouraged, there was no obligation for them to do so. These Zazars were referred to as "Free Zazars" and would often find themselves hounded by representatives of unprotected planets to select their planet. It was confusing why this situation would exist in the first place. Some thought that perhaps the Free Zazars enjoyed the hounding and attention. However, being Morn, that seems very unlikely. The most likely reason is that a lot of Morn enjoyed the fight, not so much the cause, and placed very little importance on committing themselves to a particular planet.

Just as the Royal Alliance Council had strict rules surrounding it, so too did the Zazar Corp. One of those rules, established to keep the Zazars focussed entirely on the Corp and the war against the Skurj, was summed up in the Zazar motto; "Only and Always". What this meant was that once one becomes a Zazar, they are now and forever only a Zazar, forfeiting any other title or position they held previously, no matter what that title or position was. It had never really been an issue, as the Morn did not tend to hold any other title or position in Exom.

-------------------------------- **Zargah** ----------------------------------

On Aymyn, within the Citadel of Light, A huge spectacular looking building that is, amongst other things, home to the Royal Alliance Council and Church of Light, two very large double doors in one of the main corridors lead to a very Large Training Hall used by both Aymyn soldiers and guards alike. Due to its very large size, it is also used for practice and training for the Zazars. When in use, the building technology can construct any manor of equipment or obstacles as required. When not in use, it is just an extremely large room, reaching the equivalent of many stories high.

The doors to the training hall open and a single Aymyn guard walks inside. As he enters the hall, it appears to be mostly empty. He looks over towards the side and smiles awkwardly as he sees a familiar but very intimidating face. His expression changes as to one more of sadness as he prepares to deliver bad news. *"Lord Zargah"*, he says. *"Crom has fallen to the Skurj"*. As he stares at Lord Zargah, it becomes obvious that Zargah must be sitting down, as the guard is looking straight ahead. But not for long. The guards head slowly starts looking up, and up, and up, as Zargah stands up in front of him. The guard is now looking almost straight up just to maintain eye contact with Zargah. The expression on the guard's face is filled with a little awe, but mostly unease.

For good reason too. Zargah, the Zazar General and largest of the Morn, towers over the guard. The guard feels tiny in comparison to Zargah, which he most certainly is. Zargah is enormous. Approximately twice the height of the guard, and with such a powerfully built muscular body that has no equal. The entire size of the guard hardly even measures up to one of Zargah's arms – and Zargah, like all Morn, has four of them.

Zargah's muscular body slouches briefly after hearing the sad news, but then he stands up straight, stretches all four of his arms out and tenses. The unease that the guard was feeling before now turns to fear, and the expression on his face portrays this clearly. He knows that Zargah would never harm him. Indeed, as protector of Aymyn, and occasionally moonlighting as Queen Aura's personal bodyguard, Zargah's presence on Aymyn makes everyone feel very safe. A feeling that is hard to express when you are standing directly in front of him as his incredibly intimidating frame looms over you.

When not out fighting in the Skurj war, Zargah will spend most of his time either in the giant training hall or in the Zazar Meeting Hall only a few rooms away. On rare occasions you may find him sitting silently on his large bed in his simple, but equally large, quarters located within the Citadel. Despite coming from the planet Morntra, Zargah spends more time on, and seems to have a much stronger connection with Aymyn.

------------------------------- The Council -------------------------------

Aymyn was once a planet filled with large forests, beaches, and oceans. Now still filled with forests and oceans, the beaches have all been completely built over with super cities consisting of very beautiful and large, towering buildings. The airways are just as busy as the streets below with flying and hover vehicles of all shapes and sizes zipping around using the skyways as a highway. A very large rooftop aircraft hangar stands out dominantly on top of the equally spectacular looking Citadel of Light.

Several air vehicles, small space crafts and shuttles are parked neatly, but also randomly, on the rooftop hangar. Some belonging to members of the Royal Alliance Council.

The Council's main meeting chamber is located on the top floor of the Citadel and only a short walk from the rooftop hangar. At the far end of the meeting chamber is a large round table made from a kind of non-reflective metallic material. The tabletop is flat, however built into the table are a large number of touchpad consoles and displays that can rise out of the table should they be required. These touchpads are positioned within the table directly in front of the many chairs that surround the table. Each chair allocated to a specific Council Member.

The chairs themselves, built and disassembled using the building technology, are only ever present when needed for use by the individual council member that sits there. Appearing to rise out from the floor as required and then seemingly dissolve back into the floor when no longer in use. Three chairs, however, are never not present, even when not in use. Those being the chair belonging to the Head of the Royal Alliance Council, Queen Aura, and the chairs to either side of her. The reason for this is one that no one is aware of or have long since forgotten. The one to the Right of Queen Aura belongs to Councillor Lawn of Zenos, and the one to her left, King Steel of Eluud. Ironically, at the moment all three of these chairs are not occupied. However, there are many formed around the table that are.

Most of the Councillors look to be of Aymyn origin, though obviously not an Aymyn resident nor even call themselves Aymyn anymore. Now inhabiting and representing other planets, most can be easily distinguished by their clothing or other cultural traits which contain an originality specific to their planet. Amongst them is Councillor Orcom of Mesto, Regent Pfyne of Flayn, and Queen Klatanaria of Zo, all of whom are of Aymyn appearance and have their own individual planetary distinctions. Queen Klatanaria, for example, a slender young brunette lady, clothed in a very flattering white dress with long white sleeves, conceals herself behind a blue translucent mask covering the lower half of her face, as well as a hood and sort of half-length poncho made of the same blue translucent material. Regent Pfyne, another young lady, no older than a teenager, wears a long dark red dress covered by an equally long and heavy dark red cape complete with hood. Almost looking like some kind of priestess, only showing her arms, face and the bottom half of her long light brown hair that is not concealed under her hood, Regent Pfyne, though young, is wise well beyond her years. She is held in high regard within the council, and though she rarely speaks, when she does everyone stops to listen.

Just as she keeps herself heavily covered, her home Planet Flayn also shrouds itself in some mystery. It has a Royal Family, however, no one knows who they are. With the exception of the royal guards and court advisors who would take the secret to their grave before divulging it, Regent Pfyne being one of them, the identity of the Flayn royal family is just as much a mystery as that of the Sharlon leader, Dark.

Amongst the non-Aymyn looking species is King Prahm, a Lygon from the now Skurj ravaged planet Crom. Monarch Dllm, a grey skinned, four eyed, Crymnon from the planet Strark, who no one really knows what they look like slouched under their long black hooded cloak. And lastly, King Yord from the planet Dorcas, a dwarf like species, similar to the Lygon, only slightly larger in build and temper, and much better looking, in their opinion.

Also present are Prince Niyan and Princess Illyana, who were speaking to Commander Turrin via holoprojection earlier. Princes Illyana, being Troin, is the most underdressed member of the council. A very figure forming suit, created from her Tal, comprises of only one sleeve on her non-Tal wearing arm. Her shoulders and sides are covered, but very open in the middle, her outfit extends onto a very short bottom half that barely covers her hips. There are probably more Tal nanoparticles in her shin-high boots than the rest of her attire. Her short white-blond hair flowing freely and partially covering her face, her red, very friendly eyes look upon all those seated at the table.

EXOM - THE YOUNG KING

Currently absent from the council chamber at this time is;

Queen Aura, who will no doubt be attending very shortly.

King Steel, who is still back home on Eluud, a young Aymyn colony settled almost one hundred years ago.

Councillor Minnorse of Glintree, also of Aymyn descent, who is isolating with the rest of her planet "in a time of mourning" to commiserate the death of their planet's prince.

Regent Bassal of Tarlagon, which is a rare event, as he resides on Aymyn and nearly always attends council meetings, if for nothing more than to stir up trouble.

And finally, Councillor Lawn, a Spectre from Zenos.

The Spectres, an ascended, and what some would also call a parasitic race, that completely possesses the body of another species. The transference is absolute and permanent, only able to be done once with the spectre then literally becoming the species they have possessed. No matter what species an individual Spectre possesses, it will still be very obvious that it is a Spectre. The most obvious sign being the way they move. Before the Spectres ascended, their original body had no specific front, or back. They would move in all directions without turning around. When they possess a new body, this distinctive characteristic still stays with them. It is interesting to witness.

Councillor Lawn, who now possesses an Aymyn body, strangely is second in command of the Royal Alliance Council. Strangely, because he is not liked by, well, anyone. The Spectres come across as cold, heartless, strongly opinionated, and arrogant individuals. Though, not overly vocal, when they do speak, they speak their mind and will not be interrupted. A very intelligent race that often holds positions of leadership throughout Exom. Not all these positions are ethical. An example being Nadiri, another Spectre possessed Aymyn who is the current leader of the Jaimin Drones and definitely not a friend of the Royal Alliance.

There are several spaces around the table where it looks like chairs should be but aren't. One of them is just two spaces to the left of where Queen Aura would be sitting, to the immediate left of where King Steel would sit. The chair that would usually be in this location is where

Regent Bassal of Tarlagon, another of Aymyn origin, would be sitting. Regent Bassal has long been suspected of being a Sharlon spy. Though something he has never admitted, nor denied, however this may be to continue to stir up tension and trouble, and without any evidence to support it, this suspicion has never been proven.

The Sharlon, or "Sympathisers" as they are commonly referred to, are a movement that operates in the shadows. Utilizing spies and sabotage to weaken a planet's defence, or early warning detection, against the Skurj. Hardly anything is known about the Sharlon. Not where they are based, how many bases they have, or who are members of it other than, of course, Dark, and her righthand woman, Sabel. The Royal Alliance has captured the occasional spy here and there, but never enough to do any real damage to the organisation or uncover any more information about them.

They also do not really know the motives behind the Sharlon. Some originally thought that the Sharlon believe that the Skurj are a natural and necessary cleaning system for Exom, thus the name "Sympathisers" was forged, believing them to be Sympathetic to the Skurj. This is now no longer the most common thought, though the name Sympathiser still hangs around. However, no real idea of what the Sharlon are about, or their intentions have replaced it, other than that the Sharlon are determined to bring down the Royal Alliance Council and all that they stand for. The Sharlon remains a mystery, and a very dangerous one at that.

The door to the Council Chambers opens and Queen Aura walks in, approaches the Council table and takes her seat. There is something about her, something more royal that makes her stand out above the rest. Not her dress, which is a very elegant and long aqua green dress with gold trims, Aymyn royalty's traditional colours representing the planet's oceans and beaches, but something about her personally. She looks soft and calming while also appearing very aware and assertive. She certainly looks and feels very comfortable in, not to mentioned very fitted for, her position as the head of the Council.

King Prahm of Crom, looking very visibly upset, struggles to muster up enough strength to stop himself from slouching over the table. The council members to either side of King Prahm are trying to console him as best they can. One of them is Princess Illyana, who has constructed giant angel-like wings from her Tal that extend out behind her. Not an uncommon accessory for Troin women to wear and is often worn as a tribute to the one they call "The First Troin". Princess Illyana uses her wings to wrap around King Prahm as she attempts to comfort and support him.

Queen Aura looks softly at King Prahm who, with tears spilling down his cheek, is unable to look at anyone and stares blankly, traumatized, at the table. Aura then looks at the rest of the council at the table and can tell, based on their silence, that just like her, no-one knows what to say at this moment. No words can comfort a King who has just lost his people, his family - his entire planet. Queen Aura feels that the least she can do is acknowledge this.

"King Prahm", Queen Aura says, looking directly at Prahm with a soft and caring gaze. *"I can not pretend to know your pain"*. King Prahm looks up at Queen Aura, not at all consoled by her words and with tears still flowing, is unable to speak. *"But know this"*, Aura adds, *"you will see justice on the one who facilitated this act of sabotage which has prevented aid from reaching your planet"*, she says, hoping that perhaps retribution may offer a distraction from his pain. It didn't help. King Prahm's expression turns to one of almost anger as he listens to Queen Aura's words.

"Aid?", he responds, his voice almost shaking with anger and grief. *"You speak of aid? The Troin would never have defeated the Skurj. Hold them off possibly. Hold them off for what? Zazars you never would have sent?"*

Princess Illyana, continuing to stroke King Prahm's arm and shoulder, trying to comfort him, looks into his eyes. *"My army was not going there to defeat the Skurj, Your Highness"*, she says to him. *"We are not capable of that. But to join in the fight, help you evacuate...."*

"...You know the law, Prahm", Prince Niyan, reflective of his young age, rudely cuts in. *"The Zazar Corp is only for protected planets"*, he adds almost uncompassionately. *"Once your Zazar was killed, Crom was no longer...."*

Unwilling to listen to Prince Niyan's comments, King Prahm now interrupts him, *"I no longer care about these Zazar traditions"*, he says. *"Not when...."*

"....They are not just traditions", Niyan again interjects.

"Not!", Prahm again insists, *"not when they mean wiping out my entire race"*.

Queen Aura, knowing that Princess Illyana is only trying to comfort Prahm while Niyan is also only trying to stay factual, realizes that neither are what King Prahm needs right now. What he needs is to vent. *"Please, let the King speak"*, she says to Illyana and Niyan.

King Prahm nudges away Princess Illyana. She unwraps her wings from around him, retracts them back into her Tal, but remains holding and stroking his arm as she looks softly and saddened at him. He looks back at her briefly, before sighing and slouches back down on the table. He wants to show his appreciation at her attempt to comfort him, but unable to show anything other than his extreme sadness. *"King?"*, he replies to Aura's request of Illyana and Niyan. *"I am a King of a Dead Kingdom, on a soon to be dissolved planet"*, he adds. *"I am the King of nothing. My own family is now gone. And when my planet has been completely dissolved by the Skurj and their waste...."*. He pauses briefly as he looks over at Aura. *"Aid. Traditions. Ha!"*

Queen Aura looks visibly sympathetic towards King Prahm and then lowers her gaze, unsure exactly what else she can say. But, as head of the council, feels she needs to say something. *"I wish...."*, she says, her eyes still staring down at the table. She looks back over at Prahm, *"I wish there was something I could give you that would take all of this away"*, she adds. *"I can't. No one can. The only thing that I and this council can give you is justice. While I am certain it will not in any way take away any of the pain that you feel"*. Aura leans slightly over the council table to emphasize her eye contact with King Prahm. *"You will see justice"*, she states firmly. *"Of that, you have my word"*.

King Prahm stares back at Queen Aura, but before he can speak, the doors to the Council chambers open and Regent Bassal, a well-dressed elderly man with short grey hair and sporting a neatly trimmed goatee, enters carrying a small plate with some food on it. Looking distinguished wearing his royal blue cape, which is a traditional attire on his home-world, matching his royal blue, long sleeve, open neck collared skivvy. No matter how quietly he tries to sneak in, while attempting to avoid drawing too much attention to himself, several council members turn to watch him closely as he walks up to his position at the table. His chair constructs itself in front of him, and he sits down placing his plate on the table in front of him. Sitting next to him is Monarch Dllm the Crymnon, a species known for their appetites, who starts looking at the food on Regent Bassal's plate with serious interest.

King Prahm ignores Regent Bassal's late arrival and interruption, and remains staring at Queen Aura. *"Queen Aura"*, he says. *"You have always had my greatest of respect, and even now will continue to have. There is no better leader of this Royal Alliance. You have even surpassed your father. He'd be proud"*. Aura smiles back with gratitude at Prahms kind words. *"But"*, Prahm adds, *"until this Royal Alliance has something better than the Zazar Corp to fight with in the Skurj War, even your beloved protected planets, even Aymyn itself, will end up like mine. And what will your words mean then?"*

King Prahm slides himself off his chair, looks one last time at the Councillors seated at the table before turning and walking out the Council Chamber.

Regent Bassal casually takes a bite of the food he has brought in as he watches King Prahm leave. *"He is right"*, Bassal says after swallowing down the food in his mouth. *"We are not winning this war"*.

He looks around at the rest of the Council members seated at the table, most now looking back at him with an expression of discern, some even shaking their heads, showing their disapproval towards Bassal for him choosing to use this moment to have his lunch. Bassal looks back innocently, though knowing full well what they are frowning at.

Councillor Orcom, also amongst those frowning, looks at Bassal with a sort of sceptical intrigue. *"Which war are you referring to, Bassal"*, Orcom asks. *"We are fighting several wars. The war against the Skurj, the war against the Drone Army or the war against Sharlon?"*

Bassal casually takes another bite of his food, slightly smirking to himself, before placing his food back down on the plate and looks back at Councillor Orcom. *"Any of them"*, Bassal replies. *"All of them"*, he then adds, his gaze at Orcom almost appearing challenging.

Princess Illyana, still shaking her head in disbelief at Regent Bassal, not entirely convinced that he is even upset with the situation that he is speaking about, challenges him back. *"I thought you'd be happy about that, Regent"*, she says.

Regent Bassal turns his head very casually to look over at Princess Illyana. The expression on his face looking quite displeased, portraying a feeling of insult at her words. Illyana waits for Bassal's response, which is usually quick coming. This time, however, he remains quiet.

Regent Pfyne, gently spoken as usual, as she is both shy and humble in both appearance and demeanour, runs her soft gaze along each and every member of the council. An act that alone gets their attention. *"The Sharlon are a relatively new development"*, she says. *"At least in their current arrangement as we know them now to be"*.

Councillor Orcom is actually surprised to hear Regent Pfyne speak. *"Yes, they are"*, he says. *"But the most organized one"*, he adds, with no intention to undermine what she has said.

Regent Pfyne does not disagree with Councillor Orcom. *"Perhaps"*, she replies. *"The Jaimin Drone Army has been around a lot longer. And then we have the Skurj, who we have been fighting for thousands of years and we still know very little about them"*. The Council nod in agreement at Regent Pfyne's statement and remain quiet, waiting to hear if she has anything else to add. She does. *"What we do know is that our forces are not without limits"*, she adds. *"Theirs, for all we know, might be. We do not know where they come from. Only that they keep coming. Devouring and dissolving everything in their wake. Their by-product just as unstoppable as they themselves appear to be and dissolves the planet to its core"*.

"Stoppable only by Tription Flame", King Yord feels compelled to correct her. *"A Zazar weapon"*, he adds. *"At best we are holding it back and perhaps just prolonging this war. The sympathizers are growing in numbers. Not out of belief for the Skurj, but out of feeling futile"*.

Regent Bassal smirks at King Yord's last comment. *"I am not sure that futile is the right word"*, he says.

King Yord, who like many on the Council already has a distrust for Regent Bassal, looks searingly back. *"Then what would you call it?"*, he asks Bassal, his tone almost venomous.

Regent Bassal, fully aware of the distrust towards him, not only by King Yord but by all the council, hesitates to speak in case it adds more animosity. However, that hesitation is short lived and overwritten by his nature to speak his mind, though very diplomatically. *"Frustration"*, he replies as he looks over at King Yord, showing no sign of feeling intimidated and matching his gaze.

Princess Illyana would probably have preferred it if Regent Bassal had not spoken and shakes her head, half out of disbelief with what he is saying, and the other half out of believing the Regent's opinions are biased in favour of the Sharlon. King Yord, stays silent, completely sharing Princess Illyana's thoughts, looks away from Regent Bassal and over at Princess Illyana. Illyana meets his gaze. *"We are all aware of your empathy for the Sharlon, Regent"*, Yord remarks.

Regent Bassal unsuccessfully tries to hide his frustration behind a smile. *"Are you still accusing me of that?"*, Bassal asks.

Princess Illyana decides to ignore Regent Bassal and turns her attention back to Regent Pfyne. *"What would you suggest we do?"*, she asks Pfyne. *"Surrender to the Skurj?"*

Pfyne looks back at Princess Illyana. A surprised and equally determined gleam in her eye. *"Never"*, she replies. Her gleam starts to fade. *"But that doesn't make our defeat less inevitable"*, she adds.

Councillor Orcom looks agitated in his chair. Frustrated even, as a matter, connected but more immediate, seems to have been overlooked. *"No one here has addressed the issue that losing Crom will have on the rest of Exom"*, he says. Everyone looks at Orcom, most with a curious expression, wondering what they have missed. Everyone, that is, except for Bassal and Aura, who gaze at each other and nod, knowing that this conversation was coming. Queen Aura grateful that it has been raised after Prahm had left the room.

"No more Crom means no more Sygra Steel", Orcom says. *"What we have stored on Mesto is all we have left. In Exom. The strongest and most commonly used material for constructing our starships, buildings, tools".* Aura nods at Orcom, very aware of what this means for Exom. Bassal, on the other hand, turns and looks at Orcom with cynical interest.

"Is your concern for Exom?", Bassal asks. *"Or just for Mesto?"*

"This coming from someone who traipse in late, carrying his lunch and showing no compassion for the Crom King", Orcome replies angrily.

"I actually thought you would have been more sympathetic to Crom, Regent", Princess Illyana says as she looks over at Bassal.

"Don't worry", Bassal replies, glancing over at Illyana. *"It's not the first time I have been misjudged".* Bassal looks back at Orcom. A hint of smirk again starts to form on Bassal's face. *"Mesto, after all, is where the Sygra Steel goes to be processed after being mined from Crom"*, Bassal adds. *"Your planet has done very well for itself with that arrangement".*

Orcom sits back in his chair as he clasps and rest his hands on the table in front of him. His stare at Bassal now turning less curious and more aggressive. The issue may be valid that Orcom has raised about the now limited resource affecting Exom. But has Bassal seen through Orcom's real motive for his concern? Orcom bites his bottom lip a little as he considers his response. He decides against responding to Bassal and looks back at Aura. *"We know nothing of Sharlon other than that they have spies everywhere, sabotaging and opposing our every move"*, he says, then passes a fleeting gaze again over at Bassal. King Yord, turns and makes his gaze at Bassal a lot more obvious. *"It could be that whoever is responsible for this has done even more damage to Exom than was initially considered"*, Orcom goes on to say.

"Or was considered", Yord adds, staring even more obviously at Bassal.

Orcom again passes a fleeting gaze at Bassal on his way to looking over at King Yord, and nods.

Queen Klatanaria, who has so far remained silent throughout this entire council meeting, wades in. *"We know that the drone army grows in numbers every day"*, she says. *"Taking over more and more colony planets and enslaving the population"*, an issue affecting her personally, as many of the colony posts on the moons of Zo have been overrun, or even destroyed, by the Jaimin Drones. *"We do not know where their base is"*, she adds.

"Bases", King Yord pipes in again with a correction. Klatanaria looks over and nods at Yord, in appreciation of his correction.

"While we can defeat them with our own armies on most occasions", she goes on to say, *"the destruction they cause every time, mostly in lives, is becoming too costly. The Drones don't care. They just create more"*.

"Dam Valantriun technology", Yord remarks out loud without thinking.

Princess Illyana, taking some offense to King Yord's statement, stares at him as she rests her arm wearing her Tal on the table for all to see. It is common knowledge now that the Tal was invented for the Troin by the Valantriun .

The Valantriun , a very technologically advanced race of Aymyn, that even secretly pursued their interest in science and technology tens of thousands of years ago while still living on Aymyn when such things were highly illegal. The Valantriun , a name they had always called themselves, now live on a planet they named Valant, where they focus all their efforts on research. They do not share their research with other races. Not out of spite, but rather, just wanting to be left alone. Their view on pursuing science, though never known about while they were still living on Aymyn, would have been shunned and punished by the rest of the Aymyn, considered "Dark". For that reason, they kept themselves to themselves, and in secret. After the Assembly, they were the first Aymyn group to leave Aymyn and start fresh on another planet. To this day, they still keep very much to themselves. Which itself creates mystery and unknown, again reinforcing the Aymyn's belief that the Valantriun are influenced by the Dark, which generates even more fear and animosity towards them.

The Valantriun do not consider themselves either Light or Dark. Their interest on advancement in science and technology is not specifically to bring about change, though that is usually what it does, it could easily be used to keep things the same. Their interest is purely on exploring, learning, discovering. Something they now wish to be left alone to pursue in peace and unjudged.

Now considered the second most technological race in all of Exom, after the Pizian's of course, the Valantriun are blamed as the ones responsible for creating the Jaimin Drones. In fact, while it was definitely Valantriun technology that was responsible, it was not the Valantriun 's that created them.

When no cure for the disease that inflicted the Liassians could be found, the Liassian's reached out to the Valantriun 's for help, not expecting a response. Surprising everyone, the Valantriun s did help. They created the Tal for the Liassians. Being Valantriun technology, the Aymyn were strongly against the Liassians using it. This eventuated in a war and eventual standoff between the Liasian, now called Troin, and the Aymyn. A standoff that lasted hundreds of years. It was Queen Aura that was responsible for bringing eventual peace and friendship between the Aymyn and Troin.

King Yord, noticing Princess Illyana's Tal almost as though he had momentarily forgotten that she was Troin, looks up at her shocked by his words and apologetic. *"No offense to the Troin, Your Highness"*, he says. *"I didn't mean...."*

Queen Klatanaria comes to King Yord's rescue by butting in and continuing with what she was saying. *"And finally, the Skurj"*, she says. *"Unstoppable beasts for which even the Pizians were helpless to stop and the reason they united all the planets of Exom"*.

The Council are quiet for a moment as they think on what Klatanaria has just said. It's something that every one of them already knows only too well and made evident by the solemn expression that each of them is wearing. All except for Regent Bassal that is. Who, though also sharing the sentiment of what Klatanaria has just said, wishes to change the direction of the conversation.

"We need something that will turn the tide", Bassal says. *"We have nothing within this council that will do that"*.

Prince Niyan, a strong supporter of the Zazars, is not quite sure what Regent Bassal is trying to say. *"We have the Zazar Corp"*, he says.

Regent Bassal does not wish to argue with Prince Niyan. Well, not entirely anyway. OK, maybe he does. *"Agreed"*, Bassal says. *"The Zazars are an effective defence"*. Before he can finish what he is saying, he is cut off by Prince Niyan.

"They are the best that we have", Niyan says.

"But they are only a defence", Bassal finishes what he was saying. *"They are putting out spot fires"*.

"The Skurj do not seem to invade in large numbers", Queen Klatanaria steps in to say.

Bassal looks over at her and smiles cheekily. *"Oh, my dear, but maybe they do"*, he says.

Klatanaria looks back at him, unimpressed with both being contradicted by him as well as being called "my dear". She was no one's "dear", especially not his.

Seeing her displeased look only makes Bassal's smile stronger. He goes on, *"Just not initially. They attack first in small numbers. Usually, two or three. More than enough to destroy an entire planet. And for us, luckily small enough to be defeated by the Zazars if they get there in time"*.

"They always come back though", King Yord says. *"Still only in two or three's"*.

Bassal looks over at Yord and nods. *"True"*, he says. He then turns his attention to the entire council, and no one in particular. *"But what about after that"*, he adds. *"After those two or three have been successful. When there is no one there to see what happens. We have never seen them invade in large numbers. That's the difference. We have no idea about their numbers. What comes of the day when they outnumber us? You could no longer consider that a war. That is annihilation"*.

Feeling it is time to step in and take back control of this Council meeting, Queen Aura speaks up. *"We will have to deal with that day when and if it comes"*, she says. *"There is no benefit in us arguing amongst each other about what could possibly come when we are already struggling to deal with what we already have. Not everyone or every planet is going to survive this war. We know that. The Zazar Protectorate Code is based on that. Our losses have been and will continue to be great. How great, we don't know. Maybe absolute. But that is looking at it from only one side, and I for one do not intend to be that prejudiced. The Royal Alliance was formed to bring about the strongest, best, and most beneficial outcome for Exom, in all facets, not only war. Uniting us all. Enabling all planets, all people, and all species to survive and thrive. And, until a day comes that there is no Exom, I intend to do that. Defend, support, nourish all that I can, to my last breath"*.

Everyone on the Council sits quietly, respectfully, looking back at Aura. Some in awe at her dedicated and direct words. Other's grateful that she has stepped in and taken back control of the conversation. Though Regent Bassal does strongly feel that she is being overly optimistic.

"Your look is sanguine", he says to her.

Aura looks back at Bassal, her head slightly nodding at his comment, but not wanting to make it obviously so. *"Just have some faith"*, she replies. *"All that we can do is the best that we can. And we owe that to our people. To all people. We are not perfect"*. She again looks at the entire council in general. *"We are not even trying to be perfect"*, she adds. *"We are trying to be good. To be fair. To survive. Sometimes that involves making very difficult decisions. But our people, all our people, have entrusted us to make those decisions. They have faith in us that we will come through and do the right thing"*. She again looks specifically at Bassal. *"All I am saying is, have some faith too"*, she says.

Monarch Dllm, who is still eyeing off the food on the plate in front of Bassal, and has been this entire time, finally gives into temptation, grabs the food, stuffing it into his mouth, and in an instant, it is all gone. However, Bassal, so focused on returning gazes with Queen Aura, does not notice.

"I have faith", Bassal replies. *"I also have fear. Fear that the Skurj will end up eating our faith"*.

Everyone else at the table, however, has noticed Monarch Dllm devouring the food on Regent Bassal's plate. Amused at the situation, many start to smile.

"Right now, you should be more afraid about your friend eating your lunch", Niyan says as he smiles over at Bassal.

Bassal looks down at his now empty plate, then looks at Dllm sitting there, looking guiltily back at him. Bassal then gazes around at the other Councillors sitting at the table and notices that they are all looking back at him, equally amused at the situation.

EXOM

THE YOUNG KING

CHAPTER FOUR

-------------------------------- Eluud --------------------------------

Theorone, a Seer and the last and most gifted of the Lightning Sign's, lived on Aymyn 20,000 years ago. A large painting of Theorone along with his pet mewsie, an extinct feline species that used to live on Aymyn thousands of years ago, hangs pride of place at the altar of the Church of Light located inside the Citadel. During his time, Theorone used his strong clairvoyance gift to pre-tell many events that occurred on Aymyn, even throughout Exom, right to this day. Some that are still yet to come.

Theorone was bestowed a leadership title within the Church of Light by the chairman, who himself was a very strong Light Sign. Theorone's writings and predictions are still widely discussed to this day.

Still strongly influenced and guided by the "Church of Light", of which Aura being the Queen of Aymyn is also duty bound to be its "Guardian", Aymyn still has a very strict practice of not seeking change. In fact, if it wasn't for the Pizian's uniting Exom several thousand years ago, Aymyn would still be a civilization living in sandstone houses and barns, and not the mighty technologically advanced supercities that it is today.

The Assembly, and with it the technology to travel to different planets and star systems, presented an opportunity to the Aymyn. Those wanting to pursue a different style of life, not regulated by Aymyn philosophy and principles, could now leave Aymyn and colonize new planets and become their own people with their own beliefs and traditions.

EXOM - THE YOUNG KING

The ruling monarchy of Aymyn, and the Church of Light itself, were surprised at how many took up this opportunity. As we know, the Valantriun , who wanted to, and secretly always did, explore all areas of science, were the first to leave. Many followed, and continued to follow, for reasons of their own, over the centuries. Leaving in large colony ships, often not in the best of condition, or working order, since the Aymyn Government was not going to fund the mass departure of its citizens. These colonies would settle on other inhabitable planets throughout Exom and form their own new civilisations with their own customs and philosophies.

Eluud was such a planet. Settled a few generations ago by a small Aymyn colony ship led by King Steel's great grandfather. Like many colonies that have been settled throughout Exom, the Eluudians as they now choose to call themselves, wished to break free from Aymyn and become independent. Not out of malice or spite, just wishing to pursue their own beliefs and traditions which may not have aligned exactly with those on Aymyn.

The planet they eventually came to settle on, though history would say was not entirely of their choosing, Eluud, is a small and interesting independent planet located in one of the Outer Rim Systems of Exom. Interesting in that the planet does not rotate like most planets, having only a very slight movement, and has one side of the planet permanently facing the sun. This side of the planet, the scorched side, is completely uninhabitable. So too is the other side, which is frozen and in permanent darkness. The only inhabitable part of the planet is a thin area that runs around the centre of the planet, between the scorched and frozen sides. This inhabitable area though, due to the small amount of movement the planet does have, does experience short periods of both day and night. However, most of its time is spent in a kind of twilight.

The inhabitable part of the planet is covered in hills, mountains, and thick forests. Trees, extremely tall, as they compete against each other for the little direct sunlight that this area of Eluud has.

The atmosphere of Eluud, though very pleasant and of course breathable, has something in it that renders a lot of technology, such as lasers, scanners and even all known types of propulsion systems, ineffective. Motorized vehicles are not used, or even able to be used, on Eluud. Instead, the most common form of transport is rouk, a domesticated and majestic looking hoofed species native to Eluud, that has a large, curved horn in the middle of its forehead. The rouks are often ridden or used to pull simple carts. Laser and blaster weapons are mostly unable to be used on Eluud, or if attempted would often result in them backfiring or even blowing up. For this reason, the Eluudian population does not use such weapons. Instead, the most common weapon used by the Eluudian soldiers, and other royalty, is an extendable pole spear, called a "ronad", which is sheathed in a holster strapped to the outside of the user's shin.

In its inactive state, the ronad is cylinder shaped, about 9 inches long and almost two inches in diameter. When activated, it extends to almost six feet long, with each end coming to a sharp point and capable of inflicting significant damage. The ronad is made of Sygra Steel, making it almost impossible to break, and in the hands of a trained fighter could give any other kind of weapon a run for its money. Even if used off-world, against an enemy armed with a laser or projectile weapon, a skilled user could use their ronad to deflect lasers and other blasts. It is a very effective close combat weapon which, if required, could also be used as a spear. Ronads are not only a close combat spear weapon, however, though that is how they started out and are often used. They can be activated another way to form a new different kind of weapon. When activated this different way, as the pole extends it separates into the main shaft and a single thin strand of Sygra Steel that stretches the entire length of the weapon, pulling the ends of the shaft down into a slight curve. In this formation it resembles a long bow and is used as such.

The ronad fitted in well with the Eluudians general appearance. Their dress and clothing are very much a gothic punk style. A lot of black, sometimes entirely, with shirts, tops, cloaks, dresses, skirts and trousers of all styles and lengths. Some very revealing while some others completely cover the body from neck to toe. With the exception of uniformed staff and military, you would rarely see two Eluudians dressed similarly. Each free to express their own personal style and individuality. Including members of the Royal family.

The Eluudians live humbly but are self-sufficient and, while the population are mostly Aymyn, the name Eluudian also extends to the non-Aymyn inhabitants of Eluud. If you reside on Eluud and call Eluud your home, then you are Eluudian, no matter what your origin species is.

Positioned on a large clearing surrounded by forests and farming area on Eluud, is the Eluudian Castle, "Chassam Castle", and the gardens that surround it. Again, not overly sophisticated in appearance, looking more medieval than modern. On top of the castle is a very large horn called "The Great Horn" but often referred to simply as "The Horn". A horn that, if ever sounded, would be heard right throughout Eluud.

This horn was built to be sounded once, and only once, on a very special and specific day. The day that Eluud is chosen by a Zazar to become a Protected Planet. Protection, that if Eluud was to stand any chance of surviving a Skurj attack, which drew closer to Eluud with every passing day, was most certainly needed. Unfortunately, to this day, Eluud has never been selected so the horn has never sounded.

To both the left and right of The Great Horn, there are two much smaller horns that are used to signify an imminent Skurj attack. Though fortunately, to date, these have also never had to be sounded, the chance of them being sounded sometime in the future, potentially very near future, is not only likely but a certainty.

The planet is ruled by King Steel, a young King who inherited the throne early when his father, King Solso was killed in a battle with raiders. The raiders, comprising almost entirely of a species called Dakari, a 6-foot-tall bipedal reptilian race with no tails, but very vicious nature, are known to terrorise the outer rim systems on this side of Exom.

The Dakari Raiders attacked a small Eluudian village some distance from Chassam Castle. The Eluudian army was able to fight off the raiders, but not before the raiders had done considerable damage, wiping out the village, and of course killing King Solso.

Upon hearing of his father's death, Steel arranged a small search party that comprised of himself, a very young boy squire named Dacos, and several soldiers to search for survivors in the destroyed villages. None were found except for 2 baby girls, buried in the rubble in two different destroyed huts. Steel took the two babies back with him, raising them as his own daughters, and eventually adopted them officially and decreed that their standing is equivalent to his bloodline, holding all the privileges that comes with that. The two daughters, Det and Tespa, now the only children of King Steel, grew up to become the Princesses of Eluud and are very much loved and adored by the people.

-------------------------------- **Coolax** --------------------------------

The grounds of Chassam Castle gleam in the daylight. To the side of the main gardens is a sports oval surrounded by elevated staircase bleachers filled with Eluudian spectators. The crowd roars as a man, carrying a very large sealed rubbery sack, almost as tall as he is, filled with water, slides along the grassy ground and through a group of opponents, tripping and throwing them aside in his wake.

The game is called Coolax, originally named after a large, bloated fish found on Aymyn thousands of years ago. The object of the game is two opposing teams attempt to grab and carry the Coolax, no longer a fish these days and substituted by the large rubbery water filled sack, that is just as heavy and awkward to carry as the original fish. Once they have it, they must first take it to their side of the field, then return to the centre of the field where lays a giant mounted metal spike. They must place, or in most cases smash, the coolax down on the spike, bursting it and showering the field with water. The opposing team must do anything they can to stop them, take possession of the coolax, get it to their side of the field and then likewise attempt to get it back into the centre and burst it on the large metal spike.

It seems easy enough, and it is, other than this simple process there are very few rules. Each team needs fifteen players and can use any means to stop their opponents from reaching the spike with the coolax.

EXOM - THE YOUNG KING

It's also not polite to seriously injure your opponent. However, this sport is definitely not for the timid.

As the player continues sliding his way towards the giant spike in the centre of the field, a female opponent, who also happens to be Trill, The Eluudian Army Commander, charges through the tumbling players, using some as steps and objects to jump onto and leap herself from as though they were stationary objects and walls, and dives onto the sliding player, pinning him to the ground. She flips him over and, with both legs, kicks him off the Coolax and into the air, landing on the ground with a heavy thump some meters away from her. She flips herself over again and straddles the Coolax, wrapping her legs tightly around it. She sits up and holds her arms out as a dozen men from her opponent's team charge and pounce on top of her. Piling up they cover her completely. She manages to punch her hand through the pile of players on top of her, get it free and hold it out again, waving it in the air.

Like a charging beast, a very tall and muscularly built, shirtless man runs straight towards her and the pile of players on top of her. Picking up and tossing players aside like they have no weight at all, he grabs the girl's hand and flings her out from underneath the pile of men. The Coolax still firmly grasped between her legs, she flips and summersaults through the air, eventually landing on the ground on top of the Coolax. The strong shirtless man, reaches down and picks the Coolax up with ease. He throws it over his shoulder, lifts the female player to her feet with his other hand and together they charge back towards their end of the field.

Four more defending opponents block their path. The tall muscular man, Dacos, no longer a small young squire and now the General of the Eluudian Army, holding the Coolax with one arm, while holding the hand of his much smaller, twin sister, Trill, who also happens to be the army's Commander, stops and stares at the defending opponents blocking their path. His eyes, focused, determined, an evil smile starts to take shape on his face. Trill looks at her brother, and as though knowing his very thought, lets go of his hand, then turns and charges towards the defending players. Dacos charges at them as well. Trill leaps into the air, landing with her legs wrapped around the neck of one of the defending players, she flips herself sideways, taking him down with her. Dacos charges through the remaining four defending players, knocking them down like a ball through pins. He makes his way to his side of the field and turns around in time to watch Trill stand back up and get tackled to the ground again by the four defending players. He looks at them curiously, confused. She wasn't even holding the Coolax. Though, not against the rules, it seemed a little vindictive. He steadies the coolax firmly on his shoulder then charges back towards the defending players. More defending players come to assist their comrades. So too do many players on the same team as Dacos and Trill.

Dacos, still firmly holding the Coolax on his shoulder, charges through and throws his opponents around with his other shoulder and arm. More players on Dacos's team tackle the opponents wrestling with Trill. Trill manages to get free again, stands up and is then hit with a very solid backhand across her face by another opponent, sending her falling back onto the ground. She sits up, holds her cheek, and gives a very angry stare at the player that just hit her. He stares back at her, at first smiling, but his smile quickly fades when it dawns on him that he has just backhanded the Commander of the Eluudian army. He, being a soldier in it and under her command.

Dacos runs up, picks up the soldier and throws him onto the ground. A loud siren sounds as Dacos looks around and notices that both teams have stopped playing the game and are instead all just fighting each other. Trill also looks around and seems a little confused.

A group of men, dressed in long black coats, umpires of the game, run onto the field, yelling, and trying to break up the fighting. Trill picks herself up and stands next to Dacos, watching the fight around her, as the umpires, with the help of some other players attempt to break it up. Dacos takes the Coolax off his shoulder and pushes it onto Trill. *"Hold this"*, he says to her. She starts to struggle and buckle under the weight but adjusts herself to hold it securely. Dacos moves through the fighting teams, grabbing players, pulling them apart and tossing them aside. The soldier that had previously backhanded Trill, and only just recovering from the slight winding of being thrown to the ground by Dacos, stands up next to Trill and also watches Dacos break up the fighting. Trill looks at the soldier briefly before returning her attention back to Dacos. She throws the Coolax up onto her shoulder, then with a quick flick she throws her other hand up and back, punching the soldier firmly in the centre of his face with the back of her fist. The soldier falls to the ground again and Trill walks up towards her brother without looking back at the soldier.

As the crowd disperses, with the teams retreating to their own groups, three players from the opposing team still lay on the ground being aided by the umpires. Dacos looks over at them as Trill walks up and stands beside him again. She also looks at the injured players curiously. *"I think you did that"*, she says to Dacos.

Dacos nods as he bites his lips, looking a combination of guilty and remorseful. *"I think I did"*, he replies.

Trill watches the umpires assist the injured players to their feet and helps walk them off the field. She turns and looks back at Dacos who still seems a little pained by his actions. *"You realise that nearly all the players on the field are soldiers, don't you"*, Trill asks him.

"I do", Dacos replies, still watching the injured players and umpires leave the field.

"Well, if you continue to injure them then we won't have an army", she tells him. *"And you'll have no one to lead, dear brother"*.

Dacos looks down at Trill and smiles. *"I'll still have you"*, he says to her.

"True", Trill replies. *"What more do you need?"*, she says as she shoves the coolax into her brother's chest. Dacos grabs it as Trill turns to walk away. She stops for a moment to look up into the bleachers where she spots a familiar face, Princess Det. A very attractive young lady. About nineteen or twenty years old, though her exact age is unknown as she was found as a baby. She is wearing a black open sleeveless jacket top and black skirt, that goes down to her shins around the back and sides but short and ruffled in front. A brown belt completes her outfit, though appears to be more of an accessory than serve any purpose. Just beyond shoulder length black hair and pale

complexion. Her piercing eyes staring right back at Trill. *"Don't look now"*, Trill says to Dacos. *"Your girlfriend is watching"*.

Dacos turns and looks up into the bleachers. He immediately spots Det, sitting next to her father. The moment Det and Dacos's eyes lock, Det quickly turns away, then stands up and walks off, much to her father's confusion. As King Steel watches Det leave, her seat is quickly occupied by Princess Tespa, equally beautiful with long golden-blonde hair. She is wearing a similar outfit to Det, only with the long parts of the skirt finishing a bit higher, just below the knee, showing off her long knee length black boots. Strapped and sheathed to her left boot is her ronad. Her top has long sleeves, is completely closed in front and finished with a black and metallic corset.

A strong Wendral sign, Tespa is often seen smiling, happy and tends to bring joy to those around her. Rarely seen without her Troin girlfriend, Vessel, by her side or carrying her small, strange pet, Kako, this time she is unaccompanied by either and sits excitedly next to her father. She reaches out and grabs his arm. King Steel turns his attention from Det, who has now disappeared from the bleachers, and onto Tespa. He smiles back at her as she starts excitedly sharing some news with him.

Trill stands next to Dacos and stares up at the bleachers with him. *"And she's gone again. How unlike Det"*, Trill says sarcastically and starts to walk away. Dacos looks over at Trill and marches up to walk beside her.

"You could talk about her a little more nicely", Dacos tells his sister.

"I could", Trill responds, almost with a hint of cheekiness.

"And - she's not my girlfriend", Dacos adds.

"Only because you won't ask her", Trill says as she stares back at her brother. *"You two have been in love with each other since you were kids and neither of you say a word to each other"*.

"That's not true", Dacos replies. *"I speak to her all the time. I'm the General, she's a princess. We kind of have to. Eluud is not that big"*.

"Oh yeah", Trill says with a very disbelieving stare. *"When was the last time you spoke to her?"*. Dacos looks as though he is about to answer, then hesitates as he stops to think. Trill nods and punches her

brother firmly in the chest, though he'd hardly feel it. *"My point"*, she says and walks off again.

"And I did it", Tespa says to her father, catching his attention, though he is not exactly sure what it is that she did, as she had been talking so quickly and excitedly non-stop that his attention had already started to drift. *"You should have seen it"*, she continues. *"I think you would have been proud. I just kept persevering, got there in the end, but now my fingers are sore"*. Still not knowing what Tespa is talking about, Steel just nods. *"That happens"*, he says to her.

"It shouldn't", she replies. *"Never happened before. Maybe I am doing it wrong"*.

Steel smiles at her, still completely oblivious to what she is talking about. *"I'm sure you did it just perfect"*.

"Now all we need is for me to do it in public", Tespa says as she looks away and thinks to herself. Steel looks at his daughter very confused. He has no idea what she is talking about and starting to think he should find out. Tespa turns back looking excitedly again at her father. *"I know. How about a concert?"*, she says. *"Do you want to have a concert? I think we should have a concert. How awesome would a concert be?"*

"You want to have a concert?", Steel asks her, still trying to work out what she is talking about.

"Well, yeah", Tespa replies, looking at her father curiously. *"Haven't you been listing to what I was saying?"*, she asks him with a smile.

Steel's face starts to appear a little guilty now. *"I tried to"*, Steel replies. *"Kind of drifted off at the end somewhere. But I am back now. So, you want to have a concert?"*

Tespa smiles and hugs her father's arm. *"Yeah, maybe. We can talk about that later"*, she says. She turns and looks over the field. *"I've never understood this game"*, she says to him.

"What part?", Steel asks her.

"Any of it", Tespa replies. *"It just looks like a bunch of people running around after that blubbery thing and hitting each other"*.

Steel looks back over the field as well, then turns to her and smiles. *"Pretty much"*, he replies before turning his attention back to the field.

Tespa looks up at her father again. *"Dad"*, she says as she stares at him with an "oh really, that's all you have to say" expression.

Steel turns back to look at her and smiles again. *"That blubbery thing is a Coolax. It's filled with water. Heavy and difficult to hold"*.

"It looks it", Tespa replies.

"It is", Steel says. *"Each team needs to try and take the Coolax back to their side of the field and then back into the centre again and burst it on that giant spike. If they do that then they win the game"*.

"Doesn't sound all that complicated", Tespa remarks. *"What is everyone else on the field meant to do?"*, she asks

"Try to stop them", Steel replies. *"Well, the members of the other team anyway. Not stop your own team mates of course. That kind of defeats the purpose"*.

"So, stop them how", Tespa asks.

"Any way they can", Steel replies. *"Without using weapons or anything of course. Its sport, not gladiatorial"*.

Over at the opponent's team, the men are regrouping and addressing a serious problem. With the injured men taken out of the game, the team does not have enough reserve players to make a full team. They are one short. Without a full team on both sides the game can not continue.

"General", one of the umpires calls out as he runs to Dacos. Dacos turns to face him, looking at him curiously. The umpire stops and stands in front of Dacos. *"We are short a player on the other team"*.

Dacos looks over at the team, observing their injured men being escorted off the field and the now noticeable smaller side. *"Oh"*, Dacos replies understanding the predicament.

"Do you have any reserves that you can lend to your opposition so that the game can continue?", the umpire asks.

Dacos looks over at his own team, who Trill has now just joined and stands amongst. He does a quick head count and looks around before looking back at the umpire with a dejected expression. *"We didn't have any extra to start with"*, Dacos replies. *"I have most of my men out patrolling the outer forest which has kept our numbers stretched".*

"Without another player, the game can't continue", the umpire says and stares at Dacos. Dacos stares back at him as though waiting for the umpire to realise the solution. The umpire knows what solution Dacos is waiting for him to realise. *"Ask the crowd"*, the umpire says without blinking or changing his expression.

"Ask the crowd", Dacos replies with a nod.

"Ask the crowd", the umpire says again with a shrug and runs off towards the bleachers. He climbs up onto a small podium in front of the bleachers and faces the audience. Everyone goes quiet. That is except for Princess Tespa who is still excitedly talking to her father. Noticing the umpire standing, facing the crowd, Steel stares back at him and taps Tespa on her arm. Tespa stops talking and turns to looks at the umpire curiously. The umpire looks down at the ground, gathering his strength, then looks back at the audience and takes a deep breath. *"We are down one player"*, he shouts to the crowd. *"The game can not continue"*. Before he can go on, the crowd starts booing and yelling in disappointment. *"Unless!"*, the umpire again shouts at the audience. The crowd starts to settle down again and slowly becomes quiet, allowing the umpire to speak. *"Unless one of you wishes to step up and take the place of the missing player"*. The crowd remains quiet. Many start looking at each other, wanting to see if someone is going to volunteer. No one does. The umpire watches them, looking disappointed. A few in the crowd start talking amongst themselves again. One man yells out, *"Whose team?"*. Another yells out, *"is it the General's team?"*

"It's not the General's team", the umpire replies.

The crowd goes silent again. Dacos walks up and stands next to the umpire. His height allowing him no need to stand on the podium and still stand taller than the Umpire. *"Brave Eluudians!"*, Dacos yells out to them. *"Surely someone here, with the aid of some of my soldiers, is courageous enough to challenge my team and myself"*. Still the crowd remains silent as Trill walks up and stands beside Dacos. *"And me"*,

Trill adds shouting into the crowd. Dacos frowns, refusing to look back at his sister. *"Oh yeah, that helps"*, he says to her sarcastically.

As the crowd continues to look at each other in silence, an excited gleam appears in the eyes of King Steel as he smiles at Dacos and Trill. He stands up and stares at them. *"I'll do it!"*, King Steel shouts at them. The entire crowd gasps in surprise, including Dacos, Trill, the Umpire and especially Tespa, who is still holding onto her father's arm and looking at him with shock.

"Dad?", she says to him, her expression now starting to really show her concern.

Steel looks down at her, still smiling, then looks back at Dacos. *"This should be fun"*, Steel says and starts to make his way down the stairs of the bleachers towards the front fence. Dacos stands back beside the podium still watching his King curiously and with surprise. Trill and the umpire walk up to Steel as he is about to jump over the fence. *"Are you sure Your Highness?"*, the umpire asks him.

"About most things that matter", Steel replies.

"Are you sure you should be doing this, Your Highness?", Trill also asks him.

Steel jumps over the fence, takes Trill's hands and holds them. *"The people look forward to this"*, he tells her, smiling, and now the only one doing so. *"We have such little excitement around here"*, he says. *"Well, positive excitement"*, he adds. *"The constant raider attacks are a little discouraging"*. Steel lets go of Trills hands, removes his royal robe, and hands it to the umpire. He then walks up and stands in front of Dacos, looking up at him, and smiling cheekily. Dacos still looks down at his King, a little uncertain that he has made a good decision. *"You do remember what happens in this game, Your Highness?"*, Dacos asks him.

"Remember?", Steel replies. *"I believe I was the one who taught you"*, Steel tells him. Dacos shrugs. A fact he can't really deny. Steel taps Dacos firmly on the arm and starts to walk off towards the centre of the field. *"I used to kick your arse when you were my squire"*.

Dacos turns and looks back at Steel. *"You realise I was a lot smaller then?"*, he says.

EXOM - THE YOUNG KING

Steel, not turning back, just shrugs and replies, *"meh"*.

Dacos shrugs again, turns, and walks towards his team. Trill runs up and walks beside him.

Steel reaches his new team, the soldiers more than just a little surprised to see him there with them and not entirely sure how to react. Thinking nothing of it, Steel starts to take control of the conversation, something the captain of the team is happy to let him do. *"Now, we don't have much time"*, Steel says to them. *"They'll ring the siren soon and start the game. So, it's important that we agree on a strategy if we are to stand any chance"*. He calls them all in close together, *"Now I was thinking....."*, Before he can finish, the siren sounds signifying the start of the game. *"Well, that came around quicker than expected"*, Steel says loudly to himself. Steel waves his fist encouragingly in the air. *"Right, great chat. Let's do it"*, he says as he turns around and faces the middle of the field. He marches towards the centre, towards the large spike and the Umpire holding the Coolax. He smiles at the umpire and watches as Dacos approaches him from the other end of the field and stands at the other side of the umpire. Dacos looks at Steel, still feeling like his King has made a bad decision. Steel smiles back, his body positioned prone, and keen to start the game. *"I won't be taking it easy on you, Your Highness"*, Dacos tells him.

"I'd be disappointed if you did", Steel replies.

The siren sounds again, and the umpire drops the Coolax on the ground. Dacos runs and reaches down to grab it. However, Steel dives for it and reaches it first. He wraps himself around it and rolls out of the way of Dacos's arms before they reach him. He quickly picks up the Coolax and is about to run off with it, when Dacos reaches out, grabs him and throws him to the ground. The crowd gasps, as do a lot of the players on both sides. Steel looks up at Dacos, also a little surprised, as Dacos also looks back at him with the same expression. Steel smiles, keen and cheekily. Dacos smiles back, just as cheekily. Steel dives for the coolax again as Dacos grabs it, picks it up and starts running towards his side of the field. Dacos maybe bigger, taller, and stronger, however Steel shows him soon enough that he is not faster. Steel charges at him and catches him easily. He jumps at Dacos and almost runs up his back. He kicks him in the top of his back with both feet. Dacos immediately topples to the ground and Steel summersaults over and off him. Steel tries to grab the Coolax but notices that it is now underneath Dacos. Steel dives and rams Dacos, rolling him over. Dacos holds firmly onto the Coolax. Steel quickly stands up and then slams his entire body into Dacos's stomach. Dacos gasps, stunned, winded, and let's go of the Coolax. Steel grabs the Coolax and picks it up. Dacos reaches out for Steel's legs, but Steel kicks Dacos's hands away and runs back, with the coolax, towards his end of the field.

Steel runs quickly, frantically, towards his end of the field, holding the coolax like he has stolen it. His team watch him running towards them as they run towards the centre of the field and towards Dacos. His team makes a parting for Steel to run through and then quickly close in, closing the gap. Dacos has now picked himself up and is charging towards Steel's men, with Trill and the rest of Dacos's team close behind him. Dacos charges through the men as though they were not there. But they were there, and the impact knocks them flying sideways. The few still standing are quickly taken down when Trill throws herself sideways at them, spinning in the air and bowling all three down at once. As the soldiers hit the ground, Trill lands on her hands and knees, gets her bearings, and then runs after Steel and her brother. The rest of Dacos's team jump in and tackle Steel's men as they pick themselves up. More fighting ensues but the game does not stop this time.

Steel reaches his end of the field and, still running, turns around and continues charging again towards the centre of the field, still firmly holding onto the coolax for dear life.

Dacos and Trill run straight at him, together, on a collision course. Steel does not stop. It's like a game of chicken, though all three know that none of them are going to swerve. Steel runs directly at Dacos and Trill. He leaps and plants his foot dead centre in Dacos' Chest. This time Dacos does not stumble, which is exactly what Steel was counting on. He uses Dacos's solid frame as a springboard and propels himself towards Trill. Trill looks at Steel just as he throws the Coolax at her. It hits her in the face, the surprise and weight of the coolax knocking her to the ground. Steel lands next to her, quickly picks up the Coolax again, narrowly dodging Dacos's attempts to grab him, and resumes running towards the centre of the field.

Trill raises up her arm and Dacos grabs it as he runs past her, throwing her back onto her feet. Both Dacos and Trill tear after Steel.

As Steel approaches the centre of the field and the large metal spike, four defending players on Dacos's Team step out ahead of him, blocking his path to the spike. Steel keeps running towards them then looks back and sees Trill and Dacos hot on his heals. Steel changes course slightly, running past the defending players and away from the centre of the field. He is now actually running towards Dacos's teams end of the field. Trill and Dacos reach the giant spike and stop and watch Steel still running away with the coolax. They look at each other, very confused. The four defending players on Dacos's team come up and stand by Dacos and Trill, also watching their King run in the wrong direction with the Coolax.

Eventually Steel stops and looks up at the audience in the bleachers. The crowd is equally baffled as Dacos and his Team, wondering what their King is doing. Steel smiles, again cheekily, and turns around to face Dacos, Trill and the defending opponents. He repositions the Coolax on his shoulder and chest firmly and comfortably. He adjusts his footing, his stance, preparing himself to charge. He stares directly at Dacos. An intense and determined stare. Dacos looks at him curiously. Then steps forward in front of the spike as he realises what his King is planning on doing.

Still smiling, his stare still intense, Steel nods at Dacos. Dacos, just as Steel had just done, fixes his footing and stance then also prepares to charge. He stares back at Steel, also smiling and nods. Steel takes a deep breath, pushes his feet firmly off the ground and charges directly at Dacos. Trill looks at Dacos, wondering what is about to happen. Dacos, still focused firmly on Steel, also pushes off and charges directly at his King. Neither showing any intention of veering. Travelling at full speed towards each other, Steel pulls the Coolax around in front of him, in front of his face as he collides with full force into Dacos. There is a mighty thud. The impact bursting the Coolax between them as they both bounce off each other and fall backwards onto the ground.

Stunned, seeing a lot of black and white, with nothing else in focus, both Dacos and Steel lay flat on their backs on the ground. Water from the Coolax still raining down on them. They turn their heads and look at each other, both still unable to move. Steel starts to smile. Dacos looks a little confused but then also starts to smile, followed by a little giggle. Steel joins in with a laugh and soon they are both laying there, flat on their backs, still unable to move, laughing together.

Trill and the rest of the defending team, along with the rest of the players from both teams start to make their way towards Steel and Dacos. Trill stands over them both, looking down on them, confused about what has just happened and even more confused at them both laying their laughing. She looks back at the audience who are all sitting silent and shocked, staring at the show. Tespa, looking particularly alarmed, is making her way down the bleachers and towards the main fence.

Steel picks himself up, still looking very winded and stunned, but also still laughing. He looks down at Dacos and reaches out his hand. Dacos grabs it and Steel helps him to his feet.

"What the...!", Trill exclaims at both Steel and Dacos. Dacos, still laughing, reaches out and places his hand on Trill's shoulder. Tespa runs up and hugs her father. Steel flinches in pain, sore and injured from the collision but still smiling and giggling. Realising that he is hurt, Tespa quickly pulls back and looks at him with concern. *"Dad, are you alright?"*, she asks him.

Steel smiles at her. *"Oh, I am going to feel this in the morning"*, he says still giggling.

"You and me both", Dacos says holding his sides.

Trill steps up next to Tespa and looks at Steel firmly. *"What were you thinking?"*, she says to him.

Tespa also looks at her father in the same way and repeats Trill's question. *"What were you thinking"*, Tespa says.

Steel looks at Tespa, still smiling through the pain. *"Wasn't thinking"*, he replies. *"I was hoping. Hoping it wouldn't hurt so much"*.

Tespa looks at her father even more confused. *"You meant to do that?"*, she asks him.

Steel nods. *"I did"*, he replies. Trill throws her hands up gesturing "why" at him. Steel looks over at Trill, smiles and raises his finger for her to wait for a moment as he catches his breath. He then leans back, cracks his back into place, does a couple of twists of his torso then walks towards the now deflated and empty Coolax bladder. He picks it up, then takes a few quick steps towards the large metal spike before leaping onto the side of it and impaling the coolax on it. A siren sounds as Steel holds himself up along the shaft of the spike and looks back at the crowd as the crowd starts to cheer.

Dacos and Trill look up at Steel, now realising that he has successfully placed the coolax on the spike and won the game. They shake their heads. *"oh you...."*, Dacos starts to say but does not finish his sentence.

Tespa looks at Dacos and starts to laugh. Trill walks over and shoves Dacos, while smiling and shaking her head. Dacos smiles at Steel as Steel jumps back down off the spike, walks up to him and pats him on the back. *"Good game"*, Steel says to him.

Tespa continues to smile as she looks up at Dacos. Dacos looks down at her and smiles back. *"And that's why he's our king"*, Dacos says to her. Tespa, still smiling, nods.

Steel starts walking back towards the bleachers, raising his arms up to more cheering from the crowd. Tespa runs up, holds onto his arm and walks back with him. Dacos is also about to join them when he looks over towards the main entrance gate to the Castle gardens and notices a couple of his soldiers returning. Mounted on their rouks, they ride towards Dacos, dismounting their rooks at the edge of the field. Dacos looks at Trill, his face now looking a little concerned. Both Trill and Dacos walk to the soldiers and start speaking with them. Trill then quickly runs off towards the Castle gardens as Dacos continues to talk to his men. Steel turns and notices Dacos speaking with his soldiers and looks a little concerned. Tespa looks up at her father, still in awe of both him and the crowd cheering him. Steel looks back at her and changes his concerned expression into a smile.

Trill returns to Dacos holding his long coat in one hand and leading his rouk with her other. Dacos's rouk is slightly larger than the ones the other soldiers were riding. It also has two curved horns in the centre of its forehead instead of just one. The second much smaller and slightly further up the forehead from the larger one. Dacos throws on his coat and buttons it up. He reaches into his coat pocket and pulls out a large bracelet and fastens it to his wrist. He then raises up his hand and instantly a small cylindrical handle shaped object, his ronad, flies out of his jacket and into his hand. Though his looks very similar to any other ronad carried by the other soldiers, it most definitely is not. The most significant difference with his ronad, other than when it is fully extended is equipped with extra forklike spikes and side spikes on the ends instead of just simple points, is a feature that enables it to be summoned directly to Dacos's hand by use of a control bracelet. With a simple hand gesture, his ronad will fly out of its sheath, or anywhere it happens to be, even several meters away while fully extended, and come directly to his hand. He needs to be quick to catch it, however, Dacos's reflexes have never let him down yet. He places his ronad on a sheath strapped to the outside of his left shin. He jumps up onto his rouk, as the other soldiers do the same, and he rides off with them out through the main Castle gates. Trill turns back and walks back towards the Castle again.

-------------------------------- **Prono-4** --------------------------------

On Prono-4, a remote and barren planet in the outer rim system near Eluud, a small Laden colony has been residing temporarily and now preparing themselves to move on. The Ladens are a very peaceful group of nomadic and simple living, free spirited humanoids. They wear very simple, almost torn, white clothes that barely cover their bodies and white hoods that cover their head and upper half of their face. All female, and dressed like this, they look like slim Aymyn females, though with an obvious golden hue tone to their skin. However, seemingly hidden underneath their hoods, their heads are not Aymyn. Long pointed ears that point back and downwards. Bald rigid skull-top and forehead that finish in a couple of also backward pointing horns. They are a completely different species altogether, though still considered quite attractive.

EXOM - THE YOUNG KING

This group of Ladens are standing around a campfire engaged in a Laden "Exiting Ritual". Looking to be deep in prayer, standing straight, the top of their heads and faces covered, they sing a melodic and soothing chant. Their chant seems to influence the Flames within the campfire. The fire dances in a kind of rhythm matching the Laden's chanting, changing colours, and shooting out little sparks when the Ladens sing a particular note.

Flame plumes shoot out from the campfire and up into the air. So high, in fact, well up into the upper atmosphere, where they seem to explode into a variety of different colours. These colourful explosions can be seen from out in space and act as a signal to passing ships. A kind of Laden "Hitchhiking" signal. Passing ships will see this signal and know that there is a Laden Colony on the planet who is requesting a lift to move them to a new planet.

Not only very simple living, the Ladens are very highly respected throughout Exom. Their rituals affecting nature, promoting growth and restoration, they are seen as "Planet Healers". A kind of Terrestrial Priestess. To ignore their signal, and not offer them a ride to wherever they are going, would actually be considered rude.

Surrounding their campfire are very simple looking tents made from the same white torn fabric as their clothing. Flimsy, but looking like they serve their purpose.

A ship notices their signal and enters orbit. Before the Laden's notice it, a large weapon blast, originating from the ship, shoots down destroying their campfire. Many Ladens stumble backwards from the impact of the blast, then look up at the approaching ship, pulling their hoods back and revealing their shock and fear.

The ship, resembling a large metallic clump of dirt, with no real shape or form, obviously built more for functionality with no consideration for aesthetics, is clearly recognizable to the Ladens as a Dakari Raider ship. It fires more blasts at the site as it starts to land. Most of the Laden's scatter, helping others to their feet, then run into their tents. The Raider's ship lands, the outside doors open, and several Dakari exit, shooting the Laden's. The Ladens do not appear to have any weapons with which to protect themselves. Many are killed by the Dakari weapons while others still try to get away.

The Dakari charge at the ladens that are trying to flee, catching them easily, and slash them with long daggers, taking great joy in doing so.

Three Ladens do not run, however. Laden Elders, they stand still by the campfire and face their attackers. Hoods still pulled over their heads and faces, they make no attempt to flee and bravely conceal their fear as several Dakari approach them. The Elders, not dressed any differently to the other Ladens, are still recognised by the Dakari due to their defiant demeanour. The Dakari do not attack them, instead taking a more intimidating action and aggressively point their rifles at them. The Elders still do not move.

A lone Aymyn, an elderly looking male, walks off the Raider's ship and approaches the three elders. This Aymyn is dressed in what appears to be a tight fitting long black dress with a form fitting black overcoat fastened up to his neck. As he walks towards them, he keeps his body pointed forward, though seems to take more of a zigzag course towards them. The Elders remove their hoods as they watch him approach, their now scornful look hiding their fear. They recognise this Aymyn by, well almost everything about him, to be a Spectre.

They are correct. This Spectre, who calls himself Ador, leads the Dakari Raiders in this sector and nearby systems. He stops in front of the three elders, looking at each of them individually and then returns his gaze to the one standing in the middle. *"What have you got for me, old woman?"*, he says to her, looking completely emotionless.

"That's some nerve calling me old", the elder replies, still staring straight back at him and refusing to show any fear. *"How old is the demon inside this body that stands before me?"*, she asks.

Ador does not respond or even show any reaction to her question. He just stands there, emotionless, looking at her. He then looks at the other elders briefly before stepping in close to the middle Elder, right up to her face and stares her directly in the eyes. *"What have you got?"*, he asks again.

EXOM - THE YOUNG KING

"We are a simple Laden Colony", the elder standing to the left of the middle one replies. *"We are Planet Healers. We have nothing. The planet's we heal provide everything that we need"*.

"We are unarmed", the elder to the right then says. *"There is nothing here for you"*, she adds insolently.

Ador turns his head to look at this second Elder. *"Maybe"*, he says, still without any hint of emotion. If he had any emotions, even standing this close to the three Elders, he would not be concerned. He knows that they are unarmed. He also knows that they do not intend to run, or they would have done so already. Their defiant stance tells him everything he needs to know about them. They are not going anywhere, nor do they intend to give him anything. *"Search their shelters"*, Ador says to two Dakari that still have their rifles aimed at the Elders, as he turns and walks back towards his ship.

The Dakari walk off and start going through the tents and belongings of the Ladens. Rolling over and searching the bodies of the Ladens they have killed, though a seemingly pointless exercise given what the Ladens are wearing. Hardly the type of clothing that they could use to conceal anything

Ador stops, turns back, and looks at the elders. *"It's been a long trip"*, he says to them. *"Some of us are hungry. Some..."*, he pauses to watch their reaction to what he is about to say, *"More so than others"*, he adds. He starts rubbing a large, jewelled signet ring on his finger. The Laden Elders can no longer hide their fear. They know exactly what is about to come.

Jumping out of the Raider's ship, three very large feline-type creatures. More reptilian than animal, their piercing snake like yellow eyes stand out strikingly against their smooth black silky skin. At the end of their long powerful tail is a cluster of hardened bones capable of inflicting considerable damage. Not that they need to rely on that too much, their extendable lower jaw, that separates into toothed mandibles, is more than capable of tearing their prey apart. In horror, one of the elders calls out the name of these fierce creatures, *"Vipers!"*

The Vipers take a quick look around them, then spotting the elders, their reptilian pupils contract and focus right before they charge. All three leap straight past Ador, onto the elders, and immediately start tearing them apart. Ador, still showing absolutely no emotion, turns away and starts walking back towards his ship. Two Dakari return to the ship with him. They stand and stare at Ador, waiting for further instructions. Ador tilts his head slightly towards them but does not look at them. *"Find something"*, he says to them. *"Make this worthwhile"*.

The Dakari walk back towards the tents, passing the Vipers who are still tearing into the Laden Elders. The Dakari do not seem to be worried about the vipers and walk past them as though they are not there. Likewise, the Vipers seem to show no interest in the Dakari. Ador continues onto his ship and disappears inside.

--------------------------- **The Young King** ---------------------------

Zippin, a young girl, about sixteen years old, runs down one of the corridors of Chassam Castle. Dressed in a long black dress with long sleeves, a low plunging neckline and a wide black belt. She appears to be running from someone, or something. She drops to her knees and slides down the corridor floor until she crashes into a closed door. She picks herself up and looks back behind her. Two Eluudian guards come running down the corridor after her. She smiles cheekily at them, then opens the door that she just crashed into, runs into the room, closing the door behind her. Right behind her the Guards reach the door, open it run in after her.

Vessel, Tespa's tall and very glamorous Troin girlfriend, walks down the long balcony that goes all the way around the castle. Wearing very little other than a very small wrap skirt around her waist and a barely-there criss-cross scarf around her neck and chest, both created by her Tal, her long brown hair that reaches down to her lower back would cover more of her if she wished than any of her clothing. Ahead of her a door opens and Zippin runs out through it and onto the balcony. Vessel looks at her and chuckles slightly. Zippin spots Vessel and runs straight for her. Vessel does not move and just watches as Zippin approaches. The two guards come running out of the same door that Zippin just exited through. They spot her and run after her just as she reaches Vessel. She grabs onto Vessel and hides behind her as the guards catch up to them. The Guards stop in front of Vessel as Vessel stands there looking at them. *"Sorry, Mam"*, one of the guards says to Vessel. *"We tried to catch her before she got to this area of the Castle"*.

"She's a slippery one", the other guard says to her.

"She is indeed", Vessel replies as she reaches behind her back and wraps her arms around Zippin, giving her a backwards hug. *"It's alright, she's with me"*, Vessel tells the guards. Zippin comes out from behind Vessel and glares at the guards. *"You are here to see me, aren't you"*, Vessel asks Zippin as she looks down at her. Zippin looks at Vessel and pokes her tongue out at her. Vessel grabs her and holds her out in front of the guards. *"Lock her up"*, Vessel tells them.

"No, no. I'm here to see you. I'm here to see you", Zippin says as she giggles. Vessel smiles and nods at the guards. The Guards turn and walk away. Zippin hugs Vessel's arm as Vessel looks at her.

"Are you up to no good again?", Vessel asks her.

"Always", Zippin replies with a cheeky smile. Vessel smiles back. *"Hey, check this out"*, Zippin says to her. She rolls up her sleeve to reveal her Tal on her arm. As she stares at her arm, nanoparticles pour out of her Tal and start covering her arm, slowing making their way up to her elbow. They solidify into the beginnings of Troin armour. As the nanoparticles make their way past Zippin's elbow and continue to solidify into Troin armour, it starts to tear away at the sleeve of her regular clothing.

"You'd better stop there", Vessel tells her. *"Unless you want to wear the armour home or walk around naked"*. Zippin laughs as the armour reverts to nanoparticles again and returns to her Tal.

She smiles at Vessel. *"I can make other stuff too"*, she tells vessel. She puts her arms down and stares at Vessel as a giant set of Troin angel wings forms on her back behind her. As they take shape, Zippin spans them out to show Vessel. *"Just like the first"*, Vessel says to her, referring to the "First Troin" whom the female Troin create wings with their Tals to honour her.

Forgetting that Tal created clothing and objects will cut straight through any clothing, and most other things they contact while solidifying, a point that Vessel was trying to make to Zippin when it started to tear apart her sleeve, Zippin's wings cut through the shoulder section of her shirt. Her shirt comes apart at the shoulders and starts to drop. Zippin catches the front part of the shirt before it drops too far, then looks at Vessel and laughs. Vessel smiles and shakes her head. *"Go home"*, she tells Zippin. Zippin retracts her wings back into her Tal, turns and runs off still holding the front of her shirt in front of her. Vessel laughs as she watches Zippin run off, her back naked and the back part of her shirt flopping behind her. *"Keep practicing!"*, Vessel yells out to her as Zippin runs back inside through the door she came out of before.

Quite some distance outside the Eluudian castle walls, eight Eluudian soldiers, dressed neck to toe in a black uniform complete with gloves, large belt and with their ronad strapped and sheath to their boot, have gathered around the bodies of three dead villagers. Two of the soldiers are still mounted on their rouks, while the other six soldiers have dismounted their rouks. Three of these soldiers are studying the bodies of the villagers while the other three soldiers are holding the reins of the remaining six rouks between them.

Dacos rides up on his rouk and approaches the party. He dismounts his rouk and walks towards the soldiers and dead villagers. His rouk does not need anyone holding it and it stays where Dacos has left it. Dacos moves in closer, crouches down to inspect the bodies and shakes his head mournfully as one of the Eluudian Soldiers approaches him.

"It looks like Raiders did this", the soldier says to Dacos. Dacos, still crouched beside the bodies of the villagers, looks up to survey the landscape. Something does not seem right. Something that may not be noticeable to anyone else other than Dacos. For when it comes to noticing things, Dacos's sense of perception is second-to-none. If it wasn't for the fact that he was an obvious Parandrae Sign, one would think he shows gifts of something more.

"Either that", Dacos replies, *"or someone has made it to look that way"*.

The soldier speaking to Dacos, starts to look concerned, and a little surprised. *"Someone?"*, he asks, and then starts to look at the other soldiers.

Dacos continues to look around the scene, as well as taking in the setting of the dead villagers and ground they are laying on. *"It's too clean"*, Dacos replies. *"Raiders are not known for their neatness"*. Dacos stands up, towering with his height over the soldiers that stand near him, and completely takes in the scene. Looking all around him, even up into the air at apparently nothing. This confuses the soldiers that are watching him and wondering what it is that he thinks he is seeing. *"It's very clean"*, Dacos adds.

Dacos starts walking back towards his rouk, stopping briefly next to one of the more senior looking soldiers to speak to him. *"My sister will be on her way here soon"*, Dacos tells him. *"Don't disturb anything, and then assist her when she gets here"*.

"Yes, General", the more senior looking soldier replies.

Dacos continues walking back to his Rouk, mounts it and gallops off, leaving the Eluudian soldiers to stand guard.

Inside a large, very dimly lit room, stands three Aymyn males wearing civilian style clothing. Walking towards them is Nadiri, an Aymyn looking female, wearing a full neck to floor length, long sleeve, black coat that ends in a kind of skirt. As she walks towards them, she doesn't take an entirely direct route. Instead zigzagging across the floor. Her movements are very elegant, and at no point does she turn her body to face the direction that she is walking, instead keeping her body and head always pointing forward towards the three Aymyn males. The males look uneasy as she approaches as they know that this female, though has the appearance of an Aymyn, is actually a Spectre.

As Nadiri approaches the three Aymyn males, another figure steps out from the shadows. A very attractive Aymyn female, with long red hair, wearing a very long, but very different, sleeveless black cloak. Her eyes are piercing and emphasized by very thick black makeup. This is Sabel, and though she looks innocent, is actually a very deadly assassin and right hand to the Sharlon Leader, Dark.

While the Aymyn males feel uneasy, almost fearful around Nadiri, Sabel does not. Sabel confidently moves toward Nadiri, her walk and posture portraying her as someone who owns the room.

Nadiri walks up, stands in front of Sabel and looks her up and down, seemingly just as wary of Sabel as the three Aymyn males are fearful of Nadiri herself. And she should be. Sabel's confidence is not unfounded. Everyone in the room is only alive and standing due to Sabel's choosing it to be so. Something that Sabel looks as though she does not choose all that often. Sabel gives Nadiri a quick side glance before moving past her and towards a long table. On top of the table is a plethora of objects and devices scattered all along it. Sabel picks up one of the objects and looks at it briefly before putting it back down again and continues moving along the table. *"I was hoping your coming here would attract less attention"*, Sabel says.

Nadiri turns around to face Sabel, and watches as Sabel runs her fingers down a couple more objects on the table. *"Nothing I couldn't handle"*, Nadiri replies.

Sabel picks up another one of the objects on the table and looks at it closely. *"Evidently"*, Sabel says, as she then places the object back down on the table. She continues to walk on further along the table, not looking back at Nadiri and not afraid to have her back facing her either. *"Still, we have gone this long without drawing attention to our whereabouts"*, she adds. *"We'd like to keep it that way for a little bit longer"*.

The Spectres, being an outspoken race, and Nadiri being no exception, makes her reasons for being there a bit clearer to Sabel. *"You are not the one I have come here to see"*, she says.

Not sure if she should feel insulted or belittled, Sabel gives Nadiri another side glance before looking away again. *"You will need to wait then"*, Sabel responds, as she pulls out a chair for Nadiri at the end of the table, then walks back into the shadows and out of sight.

Dacos, still riding his rouk, rides through the Castle gates and into the Castle gardens. He slows his rouk down to a walk and, as he approaches the Castle, a small number of other rouks, sheltered in individual stables to the side of the Castle, watch Dacos approach with curiosity. Three children are playing on a cart, that is being pulled by two much smaller and younger rouks, obliviously cross Dacos's path. He stops his rouk and allows them to pass, seeming completely unconcerned.

Suddenly, from out of nowhere, another Rouk charges through the castle grounds past Dacos. It jumps over the children and cart, which the children watch on and smile with amusement, not at all scared and as though this kind of thing happens regularly. What should ordinarily be surprising, but again does not appear to be, is that this Rouk has no rider on it, but is still galloping with purpose towards the castle's large main entrance stairs. At that same moment the castle doors swing open. Trill comes running out and runs down the stairs towards the charging rouk. The charging rouk stops right in front of her and, in one leap, Trill mounts the rouk. The rouk immediately rears up, turns around and charges back towards Dacos. Dacos watches on, surprisingly calmly, as Trill rides at full speed towards him, and not looking like slowing down any time soon. Now, evidently not riding directly at him, she tears past Dacos, reaching out her closed hand to him. Dacos also extends his arm out towards her, hand in a fist, and fist pumps hers as she passes. Never even slowing down, Trill rides her rouk out the Castle grounds.

Dacos resumes riding up towards the stables and, as he does so, a brand-new stable starts to construct itself right in front of him beside all the others. Dacos jumps off his rouk and lets the rouk continue to walk into the still being built stable. By the time his rouk enters and turns itself around, the stable is completely built around it.

Dacos starts walking towards the Castle stairs, passing the children on their cart and young rouks. Two more children run up to him and start tugging on his coat. One is holding over themselves a large blanket that has random pieces of cloth and sticks sewn onto it. He is pretending to be the "Trolor Monster", a fictional creature told in many fairy tales throughout Exom. A creature so scary that even the Skurj are afraid of it.

Dacos stops, awkwardly pats one of the children on the head and smiles. He is quickly "rescued" by the Twins, two identical Albearian twin sisters, very tall and slender humanoid ladies with pale white skin and a shared consciousness. Dressed in matching but opposite long black and white skirts and sleeveless open tops, that reach right up to the top of their necks. Finished with a head covering, that is draped over their head, and hangs down to the side below their shoulders. They approach Dacos and the children, smile, lean over and start talking to the children, distracting them long enough for Dacos to continue his way up the stairs and into the Castle.

The inside of the Castle matches the outside. Walls made of large stone blocks, but also with visible wood poles and trims. The light inside is not overly powerful but fitting for a culture used to living in a twilight. Good enough to read in, which is convenient, as there is a small open library near the castle entrance area. Only a couple of shelves with books on them, along with a couch and a couple of single couch-like chairs, it is really only used by one person.

As Dacos enters the Castle, the Castle Door Sergeant, Sergeant Mew, a very pleasant, and though quiet, not unsociable person, greets him, escorted by two more Eluudian soldiers. A bearding man with tied back long hair, also dressed neck to toe in all black and finished with a long black coat that stretches from his neck to his shins, Sergeant Mew is tasked with knowing all who enter the Castle. He does this, often, by being the one to actually open the door for everyone, if he can get there fast enough. Though opening the door is not specifically his job, it is something he doesn't mind doing. Sergeant Mew often knows more than just who is in the Castle, and usually also knows exactly where they are.

"General", Sergeant Mew greets Dacos.

"Sergeant Mew", Dacos replies with a smile.

Sergeant Mew catches the large wooden Castle door before it shuts and assists it to close more quietly and properly. Dacos stands and watches, feeling somewhat guilty, as though despite his rank and position, that is probably something he should have done himself.

Sergeant Mew interprets Dacos's thoughts by the expression on Dacos's face, and smiles at him but thinks nothing of it. *"You're Sister just took off out of here"*, Mew tells Dacos.

"Yes", Dacos replies. *"I've just come back from where she is going"*.

"She seemed in a hurry", Mew adds speaking about the speed at which Trill left the Castle to run and jump on her rouk.

"She is Airy", Dacos replies. *"When is she ever not?"*

"Airy", a sort of descriptive nickname given to those of the Arandae Sign. Sergeant Mew, still smiling, and also very familiar with Trill's energetic behaviour, just nods. Dacos continues on his way, walking past Sergeant Mew, his mind focussed on speaking with King Steel. *"Sergeant"*, he turns to Mew and asks. *"Whereabouts of the king?"*

Mew looks back at Dacos, hesitates for a second before answering. *"Currently in the Meeting Hall"*, Mew replies.

Dacos notices the hesitation but pays it no mind. *"Good"*, Dacos says back to Mew, and walks towards one of the main hallways inside the Castle.

Mew, slowly turns and looks over at Dacos, still smiling, and now reveals the reason behind his hesitation. *"With Princess Det"*, Mew adds, making Dacos stop in his tracks, almost tripping himself up, and then pauses for a moment. Mew watches Dacos's reaction with amusement. Knowing that just mentioning Princess Det's name would make Dacos stumble. Not because he thinks that Dacos does not like Det, but because he knows he does. A lot. Something that is mutual, though neither of them will ever admit it, not even to themselves. It is something that everyone else in the Castle is aware of, however, and is the cause of much frustration from bystanders who just wish that Dacos and Det will get together already.

Dacos quickly recomposes himself, then continues walking towards the hallway as Sergeant Mew giggles to himself briefly, then turns and leaves the entrance area with his escorts.

The meeting room is one of the more commonly used rooms by the royal family in the Castle, though very simple in layout and decor. It consists of a large table, almost immediately in front of the doorway as you enter the room, surrounded by many chairs. A long bench seat is positioned against the wall next to the main doorway. Deeper into the room are several smaller chairs, shelves, and tables along with another doorway leading out onto the main balcony that goes right around Chassam Castle.

The same type of technology that is on Aymyn that enables them to build all required furniture at will is also available on Eluud, however, not many rooms in Chassam Castle utilize it, except for the Training Hall.

Seated at one end of the large table is Det. She does not look very happy. In fact, she looks a little worried, even annoyed. *"I have changed"*, she says defiantly. *"I am not aggressive anymore. I used to have a temper, but I can keep that under control now. It's been ages since I have lashed out"*.

She is speaking to her father, King Steel, who is seated at the other end of the table, dressed in a long black gothic style royal robe. His wavey, unbrushed dark brown hair and dishevelled looking shortcut beard makes him look like he has not tidied up after the Coolax game, but this is the usual appearance for this "young king". He is looking back at Det with a serious and somewhat disappointed expression. *"It was only moments before you entered this room"*, he says back to her.

"But I didn't hurt anyone", Det says in her defence. Steel looks down along the table and at a middle-aged woman and a young man, from appearances around the same age as Det, who are also sitting at the table. The young man looks to be beaten up, with obvious cuts and bruises to his face, neck, and shoulders along with his clothes looking as though they have been torn in some sort of scuffle. Steel looks back at Det with a hint of disbelief, as Det glances at the young man quickly, then looks back at her father. *"He doesn't count"*, Det adds.

Steel shakes his head with disappointment as he thinks about what to say. Before he can say anything, Det speaks up again. *"So, one person"*, Det says. *"I hurt one person"*.

Steel now looks behind Det at the long bench seat by the wall. Several people are seated on it, all of whom look as beaten up as the young man seated at the table. Det also turns to look at them, then quickly looks back at her father, this time with a guilty expression on her face. *"Maybe a bit more than one"*, she adds. *"One person and a bit".*

Det leans over the table, ready to defend her actions, as she looks at her father. *"It's not like...."*

But Steel has no interest in hearing it and cuts her off. *"Det! Be quiet!"*, he scolds. At a loss of what to do, or even what to say to Det's victims seated in the room, Steel can only manage to look at them sympathetically frustrated, shaking his head, with no words escaping his lightly clenched mouth. He takes a deep breath, lets it out and then speaks. *"Please go see to your injuries"*, he tells everyone else sitting in the room, *"and know that I will deal with this".* The injured group all stand up, bow, and leave the room.

Before leaving, the young man who was seated at the table, stops, turns to Det, smiles and waves. *"Bye Det"*, he says to her, but Det just ignores him. As everyone else leaves the room, Det remains sitting there, just looking straight at her father. Steel watches them leave, giggles at the young boy's words, then looks back at Det. *"And they still love you"*, Steel says to Det.

Det looks away from her father, and down at the table, looking slightly remorseful. Steel stops smiling, remembering that this needs to be a serious moment. *"This can't continue, Det"*, he says to her. *"You're a princess, not a thug. The people love you. How long do you think they will continue to love you if you go around beating them up?"*

Det looks back at her father, as though she is about to protest against what he is saying. *"It's not like I go around beating people up"*, she says to him. *"They started fighting. I broke it up".*

"You finished it", Steel replies. Det shrugs, not sure what to say. Steel's gaze softens. *"They look up to you"*, Steel adds. *"You represent the best in us".*

A that moment, Tespa skips excitedly into the room. She has her hood pulled up over her head and a backpack strapped to her back. Something that she is hardly ever without.

Oblivious to what is happening in the room, and only knowing that her father is in there, Tespa interrupts as she skips into the room. *"Dad,*

I saw.....". She says, before stopping herself after noticing what she is walking in on. Seeing both her father and Det seated at the table, staring at each other silently and awkwardly, Tespa starts walking backwards towards the bench seat along the wall. *"It can wait"*, she adds. She sits down, looking very embarrassed to have interrupted something, and sits there quietly

Det does not turn to acknowledge Tespa's entrance. Though knowing Tespa is there, she continues to look at her father as though she is not. Steel looks over at Tespa, wanting to smile, but also needing to stay in a serious appearance. He looks back at Det and continues to address her. *"You're a princess, not a combatant"*, he says to her.

A high-pitched muffled voice, coming from Tespa's direction, can be heard joining in the conversation. *"Princess"*, it says. Steel glances quickly over at Tespa, who is just sitting there, innocently looking back at him. Det continues to ignore everything other than her discussion with her father.

"You're a King and you're a combatant", Det says. *"And the people still love you"*.

Again, a high-pitched muffled voice, coming from Tespa's direction, speaks up. *"Love you"*, it says. This time Steel tries to ignore it, as Tespa still sits quietly, looking very innocent.

"I don't fight our own people", Steel replies to Det.

Once again, the same high pitched muffled voice comes from Tespa's direction. *"I don't fight"*, it says. This time Steel and Det both turn and look at Tespa, both with a frustrated expression. Tespa continues to sit there quietly, innocently, and just smiles back. Steel and Det return to facing and addressing each other.

"I wasn't the one fighting", Det says. *"They were. Mostly"*.

"Mostly", the high-pitched muffled voice coming from Tespa's direction repeats. Instantly Tespa stops smiling and scolds back, *"Kako!"*. There is silence. Tespa sits there quietly and smiles as Det and her father try to ignore her and remain focussed on each other.

"I don't get what the big deal is", Det continues as she stares angrily back at her father. *"You break up fights all the time. You are always going out to a battle somewhere"*.

EXOM - THE YOUNG KING

"When I fight it is to protect our people", Steel replies shaking his head, wondering how she can see a comparison between going out to fight an enemy of the kingdom and a hallway brawl.

The door to the room opens again, and this time Dacos enters. Noticing very quickly what is going on by the intense staring that is going on between Det and her father, Dacos steps back and stands beside the doorway so as to be out of the way and away from the conversation. He had been prewarned by Sergeant Mew that Det was in here with her father, but what Mew had not warned him about was why. Perhaps he didn't know. Dacos looks over at Tespa wondering what he has just walked in on. Tespa looks back at him and smiles uncomfortably, feeling his awkwardness.

Det and Steel do not acknowledge Dacos entering the room, instead keeping themselves focused on the intense conversation that is happening between them. *"So, take me with you"*, Det adds as a rebuttal to her father's last statement. *"Let me fight with you"*.

Again, Steel shakes his head. This is not the first time that Det has asked to go out and battle beside him. Or battle instead of him. Or just go out and battle in general. All Steel has wanted is for Det to behave like a princess, stay safe, not fight, not scuffle, and especially not go out into battle. *"We are not having this discussion"*, he replies, trying to stop the topic from branching off in that direction again.

"We never have this discussion!", Det huffs as she stands up from the table, turns and storms towards the doorway. Still ignoring Tespa, even looking like she is going to completely ignore and not acknowledge Dacos, she walks past Dacos with her eyes pointing firmly towards the doorway. Annoyed at Det storming off before the conversation is finished, Steel calls out to her, *"Det!"*. Det stops momentarily. Not in response to her father calling out to her, but instead to look up at Dacos who is still looking awkward standing beside the doorway. *"He's your king"*, she says to Dacos snidely, then continues out through the doorway. Dacos stands there, speechless, and only able to watch, then looks at Steel all wide-eyed and innocent, still wondering what has just happened. Steel looks back frustrated at Dacos. *"She's your girlfriend"*, Steel says to him.

C.C.DAVISON

Dacos tries to appear confused by Steel's words and retorts back, *"Hardly. But she is your daughter"*.

"And on that note", Tespa joins in as she stands up quickly, *"I will go and see if My Sister is alright"*. Tespa walks over to the doorway and looks up at Dacos. *"Or anyone else she happens to pass on her way"*, she adds with a kind of anxious smirk.

As Tespa turns and leaves the room, the contents of her backpack, which also happens to be the source of the muffled high pitch voice that was interrupting Steel and Det earlier, can be seen through the large transparent front section. Sitting on a tiny chair, is a small blue hairless creature, about fifteen centimetres tall, wearing a white shirt, yellow boots, and a very happy grin. This is Kako, Tespa's little pet friend. As Tespa leaves, Kako, with his wide black eyes and what looks to be a permanent excited expression, stares back at both Steel and Dacos. *"Allo, I'm Kako"*, he says.

Tespa has had Kako for a very long time, since she was a young girl in fact. No one is quite sure what he is, or where he comes from, but he is certainly a jolly little thing that Tespa loves and carries with her almost everywhere. Though perfectly capable of getting around on his own, and does, especially when trying to escape from Tespa when she tries to dress him. For some reason he prefers to only wear one boot instead of both. While travelling, he usually stays inside his purpose-built backpack and happily watches the world while seated on his small chair. Saying very little, often repeating words or small phrases when not continually introducing himself, he is always friendly and smiling.

Walking confidently and proudly down the corridor, Vessel spots Tespa leaving the Meeting Hall. Smiling, she approaches Tespa. *"Your sister seems to be in her usual form"*, Vessel says to Tespa as she walks up, places both hands on Tespa's shoulders in a flirty embrace. Tespa responds by placing her hands on Vessel's cheeks and gives her a passionate kiss on the lips. Tespa then pulls back and smiles. *"I'll be back"*, Tespa tells her as she turns both herself and Vessel around before breaking off and continues down the corridor backwards. Vessel looks at Tespa a little confused but more amused. *"Where else would you go?"*, Vessel calls out to her. Tespa blows her back a kiss and then turns around and walks forward down the corridor. Vessel's attention is drawn to Kako, still seated in Tespa's backpack, and staring back at her. *"Allo, I'm Kako"*, Kako says to Vessel, still sporting his apparently permanent happy smile. Obviously very well acquainted with Kako, Vessel smiles back at him. *"I know, Kako"*, she says back to him. Kako appears very pleased with Vessel's acknowledgement and his smile now becomes even happier. *"I'm Kako"*, he says again.

Tespa, still walking away, turns around again and once again walks backwards down the corridor as she looks back at Vessel. *"If you are going in to see my father"*, she calls back to Vessel, *"you should probably cover up more. You know how much of a prude he is. Though he would never say anything"*.

Vessel, almost laughing, smiles back at Tespa. Vessel has never felt embarrassed about the way she dresses around King Steel. Or anyone else for that matter. And, just as Tespa said, no one has ever said anything to her to make her feel so. Just to humour Tespa, Vessel constructs giant angel-like wings on her back from her Tal. She grabs hold of them and wraps them around herself while never taking her eyes off Tespa. *"How's this?"*, she asks Tespa.

"I wish I could be as bold as you", Tespa replies as she giggles. Tespa turns back around again and continues down the corridor. Seeing Vessel again, and just as excited as though it is the first time, Kako smiles at her excitedly. *"Allo...."*, is all Kako manages to say before he is cut off by Vessel.

"Bye Kako", Vessel says and smiles back at him as she watches them walk away

Inside the Meeting Hall, Dacos moves away from the doorway and walks towards Steel. Steel is still seated at the table. His thoughts still on Det. He looks up at Dacos curiously. *"When are you going to take her off my hands?"*, Steel asks him. *"You can't be waiting for my blessing, surely. If so, then you have it"*.

Dacos attempts to play all innocent, pretending not to know what the King is talking about. *"Tespa?"*, Dacos asks in an attempt at deflection. *"In case you hadn't noticed, she already has someone"*.

Not buying into Dacos' unsuccessful attempt at naivety, Steel just looks back at him and shakes his head. *"Don't give me that"*, Steel says, then clarifies, *"Det"*.

Dropping the facade, Dacos calmly speaks his mind. *"Have you considered letting her join the army?"*, he asks.

Steel looks back at him with a look of disbelief, which slowly turns to one of amusement. *"That is not what I meant, Dacos"*, Steel replies. *"But you'd like that, wouldn't you?"*, he then adds with a smirk.

Dacos ignores his king's suggestive comment. *"You can't deny her fighting ability"*, he says, still just standing there looking innocently back at Steel. Steel's amused expression quickly fades.

"Don't remind me", Steel replies.

"Sometimes I think she can out do me", Dacos adds, more matter of fact than defiantly. *"Even you. Perhaps the both of us"*.

"Which is why it is up to the both of us to make sure that it never comes to that", Steel replies. *"She is a princess. I wish she'd behave like one"*.

Dacos looks at his King with intrigue, wondering if he should continue saying what is on his mind. Almost encouragingly, Steel waits for Dacos to do so, so Dacos does. *"She was decreed a princess"*, Dacos says. *"Not born one. You should know, you decreed it"*. Steel looks away, not knowing any rebuttal to Dacos's comment. *"I am just saying, maybe she has a different nature to the one you have in mind for her"*, Dacos explains, noticing his king's silence.

Dacos's words make Steel smile, but not due to any reason that Dacos may think. *"Nature?"*, Steel says to Dacos cheekily with a smile. *"I am sure it's more than just her nature that has you interested"*. Dacos stares blankly back at Steel, again pretending to not know what he is referring to. Once again, not buying into Dacos's pretend ignorance, Steel just shakes his head and looks at his royal coat, then starts trying to adjust it. *"Fine, continue playing that game"*, Steel adds. *"You've both been playing it since you were children"*.

"Is that so?", Dacos asks.

"It is", Steel replies.

Dacos shrugs. *"I am obviously easier to read than she is"*, Dacos says. Steel laughs at Dacos's words as he stands up, having no luck adjusting himself while sitting down, and starts to work on his lapel, making sure that each side appears even.

"Oh, you can read her", Steel responds. *"The bravest General in my army, who takes chances with his head and his heart in battle, won't take the same chances on my daughter and ask her out"*.

"Well, she is your daughter", Dacos now replies confidently. *"And I run the risk of losing a lot more than just my head and heart by taking a chance on her"*.

Steel glances up at Dacos curiously. *"Not from me you wouldn't"*, he says to Dacos.

Dacos looks back at Steel with a sincere expression. *"There are scarier things than you, my king"*, he says. *"Have you met your daughter?"*, he then asks rhetorically.

Not sure how to respond to that, or even if it deserves a response, Steel just frowns at Dacos. His expression then softens as he appears to get lost in thought. *"I know we don't practice the old Aymyn customs on Eluud anymore"*, Steel says. *"Not that we ever did. But I still wonder if we had the old revealing ceremonies what sign she would be"*.

"Parkendal, I would imagine", Dacos says.

"Parkendal, we would hope", Steel responds. *"She certainly has the stubbornness"*.

"You can talk", Dacos says jokingly to his King. Steel looks back at him wondering if he should feel insulted. Dacos smiles and continues. *"You are an obvious Arandae, almost as airy as my sister. Perhaps stubbornness is something that happens when you're royal"*. Steel again does not know how to respond, and yet the more he thinks about what Dacos has said, the more he thinks it makes sense.

Steel shrugs softly before returning his thoughts back to Det and her Sign. *"Well, she is certainly hot headed"*, he says out loud as he thinks, trying to reassure himself that Det would be Parkendal. Dacos can see

Steel lost deep in thought, and also the uncertainty expressed on his face.

"You don't seem convinced", Dacos says.

Steel looks up at Dacos, his uncertainty now starting to look more like concern. *"It's a scary thought to entertain"*, Steel replies. Steel snaps himself out of his thoughts and changes his concerned expression into a smile. *"Which, I guess, is why we don't anymore"*, he then adds.

Steel pauses for a moment and stands still as he looks to be in deep thought. Dacos looks at him with intrigue, wondering what he is thinking about. *"Is everything alright, Your Highness"*, Dacos asks him.

Still deep in thought, Steel looks up at Dacos as though bringing him into it. *"She wasn't always like this"*, he says to Dacos.

"We're still talking about Det?", Dacos asks.

"I mean she was never the happiest of kids", Steel continues not really having heard Dacos's question. *"She used to have such terrible nightmares when she was really young. Not just at night either. I'd often find her huddled in a corner, trembling"*.

"Well, she had a pretty traumatic start to life", Dacos says.

"Don't we know it", Steel replies, now looking more present. *"They both did"*, Steel adds. *"But Tespa never had the nightmares or day terrors. Not that I knew about anyway"*.

"You'd know if she did", Dacos says. *"She is a strong Wendral Sign if ever there was one. She'd tell you all about them"*. Dacos pauses and smirks. *"With a smile on her face"*, he adds.

"That she would", Steel replies. *"Never scared to show her emotions"*, Steel adds as he smiles thinking about Tespa. His smile fades into a more serious expression as his thoughts return to Det. *"But so did Det"*, Steel says.

"Det showed her emotions?", Dacos asks. *"That I'd like to see"*.

"Yes, she did", Steel replies. *"Until she didn't"*. He looks at Dacos and Dacos stares back. *"She just suddenly closed off. Shut herself out to everything"*, Steel tells him. *"Emotionally anyway"*, Steel adds. *"Physically she shut herself off to nothing"*.

"And now she is just angry all the time", Dacos says with a hint of a laugh.

"Well, I wonder if she is", Steel replies. *"I don't think she lets herself feel anything. Or tries not to at least. I am not sure which is worse"*.

Dacos looks down and raises his eyebrow as he thinks about it. With all his heart he would very much like her to feel something. Steel notices Dacos standing there, thinking, and knows what he is thinking about. Steel smiles at him. *"I am sure there some things that even Det can't stop herself from feeling"*. Dacos looks up at Steel. Steel gives him a wink. Dacos looks back down as he continues to think about it.

Feeling that this conversation has gone on long enough, and time to address why Dacos is really in the room with him, Steel changes the subject. *"So, if you have not come to ask for my daughter's hand, then why do you grace me with your presence?"*, Steel asks Dacos.

Dacos walks further into the room and closer to Steel. *"You've heard about the dead villages that were found outside the Castle grounds?"*, Dacos says. Steel had heard the news, but no more than anyone else and was waiting for any extra information that Dacos or his sister could provide.

"What can you tell me?", Steel asks.

"It looks like another raider attack", Dacos replies.

Steel had suspected as much. Raider attacks were common in Eluud. They are the very reason his father was no longer with them, and they had been slowly increasing in frequency. *"I see"*, Steel says thinking that is pretty much going to be the end of the report. Dacos stands there looking back at Steel, not saying another word, and waiting to see if Steel picks up on his silence. Not quite sure exactly what he is picking up on, Steel looks curiously at Dacos. *"You didn't come in here to tell me about another Raider attack"*, Steel says.

"No", Dacos replies. *"I said it looks like another raider attack"*.

Steel now starts to pick up on what Dacos is not saying. *"You don't think it is?"*, Steel asks.

Dacos just stands there, looking at Steel and shakes his head. *"No, I don't"*.

"What do you think it was?", Steel asks curiously, never having reason to doubt Dacos's suspicions. In fact, often relying heavily on them.

"I don't know", Dacos replies. His words hesitant, as though still thinking about the question as he answers. *"I mean it could be"*, he adds. *"The Dakari are known for their gorilla assaultive style and small random attacks"*.

Steel focuses on the possibility that it was Raiders and reflects on other recent attacks. *"The number of Raider attacks lately have increased"*, Steel says. *"Turning up everywhere and anywhere. Which is strange because there have been no reports of Drop Ship remnants around"*. Drop ships are what the Dakari Raiders use to land on Eluud. Since ships can not land normally on the planet, under their own power, the Dakari created ships without engines that they simply drop to the planet from orbit. Made to withstand the impact, well usually, the occupants inside leave the ship after it has crash landed.

"They usually scavenge and salvage most of the wreckage", Dacos says. *"But you are right, there is usually some trace left behind"*.

"They are obviously getting here somehow", Steel says. Steel then remembers Dacos hesitancy to conclude that this was a Raider attack. *"But you don't think this was one of them?"*, he adds.

Dacos just stares back at Steel and shakes his head. *"No"*, he replies. *"It did not seem vicious enough for the Dakari"*. On any other planet the Dakari will shoot their targets with their long laser rifles. However, on Eluud, with such weapons being ineffective, the Dakari will slaughter their victims with long dagger like weapons, and occasionally also their long razor-sharp claws, seeming to take great pleasure in the kill. Occasionally they will forget that they are on Eluud and still attempt to use their laser rifles. This never works out well for them. One thing the Dakari are not known for is leaving an attack site tidy. Of course, this was something that Dacos picked up on when investigating the attack site. Even when Dacos was a child, his suspicions were something that Steel had learnt to trust. This in mind, although he still does not know what has happened, he takes comfort in knowing that Dacos will find out.

"And that is why you are my General", Steel says to Dacos. *"I have known you for a very long time, Dacos. I have learnt to trust your gut. You pick up on things that no one else does. If you are saying there is*

something not right about this, then I have every confidence that there is something not right about this. Just as I know that YOU will work it out".

"So, no pressure then?", Dacos replies with a sarcastic look about him.

Steel throws Dacos a sneaky side glance as he reaches into his pocket as if to feel for something. *"You'll be fine. You always are".* Whatever Steel was looking for in his pocket, it's not there, and he pulls his hand out empty and looks around the room. He notices Dacos watching him, so stops looking around and smiles back at him cheekily. *"Now, speaking of working things out",* Steel starts to say to Dacos. Dacos smiles knowingly at Steel, aware of where he is directing the conversation.

"Yes, on that little project", Dacos replies. *"I have uncovered some information that puts an interesting perspective on Aymyn".*

Steel looks at Dacos curiously. This was not quite what he was expecting to hear. *"On Aymyn",* Steel asks Dacos.

Dacos walks over and stands next to Steel. He pulls out a message stick, a pencil thin footlong metallic bar, that when activated produces a holographic screen. He activates it, producing the holographic screen which appears to have a large amount of text on it, and shows it to Steel. As Steel begins to read the information on the message stick display, he appears visibly taken back. He looks at Dacos confused. *"Troin?",* he asks as though some part of the information on Dacos' screen doesn't seem to make sense.

Before he responds, Dacos turns back and looks at the doorway and notices Vessel standing there, wings still wrapped around her. How long she had been standing there he did not know. Realising that she has been discovered, not that she was hiding, Vessel walks into the room. *"Is someone talking about me?",* She asks as she walks over to Steel and Dacos.

Also surprised to see Vessel there, Steel looks at her and smiles. *"Vessel",* he says. *"You just missed Tespa".*

Vessel continues to casually walk towards him. *"No, I didn't",* she replies. *"She'll be back apparently".*

Steel notices how Vessel is dressed, and while not the prude that Tespa has made him out to be, he does look strangely at the way Vessel has her wings wrapped around her. Noticing his curiosity, but not particularly bothered about it, Vessel shrugs at him and brushes off his look. She walks over to Dacos and starts reading the screen being projected by the message stick that he is holding. Like most Troin, Vessel has the old "better to ask for forgiveness than permission" attitude in abundance. And, typical of Troin of the Royal Line, she also rarely asks for forgiveness. Dacos stares at her curiously before deactivating the message stick. The holographic screen disappears, and Vessel gives Dacos a friendly side smirk then looks back at Steel.

"So, spill", she says. *"I heard you mention Troin. And since I am the only Troin here..."*

"That's hardly true", Dacos interrupts to correct her

"In this room", Vessel adds to combat Dacos's correction. An awkward, but friendly silence falls between Dacos and Vessel as they remain staring at each other. They both have a great deal of fondness and respect for each other, but very different characters.

"I am still surprised there is not a great deal more Troin here", Steel says, joining in the conversation, more to break the silent standoff that seems to be taking place between Dacos and Vessel. *"Eluud's atmosphere doesn't allow for much in the way of technology and weapons"*, he adds. *"Not even our Ships can launch or land under their own power. Yet Troin technology, or at least their Tals"*. Steel pauses as he looks at Vessel's Tal curiously. Vessel looks at Steel, then also looks at her own Tal before looking back at Steel, waiting for him to finish his sentence. *"They seem to be very much unaffected here"*, Steel continues. *"Even the weaponry it creates works here"*. Steel looks back at Vessel. *"Why is that?"*, he asks, thinking perhaps she may have some answers. She doesn't.

Vessel shrugs her shoulders. *"As much as they control our biology"*, Vessel thinks as an answer, *"our Tal's are also controlled by our biology. That might be the difference"*. She can see that her theory is no less confusing to Steel than not having any clue. Her expression becomes more solemn and innocent. *"I have no idea"*, she says, thinking that is what she should have just said in the first place. *"I was never too interested in the how and why of things on Liass. Just what I could do with it"*, she adds. Steel smiles back at her and nods, whereas Dacos lets out a quick laugh, probably a bit louder than he intended.

"Spoken like a true royal", Dacos unthinkingly blurts out.

"Hey!", Steel responds, as he looks up at Dacos, showing his offense to that comment. Dacos looks back at Steel apologetically, wanting to eat his words as he thinks about them. Almost everyone he knows and deals with is royalty after all.

"Not including you, Your Highness", Dacos quickly says. *"Or anyone else here. Or any other royalty that I know for that matter"*. Dacos can feel himself inside the hole he has just dug. *"Forget I said it. Please"*.

Steel lets Dacos off with a smile. He was not really offended. Steel sees the funny side of most things, sometimes inappropriately, and is also well known for speaking faster than he thinks. Likewise, Vessel also shrugs off Dacos's comment.

"You could hardly consider me real royalty", she says. *"On Liass, I am 24th in line. I would have to kill a lot of people before I could take the throne"*. She looks cheekily at Dacos. *"Don't think I didn't consider it"*, she adds.

Dacos looks surprised at Vessel's comment, wondering if she was being serious. Vessel just winks at him. She then turns to face him completely and starts poking him, not hard, sort of jokingly, but enough to get his attention as was her objective. *"And just what did you do to Det?"*, she asks him. *"She tore past me like a charging Rouk. I guess, not really all that unlike Det"*, she adds.

Dacos holds his hands up in front of him and shakes his head. *"It wasn't me this time"*, he replies. He then thinks more about it, *"or any time"*. He puts his hands back down and stares back at Vessel curiously, *"Why are you accusing me?"*, he asks. Vessel ignores his question, and through the process of elimination, now concludes it must have been Steel that upset Det and gives him a stern look.

"Guilty", Steel says as he throws his hands up.

Not really being able to scold the king, and Det's father, Vessel quickly decides to change the topic and returns her attention back to Dacos. *"You asked her out yet?"*, she asks Dacos. Dacos looks over at Steel, trying to look confused but appearing more annoyed. This is now the second time in only minutes that he has been asked about getting together with Det, and by two different people.

"Told you", is all Steel replies as he looks back at Dacos and shrugs.

There was no longer any point in trying to play naive about the unspoken attraction Dacos has for Det. However, there being no point was not reason enough to stop Dacos in continuing to give the pretence of denial. Exactly who he thought he was fooling, however, is anyone's guess. Most likely, only himself. The truth though, surprisingly, is that, if pushed, Dacos would gladly admit it to himself, even if not to others. However, even with his extraordinary observation ability, he has never been able to read Det. Not what she says and the way she talks to him anyway. Which is hardly that surprising. If Det was interested in Dacos, just like Dacos, there is no way she would admit it. Many say that if Dacos paid attention to certain things that Det did around him, things that Det herself would never admit to, then the message would be clear. Given that Dacos's observation skills are considered legendary throughout Eluud, it is believed that his feelings towards Det have either blinded him to her, or that he doubts and dismisses what he sees. Others offer a simpler explanation. He is just shy and feigns ignorance to hide this.

Vessel reaches out her hand and places it on Dacos's chest. *"Take this message from the heart"*, she says to him. *"Listen to yours a bit more"*.

Steel smiles, silently pleased that someone else is saying to Dacos something that he has been saying to him all along. Especially someone like Vessel, who has never been afraid to take chances. and wear her heart on her sleeve. Figuratively of course, as she never wears anything with sleeves.

As Steel watches the interaction between Dacos and Vessel, he thinks back to Vessel's own civilization and background. Though probably not strictly applying to Vessel herself, as she lived with the

Troin Royal Family, the men and women on Liass do not live together. In fact, they lived nowhere near each other and had virtually nothing to do with each other. On any given continent the men would live on one side, concentrating their time and efforts on their military training, which at times could even take the form of gladiatorial-like combat. The women would live on the other side, acting as the providers, farmers, and supporters of the Liass population. This is not to say that the women were not combat ready. Combat training and the use of the Tal, as no Troin could live without one, was a very large part of Troin life. Vessel herself is a very skilled and capable warrior. It was just not traditional for the women to be part of the Troin Army. Though there were many that formed part of the royal guard, and Princess Illyana's Personal Guards were only women.

"You should listen to her", Steel says to Dacos. *"She probably understands women more than most. Definitely more than either of us"*.

Vessel turns and looks at Steel, feeling flattered, but also a bit confused and taken back by his words. *"Just because the sexes live separately on Liass"*, she says, *"does not mean that I understand mine any better than anyone else"*. She looks back at Dacos and thinks to herself that his problem is not anything that she can educate him about. His problem has nothing to do with understanding women - his problem is understanding and trusting in himself. *"I think you need to accept what is right in front of you"*, she says to him.

Again, there is only silence as Dacos and Vessel stand looking at each other. This time it does begin to feel a little awkward. Feeling that they have reached the end of this conversation, and in fact every conversation that has been started since being in the Meeting Hall, Steel decides that this is a good time to make his exit. *"Well, as Dacos was so kindly reminding me"*, Steel pipes in, getting both of their attention, and now focused on him instead of each other, *"I need to get ready to head back to Aymyn"*.

Dacos looks at Steel with some confusion as he does not recall having this conversation with him. *"I was?"*, he says curiously to Steel.

"You were", Steel replies as he walks past them both and places his reassuring hand on Dacos's shoulder. *"Brief by my shuttle before I leave"*, he adds as he continues walking towards the doorway.

"Yes, Your Highness", Dacos responds as he watches Steel walk out of the room. Dacos looks back at Vessel, who is still just standing there looking at him. Again, there is only silence as they both stare at each other. With neither a smile nor frown, Vessel pokes Dacos in the chest one more time before turning and walking out of the room. Dacos stands still and does not watch her leave.

THE YOUNG KING

CHAPTER FIVE

Inside what can only be described as a very advanced looking spacecraft, an invisible being, that creates a kind of shimmer as it moves, walks over to a very sophisticated looking wall console. The many shallow holographic display screens on the surface of the wall flicker and distort as the being's invisible hand waves through them, stopping at a particular display with a large button on it and appearing to press that button. A large draw style capsulated bed starts to move out from inside the wall. The bed itself looks very comfortable. Surrounding it, built into the outer structure of the capsule, are a number of smaller consoles and display screens. On the bed, laying on her side, is a woman with blond hair. The length of her hair is unknown as she is covered up to the neck with a thin foil like blanket. A screen built into the top of the bed is displaying a large amount of information. Information such as heart rate, brain activity and biorhythms amongst other things. At the top of the screen is a single name, R'Vian. The name of the Valantriun woman asleep in the bed capsule.

As she sleeps, the shimmering hand presses softly down on her foil blanket, appearing to try and wake her up. R'Vian remains sleeping. The screen displaying her readings presents the results in coloured wavey lines. Most of the lines are blue, meaning that things are within acceptable parameters. The line representing her heart rate appears to be a little raised and is not blue, but instead an orange colour. More noticeable is one line that is red. This particular line represents her brain activity. It is very elevated. She is having a nightmare.

An enclosed hover vehicle sits parked on the side of a built-up street lined with large apartment buildings. Sitting inside the hover vehicle, on the driver's side, is a very panicked looking young Aymyn man. Not just panicked, but also looking extremely agitated, frustrated, and impatient. This is Kaylen, R'Vian's husband.

He is trying to use a pair of really advanced looking binoculars. Looking through the vehicle's windows and out into the streets. He scans up and down, even looking at the buildings. When used correctly these binoculars can actually see straight through walls. However, he is not using them properly. In fact, he doesn't know how to use them at all and can see nothing through them.

R'Vian, looking and dressed like any other Aymyn, in all black, boots, trousers, open long sleeve shirt with the sleeves folded up partially concealing a very sophisticated electronic arm devise wrapped around her left forearm, runs out the door of one of the apartments. Her blond hair shoulder length and her eyes red like all Aymyns. Yes, despite people's fear of Valantriun s, the Valantriun are still Aymyn. With her other hand she is holding the hand of her young child. Barely older than a toddler, she has long dark hair the same colour as her father's. Strapped to her shoulders is a small backpack, mostly empty except for a couple of toys and a comfort blanket.

R'Vian picks up her daughter, opens the passenger side door to the hover vehicle and quickly jumps inside. Kaylen lowers the binoculars and looks at her, still looking frantic. He throws the binoculars onto the back seat. *"I don't know why you keep giving me these things"*, he says to R'Vian. *"I never know how to use them"*. He starts shaking the steering controls in panic and frustration. *"Quickly, shut the door!"*, he yells at her.

R'Vian closes the door with barely enough time before her husband quickly drives off, speeding down the chaos filled city streets. People in their hundreds screaming while running out of buildings, branching off in all different directions, but most of them running in the same direction that Kaylen is driving. More hover vehicles dart up the road, some colliding with and driving right over running people, not stopping or even slowing down to look back.

Inside their vehicle, R'Vian is busy trying to buckle her daughter into the back seat as Kaylen zig zags through traffic of vehicles and people. They are on the Aymyn colonized planet Tradori. Long ago started out as a simple colony, now a metropolis society, busy city streets with large buildings and towers. Unfortunately located in an outer rim system, systems prone to Skurj attacks. An attack that unfortunately is happening right now.

The population of Tradori scurry to the only evacuation centre in the area, to board waiting carrier starships and flee the planet.

R'Vian finishes buckling her daughter into her seat, then looks through the back window, watching more and more people running out of their buildings and up the street in the same direction that her husband is driving. A Skurj crashes through one of the building walls and out onto the street, knocking over and devouring people as they almost run straight into it. Horrified, R'Vian looks up and can see a second Skurj on the roof of another nearby building, tearing through more people who have cornered themselves up there. The Skurj then stands upright and spews the blue-grey mazzie bile into the air.

R'Vian turns around and sits properly in her seat next to her husband. She places her hand on his arm to try and comfort him, worried that, in his panicked state, he could potentially have an accident.

"I thought you said your people would come and get us", he turns to her and says, his frustration vocally dominating over his panic.

R'Vian pulls back her sleeve to completely reveal the electronic device that she is wearing, covering her entire arm from the elbow down to her wrist. Built into the device are several displays and lights, some of which are flashing. R'Vian examines the flashing light pattern as though it means something. *"They are on their way"*, she says. *"But they are not going to get here in time"*. She puts her hand back on her husband's arm, again trying to calm him down, but knowing that her news is not what he wants to hear. *"We need to get to an evacuation point and escape like everyone else"*, she tells him.

Kaylen continues to drive erratically, speeding down streets and skidding around corners. *"Why didn't the Skurj Sensors detect their approach?"*, he asks R'Vian, keeping his eyes focused on the road. *"That's what they are there for"*, he adds. *"That would have given us enough time"*. But he is asking questions that even R'Vian can not answer.

"I don't know. But they didn't", R'Vian replies as she squeezes his arm softly and supportively.

"I bet it was those blasted Sharlon again", Kaylen says.

Crom had not been the first planet to have their sensors sabotaged by the Sharlon. It had been happening for quite some time. Planets receiving no warning from the Early Warning Sensor Systems surrounding all inhabited planets. Sabotage that was always blamed on the Sharlon, and rightfully so, as in every occurrence they were the ones responsible. However, no one ever understood why. What did the Sharlon have against everyone? Why do they keep facilitating Skurj attacks on unprotected planets?

Kaylen makes a sharp turn, skidding their hover vehicle around a corner and into an alleyway. He tears down it with increasing speed. He can see the main road up ahead which leads to the evacuation centre. While speeding towards it, another vehicle, also traveling at considerable speed, shoots out from one of the side streets and straight into them, sending Kaylen and R'Vian's vehicle flipping and hurtling across the alley.

Their vehicle comes to rest on its side. All is still. There appears to be no movement coming from inside their vehicle.

Two occupants from the vehicle that collided with them, a husband and wife, exit their vehicle unscathed. They look shocked at R'Vian and Kaylen's upturned vehicle and, after looking at each other to make sure that they are both alright, they run over to offer assistance. The man reaches up and tries desperately to open the passenger door, R'Vian's door, the only door they have access to as the driver's side door is lying flat against the road. It's jammed shut from the collision and doesn't move. The couple look at each other, concerned and not knowing what to do. The question crosses their mind; Do they stay and try to help, or do they continue to quickly make their way to the evacuation centre? They are desperate, confused, and scared. The man tries again to open the door. Still without any success.

"Are they OK? Can you see anything?", the woman asks her husband.

The male jumps on top of the upturned vehicle and tries to look through the window. A large glowing red circle starts to appear on the door beneath him as though someone is cutting through it from the inside. The man jumps back off the vehicle just as the circle cut-out is completed and pushed out of the vehicle's door. An arm reaches out through the newly cut out hole. It is R'Vian, her electronic arm device now seemingly equipped with spinning laser cutters zipping around her wrist. The laser cutters retract back inside her arm device as R'Vian pulls herself up out of the vehicle. The couple start stepping backwards, looking very alarmed to see R'Vian.

"It's a Valantriun !", the man shouts as the couple both turn and run off down the street.

"Wait!", R'Vian shouts after them, but it's of no use. The couple flee around a corner in the direction of the Evacuation Centre. R'Vian kneels on top of the vehicle and looks back inside at her husband and daughter who are alive and conscious. She reaches inside and Kaylen passes her their daughter. R'Vian pulls her out of the vehicle and climbs down off it with her. She stands her daughter beside the vehicle and pulls out her blanket from the small backpack. The girl stands shaking, not saying a word, takes her blanket from her mother and holds it close to her chest and face. R'Vian gets down on one knee and strokes her daughter's face. With her other hand, she is using her arm device to scan her daughter for any injuries. The device emits a strong red laser beam that covers R'Vian's daughter. R'Vian studies the screen on her arm device and sighs with relief. She smiles at her daughter and kisses her on her forehead. *"Stand right here. Don't move"*, she tells her.

R'Vian quickly climbs back up on the hover vehicle, kneels down again and peers in to see her husband. She reaches in and extends her hand to him. *"Grab my hand"*, she tells him.

Kaylen grabs her hand and tries to pull himself up out of the vehicle when he suddenly stops and pulls back in pain. *"Ahh!"*, he exclaims. *"I think I've broken my leg"*.

R'Vian pulls her hand back and, using her arm device, runs the same scan on Kaylen. Looking at the screen on her device, she nods with a less relieved expression as she bites her lip. *"My people can fix that"*, she tells him. *"But we've got to go"*.

"I'm going to slow you down", Kaylen says to R'Vian. *"Take her and go"*.

"Can't do that, dear husband", R'Vian says in an effort to destress him just a little. *"Keeping my family safe is the part of my job that I like. Don't sap all the fun out just because the world is ending"*.

"Even while under attack from the Skurj, Aymyn still fear Valantriun s", Kaylen says as he stares at the device on R'Vian's arm. *"It makes no sense. There is nothing scary about you"*, Kaylen adds.

"Oh, you'll see scary if you don't get out of this vehicle", R'Vian replies as she reaches out her hand to him again. Kaylen grabs hold of it and together they are able to pull him out of the vehicle. Kaylen sits on top of the vehicle as R'Vian jumps back down and grabs her daughter's hand. She then reaches up and helps Kaylen down off the vehicle, then helps him to stand. Kaylen winces in pain but tries to work through it.

He looks at R'Vian and notices that her right eye is bleeding, something no one had noticed before. *"Your eye"*, he says to her. R'Vian wipes her eye with her arm, then looks at the blood on her arm and shakes her head.

"Have to fix this later as well", she says.

Kaylen looks at R'Vian concerned, thinking that she is not considering the severity of her injury. *"We are not talking about a broken leg"*, he says. *"Your eye is literally bleeding"*.

Not seeming to show any interest in Kaylen's concern, she places her hand on Kaylen's shoulder and looks up the street towards the direction of the Evacuation Centre. *"It's alright. They can build me a new one"*, she replies casually.

"A new eye?", Kaylen replies almost disbelievingly.

R'Vian's attention is now completely on where they are and where they need to go. Almost as if they had momentarily forgotten that there was Skurj around, and now just remembering again that that's the reason why they and everyone else is fleeing, R'Vian suddenly looks up and all around her in a panic. Kaylen also again starts to panic and looks all around him as well. Neither of them sees any signs of Skurj. However, they both know that with the way the Skurj move, and can crash straight through buildings, that doesn't mean much. R'Vian looks back towards the main street ahead of them. *"We need to go that way"*, she says. Then, still holding her daughter's hand, she grabs Kaylen's arm and wraps it around the back of her neck. Slowly, they all walk towards the main street.

Reaching the evacuation Centre, a large, raised, fully encompassed building on the outskirts of the city, R'Vian and her family join the huge crowd of people who are also attempting to flee the planet. Inside the building, guards and soldiers are standing at a large, gated wall directing people through to awaiting space transport ships, as people push and shove each other to get there.

Kaylen, with his wife's help, who is also still holding their daughter's hand, starts to head towards the gate when he notices that R'Vian's electronic arm device is still exposed for all to see. *"Your thing"*, he says to her nodding towards her arm. R'Vian at first looks at him confused, but then looks at her arm and realises what he is trying to tell her. She tries to roll the sleeve of her shirt down to cover it, but it won't stretch over the device. She presses a small screen on the device and the device opens, coming apart on a hinge and she takes it off her arm. She reaches down and grabs her daughter's backpack. Her daughter looks at her, wondering what she is doing, as R'Vian slides the backpack from her daughter's shoulders. She places the device in the backpack and then throws the backpack over her own shoulder.

The soldiers at the gate see R'Vian and her family and, along with many more in the crowd. Noticing that they have a small child with them they assist in directing them to one of the awaiting transport ships. Among those also being directed are the couple who had just before collided with R'Vian and her husband's vehicle. They spot R'Vian and her family and again look alarmed. They approach one of the soldiers and start speaking to him. The soldier looks over curiously at R'Vian and her family.

"You!", the soldier calls out to R'Vian and her husband. *"Wait there!"*. R'Vian and Kaylen both stop and look back at the soldier confused. A sinking feeling starts to overcome them, and they look at each other worried about what the soldier wants. The soldier approaches them, bringing a second soldier with him. The soldier grabs R'Vian's arm and pulls up her sleeve. R'Vian stares at him as he looks at her naked arm. He looks up at her, a scornful distrust in his eye. R'Vian just stares back at him blankly, not wanting to show any expression that could be interpreted negatively. Yet, inside, that sinking feeling continues to grow.

Kaylen grabs R'Vian's arm and pulls it free from the soldier's grip. *"What are you doing?"*, Kaylen asks the soldier, his voice still both panicked and frustrated. The soldier stays focussed on R'Vian. He looks her up and down and notices the small backpack that she is holding. R'Vian can see where he is looking and tries to slowly move it out of sight. It's too late. The Solder grabs the backpack, yanking it from R'Vian. R'Vian tries reaching for it again but the soldier has now already opened it. R'Vian freezes, as too does Kaylen, as they watch the expression on the soldier's face change as he looks inside the pack. He reaches in and pulls out the arm device, looks at it fearfully, then looks at R'Vian. The accusation and his suspicion now confirmed. His expression now one of both fear and loathing, he yells out, *"They're Valantriun "*.

R'Vian's shoulders drop, that sinking feeling hitting rock bottom, she sighs and lowers her head. She then reaches out and grabs the soldier's arm to plead with him as Kaylen looks on helplessly. *"Only I am Valantriun "*, she tells the soldier. *"My husband and daughter are Aymyn"*. R'Vian grabs her daughter's hand again and places it in Kaylen's. She looks at Kaylen. *"Go. You go"*, she says to him. Kaylen shakes his head no, his panic and frustration now replaced with fear and sadness. R'Vian turns back to look at the soldier. *"Let them go.*

They are not Valantriun ", she says to him. But the soldier has no interest in hearing her out. He looks at the other soldier, anger still expressed strongly in his face and words. *"Get them out of here!"*, he yells, pointing back towards the Evacuation Building main entry doors.

The second soldier starts pushing them backwards through the crowd. Kaylen winces in pain from his broken leg as he almost stumbles over from the soldiers pushing. R'Vian snatches back her backpack and arm device from the first soldier, then grabs her daughter's hand. She pushes the second soldier away and stares at him defiantly. The soldier stops and looks back at her, his face looking somewhat concerned as he wonders what this Valantriun may do to him. R'Vian turns back around, grabs Kaylen's arm, again wrapping it around the back of her neck, and helps him move back out through the crowd to where they had just entered the building.

As they reach the buildings main entrance once again, they turn back and look back at the crowd still piling through the gates, being directed by the guards and soldiers. Kaylen looks at R'Vian despairingly. *"What now?"*, he asks her. R'Vian looks back at him, her gaze expressing her feeling of anguish. She looks down and helps Kaylen and her daughter through the main entrance doors and back outside the building.

Noticing a long bench seat along the outside of the building wall, not too far from where they are standing, she takes Kaylen and her daughter over to it and sits them both down. Again, she places her daughter's hand in her husband's. *"Stay here"*, she tells Kaylen. *"I'll find....."*, she hesitates as she thinks about what she could possibly find that could help them, *"Something"*, she adds. Kaylen looks up at her with a feeling of futility but needing to stay hopeful.

Not even knowing where to start, R'Vian runs off, carrying the backpack and heads back down the street. She runs deeper into the city and sees a small group of people running in a terrified panic, unsure where to go. A small, single piloted shuttle lands on the road just down from them. The door opens and the pilot steps out. *"Over here!"*, he calls out to them. The group see him and start to run towards the shuttle. Then suddenly stop. Horror on their faces, they start stepping back, turn and run away. The pilot watches on confused then, feeling something behind him, slowly turns around. He barely has time to look at the Skurj that has stepped out from behind his shuttle when the Skurj swoops in and eats him.

R'Vian freezes in terror as she watches the Skurj devour the pilot. The screams from the group running away gets the attention of the Skurj and, when finished with the pilot, it takes off after them. All R'Vian can get herself to do is stand there, still frozen, and watch. She watches the group run around a corner and down a small alleyway pursued quickly after by the Skurj. When out of her sight, R'Vian looks back at the shuttle, its door still open. Making herself move, she quickly runs to the shuttle and goes inside.

Noticing that no one else is in there, she takes a seat at the helm, closes the door, and starts to take off. The Shuttle under-jets pushes it up off the ground, R'Vian hovers the shuttle at around the same height as the building roofs that line the street. Then, turning the shuttle around, she flies it back towards the Evacuation building where her husband and daughter are waiting.

As she approaches the Evacuation Building, she sees Kaylen, still holding onto their daughter's hand and both still seated on the bench seat along the side of the building wall. R'Vian looks for somewhere to land. She sits the shuttle down in the middle of the street just below the stairway that leads up to the Evacuation centre. Kaylen looks at the shuttle curiously as R'Vian watches him through the shuttle's view screen. She presses the button to lower the shuttle doors and is just about to stand up and exit the shuttle when, to her horror, she notices another Skurj approaching the Evacuation building. Approaching Kaylen and her daughter.

R'Vian quickly runs out of the shuttle, but only in time to see her husband notice the Skurj right before it jumps down on him and her daughter and eats them. R'Vian screams and runs towards the Skurj as it finishes eating her family, then it stands straight up and starts spraying regurgitated mazzie into the air. As the Mazzie showers back down, the Skurj charges towards the Evacuation Centre, crashing through the building wall and goes inside.

EXOM - THE YOUNG KING

Mazzie droplets start hitting the street near R'Vian. R'Vian stops in her tracks and then starts to back away as more mazzie hit the ground near her. She runs back towards the shuttle as she raises her arms above her head to shield herself from the falling mazzie. Large drops hit her arms. She stumbles and falls to the ground in pain as more large droplets land on her legs. She picks herself up as the mazzie starts to eat through her trousers and arms.

She reaches the shuttle, kicks off her boots, hastily pulls down her trousers and throws them outside the shuttle, but the mazzie has already dissolved through to the skin on her legs.

She runs inside the shuttle, quickly sits down at the helm, closes the door, and lifts the shuttle into the air. Again, just hovering the shuttle meters above the ground, R'Vian stares through the view screen, looking at where her husband and daughter has just been sitting only moments before. There is nothing left there now. No husband. No daughter. Not a trace of anything that meant everything to her. Her mouth held open in shock, tears starting to make their way down her cheeks, she struggles to draw breath as she stares at the empty bench seat outside the smashed in wall to the Evacuation Building. The pain she is feeling inside, in her heart and soul, almost blocking out the pain from the mazzie on her arms and legs eating away at her. She looks down at her arms and legs, the flesh dissolving away revealing muscle, then bone. She looks back again at the empty bench seat before throwing her head back and screaming into the air. She pushes the helm controls forward at the same time and the Shuttle shoots straight up, bursting through the atmosphere and into orbit.

A second, then a third Skurj approach the Evacuation Building and charge inside, attracted by the loud screaming. The screaming starts to fade, then goes silent. Soon after, the three Skurj burst back out through the building walls. Two run off in opposite directions as the third stands up on its hind legs and spews mazzie into the air.

Sometime later, in orbit above the planet, R'Vian's shuttle is just drifting as though no one is flying it. Against the backdrop of stars in the distance, a cloud starts to form near R'Vian's shuttle. The cloud starts swirling into a circular whirlwind and at the centre a dark void appears. A large cylindrical shaped craft appears from within the dark void and travels out and towards R'Vian's shuttle. The swirling cloud and void then dissipate revealing again the stars in the distance.

Light starts to break through the cylindrical craft as a door, many times the size of R'Vian's shuttle, opens revealing a large hangar inside the vessel. A single piercing beam of light shoots out from just below the large hangar door and makes contact with R'Vian's shuttle. Immediately the shuttle stops drifting and is slowly pulled into the large hangar inside the cylindrical craft.

Inside the shuttle, there is no one sitting at the helm anymore. The shuttle looks lifeless and just operating on its own. A large glowing circle starts to appear on the inside of the shuttle's main door, looking a lot like the same kind of circle that appeared on R'Vian and Kaylen's hover vehicle when R'Vian cut her way out, only this one is a lot bigger. The glowing circle fades and then the same circular patch is pulled out from the door revealing two male figures, Aymyn in appearance, standing outside the shuttle.

Both dressed in large, hooded cloaks, they walk through the circular cut-out in the door and into the shuttle. They walk up to the helm and noticed that no one is there. They look at each other confused, wondering how the shuttle came to be here. More significantly, it was a signal coming from inside the shuttle that brought them here. They walk on past the helm controls and look down on to the floor, where they notice R'Vian laying there, barely conscious, with the mazzie having already dissolved most of her arms and legs. The two males look at each other briefly, then one looks back at R'Vian and pulls back his sleeve to reveal an electronic arm device identical to the one that she had been wearing. He presses a button on his arm device and a slim barrel shoots out from it, extending just past his hand. A small cutting Flame, like that of a blowtorch, then comes out of the barrel as the male starts to crouch down next to R'Vian.

Still watching over a sleeping R'Vian in her capsulated bed, again the invisible being attempts to wake her up. The shimmer from its hand moving as it slowly pulls the thin foil blanket back. Still asleep, R'Vian reaches out from under the blanket with her metallic, cybernetic, skeleton hand and pulls the blanket back up. The Invisible being again pulls down the blanket, this time further, revealing that it is not only R'Vian's hand that is cybernetic, but her entire arm. Again, trying to stay asleep, R'Vian pulls the blanket back up to cover her.

The invisible being decides to leave her to sleep and moves off again, creating a faint shimmer as it makes its way to the main doors of the Valantriun ship. The doors open and the Invisible being exits.

As the doors close behind it, R'Vian's eyes open, the sound of the doors waking her up. She lays there, just listening, not seeming too alarmed. In fact, not alarmed at all. She closes her eyes again and yawns. Then reaching over the side of her capsulated bed, eyes still closed, R'Vian fumbles around and eventually presses a large button. The side of the capsule starts to lower and disappear completely under the bed. R'Vian opens her eyes and pulls back the foil blanket and sits up on the bed, dangling her legs over the side, revealing the full effects of her augmentation. Both her arms and hands have been replaced with a cybernetic skeletal prosthesis. As too are both her legs right up to her hips. As she sits there wearing only a simple white t-shirt and underpants, the rest of her body appears to be unaltered, though her shoulder length blonde hair is now much longer, reaching down past her shoulder blades. Not a product of any augmentation however, the hair length was a result of time. A few years have passed since she lost her family on Tradori and was discovered drifting in the shuttle by her own people.

Kaylen was often left baffled by the way R'Vian would casually mention that her people could replace body parts. It was these very same cybernetic replacements that were used to rebuild R'Vian's arms and legs after the mazzie had dissolved hers. There are definite advantages to cybernetic augmentation. Her new arms and legs are a lot stronger and faster than the ones she was born with, with an emphasis on a lot. As she had also told Kaylen, her people also built her a new eye. Though, this was not something you could tell by looking at it.

She finishes waking up and stretches before standing up. She walks over to the ship flight controls, pressing a couple of buttons, and a holographic map of the area appears in front of her. On it she can see the location of her ship, as well as that of the invisible being which is represented as a green dot moving away from her location. She taps the hologram, and it ripples then expands, showing a much larger map of the area. More and more dots appear, this time they are red and blue. She studies it intriguingly, then waves her hand through the hologram and the hologram disappears.

She walks over to another wall within the ship and places her hand on it. The wall lights up with a strong glow. R'Vian turns around, her back now facing the wall, she leans up against it and stretches out her arms. Nano particles, not dissimilar to those in the Troin's Tals, come out of the wall, covering her arms, legs, hands, and feet, and instantly start to completely fill in her cybernetic augmentations with a kind of dark grey, almost black, material.

Once the process is complete, R'Vian stands there looking whole again, her cybernetic skeleton covered over by this dark grey metallic material. Her arms, legs, hands, and feet, now look like dark grey metallic arms, legs, hands and feet. She steps forward, away from the wall, and stands still again, arms still stretched out. The process appears to start again, but this time the nanoparticles are no longer rebuilding her body, they are instead building her clothing. For such sophisticated technology, the clothing it is building on her body appears to be nothing special. A simple pair of dark brown trousers and black boots. Really just enough to cover her lower body augmentations.

Once dressed, the light in the wall dims and turns off. Two sliding cabinets come out from the wall and open, one on each side of R'Vian. The cabinets contain a large amount of sophisticated weaponry and clothing. R'Vian pulls from a cabinet a belt and body holster ensemble and puts it on. She then starts loading it up with an assortment of weapons and gadgets of all shapes and sizes. She finishes off with a pair of long black gloves and walks away from the cabinets. She walks to another drawer, touches it and it opens to reveal a very familiar looking electronic arm device. Positioned next to it is a strange looking flexible metallic strap. R'Vian picks up the arm device and slides it onto her arm and closes it. She then picks up the metallic strap and, with a flick of her hand, it wraps around her wrist. She closes the drawer and walks off, grabbing a large green hooded cloak from a hanger and throwing it around herself.

She walks towards the main doors and stops, turning to look at a small parcel shelf just inside the doorway. On the shelf sits a small backpack, the one that belonged to her daughter. The only thing she has left of her family. R'Vian reaches into the shelf and places her hand on the backpack. She pulls it out and holds it to her cheek, feeling the texture of the material against her skin. Her eyes stare blankly for a moment as though she is again reliving the last moments with her daughter, she then takes a deep breath and focusses again. Still holding the backpack firmly, she walks towards the main doors, they open in front of her, and she steps outside.

Dense forest and trees cover the area surrounding the Valantriun ship, with the exception of about a 100-meter area all around the ship that looks as if the powerful Valantriun engines have incinerated all that was there while it was landing. The ground is not scorched however, just cut down; you could even say appears neatly mowed.

Just as fascinating on the inside of the ship, the outside of the ship is also truly awe inspiring. Shaped like a sphere that has been cut into a quarter wedge, the outer hull of the ship has a smooth reflective metallic surface. Though nowhere near the size of the cylindrical shaped Valantriun craft that rescued R'Vian while in the shuttle, this wedge-shaped ship is still on the large size when compared to most medium sized ships.

R'Vian steps away from her ship, pulls her sleeve back and touches a small console on her arm device. The ship's doors close and the ship starts to emit a blue light underneath it. Slowly the ship starts to ascend into the air, pushed up by these blue lights, the Valantriun 's own version of Stilts, something that is needed on planets like Eluud, where ships can not launch or land using their own engines. Stilts are basically long, quickly constructed and deconstructed, powerful poles, which used to be made from Sygra Steel, but lately has been replaced with advanced laser light technology that can be fired from large cannons. These stilts, acting as a bridge between the ship and surface, extend or retract to raise or lower the ship in and out of orbit, either bringing the ship in to land or placing it beyond the planet's atmosphere where it can then operate under its own engines. If it were not for Stilts, which the Chassam Castle can now fire from large laser cannons positioned on the flightdeck itself, no one would ever be able to land on or leave Eluud.

The Valantriun ship rises higher and higher until it enters orbit. R'Vian moves a sliding knob on the screen on her arm device and the Valantriun ship fires its engines. The Valantriun stilts disappear along with the ship as it launches itself away from the planet. How far it has gone only R'Vian knows, as she is the only one remotely controlling it.

R'Vian, now standing in a large, flattened area surrounded by forest, throws her daughters backpack on the ground and instantly it starts to expand and take the form of a simple tent. Two large metal anchoring poles, about eight inches in width, stick out from the ground about three feet at each side of the tent. R'Vian walks over to each one, presses the sides, opening them up and revealing a further assortment of technology, weapons, and gadgets inside. She closes them both without taking anything out and again presses a button on her arm device. The two poles lower into the ground, lying flat with the ground surface.

She looks over her campsite, taking it in. Meanwhile, hiding amongst the trees in the forest behind her, three Dakari peer out, watching R'Vian with interest. Noticing that she is alone, they start to slowly move out of the cover of the trees and towards her. R'Vian hears them and quickly turns around to face them. The moment she sees them she reaches under her cloak and pulls out two large weapons. She does not aim them, but instead holds them pointing down beside her. She stares back at the Dakari, who now speed up and approach her more aggressively. In response to R'Vian pulling out her weapons, the Dakari aim their rifles and fire at her. Instead of hitting her, their rifles blow up in their hands, killing all three Dakari.

R'Vian watches on calmly and seems somewhat amused at what has just happened. She places her weapons back under her cloak as she walks towards the Dakari that now lay dead on the ground. She glances down at them, examining their exploded rifles and consequently lethal wounds, before looking around her and into the forest, checking for any more unwanted company. Feeling confident that she is now alone, she looks back at the dead Dakari and smiles. *"This is going to be easier than I thought"*, she says as she giggles to herself.

EXOM

THE YOUNG KING

CHAPTER SIX

------------------------- Always Together -------------------------

Steel strolls out the large doors of Chassam Castle, stops on top of the stairway and looks out over the Castle gardens. Taking advantage of the short daylight each day that Eluud experiences, many Eluudians are also ambling around enjoying the sunlight. Steel takes the first step down on the stairway, when the Castle doors open again behind him. He stops, turns around and sees that it is a Castle guard walking out. Thinking nothing of it, Steel is about to turn back and continue down the stairs, when he notices the guard walks towards him the moment he sees Steel there. Steel turns to face the Guard and smiles curiously.

"Your Highness", the guard calls out to have the King's attention, which he already had. *"Your ship is ready. Your escorts are ready to go whenever you are"*.

Steel places an acknowledging hand on the guard's shoulder, smiles, nods, then turns back around and continues to walk down the stairs and into the gardens. At the bottom of the stairway, sitting on a garden bench all by herself, is a young girl. She watches the King come down the stairs, but the moment that Steel looks at her, she looks away. She doesn't look out of place, dressed normally for a child on Eluud, but sitting alone with no one else around her is making her stick out to the King. Steel stops and stares at her, knowing how awkward that would make her feel, and hopefully look at him so that he can smile at her. She does look at him, but quickly and out of the corner of her eyes, then looks back off into the gardens pretending that she is not.

EXOM - THE YOUNG KING

Somewhat amused by this behaviour, Steel smiles anyway, then to make things even more awkward, he walks over and sits down next to her. He stares at her closely, obviously, all the while the young girl keeps staring directly ahead into the garden, trying her hardest not to look back at him. Eventually Steel also stares off into the gardens, in the same direction that the young girl is looking and tries to work out what she is looking at, though suspecting it is really nothing.

"I do hope that there is something interesting over there, and you are not scared to look at me", Steel says to her while still looking out into the gardens. The young girl looks up at Steel. Shyly, but with a hint of rebelling against her instinct not to. Steel looks back at her, glad that she is finally looking at him, and gives her a cheeky smile. *"I am not really that scary, am I?"*, he asks her. The girl smiles back at him, but still seems too shy to speak. *"I didn't think so"*, Steel says to her as he nods and continues to smile. *"I mean, I try to be, sure"*, he adds. *"No point being a King if you can't go around scaring people, now is there? Where's the fun in that? "Oh look, it's the King. Which one? The one that's not scary. Let's throw dirt at him and eat all his fruit""*. The young girl tries very hard not to laugh and succeeds. Steel reaches into his pocket. *"Do you want some fruit?"*, he asks her. *"I usually..."*, he starts to say but stops when he pulls his hand back out realising that his pocket is empty. He looks at his hand, then looks into his pocket, and then back at the young girl, his face all innocent. *"Nope, no fruit"*, he says. He starts to smile at her again. *"See, that wouldn't happen if I was scary"*, he adds. *"My pockets would be filled with fruit. I'd be known as the Fruity King!"*. He stops for a moment as he thinks to himself, *"Actually, not so convinced I'm not called that now"*, he says out loud. The girl continues to Smile, amused at her king's comments.

Feeling that he is making some sort of progress, Steel turns his body and looks at the young girl with his full attention. *"Why are you sitting here all alone?"*, he asks her. *"Where are your parents?"*.

The girl stops smiling. Her eyes slowly starting to reflect her sadness at Steel's question. *"Gone, Your Highness"*, she replies.

Not catching her meaning, Steel presses further. *"Gone where?"*, he asks her.

C.C.DAVISON

The young girl again looks away. This time with no pretence, only sadness. *"Gone. Just gone"*, she answers.

Now Steel does catch onto what she is saying and looks at her speechless, not sure what to say, so also looks away. *"Hmmm"*, strangely is all he can manage to say back to her. He looks back at the young girl as if he has thought of something to say, but then looks away again when he realizes that he hasn't. He sits quietly, feeling like he should say something to break this awkward silence. Another joke perhaps? No, that would not be appropriate. No, it's time to dig a bit deeper inside himself, he realises.

"My father is gone too", he says to her, still looking away. Steel turns his head again to look at the young girl to gauge her response. There isn't one. *"You wouldn't have known my father. Long before your time"*, Steel says to her. *"But you have probably heard of him"*.

"King Solso", The young girl replies, but still does not look at her King.

"It's a start", Steel thinks to himself, and is pleased that she is responding. *"King Solso"*, he says as he nods at her. *"I was older than you when he...."*. Steel stops himself from saying what he was about to say next and rephrases. *"Was made gone"*, he finishes saying. *"But still...."*, he says and pauses again, momentarily in deep thought, thoughts of his father, happy and loving thoughts, then continues. *"No one is ever really gone"*, he says. *"Not while there are things around us that they have touched. Our heart being one of those things"*.

The little girl looks up at Steel, feeling his genuineness and taking some comfort in it.

"You know my daughters?", he asks her curiously. A silly question when he thinks about it.

"Of course", the young girl replies, with a tone that acknowledges that it was indeed a silly question.

"Of course", Steel says back, chuckling to himself. He recomposes himself and looks back at the young girl, now with a more serious, but still soft look. *"We have this thing, you know"*, he goes on to say. *"A thing we do with our hands. Let me show you. Put your hands like this"*. Steel holds his hands out and shows the young girl a special hand signal.

His thumb, middle and ring fingers crossing over the ones on the other hand, and his index and little fingers touching and pointing straight up. The young girl tries to copy it and Steel helps her until she has it. The girl looks at her hand in that position. *"Now, hold your hands to your chest, like this"*, Steel says and shows her. The young girl follows suit. *"That's it"*, Steel says, smiling at her. *"That there has a special message"*, he explains.

The girl looks intriguingly at her hands and then looks equally intrigued at Steel. *"What's the special message?"*, she asks.

Steel's smile softens, changes from one of just happiness to now one that seems to show a deeper feeling of care. *"It means, no matter where you are"*, he says to her, *"no matter where I am, near, far, or....gone, we are always together. Always caring, loving, no matter what"*. The young girl looks up at Steel, not smiling, but her eyes expressing the same level of care that Steel's are expressing. *"We call it the "Always Together Sign""*, he tells her.

The young girl looks back at her hands and the sign she is making. Steel watches her and smiles before looking back over the gardens. He notices in the distance, standing on a footpath that crosses the gardens, Tespa talking to Det. Det still looks sour. Tespa gives her a hug anyway and then runs off. Det continues walking down the garden path, when she senses that she is being watched and looks over and sees her father looking at her. Steel just sits there, watching her, with a soft, curious and friendly expression. Det looks back at him with a grumpy expression on her face, having not forgotten their last encounter. She then realises that he could, and should, also be looking at her equally grumpy, and he isn't. Instead, Steel smiles at her, then makes the "Always Together Sign" hand signal that he has just taught the young girl and holds it to his chest. Det, still determined to hold her grumpy expression, looks away as though trying to ignore him. She then looks back, and a small glimpse of a smile starts to appear on her face, though she tries hard to fight it. She does the hand signal back at him before again looking away and continuing her walk down the path.

Before she gets too far, she walks straight into Dacos, literally, and bounces off him. Surprised, not expecting him to be there, she looks up at him. Then overwhelmed with an awkward embarrassed feeling, looks away and runs off towards stairway, past her father and to the Castle main doors. Dacos watches her run off, feeling rather confused, then shrugs it off as he sees Steel sitting with the young girl across the garden. Steel gives him a wave, Dacos nods back at him and continues walking down the path.

Tespa and Vessel, who are now walking together the opposite way along the path, see Dacos and head towards him. Tespa is talking to Vessel and seems to be deep in conversation as they approach.

"Not always", Tespa says to Vessel.

"Mostly", Vessel says back to her.

Tespa looks up at Dacos, stops and smiles. Noticing this, Dacos stops as well.

"You will know", Tespa says to Dacos. *"Tell Vessel I'm right"*.

"About what?", Dacos asks curiously.

Tespa looks at Dacos with a jokingly frown of disappointment. *"Does it matter?"*, she replies. *"Just tell her I'm right"*.

Obeying his princesses' instructions, Dacos looks at Vessel and shrugs. *"Apparently, my Highness is right"*, he remarks sarcastically to Vessel. Vessel glares at Dacos, completely unamused, and can only manage to raise a single eyebrow as Tespa smiles contently at her.

"Told you", Tespa chirps with glee. Vessel now turns her glare to Tespa.

Having no idea what he has just been pulled into, and feeling like he does not want to know, Dacos looks back at Tespa. *"If you are looking for your father, he is just over there"*, Dacos says to her pointing over to Steel. *"He'll be leaving soon"*.

Tespa looks over at her father still sitting and talking to the young girl. Steel spots Zippin in the gardens and beckons her over. Zippin skips over and sits to the other side of the young girl as Steel introduces them. Zippin smiles at her, grabs her hand excitedly and points over at something in the distance. The young girl looks at where Zippin is pointing with curiosity. Zippin stands up and gestures to her to come with her. The young girl stands up and runs off with Zippin.

"I was actually looking for Det", Tespa replies as she turns her attention back to Dacos. *"She was just here. Vessel has something to tell her"*.

Dacos looks towards the main Castle entrance. *"She took off that way"*, he says. He looks back at Tespa, *"Inside the Castle"*, he adds. *"Going back to the entrance Library is my guess. She is usually there"*.

Hearing these words, a sly cheeky smile develops on Tespa's face as she looks back at Dacos. *"Oh, you've noticed that, have you?"*, she says to him.

"It is a very busy area of the Castle", he replies, oblivious to Tespa's cheeky grin. *"I am always coming and going through there and often see her there, reading. She reads...A lot"*, he adds.

Tespa remains smiling, just as sly and cheekily. *"I don't think she is there to read"*, she says to Dacos. *"I think what she is really there to study lies outside of those books"*. Tespa winks at Dacos and walks off towards the Castle. Vessel stands there looking at Dacos, who is still looking as innocently unaware as usual when it comes to Det. She shakes her and head follows Tespa, throwing one final comment back at Dacos, *"Oblivious!"*

------------------------------ **Concerned** ------------------------------

The Queen Mother, King Steel's mother and former Queen of Eluud until the death of King Solso, has now taken up position sitting inside the Meeting Hall inside the Castle. The same room that Steel and Det had been arguing in earlier. The Queen Mother is an elderly lady that actually holds her age rather well, some would say very well, looking decades younger than she is. Dressed neck to toe in black cloth and leather clothing. Wearing a split black cape similar to Dacos's, only hers has a large black hood that she will often wear inside or out at will, regardless of her environment, as is her privilege to do so. It is not as though anyone is going to ask her to remove it. She is the former Queen after all. And besides that, the Eluudian's really don't care what people wear. Black seems to be a strong recurring theme, however. Almost as though it is the only colour anyone wears on Eluud.

The Queen Mother is sitting at the large meeting table speaking with an Eluudian man called Bajen, one of the Royal Advisors within Chassam Castle. By appearances, a young man to be holding an advisory position, but his eyes tell a different story. A confident piercing stare that portrays that he knows far more than he ever says. Dressed also entirely in black. Black trousers, black vest that is fashionably short and tight, all covered over by a long black coat that stretches to the floor.

As the Queen Mother and Bajen talk, the Albearian Twins enter the room and approach the Queen Mother. They stand there gracefully, silently, and humbly looking at the Queen Mother, not wanting to interrupt her conversation with the Royal Advisor. The Twins will not often interrupt anyone, always courteous and refraining from anything that could even remotely seem rude. So, the fact they have walked into the meeting hall and approached the Queen Mother is enough to suggest that what they have to say is important.

The Queen Mother looks away from Bajen and to the Twins, curiously. *"Is everything alright?"*, she asks them. Bajen takes that as his queue to leave, knowing that what he is discussing can always wait and be continued later. He bows to the Queen Mother and quietly leaves the room.

The Twins walk up closer to the Queen Mother and speak. Having a shared consciousness, the Twins will often speak as one. Not at the same time but will often finish and continue each other's sentences.

"Queen Mother", the first twin says.

"So sorry for this intrusion", the second twin adds.

The Queen Mother smiles at the twins and shakes her head reassuringly. *"It is no intrusion"*, she says back to them. The Twins look at each other before looking back at the Queen Mother and continuing.

"We are worried", the first twin starts to say.

"Queen Mother. Not really worried", the second twin takes over.

"Concerned", the first twin finishes.

"We are concerned. There is a real",

"Uneasy feeling among",

"Many in the community", the twins say, finishing each other's sentences.

EXOM - THE YOUNG KING

The Queen Mother has also seen this as she walks the Castle grounds and mingles with the people. Even closer than that, she has also seen it within the Castle walls amongst the soldiers and staff. *"Yes, I have noticed that as well"*, she tells the twins.

The Twins continue. *"With the Raider"*,

"Attacks increasing in frequency and the Skurj",

"Getting closer every day. People",

"Are worried. And we are concerned",

"For them", the twins continue to say.

The Queen Mother sighs and nods, feeling and relating to the Twins' concern. *"Tensions are certainly increasing, and something needs to change"*, she says to them. *"My son will be leaving to go to Aymyn again shortly. I know that he makes every council trip double as an appeal to convince a Zazar to choose Eluud as their protectorate"*. She reflects on the challenges that she knows Steel faces every time he goes to Aymyn. *"Change is not something the Aymyn do very well"*, she adds.

This information is something that the Twins are very aware of. *"We stay hopeful that one day"*, the first twin starts to say

"He will be successful in his appeal", the second twin finishes.

"But it has been so long and",

"The horn has never sounded. Eluud stays unprotected and the people",

"Are feeling that lack of security more now",

"Than before", the twins say.

"We feel for the people", the first twin says as both twin's faces start to express a great deal of sadness.

The Queen Mother smiles at the sisters. Their compassion is something that can never be questioned. So too their devotion to, not only the people of Eluud, but all people in general. *"I know you do"*, the Queen Mother says as she stands, reaches up, and touches the sisters on their arms. Ordinarily she prefers to touch people on their cheek when she wishes to make a connection with them. However, due to the Twins towering height, even standing at least a foot taller than Dacos, their arm is all the Queen Mother can reach. *"Such beautiful ladies you are"*, she says smiling at them sincerely.

C.C.DAVISON

The Queen Mother sits back in her chair and looks softly into the Twin's eyes. *"I wish I could offer more words of comfort"*, she says to them. *"When you are as old as I am, you take comfort in the days you have and have had. Every day that we see the sun, even on this twilight planet that we call home, I count as a blessing"*. She looks away as she thinks to herself. *"I feel that there is a fight coming to turn the tides on things"*, she says. *"Something definitely needs to change"*.

She reflects on her own words for a moment, then looks back again at the Twins. *"But I feel and share your concern"*, she says to them. *"All we can do is continue to watch, hope, learn. We'll see what advances my son makes on Aymyn with the Council and Zazar Corp"*. She looks down briefly, feeling that she is not really offering much that can alleviate any fears or bring a much-needed comfort to the people of Eluud. Her mouth closed, she clenches her teeth and sighs. She takes a breath and looks sincerely up at the twins again. *"I appreciate you bringing your concerns to me"*, she says to them. *"I wish there was more that I could do about them"*.

The Twins start to worry that their conversation with the Queen Mother may have saddened her. *"We did not wish"*, the first twin starts saying,

"To upset you", the second twin finishes.

The Queen Mother smiles reassuringly at the sisters. *"You haven't"*, she replies. *"You are expressing what we all feel. Please keep doing so"*.

The sisters blink and curtsy at the Queen Mother before turning around and gracefully leave the room. The Queen Mother sits quietly in her chair for a moment, staring off at nothing in particular, before speaking once again. *"Are you happy sitting there, hiding away, listening in on conversations?"*, she says out loud, seemingly to no one. But it wasn't no one.

In the corner of the room, before unnoticed, is Orlow, King Steel's uncle and younger brother of the late King Solso. A very skinny and strange, perhaps eccentric, man that is known to say the strangest, and often inappropriate things. He is often seen on his own, eating a piece of fruit, something that he is very fond of and usually has some stored in his pocket, preferring his own company and that of the toys he tinkers with and makes for the children of Eluud. Toys that he will randomly place around Chassam Castle and the grounds for the children to find.

Ironically, he finds regular people - well, all people – strange, so will avoid most direct company if he can. On this occasion he is sitting by himself tinkering with some small rouk-shaped object. *"I am not listening"*, he replies. *"Have no interest in private things"*. He holds up the small model of a Rouk that he appears to have been working on. *"Prebus here though"*, he adds, *"he hears everything"*. He holds the toy rouk up to his face. *"Don't you?"*, he asks the toy rouk. *"Yes, he does"*, he answers for it.

The Queen Mother, always disappointed with Orlow and his comments, turns to look directly at him. *"If you took the same interest in comforting the people of Eluud, as you do in those trinkets"*, she says somewhat angrily at him, *"things would have been much better between you and your brother"*.

Orlow still does not look at the Queen Mother and continues tinkering with his toy rouk. *"No interest"*, he replies. *"Trinkets don't argue back"*.

Never getting the kind of response that she wants from Orlow, and unsure why she continues to expect differently, she just shakes her head gently with frustration. *"For someone who says they don't like to argue"*, she says to him, *"you tend to take a contrary position to most things"*.

Orlow persists with not looking at the Queen Mother, and instead starts talking to his rouk model. *"Do you know what she is talking about? I'm not really listening"*, he says to it.

Wishing to end this conversation now, even starting to regret having ever started it, the Queen Mother scours at Orlow. *"Enjoy playing with your toys, Orlow"*, she says to him as she looks away, removing him from her sight.

"Not toys. Creations. I create", Orlow replies, feeling the need to correct her, not at all bothered by her frustration, or perhaps not even noticing it. He starts talking to his toy rouk again, *"I made you. Yes, I did. Who's your daddy? I'm your daddy. Wait. What?"*. He looks away

and thinks briefly to himself, but then shrugs it off and looks back and smiles at his toy.

The Queen Mother stands up to walk away but stops momentarily to laugh as she reflects. *"To think I could have ended up married to you instead"*, she says to Orlow. *"I definitely ended up with the right brother"*.

And this is where Orlow, true to form, says something really inappropriate; *"But I'm still alive"*, he says.

Before The Queen Mother can start walking again, she is struck speechless by Orlow's remark. She looks scathingly over at him. And with her gesture Orlow realizes the tastelessness of what he has just said. He looks up at her, his face expressing his concern and shock over his own words. *"Yeah, that was inappropriate"*, he says, more to himself than to her. He returns his attention once again to his toy rouk. *"There was a line there - and we just crashed straight through it"*, he says.

The Queen Mother shakes her head angrily, still completely speechless, and walks out the room.

She furiously walks down the corridor and into the Entrance area of the castle. She notices Steel talking to Sergeant Mew and the Flight Commander. She stops and stands there watching them. Steel looks over at her and smiles. Still very much angry at Orlow's words, she is unable to smile back.

Sergeant Mew and the Flight Commander look over at her as well, then look back at Steel, who now has stopped smiling as he notices his mother's angry expression. He nods at Mew and the Flight Commander. They both head off in different directions as Steel walks over to his mother.

Instead of asking her the obvious question of what it is that is making her look so angry, Steel instead decides to point out something completely different. *"Have you ever thought that our walls would look better in a kind of burgundy shade?"*, he asks her. The Queen Mother just stares at Steel, shaking her head, knowing that he is really not expecting an answer, and if he is then he's going to be waiting a while.

As she remains silent, Steel smiles at her again, making her shake her head at him again. A very slight smile now starting to appear on her face. *"Back off to Aymyn?"*, she asks him.

"You're not going to burn the castle down or anything while I'm gone, are you?", he replies.

"Not the castle", The Queen Mother replies. *"Some people in it, maybe"*, she adds with a nod, followed by a slight smile. Steel smiles back at her.

The Queen Mother reaches out and straightens up the Lapel on Steel's royal coat. *"Mum, stop"*, Steel says, looking around all embarrassed. She does.

"Missed you at the Coolax game", Steel says to her.

"Why would I go and watch that?", she asks him. *"It's barbaric. Your father used to make me sit through it. Never liked it then"*. Steel shrugs at her. She looks seriously into Steel's eyes. *"Don't think I didn't hear what you did though"*, she says to him.

"I was pretty awesome", he says to her, a huge proud grin on his face.

"Pretty foolish, more like it", she replies. *"You could have been really badly hurt"*.

"Well, I kind of....", Steel starts to say, but his mother does not let him finish.

"You are a true Air Sign", she says to him. *"Running off into danger at every chance. It's not healthy"*.

No longer smiling, Steel bites his lip and stays silent as he looks at his mother, wondering who she is really talking about.

"Some people actually feel fear, you know", she says to him. At that moment Det walks into the entrance area. She notices her father and grandmother standing there and stops still, not wanting to approach them. The Queen Mother and Steel look at her. *"Not everyone"*, the Queen Mother says, then looks back at Steel. *"But most"*.

------------------------------ **Apprehension** ------------------------------

Later that day, as the sunlight begins to fade and makes way for the usual twilight that Eluud experiences, the giant laser stilt cannons, that are built into the flight deck just outside Chassam Castle, are all fired up and pushing King Steel's shuttle into orbit. Shuttle by name only, in fact it is a medium-sized oblong shaped vessel, piloted by his two guard escorts from its decent sized bridge, the shuttle contains a few rooms with which to comfortably transport a small group of people over considerable distances.

Once it leaves the atmosphere of Eluud, the underside of the shuttle starts to extend out its sides, changing the shuttle from an oblong shape to a complete circle. It fires its own engines, launches away from the stilts and disappears. The Giant cannons shut down and the laser stilts also disappear as the cannons return to their resting position.

In the darkness of space, just outside the atmosphere of Aymyn, a cloud forms and starts to swirl. In the centre of the swirling cloud, a dark void, and speeding out of it a large Troin Starship. As soon as the Starship has passed through the void, the swirling cloud dissipates and along with it the dark void in its centre. The Starship, pushed by its powerful point engines, heads towards Aymyn and joins three more giant Starships already orbiting the planet.

One of the Starships has already launched a smaller ship, like that which Vice Commander Ardok had crashed earlier, which has now entered the atmosphere of Aymyn and makes its way to the Rooftop hangar of the Citadel. It lands, its doors open and Commander Turrin and Vice Commander Ardok step out onto the hangar, followed by many Troin crewmen. Without any hesitation, they walk straight towards the Citadel's main rooftop entrance and go inside.

They are immediately greeted by members of the Royal Alliance Council including, King Yord and Princess Illyana, along with a couple of Princess Illyana's personal Troin guards. Two large sliding doors, separating the entrance hall from the main corridor, open automatically as Queen Aura and her handmaiden, a young long dark haired and rarely spoken lady, dressed in a full-length teal dress with metallic gold ornamentation around her shoulders and upper arms, walk through to also welcome Commander Turrin and his men. The Queen is also escorted by several Aymyn Soldiers, who themselves are led by the

Aymyn General, a serious looking and battle-hardened older man who does not smile.

Commander Turrin looks at the Queen and her entourage and is surprised to see such a heavy military presence. Queen Aura, seemingly wanting to avoid drawing any attention to it, smiles at the Commander. *"Commander, so glad you made it in one piece"*, she says to him, smiling warmly and welcomely.

"I prefer it that way", Commander Turrin replies, trying to hold his attention on Queen Aura but visibly distracted by the large presence of her soldiers.

"As do we", Aura responds even more warmly.

Vice Commander Ardok walks up and stands beside Turrin, also aware of the company they have around them, but seems to be less suspicious of it than his Commander is. *"So, what is it that we can do for you, Your Highness"*, Commander Turrin asks, partly wanting to get straight down to business, but mostly wanting to find out the reason for the military entourage. Turrin can't help but notice that Queen Aura does not move any closer to him as she continues to speak to him, instead staying back with her handmaiden and soldiers.

"Well", Queen Aura starts to say, *"while our resources are stretched, we require the assistance of yourself and your crew, if you will all indulge us, with apprehending the Skurj Sympathiser that we believe is responsible for disabling the satellites that prevented you from getting to Crom"*.

"Couldn't your Zazars have done that?", The Vice Commander asks her, waging in on the conversation.

Now, no longer holding a smile, Queen Aura looks directly at Vice Commander Ardok. *"Probably not so delicately"*, she replies.

"I dare say, it is also not exactly their job", Turrin says looking at both his vice commander and Queen Aura.

"Correct", Aura replies with a nod back at Turrin.

Still sensing very strongly that something more is going on here, Turrin looks over at his Princess. Though not at all uncommon for her to have while both off world and even back on Liass, her Troin guards also being there at this moment, adding to the military presence before him, was starting to make him feel even more uneasy. Then there was also King Yord's tense disposition. Though usually only ever either jolly or agitated, the fact that at this moment he seemed the latter was not helping Turrin's concern.

Turrin looks back at Queen Aura, very much wanting some sort of clarity on this situation. *"What is it that you would like us to do?"*, he asks her.

"Well, the first thing I'd like", she starts to answer, looking confidently at Commander Turrin, *"is for you to arrest your Vice Commander"*.

Every one of the Troin crewmen are taken back and look at Queen Aura confused. But not nearly as confused as Commander Turrin or Vice Commander Ardok himself.

Ardok feels the gazes of his crew and Commander upon him as he looks back innocently confused and shocked. Believing that some kind of mistake or misunderstanding is happening here, Commander Turrin returns his attention back to Queen Aura. *"Your Highness?"*, he says to her, almost waiting for her to drop her serious look and start laughing, revealing the elaborate joke that is being played out.

"Wait, what's going on here?", Ardok also asks Aura, still looking very confused.

Not moving, nor changing her expression, Aura looks directly at Ardok again. *"The Sharlon are not the only ones with spies, Vice Commander"*, she says to him, before returning her attention to Turrin once more. *"Commander"*, she continues, *"it was your Vice Commander that destroyed those satellites from your very own scout ship, which prevented you from reaching Crom"*.

Vice Commander Ardok lets out a laugh as though Queen Aura is joking. However, Turrin does not seem so amused, or less concerned. *"You're not serious"*, Ardok says to Aura.

"Very serious", Aura replies, not looking back at him but instead keeping her attention on Commander Turrin.

Still not entirely sure about what he is hearing, Turrin looks over again at the Troin Princess. If anyone will clear this up, then certainly it will be her. Princess Illyana looks back at Turrin, her eyes sincere and her face in a sad frown. *"Sadly, as Queen Aura has stated, we do have more proof"*, she says to him. *"However, you only need to check the records on the scout ship to confirm for yourself"*.

Commander, now seeming less confused, nods at his princess. *"The scout ship"*, he says, then looks at Ardok, *"that was destroyed"*.

"I am happy for us all to view the evidence together, Commander", Aura steps in and says, *"after you have apprehended your Vice"*.

Turrin keeps his eyes focused on Ardok. Ardok looks back at him curiously. *"You don't seriously believe this"*, Ardok says to him. *"This is ludicrous"*. Ardok looks at the rest of the Troin Crewmen who are also looking less confused and now more suspiciously at him. *"Absolutely ridiculous"*, Ardok adds. *"Almost as ridiculous..."*, the Vice Commander stops speaking as he looks back at Queen Aura and shakes his head in disbelief and disappointment. *"As me continuing on with this charade any longer"*, he finishes off by saying, and raises his arm as his nanoparticles pour out of his Tal, covering his body, and solidify to form Troin armour. A pistol also forms in his hand. He turns, aims, and fires at Commander Turrin. A lethal blast that would have killed him had Turrin not also activated his Tal, producing a medium sized shield, and deflects the Vice Commanders blast. The impact of the blast against his shield at such a close distance makes Turrin stumble backwards. Turrin quickly regains his balance however, and at the same time, Troin armour also forms all over his body.

The rest of the Troin crewmen also use their Tals to form body armour, weapons and shields and immediately take aim at Ardok. Troin Nanoparticles again pour out of Ardok's Tal, producing a very large floor to head-height shield. He holds the shield directly in front of him, bracing himself for the barrage that will inevitably follow. It doesn't take long. The Troin crewmen commence firing on their vice commander, their blast absorbed by his large Troin shield.

Also, using their Tals, Princess Illyana's personal guards produce even larger floor to head-height shields, identical in most ways to the one that Ardok has constructed, only wider. They grab Princess Illyana and King Yord, pulling them back behind the shields with them.

C.C.DAVISON

Protecting her Queen, Queen Aura's handmaiden pulls Aura back around a corner, using the wall as protection as the Aymyn soldiers also commence firing at the Vice Commander. The Troin soldiers all step between the Vice Commander and Aymyn soldiers, not so worried about any crossfire as their body armour and shields will absorb the blasts, unlike than the unprotected Aymyn soldier's uniforms.

The entire corridor is filled with a volley of weapon blasts, most aimed directly at Vice Commander Ardok. Ardok struggles under all the impact but manages to hold his own and return fire. He makes his shield even larger, both in length and width, reducing the number of blasts that are missing his shield and hitting his body. He starts to step backwards as though attempting to retreat to the landing pad and back to the Troin shuttle. The firefight continues ferociously, neither side relenting or winning. The Troin crew and Commander unable to surround Vice Commander Ardok as he continues to make his way backwards. Given the strength of the Troin Shield, even against their own weaponry, that unless someone is able to get past the one that Ardok has created and protecting himself with, this fire storm could continue almost indefinitely.

Suddenly, what looks like a glowing red rope darts out from somewhere behind the Vice Commander and wraps around his Tal Arm. Before the Vice Commander even has time to look at it, the glowing red rope cuts straight through his armour and severs his arm right off. His arm and shield drop to the floor, exposing him and leaving him open to the weapon blasts that subsequently hit his body, being fired from both the Troin and Aymyn soldiers. Ardok stumbles back from the impact of the weapon blasts, and in pain from his severed arm, as his body armour and shield start to decompile back into nanoparticles, which then return back to his Tal. Even his underclothes, such as his singlet, shorts, and shoes, which were also constructed by his Tal, begins to quickly decompile.

The Troin and Aymyn soldiers stop firing at the Vice Commander. As the flashing and smoke from the weapons fire starts to clear, all that remains of the Vice Commander is his naked, one-armed body, having just fallen over in pain, and his severed arm, still wearing his Tal, laying on the ground in front of him.

In excruciating pain, Ardok stares at his severed arm. The Tal, now no longer detecting a living Troin attached to it, only an arm, starts to change from the lattice shaped armband to a much smaller and simpler looking bracelet. This is what the Tal looks like in its inactive state. That is, when it is not attached to a Troin.

The glowing red rope vanishes. Then, stepping out from behind Vice Commander Ardok, holding his Tription Handle, is Zargah. Though looking like he hardly needs it, Zargah is wearing a small amount of light metal armour, gold in colour, over his shoulder blades and across his chest. To the corner of his chest plate is a small insignia that is worn by the General of the Zazar Corp.

The Troin Crew and Aymyn soldiers surround the Vice Commander, weapons still pointing directly at him. Zargah charges through, pushing both the Troin and Aymyn soldiers aside as though they were made out of feathers. Zargah grabs Ardok with all four of his arms, his hands almost completely encompassing most of Ardok's body, and lifts him into the air with considerable ease. Snarling angrily at Ardok, Zargah's first instinct is to squeeze and kill him, which he is just about to do when Queen Aura comes out from behind the corner. *"Zargah! Wait!"*, she calls out. Zargah stops squeezing and snarling, but still holding the Vice Commander tightly, looks over at Queen Aura. Princess Illyana's personal guards retract their large shields back into their Tals as both King Yord and Princess Illyana step out from hiding. Queen Aura walks closer to Zargah and the Vice Commander. She looks up at the Vice Commander, still held high off the ground, encompassed in Zargah's huge hands. Aura then looks fondly at Zargah, pleased with his actions, and softly strokes his arm. Zargah looks at Aura, his gaze also soft and full of fondness. He looks back at Ardok and snarls again, before returning his attention to Aura, and with it his expression changing back to one of gentleness. It is not a look anyone expects or experiences from Zargah. His tough and hardened exterior projecting a very strong "Get out of my sight" message, which most people will oblige without any hesitation. Though on some rare occasions, and only when he is with Aura, will people experience a softer side to Zargah.

Zargah has been the Zazar protector of Aymyn for a long time. He has watched Aura grow into the Queen that she is today and Head of the Royal Alliance Council. Their bond and connection is incredibly strong.

Aura asserts her attention back onto Ardok. His eyes glazing over as his body starts to go into shock, he looks back at her defiantly. *"Vice Commander"*, Aura says to him, *"you will be held to account for your sympathizer actions that have resulted in the destruction of an entire planet and race"*.

Ardok looks over at his Princess. She looks back at him, her face expressing both her anger and disappointment. Commander Turrin, his armour, weapon and shield already fully retracted back into his Tal, and standing again in only his shorts and singlet, walks over and stands next to Aura. *"Doesn't look like you really needed our help"*, he says to Aura as he looks up at Zargah and the naked and wounded Vice Commander viced firmly in Zargah's grip.

So focussed on Zargah and the Vice Commander, Queen Aura has almost forgotten that Commander Turrin is standing there. She turns and faces him, smiling at him once again. This time her smile is one of relief and appreciation than merely welcoming. *"Your assistance in bringing him here to be apprehended is most appreciated"*, she says to Turrin.

Before Turrin can respond, Zargah interrupts. *"Where will I take this one?"*, Zargah asks Aura as he gives the Vice Commander another little squeeze.

King Yord steps forward, closely examines Vice Commander Ardok, then looks up at Zargah. *"He is to be transported to Borhm"*.

Queen Aura looks at King Yord confused. In fact, beyond just confusion. Hearing the name Borhm, Aura looks completely horrified. Commander Turrin looks at Queen Aura with the same expression on his face. *"You are going to sentence him to Carpaga?"*, Turrin asks Aura, the pitch of his voice heightening as his throat seems to constrict even saying the words.

EXOM - THE YOUNG KING

Queen Aura remains looking at King Yord, her mouth open but speechless, as King Yord remains steadfast and maintains eye contact with the Vice Commander. *"The Sympathizers are far too organized"*, Yord starts to explain. *"Not even a death sentence is acting as a deterrent against their atrocities".*

Listening to King Yord's words, Princess Illyana nods in agreement, but visibly something she is not finding easy to do. She looks over at Queen Aura who looks back at her, wanting Princess Illyana to make a different suggestion. Illyana can see the anguish in Aura's eyes and acknowledges it with a nod, her own eyes showing that it s a decision she is also struggling with. Nonetheless, it is a decision she is choosing to stand by. Illyana turns her attention to Turrin. *"Our Vice Commander's actions alone have meant the deaths of millions"*, she says to him. Then turning her attention to Ardok, she says, *"It seems fitting that he should feel every one of them".*

And feel them he most certainly will. Carpaga, a place that conjures nightmares in those that know of it, is neither a life sentence nor a death sentence. It is a life full of death sentences. Continual and never ending. The worst kind of sentence that can ever be levied on anyone. Reserved for perpetrators of atrocities such as genocide, or worse, whereby a simple a death sentence does not seem sufficient, and which Vice Commander Ardok's actions certainly equate to the assisting of, sentencing to Carpaga is an extremely rare event. Though, once, Councillor Lawn did try to have it imposed on an individual who intentionally damaged his transport shuttle.

Ordinarily, such a decision requires the entire Royal Alliance Council to vote on. However, on this occasion, as Vice Commander Ardok is a member of the Troin Army which, though assists the Royal Alliance does not fall under the authority of the council, the decision ultimately rests with Princess Illyana. A decision, it appears with much trepidation, she has made. Even Zargah looks at Queen Aura uncertain if he should be following the instructions being given to him. Very reluctantly, Aura looks up at Zargah and nods. She stares into Zargah's eyes, feeling very uncomfortable with the permission that she is giving him and hoping to find solace in his returned stare. All Zargah can offer back in his gaze is an understanding of their mutual discomfort. He looks over at King Yord, then Princess Illyana. Illyana looks back at him, her expression certain but disheartened. King Yord's temperament more resolute. Zargah looks away, then walks off carrying Vice Commander Ardok, leaving the councillors, Troin and Aymyn Soldiers silently staring at each other.

------------------------------------ Hope ------------------------------------

Missing all the excitement, having just landed on the Aymyn landing bay, King Steel, along with an escort of two Eluudian guards, walks off his shuttle. He crosses the landing bay and continues walking towards the entrance of the Citadel, as his escorts stand guard just outside his shuttle.

He passes a class of young school children who are seated in a circle on the outside hangar floor. Two teachers are also with them, distinguishable by their all-red clothing, the Aymyn traditional colour worn by those whose occupation involves teaching or the instruction of others. One teacher is standing in the centre of the circle speaking to the children while the second teacher is outside the circle walking around observing them. The students are focussed on the lecture being conducted by their teacher standing in the centre of the circle. The teacher is holding a small cube-like object that is made from malleable material. She throws it to the ground, and it bounces back up into her hand. She then gently throws it at one of the children, who catches it, looks at it and throws it back to her. She throws it to another child, who attempts to catch it but misses. It flies past him and lands in front of Steel. Steel abruptly stops walking, looks down at the cube-like object and, with his foot, flicks it up off the ground and catches it. He crouches down on one knee, and with a very friendly smile, hands it to the child who missed catching it. The child smiles back at Steel as he takes it from him. Steel looks up at the teacher who also smiles back at Steel, before being hit in the face by the cube-like object which the child has now thrown back at her and caught her unaware. The children start to laugh. The teacher's smile turns into a friendly frown as Steel smiles back, trying not to laugh. The teacher leans over, picks up the cube-like object and quickly throws it at another child, who stumbles as she catches it, juggling it a couple of times unwittingly. The children and teacher now all start laughing at the young schoolgirl, as she also laughs at herself.

Steel stands back up and continues walking towards the main entrance, walking past a large closed and sealed shut hangar door. As he enters the building, he passes Zargah, still holding the struggling Vice Commander in his clutches. Zargah does not even look at Steel as he passes by, not unaware of his presence, just not paying it any interest. Not even thinking to question why Zargah was walking out holding a struggling Troin Officer, almost as though it was a common occurrence, Steel continues down the corridor towards the large door leading to the Council Chambers. As he approaches, the door, almost seeming to know his intention, opens automatically.

Steel walks in casually, and immediately notices Aura sitting in her chair speaking with a Blyan. The Blyan are a deep-sea race from the ocean planet Blyanan. This particular one is the King of their race. Though, not previously at the council meeting, by the way his tube is positioned at the Council table, he looks as though he was entitled to be. That's right, a tube. A large transparent tube that stretches from the floor right up into the ceiling, filled completely with a clear liquid. The Blyan are an interesting looking species. A head, torso and arms that look nothing remotely like the Aymyn. Their neck and shoulders have large and protruding gills, and their body is covered in scales. Below the torso their body stretches into a long fishlike tale with many fins attached to it. All up the Blyan are a lot taller than any Aymyn by at least twenty inches.

Aura notices Steel enter the chamber, makes eye contact with him and then looks back at the Blyan King. *"This is a very important conversation, Your Highness"*, she says to him. *"Do you mind if we continue it in a little while?"*. The King of the Blyan turns around, sees Steel walking in and then turns back and faces Aura. It blinks politely then darts up towards the ceiling. The ceiling of the tube opens and the

Blyan and all the liquid in the tube shoot up into it. The tube ceiling then closes again, and the entire tube rescinds into the floor.

Aura watches the tube disappear, then looks over at Steel again and smiles. *"Missed all the action again I see"*, she says to him, referring to the recent event with the Troin Vice Commander.

The Doors to the Council Chamber close behind Steel as he continues to walk in. *"Seems to be my fate"*, Steel replies, having no idea what it is that he has missed.

Aura stands up and walks around the table towards him. She does not stop. She throws her arms around him and gives him a very passionate kiss before pulling back slightly to just look and take him in. *"Missed you"*, she says to him, her entire face and eyes smiling.

Queen Aura and King Steel have been together for a very long time. Starting soon after Steel joined the Royal Alliance Council. It was pretty much love at first sight for them and currently they are the only romantically linked couple on the Royal Alliance Council. Their relationship, though very strong, does have its obstacles. The main one being that they live on completely different planets, and in different systems, within Exom. The other being that although Aura has no other family herself, Steel most certainly does. This on top of their commitments as King and Queen of their respective planets, along with Aura's additional commitments as Head of the Royal Alliance Council, their time together is never as much as either of them would like. However, they make it work.

Queen Aura takes Steel by the hand, leads him around the table and they take their seats. Seats that are conveniently next to each other, being two of the three seats that never retract into the floor. Steel gets comfortable in his chair. All the while Aura never let's go of his hand or stops looking and smiling at him. *"I couldn't help but notice on the way in that the reserve hanger was still confined"*, Steel says to her, smiling back while also looking at her curiously. *"Are the Pizians still tinkering with their portal technology?"*

"It's compression Drive technology", Aura replies. Not exactly the conversation she was expecting Steel to start with, she giggles knowing

to always expect the unexpected with him. *"And if it wasn't for that, you wouldn't be here"*, she adds.

Steel can't argue with her statement. If it wasn't for the Pizians and their Compression Drive Technology, then interstellar, or even interplanetary, travel would not be possible. The Compression Drive, a specialized engines on almost every ship and shuttle in Exom, creates temporary miniature wormholes in space which vessels pass through to travel vast distances and reach their destinations throughout Exom. The technology has its limits, and often several wormholes are needed to travel large distances. For Steel to travel from Eluud to Aymyn he needs to stop and create several new wormholes to travel through. The Pizians are working on improving that, and have been for quite some time, even before the Assembly, but so far have not been very successful.

"I don't mind what we have", Steel says. *"It's their experiments that make me nervous. It's all very good until they open up a new portal to Carpaga"*.

Carpaga. That name again. And hearing it again has the same reaction with Aura as the last time, making it difficult for her to maintain her smile. *"They haven't done that since"*, she replies. *"They still only have the one that we know of"*.

"That we know of", Steel replies. *"That place gives me the jeebees"*. That place gives everyone the jeebees.

Aura clears her mind of her tormented thoughts about Carpaga and relaxes a bit more. She raises Steel's hand to her face, looking at it longingly, and kisses it. *"Many here would agree with you about their experiments"*, she says, then looks at him in his eyes once again. *"But since they were the ones that united all the planets in Exom, even the council of light turns a blind eye to what the Pizians do"*. She lowers Steel's hand back down to his lap, resting her hand there. *"Everything we see around us is Pizian technology"*, she says, looking around the Council chambers. She looks back at Steel. *"We claim it as our own, but if it wasn't for them, we'd all still be living in sandstone houses and using glowing fish for our light source. There would be no interspecies or interplanetary contact. You and I would never have met. There'd be no Eluud. No Royal Alliance. We'd all still be living the old ways"*.

Steel smiles and pretends to shudder. *"Terrible thought"*, he says to her. *"Given how the Aymyn are stuck in their old philosophies and ways"*, he continues now looking more serious, *"I am surprised that the Guardian of the Light is sitting here with me embracing it"*.

Queen Aura looks suspiciously and deeply into Steel's eyes. *"Do you want the title?"*, she asks him. *"You can have it"*.

"No thanks", he replies with a laugh. *"You can proudly keep that title"*.

Aura lets go of Steel's hand and sits back in her chair, looking almost despondent with her situation. *"I don't have much choice"*, she says. *"The title comes with the crown"*.

The position of Guardian of the Light is an easier one to work in if you have a strong Light inclination. And since the emergence of pure Light Signs has become so rare over time, the last known one having died long before Aura and Steel were even born, even the Church of Light is being run by a Minister who himself is only a regular Wendral Sign, like Aura, with a strong Light persuasion.

"I'm sure that your tendency is closer to Light than mine is", Steel says to her.

"It's called persuasion", Aura corrects him. *"But who knows"*, she replies. *"I am no Light Sign. There has not been a pure Light in my family line for as long as I have known. But still, it is my responsibility to uphold the philosophy"*.

A philosophy that is often summed up with a simple saying. *"Watch the Light"*, Steel recites. Three words left by Theorone to the people of Aymyn in his writing's eons ago.

"I never understood why the Eluudians ever broke away from Aymyn in the first place", Aura says to Steel, looking at him curiously. *"Look at your history, you don't change much"*.

A fact that no one really denies. However, Steel finds Aura's statement to be a moot point. Eluud, and its ways do not change much because the atmosphere does not allow it to do so. *"It's not that we are against it"*, Steel explains. *"There is plenty that I would like to change"*.

"Oww, that sounds Dark", Aura says to him jokingly. Steel shrugs, feeling instinctively insulted by the comment, since referring to an

Aymyn, or even someone of Aymyn decent, as "Dark" is inherently an insult. However, knowing that she is only joking, Steel smiles back at her and quickly changes the topic.

"Anyway, Dacos...", he starts to say before being quickly interrupted by an excited Aura.

"Dacos is here?", she asks. Having known Steel for a long time, Aura has also watched Dacos grow up and go from Steel's squire to General of the Eluudian army.

"No", Steel replies, drowning Aura's excitement.

"That's a shame", she says momentarily disappointed. *"I like that boy"*. Aura has always had a great fondness for Dacos, believing that he has turned into an absolutely lovely young man. And, like everyone else, wishes he would hurry up and hook up with Det. *"Not quite as much Det does, I don't suppose"*, she adds.

Steel laughs to himself. Aura notices Steel's laugh and smiles. *"Are they still playing that silly game?"*, she asks, almost rhetorically. *"Pretending that they aren't completely head over heels for each other"*.

"Not that either of them would admit it", Steel replies as he shrugs with a kind of disappointment. *"Now back to what I was saying"*, Steel says trying to return to the topic he was on before he was interrupted by Aura and her excitement. *"Dacos uncovered something very interesting about you"*.

Aura looks away with a cheeky smile. *"Just one thing? That's disappointing"*. She says, throwing Steel a side glancing smile. Steel looks back at her, trying to keep a serious expression. *"Couldn't have been looking too hard"*, Aura adds. She looks at Steel, wanting to see his expression change. It doesn't. She now turns to him, moving her head closer to his and playfully smiling at him. *"Oh, come on"*, she says to him. *"There is a lot that is interesting about me. I am a very interesting person. Ask me something. I'll answer it in an interesting way. With extra interest. Just for you. But only because I love you"*.

Steel shakes his head, still trying to hold a serious gaze, but failing as a smile breaks through. He looks away, shakes his head and giggles. He recomposes himself and then turns in his chair to face Aura, again looking at her seriously. *"Troin"*, he says to her.

Knowing exactly where Steel is going with this, Aura decides not to beat around the bush. She stops fooling around and looks at him more seriously. *"Grandmother"*, she replies. *"I Never knew her"*.

"You've never mentioned it", Steel says.

"Like I said, I never knew her", Aura says again. *"As you can imagine, back in those days, with the way the Aymyn thought about the Troin, my grandfather did not really talk much about my grandmother, and she'd died before I was born"*, Aura explains. *"The basics were taught to me by my mother, but none of the customs or culture. The Troin were for a long time looked upon as the Aymyn shame and, as you know, not even accepted into the Royal Alliance until very recently"*. A very recent development that Aura herself was instrumental in implementing.

"One of my lady's finest achievements", Steel says to her, smiling with admiration.

"I don't think I am completely responsible for their acceptance", Aura says.

"Don't sell yourself short", Steel responds. *"You are the one that made that alliance happen. And because of you we now also have a valuable ally in the Troin Army"*.

Aura reflects a bit on this quietly to herself. She looks at Steel warmly and smiles. *"You know you helped with that"*, she says to him.

Steel looks at her confused. *"What? How?"*, he asks. *"I didn't do anything"*.

Aura continues to look at Steel, still smiling warmly, and nods. *"You sure did"*. Steel's confused look continues. *"You opened my eyes to how accepting other races can be"*, Aura says. *"You have always been welcoming of the Troin"*.

Steel shrugs and nods.

"Your daughter is partnered with one", Aura adds.

"Well, that kind of happened afterwards", Steel explains.

Aura chuckles lightly at Steel's response, then looks at him again with her cheeky smile. *"So, I thought"*, she continues. *"If a backwards planet and people like Eluud could be that accepting..."*

Steel interrupts Aura by tickling her ribs. *"Backwards?"*, he says.

Aura laughs and squirms trying to move her body away from Steel's tickling fingers. *"Then, the great Aymyn Empire..."*, Aura says, between giggling from Steel continuing to tickle her.

"Such a great empire", Steel says.

"Mighty. I mean mighty", Aura says, still laughing and squirming. She grabs Steel's hands and holds them, looking him in the eyes. *"Can learn to be just as accepting and welcoming"*, she adds.

Steel stops trying to tickle her and looks back at her sincerely. They sit there just staring into each other's eyes. Steel sits back and nods. *"Hmmmm"*, he says, still looking into Aura's eyes. He looks at the lapel of her dress, reaches out and touches it. Aura looks down at his hand. He pulls it open gently and looks intensely at the second layer of her dress underneath, tracing his fingers along it. Aura looks back into his eyes. *"You certainly don't dress like a Troin"*, Steel says to her, referring to the several layers of her dress. A complete contrast to the Troin, who don't wear much at all.

"I feel the cold", Aura replies, still looking deeply into Steel's eyes.

Steel looks up to meet them again. *"So, not that much Troin blood still in you"*, he says.

"Evidently", Aura replies.

Aura reaches for Steel's hand, holds it with both of hers, brings it to her face and kisses it again. She lowers it to her waist and holds it there, still staring into his eyes. Her expression now looking more curious. *"Why was Dacos looking into me?"*, she asks.

"He wasn't looking into you exactly", Steel replies, leaning back into his chair, but letting Aura keep hold of his hand. *"It's thought that the Sharlon Leader is Troin"*.

This was also something that Aura had heard and had been suggested in some conversations she has had within the council. *"Dark"*, Aura says, saying the leader of the Sharlon's name out loud.

"If we can confirm that Dark herself is a Troin, then that would narrow the search field at least a little", Steel explains. *"Perhaps put us one step closer to working out who she is. A mystery no one has ever got close to solving"*.

Aura nods back at Steel, agreeing with him. *"It is something that we have suspected"*, she says. *"It would make sense. With the exception of the Spectre led Dakari raids that you get frequently around your region of Exom, a lot of the organized attacks and sabotage have been led by Troin. Like the one you probably just saw Zargah carrying out as you came in as an example"*.

The downside of being away from the council as much as he is, there is a lot that Steel is unfortunately unaware of. *"Seems I have a lot of catching up to do"*, he says.

"If you were here more, then you'd be all caught up", Aura replies smugly.

Thinking that her statement is not fair, Steel slowly pulls his hand back and stares back at Aura with a bothered look. He is not exactly in the same situation as what she is. *"I still have a planet and kingdom to run"*, he says to her. *"And my planet and kingdom are not in the same place as the Royal Alliance Council Chambers"*.

Realizing that Steel has taken offense to her statement, which was most definitely not what she had intended, Aura reaches out and grabs hold of his hand again. *"I..."*, she says, then stops to rephrase what she is about to say and looks at him softly. *"I didn't word that very well"*. She tries to think how she can tell Steel what she wants to say without sounding selfish. She thinks deeply about it, then speaks, still not convinced that her next words are going to be any fairer.

"Steel, you do too much", she says. *"You have your delegates. You have your daughters. All more than capable of picking up the slack with running Eluud. You are a Council Member of the Royal Alliance, which in itself holds a great responsibility. We need you here more often"*. She pauses briefly before saying what she really means. *"I need you here more often"*, she says.

Her words are not lost on Steel. It is something that he would like to be able to do as well. More to be with Aura than the Council. Though in no way lessening the significance of being on the council, Steel is also under no misconception that his place on the Royal Alliance is anywhere near as important as Aura's.

"Me being here is not quite the same as you being here", he says to her. *"You are the glue that holds this council together. Everyone knows that. The council would have dissolved long ago if you weren't leading it. The Royal Alliance along with it"*.

Steel now moves a little deeper into the real issue. *"I know our situation is not ideal"*, he says to her. *"I'd have a lot more if I could. I couldn't have less"*, he adds, shaking his head. *"Not of you"*. He looks away briefly, then looks back at Aura again. *"I...."*, he starts to say, but stumbles on his words. *"I...Ah....Oh gees"*, he continues to struggle. *"Where's Tespa when you need her?"*, he says to himself.

"Tespa?", Aura asks him.

"She does this thing", Steel starts to explain. *"When you can't find the words to say, she seems to find them"*.

Aura smiles gently and nods at Steel. *"Sounds like we could both do with her"*, she says.

Steel giggles as he nods and knowing that he will never be able to say what he is trying to say, he moves on. *"As my lover..."*, Steel starts to say.

"Lover?", Aura interrupts.

Steel smiles at her. *"More"*, he adds.

"A lot more, I'd hope", Aura says.

"A whole lot more", Steel replies.

"Continue", Aura says with another cheeky smile, accepting his addendum.

"I count on you to fill me in on all the ongoings", Steel continues. *"So, then I am all up to date when I get here, and when I am on Eluud, I can concentrate on protecting my home"*.

"You do a very good job at protecting Eluud", Aura says, smiling reassuringly at Steel, hoping to see him smile back. Instead, Steel looks back at her, reflective and a little disheartened.

"Someone's got to care for it", he says. Unfortunately, something that Steel feels that no one outside of Eluud does.

"We all care for Eluud", Aura says, looking confused by Steel's comment.

"That's not true", Steel replies. *"Maybe not by you, but for most, we are seen as insignificant, a small outpost at best. Not the kingdom that has stood for generations. Even Mosqua has a Zazar protectorate, and it's an ice planet, which other than the one building complex is completely uninhabitable"*.

"It has a very popular club and health spring though", Aura replies. And she is not wrong. The Club and Health Spring on Mosqua is the most popular retreat in Exom. It is also the only thing on Mosqua. The rest of the planet being just as Steel has described, completely made of ice and uninhabitable. The minerals trapped in the ice on Mosqua have amazing healing properties. Yet strangely loses these properties when taken away from the planet. Hot springs were built on the planet, liquifying the ice into a warm bath. People travelled all over Exom to relax, rejuvenate and heal in these hot springs. The area was commercialized with the introduction of a large building complex, containing nightclubs, bars, hotels, and of course the hot springs themselves. Though the most famous and popular resort in Exom, many like Steel, feel that having its own Zazar protectorate, when many fully populated planets do not, is a bit unreasonable.

Aura's comment was actually to try and lighten the mood. However, judging by Steel's dismayed expression, she quickly realises that her attempt at humour has not made Steel feel any better. *"Steel, Eluud is valued"*, she says to him.

"Then why has no Zazar selected it to be their protectorate?", he asks her. Not so much for her to answer, but more to support his statement that Eluud is not valued. *"Why are we still an unprotected planet? The Skurj War is closer to Eluud than it has ever been before. It will be within my lifetime, and I fear very soon, that we will be wiped off the map"*. Steel takes a breath to settle himself and stop himself from getting worked up. He was not intending on embroiling Aura into such an emotional discussion. He simply wanted her to understand why he needs to spend so much time away from Aymyn. *"My people are scared"*, he adds. *"I'm scared for them. My place has to be with them as a priority"*.

He is not telling Aura anything that she doesn't already know deep down. Sadly, also aware that what he is saying is true, though, like Steel, wishing it wasn't. She turns and looks at the table, as her mind drifts to thoughts of the Skurj war and the planets that are continuing to be destroyed by them. *"We lost Crom today"*, she says to Steel, still looking down at the table as she relives the pain and grief she could see in Prahm's face and body.

"I heard", Steel replies, as he joins Aura in her sad reflection and turns and stares blankly at the table as well. Steel's thoughts turn to the Crom royal family, who he had gotten to know quite well during his time on the Council. He had spent a great deal of time with them, not only on Aymyn but also on visits he has personally taken to Crom since Crom is in a system not that far from where Eluud is. King Prahm has even visited and stayed with Steel on Eluud as Steel's guest. *"Prahm?"*, he asks Aura, bracing himself to receive more bad news.

Aura realizes that Steel is thinking that Prahm was still on Crom during the attack. At least she has one thing that she can say to help improve this sad moment. She turns to face Steel, reaching out to touch his face and raises his head to look into his eyes. *"Oh no. He's here"*, she says with a smile. Her smile fades naturally. *"Who knows for how long"*, she adds.

Steel looks back at Aura, taking at least some comfort in that small fact. *"His family?"*, he asks hopefully. Aura shakes her head and looks back down blankly at the table. Unfortunately, there was no other good news that she could add. Just as she could not when speaking to King Crom himself.

Steel again reflects on his own planet and what he had just been saying. *"This is my point, Aura"*, he says to her. She looks up to look at him again. *"Crom is not that far away from Eluud"*, he adds. *"There are Zazars that have not yet selected a planet to be their protectorate. Why can't just one of them choose us?"*.

Sadly, this is a question that Aura can not answer. Neither her, nor the council, have any control over what planet a Zazar selects or when. It is the right and privilege of a Zazar to select a planet of their own choosing, whichever planet that should be, to be their protectorate.

"Even as head of the Royal Alliance Council, I can not force any Zazar to make that decision. You know that", she tells Steel.

Steel is well aware of this, as is anyone and everyone who is aware of the Zazars. *"I'm not saying that"*, Steel says. *"The Zazar General, the biggest goddamn morn to ever walk, the Aymyn protectorate - and apparently your own personal bodyguard"*, he adds with a playfully but serious look.

"He doesn't like you that much either", Aura responds with a slight smile as she returns Steel's sarcastic look.

Steel sighs, not sure what else he can say. Aura looks back at him, feeling concerned and not knowing what to do or say to comfort him. She is not sure why he mentioned Zargah. Was he hoping that Zargah could persuade the free Zazars to select Eluud? Little did Steel know; Aura had already asked Zargah if he would do that. She is not sure how Zargah asked the other Zazars this request. The Morn are not very talkative. Even their strategic meetings usually only involve a couple of one sentence statements, a bunch of grunts and a few sighs. When Aura asked Zargah how he went, he replied to her with a similar grunt. *"That good, huh?"*, she said to him. To which he responded with only a sigh. The Morn are also an incredibly stubborn bunch, even amongst each other.

Steel sits silently for a moment, again stuck for words and caught deep in his thoughts. His love and devotion for his planet, his people, his family does not even need words to be heard. It is incredibly clear to Aura, as it is to all who know him. He makes absolutely no secret of it. His wish is that others could also feel and see what he feels and sees. *"If only they could see us"*, he says out loud, still deep in his own thoughts.

Aura can not only see Steel's pain and frustration. She can also feel it. His words, thoughts and feelings echo inside her every day, whether he is with her or not. She may not be Steel's Queen, but she loves his planet just as much as her own. If she had the power to persuade a Zazar to select Eluud, then she would most certainly use it, even though her Parandrae nature would also make her think about all the other unselected planets that then may not be selected due to this decision. Yes, even though there is that, she still wishes she could.

Steel looks at Aura again with such sad questioning eyes. *"Why don't they see us?"*, he asks her.

"We do", she replies, her voice also resonating the same sadness. *"I do. Every day I petition the Zazars to select Eluud. Every day that you are here. Every day that you are not here - Which is a lot by the way - I am constantly asking the Zazars to choose Eluud to become a protected planet"*. She pauses to sigh. Her shoulders raise as she takes a deep breath and then drop lower than when she started. *"Every day the same answer"*, she says.

Steel knows the answer. *"No"*, he says looking hopeless

Aura sighs again. *"No"*, she confirms as she looks away again. She then looks back at Steel, turning in her chair to face him completely, and again holds his hands. She looks deeply into his eyes, letting herself feel his sadness, hopelessness. Perhaps if two people could be feeling it right now it will divide the pain and make it a little easier. It doesn't. She wishes that there was something that she could tell him to make him feel better, happier, more hopeful. But in this moment, words are not what she has. All she has is all she has ever had. Hope.

"You keep telling me that I can't protect Exom with only hope", she says to him. She shakes her head and looks away again briefly, trying her hardest not to show her despair, then looks back at Steel with tears forming in her eyes. *"But it's all I've got"*. Her words start to become more laboured. As if her tears are starting to choke her as she tries unsuccessfully to hold them back. *"I'm here co-ordinating the Zazar Corp with the protected planets"*, she continues. *"Communicating with the Troin Army to get some support for the non-protected planets. Watching planets like Suskin, like Balnar 7, like Crom..."*. She takes another deep breath, still choking on her tears and words. *"Like Crom, get devoured by an enemy that we can't beat. All while holding together this Council, this Alliance and running this planet. Knowing all the while that the man I love is on another planet, with his family, and not here with me"*. She turns away, tears pouring down her cheeks. Steel tries to reach out to her, but she is still holding his hands. She holds

them even more firmly to her as he tries to move them. She takes another deep breath, forces back the tears and turns and looks at Steel again. Through her sadness she is still able to smile at him. *"I am not saying that you shouldn't be there, with your family, with your planet"*, she says to him. *"But understand that every day that you are there fighting for your planet, and I am here fighting for mine, I am fighting for yours too. I have never given up. Will never give up. And despite the constant refusals, every day I continue to ask the free Zazars to select Eluud. Even when I know that there are so - SO - many unprotected planets in Exom. And I am hopeful that one day, just one day, not too far away, one of them will say yes"*.

Steel stares into her eyes. A tear also falls from his eye. He smiles back at her, through his pain and also feeling hers. Aura readjusts her grip on his hands and makes sure that they are still being held close to her. *"I'm hopeful"*, she says to him. *"But it's all I've got"*.

EXOM

THE YOUNG KING

CHAPTER SEVEN

-------------------------- Be There Soon --------------------------

A familiar liquid looking energy pools hovers above a viewing table at the back of Sabel's dimly lit hideout. Projected within the energy pool is a single figure, seen only from the shoulders up and wearing a black hooded cloak which shadows their face completely. Sabel stands beside the table, looking into the projection and speaking with the black hooded person. *"Are you very far, my sign?"*, Sabel asks them.

"I will be with you shortly", the hooded person replies with a friendly but firm female voice. Her head tilts up slightly to look more directly at Sabel, the black shadow of her hood still completely concealing her face. A small faint window through the blackness starts to appear revealing her eyes. Beautiful Aymyn eyes. The iris red in colour like all Aymyn females. There is something about her eyes, her stare. Piercing, authoritative. The kind that if they are looking at you, you shut up and listen.

Sabel nods and steps back from the table, seeming content with that answer. She also seems very comfortable with the hooded woman who is staring at her, whereas others would very likely find it intimidating. Sabel glances over at Nadiri, who is now sitting on the chair that Sabel had pulled out for her earlier. A confident, yet equally intimidating smirk starts to form on Sabel's face as the holographic projector shuts down and the energy field disappears.

-------------------------------- Training --------------------------------

The Royal Training Hall on Eluud is not that sophisticated looking by all appearances. A large hall with random obstacles scattered around the floor, seemingly attached to it, as well as the walls. Large enough to jump onto and from, as is their purpose. Also attached to the walls are various shelves and platforms, again large enough for a person to stand on or jump to and from. Some are even suspended, dangling, from the ceiling by ropes. One suspended platform appears to be broken, and is dangling precariously from the ceiling, the other end of the rope almost reaching the floor. It has been like this for a very long time, and no-one has fixed it as, the way it is, presents another unique and useful piece of training equipment. The entire layout seems to be perfectly designed for some serious parkour training; an activity that is very commonly applied to the combat training practiced on Eluud. Senior officers like Dacos, or just members of the royal family can occasionally be seen zipping through obstacles in the hall. Their ronads fully deployed, ranging through a variety of combat routines, usually adlib, jumping and diving from object to object, while striking and stabbing others.

In its "Advanced Mode", small, about one meter or so high, catapult-like machines will rise out from the floor. These machines are constructed and deconstructed using the building technology that is commonly used throughout Exom. Strangely, it is one of the very few places on Eluud that this is used. The catapult machines will fire small, about one-inch wide, metallic balls randomly, and at various speeds at anyone standing in the hall training area. The speed can be set by the user and can range from "Quite Fast" to "Very Fast". The idea is to dodge, or deflect using a ronad, these balls. Though non-lethal of course, you still would not want to be hit by one of these catapulted balls. On your body they will leave a nasty welt. On your head it could very well render you unconscious. Advanced mode is not used a lot.

This Training Hall adjoins Chassam Castle with its only entrance being a single door leading outside into the main Castle gardens. Just inside the doors is a short recessed open entrance area, only partially walled off from the main training hall. To one side of the hall, the same side as the entrance, bench seats line the entire length of the wall.

Standing in the middle of the Training Hall, holding her fully deployed ronad and practicing various routines, very slowly, is Tespa. Tespa has never used the Training Hall in its advanced mode, and very probably never will. She is also not utilizing any of the objects located around the hall or on the walls. She is simply going through her routine, walking, turning, holding and swinging her ronad at a slow and precise pace, while concentrating on her breathing and every movement.

She slowly thrusts her ronad at an imaginary enemy, breathing deeply and steadily, when the door to the training hall swings open and Det walks in carrying her gym bag. Det immediately notices Tespa in the hall. She stops and watches her, observing curiously, and cynically, her very slow movements.

Tespa also sees Det and smiles at her while not breaking her routine. Det does not smile back and continues to watch Tespa while placing her bag down on the floor. Det has never understood the seemingly incredibly relaxed pace that Tespa goes through her routine. *"You had better hope that your enemy is as slow as you are"*, Det says to her.

Tespa, very used to Det's sharp remarks, stays unaffected by her comment, and remains completely focussed on her routine. *"Just making sure I get it right"*, Tespa replies.

Det looks away and starts walking through the hall, acquainting herself with where each obstacle is situated. Though, with the number of times that Det has trained in this hall, she would be thoroughly familiar with every object, ledge and piece of rope in it, and where it is located. She casually throws one more comment at Tespa as she walks past her. *"Not much good if they are faster"*, she says, then continues to walk around the room, taking everything in.

Tespa follows her with her eyes, doing her best to ignore her. *"A tree would be faster"*, Det mumbles under her breath, but loud enough for Tespa to hear. Tespa gives Det a sideways glare, still not reacting to her words and continues with her routine uninterrupted. Det bends over and removes her ronad from her leg sheath and activates it. The pole spears extend out from the handle as Det runs straight towards a wall, leaps at it, and pushes herself off it with her legs. She lands with one leg on a large cube, pushes herself off that and towards another wall in front of Tespa. She then pushes herself off that wall and, with her ronad raised above her head, she lands in front of Tespa, bringing the ronad down with a lot of force, and stopping it only inches above Tespa's head.

Not flinching, knowing that Det would never actually hurt her, though not a belief many share, Tespa calmly looks up at Det curiously. She then looks up at Det's ronad, still being held inches above her head, and gently taps it away with her own ronad, then continues on with her routine.

Det stands there watching Tespa and just shakes her head, both disappointed and frustrated with Tespa's lack of reaction.

Tespa looks back at Det. *"Would it kill you to be nicer?"*, she asks her. Det stays expressionless, watching Tespa. *"Maybe"*, Det replies.

"You really need to feel more", Tespa tells her as she continues on with her routine.

Det brings the end of her ronad up close to her face and looks closely at the point. *"No time for feeling. Need to focus"*, Det replies.

"Can't you do both?", Tespa asks her.

"Nope", Det replies, still looking closely at the point of her ronad.

Tespa stops her routine and turns to look at Det and shrugs. *"And why not?"*, she asks Det.

Det stops looking at the point of her ronad and looks over at Tespa. She looks away for a moment, as if to think about what to say, then looks back at Tespa. *"When I let myself feel, people become blurry"*, Det replies.

Tespa's head starts to shake with confusion over what Det has just said. *"People become blurry?"*, she asks. *"What do you mean blurry? Like, do you mean they....What do you mean they become blurry?"*

Det shakes her head, not wanting to explain it to Tespa, so she doesn't, then launches herself into her own training routine. Her routine is very different to Tespa's. Like she had just done before, she runs and jumps off walls and obstacles, this time while spinning, lunging, and swinging her ronad around as though attacking invisible enemies. Det trains with speed and exerting strength and power in each push, kick, spin, thrust and swing of her ronad. All the while Tespa continues at her own much slower, relaxed pace unperturbed by Det darting off walls and obstacles around her.

The door to the training hall opens again and this time Dacos enters. Knowing that both Tespa and Det would be there, he closes the door behind him and stands just in the entrance area watching them train. Det sees him standing there but does not acknowledge him, instead continuing her running, jumping, and spinning while thrusting and swinging her ronad.

Tespa also notices Dacos standing in the entrance area. She stops training and smiles at him. Dacos smiles back and starts to walk towards Tespa, staying very aware of Det zipping around the hall. *"Hey Dacos"*, Tespa calls out to Dacos as she deactivates her ronad and turns to face him.

Det, on the other hand, is not so welcoming. *"Coming through!"*, Det yells out as she leaps and kicks herself back off the wall right beside Dacos, swinging her ronad at him. Dacos quickly ducks out of the way, narrowly avoiding being hit. Det keeps moving, without breaking so much as a step, or even acknowledging that she almost, possibly deliberately, took off Dacos's head.

Dacos watches Det continue to fly through her routine, a little confused at her antagonism, but shrugs it off and looks back at Tespa as she walks up to him. *"What brings you here?"*, Tespa asks him. She then smiles as she glances over at Det still darting about, knowing full well what brings Dacos there. She looks back at Dacos, her smile turning into a cheeky smirk.

Dacos returns her smirk with an intriguing glance. *"Just checking on you. Doing my job"*, he replies.

Det comes flying through again, ronad again swinging down towards Dacos. Dacos stretches out his hand beside his leg. Instantly his ronad flies out of his leg sheath and up into his hand. He quickly activates it and blocks Det's attack, flicking her ronad out of her hands and across the hall. Det stops and glares at Dacos. Dacos still only looks curiously back at her, then retracts his ronad and returns it to his leg sheath. Det turns away from him and walks across the hall to collect her ronad.

Tespa is amused by what has just happened but does not want to say anything. Instead, she chooses to comment on the actual disarming technique that Dacos just used on Det. *"Can you teach us that?"*, she asks him.

Dacos looks at Tespa then back at Det, then back at Tespa again doubting that teaching Det anything that could be used against him would be a good idea. *"Do you think that's wise?"*, he replies.

Det, having just picked up her ronad and now holding it again, does not deactivate it. She walks back, stands next to Tespa and looks quietly at Dacos.

"Yes. Come on. We'd love to learn it", Tespa says to Dacos. Tespa nudges Det for her to join in, but Det just stands there quiet and expressionless looking at Dacos. Dacos looks at both Det and Tespa as he thinks about it some more. Then gives in and shrugs.

"Alright", he says. He stretches out his hand, summoning his ronad back to his hand again, activates it and starts spinning it around. *"It's all in the wrist"*, he explains. *"Not just yours, but your opponents also. If they are holding their weapon too hard and rigid, which they will be if they are coming in angry or inexperienced, then their grip will feel strong to them but it's not. If their wrist and arm can't move with the momentum, then their hold on their weapon is not going to be strong"*. Dacos continues to swing his ronad around doing even more tricks. *"Strong but flexible"*, he says. Dacos then stops swinging his ronad and holds it out firmly in front of Det. *"See, holding it like this is wrong"*, he explains, *"because all my..."*. Before Dacos can finish his sentence, Det flicks Dacos's ronad with her own. His ronad flies out of his hand and across the hall. All the while Det never takes her eyes off Dacos or shows any reaction. Dacos, taken by surprise, as is Tespa, stares stunned back at Det.

Tespa runs over and picks up Dacos's ronad, something she did not really need to do considering that Dacos could simply summon it back to his hand at any time, while Dacos and Det continue to stare at each other. Tespa examines Dacos's ronad, always curious by the way it is different to hers and Det's with its extra blades and spikes at each end. She deactivates it and walks back to Det and Dacos. Not thinking, she hand's Dacos's ronad to Det instead. Det takes it casually, as though it was hers, and stands there holding it while still staring at Dacos emotionless.

"You seemed to pick that up quick", Dacos says to Det.

"Yep", Det replies. Det retracts her ronad, then opens her other hand, letting Dacos's ronad just drop to the ground. She then walks over to pick up her gym bag and walks out of the training hall.

Dacos and Tespa stand there watching Det leave and then look at each other in silence. Tespa smiles uncomfortably. *"Well, this is awkward"*, she says to him. Dacos nods as he stretches out his hand again. His ronad instantly moves from the ground and into his hand. He places it back onto his leg sheath and smiles back at Tespa.

----------------------- The Trolor Monster -----------------------

The Royal Alliance Council has reconvened, and the Councillors are all once again seated around the Council Table. Steel is still in his chair next to Aura, as they both sit there looking completely professional and not making any physical contact with each other. Though, their relationship is far from a secret, they refrain from flaunting it publicly, especially during Council business.

Councillor Lawn is also there, seated in the other permanent chair to Aura's right.

Since Steel has been away for a while, he sits there quietly, listening and trying to catch up on what he has missed. He does not want to appear ignorant to anything, so as topics are discussed, topics he knows nothing about, he nods like he is completely aware of them and agrees with what the other councillors are saying. Sometimes he finds himself ignorantly pretending to agree with two opposing sides of an argument at the same time. This is often met by confused looks from the other councillors to which Steel will just politely smile, sit back quietly in his chair and avoid making eye contact with anyone.

Then a topic comes up that he can't even pretend to know anything about.

"Are we any closer to knowing what launched from Blyanan and is moving towards the inner systems?", Queen Klatanaria asks the Council.

"If we did, you would know about it", Councillor Lawn replies somewhat coldly. Klatanaria frowns at Councillor Lawn, not liking his tone. But then again, he is a Spectre, so his tone is not often liked. *"Those that are here often enough to attend these Council meetings, anyway"*, he adds as he sends a sideways stare towards Steel.

Still focused on Klatanaria's question, it takes Steel a moment before he realizes that Lawn is speaking about him. He looks at Lawn, not knowing if his comment was intended as a dig. Being a Spectre, it probably wasn't and was just Lawn stating an observation and opinion without any tact as usual.

"You can talk", Steel rebuts with a smirk. *"You miss almost as many as I do, and you live here"*.

King Yord finds Steel's comment amusing. *"Can you blame him?"*, King Yord says to Steel, then looks at everyone else seated at the council table. *"Who would live on Zenos?"*.

Councillor Lawn looks at King Yord, showing no expression or feeling of having just been insulted. *"I represent Zenos. It is my planet"*, Lawn says. *"However, with this body I do prefer the comforts of Aymyn over the swamps of my home world"*.

Prince Niyan laughs under his breath as he looks away from Councillor Lawn. *"Maybe you are just too scared to return in case more of your kind take over your body"*, Niyan says to him, still choosing not to look at him.

Again, Lawn seemingly takes no insult to the remark. He looks at Prince Niyan, blankly, almost innocently. *"Yes"*, Lawn replies.

Councillor Lawns response has Steel Intrigued. He at first looks confused, his eyes darting all over the place as he thinks about what Niyan and Lawn have just said. He knew that the spectres could possess and take over completely an Aymyn body, or the body of any species for that matter. However, he did not know that once they had done this, that they themselves were then also vulnerable to another spectre taking them over. *"Is that even possible?"*, Steel asks Lawn, now able to keep his eyes focussed in one place.

Councillor Lawn turns his attention back to Steel. *"Yes"*, he replies.

"Really?", Steel asks him again.

"Yes", once again Lawn replies.

Steel continues to look at Lawn with intrigue. *"Like, that is actually a thing that can happen?"*, he again asks.

"Yes", Lawn replies again.

The concept is mind-blowing to Steel, sparking questions all throughout Steel's brain. *"Like another...."*, Steels starts to ask before a frustrated Aura abruptly turns to Steel and snaps at him. *"Steel! He said yes. It's a thing. It can happen"*, she says, her eyes piercing like a mother telling her child to shut up.

Steel sits back quietly and thinks about it. This time lost in his own thoughts and not the conversation that is trying to take place at the Council Table.

"How many probes do we have out searching....", Klatanaria starts to ask before Steel, still fixated on his conversation with Councillor Lawn, looks back at Lawn and interrupts.

"How does that work exactly?", Steel asks him.

Annoyed at being cut off, Klatanaria glares at Steel. Her expression showing more confusion than annoyance, as she is actually quite fond of Steel and his, at times, childlike innocence. Aura, however, is definitely showing her frustration as she snaps at Steel again. *"Steel!"*, she scolds at him, turning in her chair to look at him directly.

Only now realising that he has rudely interrupted Klatanaria, he looks humbly apologetically at her. *"I'm so sorry, Your Highness"*, he says to her. *"This has just got me intrigued"*. Klatanaria nods and smiles at Steel, unable to show any annoyance at him, finding his curiosity in the subject amusing. Steel looks back at Lawn again, unable to move past the subject. *"So, what happens to you if another Spectre takes over your body?"*, he asks Lawn.

Again, Lawn shows no emotion in his words. *"My mind will be gone"*, Lawn replies.

Steel knows that when the Spectres leave their organic, jellyfish-like, bodies and ascend into beings of pure energy, that energy is actually what they refer to as "their mind". So, when Councillor Lawn says that his "Mind will be gone", what he is really saying is.... *"You will be dead?"*, Steel asks.

"I will be dead", Lawn replies.

"Like the person who was the original owner of your body", Steel asks, knowing that this is also what happens to the people or creatures that the Spectre possesses.

"Correct", Lawn replies.

Princess Illyana sits back in her chair and looks at the other Councillors seated at the table. *"Is anyone else finding this conversation a little morbid?"*, she asks.

Aura certainly is and tries to get the council back on track again. *"I think we should stick to the subject that has been addressed by Queen Klatanaria"*, she says to everyone at the council table, then turns and looks specifically at Steel. Steel looks back at her innocently, and again in that moment feels bad for interrupting Klatanaria and apologises to her once more

"So sorry. Yes, please continue", he says.

Queen Klatanaria picks up from where she was interrupted. *"How many probes do we have searching for whatever it is that left Blyanan?"*, she asks the other councillors at the table.

"We do not know what we are even looking for", King Yord replies as he leans forward and clasps his hands together on the table.

Steel again finds himself back in the position of not knowing what the council is talking about. Probes searching for something? Something that left Blyanan? Already feeling embarrassed about interrupting Klatanaria, and now not wanting to appear completely ignorant to what she is talking about, Steel looks at King Yord and addresses his statement instead. *"Slow down, can you explain that a little bit more"*, Steel says to him. *"I'm sure there are people here that don't quite understand that. Not me of course, I understand it completely. But, you know, some people might not"*. Steel continues to look at Yord seriously, but inside he is smiling, thinking to himself, "nailed it!".

As Aura looks at Steel, it dawns on her that Steel has missed more meetings and has been out of the loop more than she had realized. Steel looks back at her and, noticing the way that she is staring at him, he realises that she has seen straight through his attempt at feigning comprehension. He smiles at her uneasily and then looks down at the table feeling a little embarrassed. She looks around at the other councillors at the table and, judging by their expressions, she can tell that they also clearly know that Steel is lost, with no clue what they are talking about. Aura looks back at Steel, staring at him once again, her gaze warm and in no way judgemental. *"What do you know about Blyanan?"*, She asks him.

Steel's starts to smile. If she is asking about the planet, the history and state of the planet, then finally, something that he can answer. Steel feels that he knows quite a bit about Blyanan. *"It's the unprotected liquid planet on the outer rim that has never been touched by Skurj, and home to the fish like species that you were speaking to when I arrived"*, Steel replies as he looks up confidently at Aura. Feeling content that he knows enough about Blyanan, he jokingly smiles at the other Councillors. *"I don't know that much about it"*, he says sarcastically.

"It has been touched by Skurj", Aura corrects him. *"And it used to be protected"*.

Steel smile quickly disappears as he looks away, again feeling called out, again feeling a little embarrassed. *"I told you I didn't know much about it"*, he says again, this time not so sarcastic.

Aura looks at Steel, caringly. It was not her intention to embarrass him. She only wants to fill him in on a subject that has now become apparent to everyone at the table that he does not know anything about. *"Blyanan was a protected planet. They had a Zazar"*, she tells Steel.

They had a Zazar, Steel thinks to himself, his face now expressing his surprise and confusion. He looks up at Aura again. *"Had?"*, he asks her.

Aura nods. *"He was killed during a Skurj attack. On Blyanan"*, she tells him.

Steel sits back in his chair looking both intrigued and confused. He did not know that.

"Many Zazars were", King Yord adds.

Steel looks over at King Yord. He did not know that either.

"That is correct", Aura again steps in to explain. *"Like the Blyan, the Skurj are able to survive in the acidic liquid that Blyanan is composed of. Not even our Morn Zazars can do that. During the Skurj Invasion of Blyanan, the Zazar Corp attempted to intercept the Skurj using submersible crafts. However, being inside these crafts and the Skurj being outside, the Zazar's Tription weapons were not able to be used to fight them"*.

"Only by going outside the crafts could they still be holding their Tription handles and produce the Flame", Yord adds.

"But outside the crafts", Aura says, *"the Zazars were quickly affected by the pressure and acidity of the liquid planet, while the Skurj were not, and, well, they were just no match"*.

"Many Zazars and Blyan were killed during that battle. No Skurj was injured", Yord says as he looks down feeling mournful.

Steel can see the sincerity in Aura's eyes, as well as the sadness in Yord's demeanour, yet feels even more confused now than before this conversation started. He knows that Blyanan is still around. He just saw a Blyan with Aura earlier in this very Council Chamber. *"I don't understand"*, Steels says, unable to hide his confusion. *"The Skurj attacked the planet. They could not be stopped. How is there still a planet?"*

King Yord's sad expression changes into a smile. He looks up and smiles at Steel. *"This is where it gets interesting"*, he says.

Steel looks back at Aura, eagerly waiting for her to tell him the "interesting" part of this story.

"It looked like all was lost", Aura starts to explain. *"The Zazars had no choice but to retreat. But you know the Zazars, they would never do that. When for some, to this day, unknown reason, the Skurj just stopped"*.

Steel is taken aback. That does not sound like the Skurj at all. *"Stopped?"*, Steel asks, looking confused at Aura, then looking at the other councillors seated at the table, all of whom look back at him and just nod.

"Stopped, turned around and left", Yord replies.

Steel is taken aback even more. *"Left?"*, he asks, almost disbelievingly. Aura nods. None of this is sounding right to Steel, and he starts to wonder if he is understanding them correctly. *"Left the planet?"*, he asks. Aura continues to nod. Steel sits there looking extremely confused.

Regent Bassal stares at Steel and smiles at his confused expression. *"You look as confused as everyone else who has heard this story, Your Highness"*, Bassal says to him.

Steel goes over the story again in his head. It not making any more sense the second time, or even the third. *"How have I not heard of this?"*, Steel looks at the council and asks out loud, his confused expression unable to be any more apparent.

Prince Niyan looks at Steel, suspecting that he has actually heard the story, but does not realize it. It is a story that everyone has heard. *"The Legend of Trolor?"*, Niyan says to Steel, waiting to see if it rings any bells.

It does. Steel does have a faint recollection of a story about the Legend of Trolor. But, having no idea where Trolor is, just assumed it was a made-up name. *"Trolor is an actual place?"*, Steel asks.

Trolor is an actual place. *"It is a level within the liquid layers of Blyanan"*, Aura replies. Blyanan, being a completely liquid planet, does not have any continents or islands to name, so the depth layers of the planet have been named instead. Trolor is one of the deepest depths of Blyanan. Not even the Blyan can go that far down. The pressure would crush them.

"The Trolor Monster?", Niyan says to Steel, seeing if that too may also ring a bell.

Steel has definitely heard of that. Everyone has heard of that. *"A monster that scares away Skurj. A fairy tale that kids play with"*, Steel replies. The Council all just look at Steel, and again Steel starts to feel like he is the only one in the room that didn't know something important. *"Wait? The Trolor Monster is real?"*, Steel asks. *"There is actually something that scares away Skurj?"*.

Aura notices Steel's mind boggling, overwhelmed trying to piece everything together, now not knowing fantasy from reality. *"The Trolor Monster is a fairy tale"*, she tells Steel. *"We do not know what stopped the Skurj and made them leave Blyanan. Not even the Blyan know. It has always been a mystery"*.

"So, stories, legends and monsters have been created to explain it", Princess Illyana says. *"We may never know what made the Skurj leave"*.

"Scared away", Niyan says, confident that it is an explanation.

"Perhaps", Illyana concedes, but uncertain.

"And too this day Blyanan has never been attacked by the Skurj again", Niyan says in conclusion as he looks over at Steel and then the rest of the councillors at the table.

Now with all the pieces, Steel is able to compile the whole story in his mind. The Council notices that Aura is staring at Steel, watching, and waiting for him to get all his thoughts together. She can see that this was big news for him.

Regent Bassal can also see Steel's mind turning. He smiles slightly, finding it somehow curiously amusing. *"Which brings us back to Queen Klatanaria's question"*, Bassal says, looking at all the councillors at the table. *"What are we doing to track this object?"*. Bassal then returns his attention to Steel again, still taking joy in watching the story unfold in his head, a story that he has just gone and added another piece to.

As Steel adds this last piece to his already overwhelmed brain, Steel's mind flashes back to Queen Klatanaria's original question; "Are we any closer to knowing what launched from Blyanan and is moving towards the inner systems?"

"Something left Blyanan?", Steel asks out loud. Not looking at anyone in particular, and not expecting an answer. More still just piecing everything together.

EXOM - THE YOUNG KING

Prince Niyan smiles at Steel's question, as he looks around at the other councillors and can see them all nodding. *"He's catching up"*, Niyan says.

Bassal looks back at Niyan and also nods. *"He's catching up"*, Bassal replies.

Steel continues to vocalize his thoughts. *"So, there was something in Blyanan that scared away the Skurj"*, he says out loud to himself. Prince Niyan is pleased with Steel's use of the term *"Scared away"*. *"We don't know what it is"*, Steel continues as he puts all the pieces together. *"Now, something has left Blyanan and is heading this way, and it is something that we do not know what it is"*.

Aura can see the conclusion that Steel is heading to. *"Just because both situations involve something unknown is no reason to draw a conclusion that both unknowns are the same thing"*, she says to him.

Steel looks eagerly at Aura. As though this unknown worrying news is something to get excited about. *"But what if they are?"*, he says to her.

King Yord starts to look at Steel intensely. *"Your excitement concerns me, King Steel"*, he says to him. *"You are talking about something that is even scarier than the Skurj. I am not sure that is a good thing"*.

Steel looks at King Yord with the same excitement. *"Something that scares the Skurj"*, he says, his eyes smiling. *"How can that not be a good thing? What else could it possibly be?"*

What indeed. The room goes silent. A thought is going through some of their minds, but no one is prepared to say it. Then the silence is broken by the one least expected to do it, Regent Pfyne. *"An Alpha"*, she replies.

Those words aid the silence to be maintained in the room. Everyone knows what Regent Pfyne means by "An Alpha". An Alpha Skurj. The mother of all Skurj. Larger, much larger than regular Skurj. One has never been seen and the concept of it is mere speculation and theory. However, it is a theory started by the Pizian.

No one has ever seen the Skurj breed or multiply, but obviously they come from somewhere. It is believed that with the way the Skurj devour planets and everything on them, should an Alpha Skurj exist, it will reside on a planet that no other Skurj would attack. It will also not require much in the way of defence or protection so will not need many, or even any other Skurj around. It may have a small number that serve it, but it is believed in general all other Skurj will stay well away from it. If there was an Alpha Skurj on Blyanan, then the Skurj's retreat from that planet, combined with the fact they have never returned, would make a lot of sense.

If what has launched itself from Blyanan is in fact an Alpha, then not only does that leave Blyanan vulnerable, but it also leaves the question of what is going to happen to the planet the Alpha ends up on?

Steel looks around at all the concerned faces around the table. He starts to feel guilty that his is not amongst them. Strangely the thought of an alpha does not scare him as much as it appears to be affecting the others. Perhaps it is because he is thinking of it as just another Skurj, which is scary enough, and not overthinking it as much as everyone else appears to be. Sensing the tension in the room from just the thought of an Alpha Skurj, Steel tries to lighten the mood. *"I think I may have dated one of those in the past"*, he says. Appearing surprised, perhaps it was shock, at Steel's comment, Aura looks at Steel with an expression that screams loudly, "What??". Steel looks at Aura and smiles with hilarity. *"Don't worry, it was before you"*, he tells her.

Steel winks at Aura, but his humour is lost on her as she just shakes her head at him. Noticing that his attempt at humour has failed, he tries to address the situation more seriously. *"If it is an Alpha"*, he says, *"we are still talking about a Skurj. We should be able to detect it with the sensors. And I'd imagine it would be hard to miss"*.

The way the council sees it, finding it is only half the problem. What to do when they find it is the other half.

"Even if we do find it. What then?", King Yord asks the question that many around the table are thinking. *"How do we kill it? A creature this size will be even harder than the regular Skurj"*.

Steel doesn't see it that way. *"It will still be a Skurj"*, Steel replies. *"We have not found anything that Tription weapons can not penetrate. I am sure the Zazars will handle it just fine"*, Steel adds confidently. He then looks over at Aura, *"Assuming it lands on a protected planet of course"*, he says as a little dig.

Aura takes Steel's comment a bit more seriously. Although probably meant in jest, he actually has a point. Being a Skurj, if an Alpha does land on an Unprotected Planet will the Zazar code still apply? Knowing the Council and their unbreakable rules, Aura has a strong feeling it will, unfortunately.

Then Steel adds another thought. *"But do we need to kill it?"*, he asks.

The council all look at Steel, shocked by his question. *"It's a Skurj"*, Klatanaria replies.

"No, hear me out", Steel quickly tries to explain. *"If it is what we are all saying, and that is a pretty big if, and all the unknowns align, it has been on Blyanan this entire time and no harm has ever come to the planet or its people"*.

Regent Bassal likes Steel's thinking. He is not sure he agrees with it but is intrigued at the fact that Steel is considering options and concepts outside of what the rest of the council would consider. In a way it takes the attention off himself. For now, Steel is the one with the "Sympathetic" view. But Bassal can not help himself from challenging Steel's conclusion.

"We do not know how long it has been there", Bassal says to Steel. *"For all we know it could have been there before the Blyan, perhaps even before Blyanan is the planet that it is today. Hibernating all this time. It may have destroyed the original planet, reducing it to nothing, fell asleep and over millions of years Blyanan reformed into this liquid planet we have now"*.

Princess Illyana laughs at Bassal's comment. *"Fell asleep?"*, she says to him.

Bassal looks at Illyana and shrugs curiously. *"Is my notion, or even that of King Steel's any more bizarre than proposing that the Trolor Monster is real?"*

Aura again steps in to regain control of the council. *"Which again leads us back to; we do not know what it is"*, she says. *"Until we do, we can all speculate as much as we like, but it will only be speculation. And*

I, for one, would prefer to deal with facts. So, we will endeavour to find out what is being done to gather these and will reconvene this conversation when we actually do know more".

The Council all remain quiet, looking at Aura like a school principal who has just told them all to sit up straight and listen. Steel looks at Aura in awe at the way she can so quickly bring the council back under her control. He turns and looks at the rest of the council and smiles. *"And that's why she's our leader"*, he says to them.

EXOM

THE YOUNG KING

CHAPTER EIGHT

------------------------ Dens to the Slaughter ------------------------

Dens, medium sized hooved animals that were native to the unprotected planet Rollig, were bred on huge farms as cattle. They were prolific breeders, and when fed well, plumped up very nicely. Slow moving but excitable creatures, they seemed to get most excited about being slaughtered. Rounding them up was never a problem, and the more they watched their fellow dens enter the abattoir, and what ensued within, the more they seemed keen to join them. They had one purpose in life - to die. In fact, Den farmers had a more difficult job trying to keep dens alive long enough to fatten them up to make their life, and death, worthwhile. It was not uncommon for a large number of dens to break free from their barn and be found later, having taken themselves to the slaughterhouse. Some even trying to start up the lethal equipment, while others lined up patiently to be the first to go through the "expiration" process.

There was a theory that perhaps these animals were all born depressed. However, other than the enthusiastic pace they took to meet their demise, they generally all seemed very friendly, affectionate, and happy. In many ways, being such a lovely animal, it seemed a real shame to eat them. However, any guilt associated with that soon faded - as they were very delicious.

The Skurj, also finding the planet Rollig delicious, like they did all planets and their inhabitants, eventually ate all the dens, along with the planet Rollig itself, making them now an extinct species. Turns out that no one thought to export den breeding farms outside of Rollig.

Though the dens themselves are now long gone, the stories of their existence, and nature, has lived on. Spoken about frequently throughout the outer rim systems, and even planets in the Mid System, like Aymyn.

The corridors in most of the buildings on Aymyn, very different to the halls and rooms on Eluud with their low natural light, are always brightly lit, even during the night. White walls being most commonplace and adding to the bright ambiance, it is difficult to know exactly what time of day it is on Aymyn while inside. The Citadel of Light is no exception, with most facilities operating and being accessible around the clock.

Walking up one of the corridors of the Citadel is the Aymyn General, accompanied by three Aymyn Soldiers. The General is quiet, his eyes instinctively examining every wall, door, corner, and vent as he walks along. His soldiers, however, seem to have a lot to say and more invested in their conversation with the General than where they are going.

They are about to walk past the large main doors leading to the Main Training Hall, when they open. The General stops and holds his arms out, stopping his men from stepping out in front of it, as they seem less aware than he is. A large hoverbed comes out from the training hall, being pushed by three Aymyn workers, dressed in long white overalls. A sheet has been carefully thrown over the hoverbed, completely covering what, based on its shape, appears to be the body of a very large creature. So large is the hoverbed and creature that is laying on it that, if it wasn't for the fact the hoverbed is lifting itself, many more workers would be needed to even attempt to move it.

Only once the workers are outside the Training Hall do they notice the General and his soldiers. They look at him and nod, appreciative of him halting both himself and his men so that they can come out. As the large doors close behind them, the General looks down at the hoverbed and a frown of disappointment starts to take shape on his face. He returns his gaze to the workers. *"Another one"*, he says to them.

The workers stop pushing the hoverbed and give the general their full attention, not accustomed to being spoken to by him and a little unsure of how they should react. One nods. *"Makes twenty-three today"*, another says.

Two of the soldiers look at each other curiously, while the third looks even more curiously at the workers. *"Twenty-Three that have died attempting the Zazar Test?"*, the soldier asks them.

"Yes", is all one of the workers replies as the others shrug and nod.

"And how many in total have attempted the Zazar test today?", the same soldier asks.

"Twenty-Three", the worker replies.

The soldier smirks inappropriately. *"Perfect Score"*, he says as he nods.

"Always is. Sadly", the worker replies as he motions to his colleagues to continue moving the hoverbed. The workers continue pushing the hoverbed up the corridor as an Aymyn guard, who had been watching the interaction between the soldiers and workers, walks up to the soldiers. The guard, having been stationed around this particular area most of his shift, has been watching hoverbeds being pushed out of the training hall all day. A very sad and regrettable sight. Zazar-wannabes attempting the Zazar test only to fail and lose, with it their lives in the process.

The guard looks at the soldiers, all still looking at each other and talking while the General just watches, quite sombrely, the hoverbed being pushed up the corridor. *"Like dens to the slaughter"*, the guard says to the General.

Without so much as a blink, the General casually turns his head to look at the guard. His gaze seemingly questioning why the guard is standing there. *"You thinking of trying out?"*, the General asks the guard.

"The Zazar Test?", the guard responds, his reaction showing his apparent surprise at the General's question. *"With less than a 1% survival rate, and a much less success rate. No. I will leave that for the Morn"*, the guard answers.

Again, the General does not react to the guard's comment, but instead just nods towards the direction of the workers pushing the hoverbed. *"Most of them don't make it either"*, the General tells the guard.

-------------------------------- **Too Close** --------------------------------

Nearing closer to the permanently dark side of Eluud, is a large hillside. Appearing innocent enough, looking like just an everyday hillside, some areas are dark and black, showing nothing interesting at all. Until, that is, you pass through the shadow-tech cloak that covers it, creating these black areas, and see what is being hidden. Built into the hillside is a large metal door. Strong, as though used for a bunker or bomb shelter, this door is hidden for a reason. It is the main entrance leading into a small Sharlon Secret base.

Two Aymyn-looking males approach the door. One of the men, a rugged looking man wearing black trousers, t-shirt and jacket is Kargon. The other, much younger looking and dressed in a long black overcoat, with a single sleeve rolled up revealing a Tal on his arm, is Grail. Both men are Sharlon agents.

As they get closer to the large metal door, another figure steps out of the shadows. This figure also has a humanoid shape to him, though a very large build. It is difficult to know exactly what species he is as he is completely concealed under a large black hooded robe, his face blacked-out completely by shadow tech. Strapped to each of his forearms are metallic bracers and only his hands naked and exposed. Very large hands. One that is holding and dragging behind him an aptly suited large pole axe. The metal of the double-sided axe itself almost half the size of the man carrying it, with a handle being even taller than he is.

This is The Guardian, a Sharlon henchman and guard to this particular secret hideout, with his size and appearance alone enough of a deterrent. He moves slowly, but purposefully towards Kargon and Grail as they approach, and raises his hand gesturing for them to stop.

They obey, having no intention to quarrel with this large figure before them.

The Guardian pulls out an electronic tablet from within his robe. Making sure not to reveal the screen to either of the Sharlon agents, he looks down at the tablet and speaks in a low but powerful tone. *"Entry Code"*, he says to them.

Both Kargon and Grail look at the Guardian, more than just a little intimidated but trying their best not to show it. *"Four Zero Nine"*, Grail starts to recite. He glances over at Kargon briefly. *"Sigma seven nine seven ogon three"*, Grail finishes as he looks back at The Guardian.

Still appearing to be staring at his electronic tablet, The Guardian compares the code recited to him by Grail with the code displayed on his electronic tablet. It matches. The Guardian lays his hand on the tablet screen and the large metallic door starts opening slowly behind him. The weight and strength of the door visible in its encumbered movement.

Being Kargon's first time to this hideout, he watches the door open and eagerly tries to peer inside before taking a step towards it. He looks back at The Guardian curiously. This process seemed a little too simple, he thinks to himself. Give the big guy a code and he lets you in. This is not Grail's first time here, however, and he is all too familiar with the process. He also knows who awaits them on the other side of that door. Someone much more intimidating than The Guardian. This Hillside hideout is the same one that is occupied by Sabel.

The Guardian leads Kargon and Grail inside the hillside entrance. As the large metallic door closes again behind them, there is coincidental movement on top of the hill. Four small laser stilt cannons, like those used on Chassam Castle's landing bay, only a lot smaller, rise from the ground. Each fires a single laser stilt up into the air and focus on a single point. That point being the bottom of a small shuttle. Only the bottom of the small shuttle can be seen as its engines rumble and conk out as it enters Eluud's atmosphere. The shuttle now completely suspended and being lowered down by the laser stilts.

Meanwhile, at Chassam Castle, one of the Communication Officers that monitor all the sensors and transmissions to and from Eluud has been walking the castle corridors to seek out Dacos. He finds him on the balcony that surrounds the castle, standing by the railings and looking over the palace gardens. Things seem peaceful but even Dacos wonders for how long. The Communication Officer approaches Dacos as he is about to walk away. Dacos sees the Officer and turns to meet him. The Officer was not expecting Dacos to turn towards him and is taken by surprise.

"Ah, Sir, ah", the Communication Officer stutters. *"Outpost reports are indicating Skurj activity approaching the Third Sector"*. The Third Sector, the name given to the system of planets separating Crom's and Eluud's systems. So far, a system that has been untouched by the Skurj, and this latest development showing that that the Skurj war is traveling towards Eluud.

Dacos looks at the Communication Officer and nods, seeing clearly in his face that this is more than just a report about another system. What the Communication Officer is not saying, but is clear by the fear in his eyes, as most will have when hearing this news, is surmised in Dacos's reply, *"This is getting too close now"*.

The Communication Officer stands staring at Dacos, waiting for a word or instruction. *"Send a communication through to Aymyn"*, Dacos tells him. *"We need to inform the king"*.

"Ok. Yes. Yes Sir", the Communication Officer replies, as he continues to stand there, not moving, just staring at Dacos.

Dacos stares back at him curiously, wondering if he has more to tell him. However, the Communication Officer does not say anything. Dacos nods as he lets the Communication Officer's eyes speak for him. *"You're worried"*, Dacos says.

"Very much so, sir", the Communication Officer replies, relieved that Dacos has said the words for him.

"Yep. Me too", Dacos tells him, knowing that the Communication Officer is not alone with that feeling. It is a sentiment shared by many, especially those aware just how close this is. Dacos tries to think of something that he can say to the Communication Officer to offer any

comfort at all, even if only a glimmer of hope, but struggles and starts to bite down on his lip instead. He turns and appears to look out over the Castle gardens again. However, his thoughts have him much further away and he is not really looking at anything. He nods to himself as he processes his thoughts, then turns back to look at the Communication Officer again. *"The Third Sector is not quite on our doorstep just yet"*, he tells him. *"But warrants concern. Are there any Troin ships in the area?"*, he asks the Communication Officer.

"I don't know", the Communication Officer replies. *"But I can find out"*, he adds, looking a little less helpless.

Dacos makes himself smile, reassuringly and places his hand on the officer's shoulder. *"Find out"*, Dacos tells him. *"And send that message to Aymyn"*.

This time the Communication Officer does move. He turns and walks back the way he came, passing the Queen Mother on the way who is also standing on the balcony by a doorway. *"Ma'am"*, he says to her and bows his head as he walks past. The Queen Mother looks back at him briefly, giving him a returning nod, before returning her attention to Dacos and staring at him inquisitively.

Dacos notices the Queen Mother standing there watching him, the hood of her long black cloak pulled up over her head. He could see by her expression that she was trying to read the situation. Even if she didn't know the particulars, which she probably did, she could read Dacos's body language just as clearly as everyone else. She does not approach, choosing instead to stay where she is and just observe.

So, Dacos decides to approach her. She watches him walk towards her, not taking her eyes off his. He stops in front of her and tries to read her expression as well. Judging by the way she has not asked him anything, he concludes that she has already heard the news. *"You've heard?"*, he asks her.

"I have", she replies with a nod, still just looking at him.

They both stand silently looking at each other. The Queen Mother trying to gauge how Dacos is feeling, and Dacos knowing that he does not need to pretend to be unaffected by the situation in front of her.

She can see his concern and, because of this, chooses not to show any back.

"While we still have time - there is still time", she tells him.

Dacos tries to take some comfort in those words, but struggles, and looks away. *"I hope so"*, he replies. And with those words, Dacos walks off. The Queen Mother watches him walk away, making his way down the external staircase which leads back inside the castle. She then holds her hood closer to her face as she opens the door in front of her, steps inside and closes the door behind her.

-------------------------------- **Dark** -----------------------------------

A door at the rear of the Sharlon Hideout on Eluud opens and through it walks a lone woman. Far from overly dressed, wearing a very scant black backless leotard-like outfit that finishes in a dress-like tail behind her, she struts almost seductively into the darkly lit room. Her legs, side, back and arms are bare, with the only other pieces of clothing being a pair of thin short black boots and a light but long black cape with attached black hood. The hood pulled up over her head, almost completely shadows and blacks out her face, presumably with the aid of some Shadow tech like The Guardian's. A thin window of light across her face, stretching from temple to temple, is the only area of her face that is not concealed in shadow. This window of light reveals her luring and piercing red eyes.

Her minimal attire and assured stride could possibly be attributed to the fact that she is also wearing a Tal. This confident Troin woman, dressed in black, is of course Dark, the leader of the Sharlon. Looking straight ahead, she steps straight out onto the raised mezzanine area that overlooks the rest of the hideout main floor. Sabel steps out beside her, seemingly coming out of the shadows, and walks next to her towards the centre of the mezzanine. *"Good to see you finally made an appearance, My Sign"*, Sabel says to Dark, also looking straight ahead and not at her. *"I was beginning to wonder if I had imagined you"*.

At first Dark does not react to Sabel's words, her eyes focussed on an old wooden throne-like chair near the front of the mezzanine. But then she stops and looks at Sabel with an almost amused but intrigued expression. Sabel returns her look, slightly raising her eyebrow to the mix, as a very brief and faint smirk starts to form on one side of her mouth.

Dark looks away and continues across the Mezzanine stage as both Kargon and Grail, who are standing to the side on the floor below the mezzanine, watch her with great interest. She makes her way to the chair and sits down. Though seated at a fairly average height from the ground, the chair's width emphasizes Dark's slender frame, looking as though it could fit two of her, or at least another half, seated side by side.

Dark sits back in the chair, resting her arms on its armrests. She looks down over the floor below her and is silently greeted by Nadiri staring back up at her. Dark stares directly into the eyes of Nadiri. A serious stare, though showing no hostility, her confidence is enough to unsettle even a spectre. Nadiri steps forward to address Dark. *"My Sovereign, it is good to see you in person at last"*, Nadiri says.

Dark's stare does not change. *"Your visit here is not without consequence, Nadiri"*, Dark replies, her words almost piercing Nadiri and, though a spectre would never think to apologize for anything, if there ever was to be a moment for that to change, Nadiri is feeling it right now.

"An unfortunate event", Nadiri says. *"One I believe was sufficiently concealed"*.

"Our definitions on that would seem to vary", Dark replies. Dark hardly blinks as she continues to stare at Nadiri, almost staring through her, into her. Nadiri begins to feel uncomfortable, a rare, almost unheard-of situation for a spectre. Nadiri tries to maintain eye contact with Dark's stare but finds herself starting to look away awkwardly. Sensing Nadiri is feeling uneasy, Dark softens her approach. *"Nonetheless, we do have much to discuss"*, Dark says to her.

Relieved with the change in Dark's approach to her, Nadiri begins to feel more at ease. *"We do"*, Nadiri replies. *"And I would like to start with the return of one of my men, who I believe you are holding here"*.

Dark does not so much as flinch, her expression and gaze upon Nadiri remaining unchanged. *"Why would we have one of your men here, Nadiri?"*, Dark asks her, again Darks eyes peering almost straight into Nadiri's soul.

"He was last seen here. Then he disappeared", Nadiri replies.

Sabel glances over at Dark. However, Dark maintains her stare on Nadiri. *"Strange that your men would be in this sector"*, Dark says to her. *"It's a long way from home"*.

"I believe she is saying...", Sabel starts to say, but stops when Dark looks at her.

"I know what she is saying", Dark says to Sabel. Dark looks back at Nadiri. Nadiri stands silent, looking back at Dark. *"Why did you have a man here, Nadiri?"*, Dark asks her. Nadiri looks away, seeming almost too embarrassed to answer.

"They were spying on us", Sabel answers for her, looking starkly at Nadiri. A slight smirk almost softens Dark's piercing gaze, but not quite.

"The question was rhetorical", Dark says to Sabel. *"She knows that"*, Dark adds having still not taken her eyes off Nadiri. Nadiri looks back at Dark, expressionless and like she has nothing to say. No need to reply, the question has already been answered.

Sabel shrugs. *"You can have him back. He was of no use to us"*, she says. Sabel looks over at Dark. *"He wouldn't talk"*, Sabel tells her. *"Just kept screaming. It was getting annoying"*, she adds.

Dark looks at Sabel. *"I don't hear any screaming"*, she says to her.

"No", Sabel replies. *"I cut his tongue out"*.

The expression in Dark's eyes change slightly as she looks curiously at Sabel. *"Was that necessary?"*, Dark asks her.

"No, but effective", Sabel replies.

Dark looks back at Nadiri, a slight smirk now appearing in her eyes. *"Well...."*, Dark starts to say.

"My Sovereign", Grail interrupts, stepping forward, somewhat rudely, almost feeling entitled with what he needs to say, and considering it more important than what anyone else could possibly be there for. *"The Troin Vice Commander is being sent to Carpaga"*, he says.

Nadiri looks at Grail, annoyed by his interruption. Dark looks like she is about to ignore Grail, not reacting to his interruption or turning to look at him. Noticing that Nadiri has stopped speaking and now has her attention focused on Grail, Dark, somewhat reluctantly, moves her gaze over to Grail. She stares at him but does not speak. Sabel, also staring at Grail, walks up and stands beside Dark. Feeling everyone now staring at him, Grail starts to feel a little less entitled than he had initially thought himself to be. Grail feels his throat start to clench but fights it back and continues to hold his resolute posture. Perhaps he thought that Dark being a Troin, just as he is, she would feel as strongly as he does about the survival and rescue of the Troin Vice Commander, he himself another loyal Sharlon Operative.

"It still confuses me as to why you authorized no attempt to intervene", Sabel says to Dark quietly, keeping her eyes focused on Grail. The situation was something that she had also been thinking about. She had been waiting to hear from Dark about steps that had been taken to facilitate the rescue of the Troin Vice Commander, or instructions on how she may assist with it. The fact that Dark has so far made no mention of it seems very strange.

Dark looks up at Sabel. Her gaze a lot softer, as it always is with Sabel. *"It is an unfortunate waste given the opportunity we had having him as part of us and his position within the Troin Army"*, Dark says to her. *"But his reckless decision in the end, after being discovered, showed that his temperament did not align with our goals"*.

Sabel takes a moment to decipher Dark's meaning. *"The reckless shooting?"*, Sabel asks, believing that Dark is referring to the Vice Commander using his Tal to weaponize, then open fire on the Troin and Aymyn Army as well as Queen Aura and the other Councillors present at the time.

"The specific shooting", Dark replies. *"A reckless decision to do so"*. Dark looks at Grail, then at Nadiri before returning her look to Sabel. *"Our approach is not single tiered"*, Dark adds. *"If we can not change the council's direction from the outside, then we must do it from inside"*. Dark again looks back at Grail. *"Difficult to do if the council and Queen are dead"*, she says to him.

Grail looks down, understanding what Dark is saying, but not sure if he entirely agrees with her response. However, he will need to swallow his diverged thoughts as he has no desire or intention to argue with her.

So far, the only one in the room who has not spoken is Kargon, who just stands there quietly, looking a bit anxious. Not at all uncommon in the presence of someone like Dark or Sabel, never lone the both of them together. Dark's back is turned to Kargon, and it appears that she doesn't even notice his presence as she again turns her attention to Sabel. *"If he had killed a member of the council"*, Dark continues to tell her, *"Then that would make them a martyr and would only serve to strengthen their resolve in their ways"*.

"He was defending himself, which is understandable", Sabel replies, now looking back at Dark. *"However, as you say, a successful shot would have set us back"*, she says, nodding, thinking, and agreeing with Dark's reasoning.

"A lot more than that", Dark says to her, repositioning herself on her chair, still seemingly oblivious to Kargon. She looks back at Grail. *"What have we learnt about the foundation sensors on Aymyn?"*, she asks him.

"While they are active it is almost impossible to examine them", Grail tells her. *"As they are a crucial part of the Aymyn system, isolating them will take some time"*.

Dark continues to look at Grail and nods slowly. *"Continue"*, she instructs him.

"Yes, my Sovereign", Grail replies as he lowers his head and bows to Dark. He turns and walks off, passing Kargon, expecting him to follow. However, Kargon does not move and seems to be still standing frozen while looking at Dark.

Still seeming not to notice Kargon staring at her, Dark turns her attention back to Nadiri. *"Nadiri, we will have that conversation now"*, Dark says to her.

Kargon now moves, pulling out a Tal bracelet from his pocket and putting it on his wrist. It extends into a full Tal armband, and from that he forms a small Troin weapon, aims it at Dark and fires. It's a direct hit. Not on Dark herself, however. It would have been, if it had not been for the fact that at that exact same moment Dark stretched out her left arm towards Kargon, constructing a small Troin shield from her Tal, and absorbs the blast from his weapon. Even, now, still with her back to Kargon, and looking in the opposite direction at Nadiri, she is well aware of exactly what is happening behind her. Without even looking at Kargon, she is aware of his presence as well as all of his movements.

She turns and looks at Kargon as he fires again and again. Each time Dark positions her Troin shield directly in the path of his blast, absorbing them. A Troin weapon takes form, protruding out from her shield, and she fires back at Kargon. Her shot hits him.

The whole thing happens so fast that Sabel barely has time to react. After Dark's first and only shot, Sable quickly runs around and stands between Dark and Kargon. Her long daggers drawn ready to protect her leader from any further attacks. It was a needless move, as Kargon falls to the ground - dead. His Tal weapon reverting into nanoparticles and returning into his Tal, his Tal then returns to its bracelet form.

Shocked and still trying to work out what is happening around him, Grail forms a Troin weapon from his Tal and points it at Kargon's dead body. Questions race through his head. What was Kargon trying to do? Was Kargon trying to assassinate Dark? And will Dark and Sabel now think that Grail was in cohorts with Kargon? If the first two questions weren't bad enough, that last question fills grail with dread. He looks up at Dark and Sabel, his weapon still firmly pointed at Kargon, his face expressing the fear and panic that he is feeling. *"My Sovereign, I had no idea!"*, he exclaims.

Sabel's gaze sharpens on Grail. Grail starts to feel faint as the blood rushes away from his head. Dark retracts her Troin weapon and shield back into her Tal, lowers her arm, and calmly looks back at Nadiri once more, seemingly unflustered by what has just happened. Sabel turns back and looks at Dark, for the first time taking a moment to express her surprise. *"My Sign, I should not have let my guard down"*, she says to Dark

Grail retracts his weapon back into his Tal, but still, unconsciously, has his hand pointed at Kargon's dead body. Dark glances up at Sabel, her eyes again soft and calming. *"We have spies. They have spies. It should not come at all surprising"*, Dark says to her. Her gaze now becomes more serious. *"Learn from this"*, she tells Sabel.

Learn from this. Something that anyone who has been around Dark long enough will hear her say at least once. It seems that Dark is seldom surprised by anything that happens. And anything that happens, that she was not expecting, she takes as an opportunity to learn from so as not to be taken by surprise again. Something that she more than encourages, she instructs, her fellow Sharlon to also do.

Sabel returns her daggers back to their sheaths under her cloak and stares back at Grail. Grail starts to feel a little more at ease, though not completely as he is aware that Sabel does not need to be armed to kill him. *"I didn't even know that he was Troin"*, he says to her. *"He was not wearing a Tal"*.

"Obviously not full Troin", Dark replies, still looking only at Sabel. Sabel looks back at her briefly, then returns her stare to Grail. *"Enough Troin blood in him to be able to use a Tal. Not enough in him to need one"*, Dark adds.

Dark then casually turns back around and looks at Grail's Tal. Grail realises that he still has his arm pointed towards Kargon, looks down at it and relaxes it down by his side. Dark's gaze moves up and across Grail's body, studying his clothing, as she thinks to herself. *"You're Eluudian"*, she says to him, raising her gaze higher to look him in his eyes.

Grail's expression changes. A feeling of insult now distracting any fear that he was previously feeling. *"My parents were Eluudian"*, he replies, shaking his head. *"My Mother was born on Eluud. My father was a soldier in the Troin Army that brought refugees to Eluud. He settled on Eluud after meeting my mother"*.

"That is fortunate for you", Dark says to him, smiling more with her eyes than her mouth.

"Not that fortunate", Grail replies, his body seeming less tense, and more at ease. More relaxed with this conversation and Dark's less piercing stare. Though he can still feel her looking straight into his soul. *"My mother died giving birth to me on this backward planet"*, he tells

her. *"My father joined the Eluudian army. Served and died under King Solso"*. Dark raises an eyebrow, intrigued by Grail's story. Grail passes a look over at Sabel before looking back at Dark. *"I have no love for Eluud"*, he says to her. *"And even less for their royal family"*.

Detecting the hurt and anger in Grail's tone, Dark gazes over at Sabel who stares back at her. Neither look that comfortable with what Grail has just said.

-------------------------------- **Carpaga** --------------------------------

Borhm, a barren and uninhabited planet near the Pizian home world. It is where the Pizian conducted many of their early experiments before the Assembly. One such experiment conducted by the Pizian on Borhm, was to create a Wormhole that would exit beyond the Void that surrounded Exom. This would enable them to reach areas of the galaxy that have so far been unreachable. Instead of creating such a wormhole, a doorway was accidently created that led well beyond the Void, or even the galaxy. In fact, it led to an entirely different region of the universe, perhaps even a different dimension, for there was nothing about it that was like anything else they had ever seen or even conformed with the laws of science.

The doorway, a two-by-two-meter pool of rippling energy called "The Portal", led to a world of landmasses and swirling energies that mixed and intertwined with each other. Destructive moving storms of pure plasma lightning were continually and relentlessly moving across the entire planet, blowing apart all forms of matter and then reconstructing it again, just as quickly, exactly as it was. Even living things that entered this area were blown apart by the fierce energy storms and then reassembled and reanimated again.

This meant that any living thing that was to enter this vicious world would be continually obliterated into dust, then reconstituted from that dust back to how they were and brought back to life. All this only to have it happen again, and again, and again. Never ending. Sometimes it could be many minutes before the plasma lightning would strike again. Other times it could be mere seconds. There was no pattern to it. And there was no escaping from it.

The doorway was only one way, with strangely no doorway, or portal, on the other side with which to return through. For anyone, or anything, that travelled through the portal there was no way back. The fate of anyone that travelled through the portal was only eternal and perpetual pain. No relief. Not even death.

This place, this world, this dimension was given a name. Carpaga.

At a safe distance the portal was of no threat, its strong gravity pull only extending about a meter. But any closer, and that gravity pull would grab you and not let go. The portal breaking down the atoms that form the object in its hold, giving the appearance of stretching it, and completely drawing it through.

The Portal seemed to hover in one spot, fixed, never moving. There was nothing within a meter around it in all directions. Anything that had been there had already been pulled through to Carpaga.

After the Assembly, the Pizians revealed the existence of the Carpaga Portal to the Royal Alliance. A decision was made by the Royal Alliance that Carpaga would become a destination for criminals whose crimes were so severe that even a death sentence was considered too lenient. A sentence, the Royal Alliance had hoped, they would not have to use very often. That the mere thought of Carpaga would be enough of a deterrent to anyone considering committing such crimes.

A ten-by-three-meter-long building, a corridor of sorts, was built around it. The portal at one end and a movable wall made of detachable blocks at the other. A single door, closer to the moveable wall side of the corridor, was the only way in or out. The wall the door is on is completely transparent, allowing anyone to see in or out of the corridor.

A sentenced criminal would be taken inside the corridor through this door, with security and officials standing outside the corridor able to bear witness through the transparent wall. The moving wall would slowly drive the prisoner towards the portal. If the moving wall itself got too close to the portal then the detachable blocks would separate from the wall and only those would be pulled through, allowing the moving wall to safely return back to its original starting point and rebuild the lost blocks.

A much larger building was constructed around the Portal Corridor. Complete with a large, enclosed viewing area. Security could open and close the door to the corridor, as well as control the moving wall, from a panel on the wall just inside the main entrance door. Outside the main entrance door lies a large hangar. Equally as large as the one on the Citadel of Light's rooftop, but rarely has anywhere near as many parked crafts and ships.

The only other room within the building is a completely separate small room, only accessible from outside the building itself and located on the opposite side of the Portal corridor. Inside this room, which has a single small window looking into the Portal corridor, a lone Pizian is situated. His job to observe and study the Carpaga Portal. The Pizians do not have individual names, none that anyone can pronounce anyway. This particular Pizian is simply called "The Watcher".

Strangely, even though there is no doorway on the Capaga side of the portal, from Borhm one can still see through the portal to Carpaga. This leaves the unanswered question of; how can the light that forms those images come back to Borhm when there is no doorway for it to travel back through. There are guesses and speculations, but since everything about Carpaga seems to defy logic and science, for most this unanswerable question remains just that - unanswerable.

Currently, gathered in the viewing area of the Carpaga Portal building, are several members of the Royal Alliance including Queen Aura, King Steel, Princess Illyana and King Yord. Also with them is Zargah and a number of both Aymyn and Troin guards. Already inside the corridor is Vice Commander Ardok. No longer naked, he is wearing simple light clothing which has been provided to him. Attached to his severed arm is a kind of metallic looking canister made to fit around the end of his arm stub to prevent him from bleeding out.

No longer wearing a Tal, he is already starting to feel the heat from the condition that affects all Troin. Not only is his body heating up, so too is his temper. He bangs his fist on the transparent wall of the Portal corridor in defiance at all those who have come to watch his sentence being carried out. *"Do you think that this ends for me now"*, he yells at them. *"It won't end with me! Your doom is more clearly written than mine. Your destruction within the jaws of the Skurj is the only certainty you have"*.

No one in the Viewing Room reacts to his outburst, instead many remain expressionless and just watch him carry on. For some, there is a faint glimpse of pity, while others seem to be showing an angrier looking expression. Not angry for what the Vice Commander is ranting about now, but rather what he has done that has led him to be here in the first place.

Ardok presses his face against the transparent wall of the corridor and looks at all those in the Viewing Room, hoping to see a familiar face other than those who are there just to witness his "execution". Hopeful that the Sharlon will not allow this sentence to be carried out and at this very moment are actively taking steps to prevent it. However, he does not see what he is looking for.

Zargah looks over at the Aymyn guard that is positioned near the main entrance. On the wall beside him is the console that controls the moving wall. The guard looks back at Zargah, Zargah nods, and the guard presses and holds down a single button protruding from the console. The Moving Wall inside the Portal Corridor begins to move towards Ardok. As the Vice Commander notices the wall moving towards him, his expression changes from anger to fear. He looks back out to those gathered in the viewing room, still hopeful of seeing a friendly face. Still none.

He looks back at the moving wall, then runs and slams his body into it, trying to knock it back. It has no effect. The wall continues to move. He leans his entire body against the wall, still trying to push it back. This still has no effect. The wall slowly pushes him towards the portal.

Panic takes hold, as he realizes that there is no Sharlon rescue plan, and with futility he cries out. *"Wait! Wait! DARK!!!"*. As the moving wall pushes him closer to the portal, he falls to his knees. He watches with dread as the floor moves past underneath him as his body is still pushed towards the portal by the wall. He looks up at the portal, now less than two meters away. *"No. Not like this. Not like this"*, he cries.

EXOM - THE YOUNG KING

The gravity pull of the portal grabs hold of him. His body starts to break down into atoms, appearing to anyone watching on as if it is elongating towards the portal. He continues to futilely push back against the moving wall, but not for long, and in no time right before the viewers eyes, Ardok disappears through the portal along with some of the blocks from the moving wall.

The moment that Ardok is no longer in the corridor, the Aymyn guard releases the button he is holding down controlling the moving wall. The moving wall stops and starts to slowly return to its original location, rebuilding itself and the missing blocks as it does so.

Zargah looks at Queen Aura. Aura is still trying to appear emotionless, but Zargah knows that she had no pleasure with this sentence being carried out. Zargah, on the other hand, does not have an issue with it, but still feels for his Queen. *"A traitor leaves us today"*, Zargah announces out loud. Aura sighs before briefly giving Zargah a sad side glance. She knows that he is right, but it does not make her feel any better about it.

The barren, rocky surface of Capaga shows no signs of life. Just strong winds, bellowing around dust and dirt. The sky is a mixture of red and grey. Many swirling cyclonic storm clouds are scattered randomly and plentiful throughout the sky. Plasma lightning sparks emitted from these eddying storm clouds burst and light the sky. Long plasma lightning bolts shoot out and hit the grounds, the rocks, and cave structures in the distance, blasting them into dust. The dust scatters in the wind then stops, drawn back together like a magnet and instantly forms back into the land and rock that it was before. Sometimes the land and rock is struck and obliterated again straight away. Other times it is left alone, for a few minutes. In the distance lies a large rocky mountain. A small cave-like entrance part way up. Swirling plasma storm clouds both outside and inside the cave blast away at it and the rocks and walls inside like any other structure in this godforsaken place. Each blast making the entrance to the cave much larger, revealing more plasma storm clouds inside the cave and mountain, before inevitably restoring the cave entrance back to its original smaller opening.

A stream of particles appears in the air just above the rocky plains of the surface, striking the ground with considerable speed. The particles quickly take shape and form into Vice Commander Ardok. Lying flat on his face on the ground, Ardok quickly turns himself over and sits up. He looks all around him with a panicked confusion. Watching the plasma storms shoot out their lightning bolts and blasting the ground around him and into the distance. Hearing about Carpaga is one thing. Being there and witnessing it for himself is completely another. The fear that fills him from seeing that everything he has ever heard is real cascades through his body. He looks up and around him for the portal he has just travelled through, but there is nothing there.

He prepares to stand up when a plasma lightning bolt strikes him, instantly disintegrating him into dust. The dust gets lifted up into the air by the swirling wind storms, then quickly drops again, coming back together and forming back into Ardok again, still sitting and about to stand up. Complete and intact, even his clothing. Ardok screams in pain, having felt every moment of being blown to dust and then being pieced back together. He collapses to the ground, bringing his arms and legs in close to his body as he lies breathless, reliving the pain he just experienced.

The lightning storms show him no mercy and he is struck again by another plasma bolt, once again blasting him into dust. Just like before, the dust comes back together and forms back into Ardok, still curled up into a ball and again screaming and crying in pain.

Through tears, he looks up and around him. He quickly jumps to his feet and starts to run. Run to where? He doesn't know. It doesn't matter. He makes it only a short distance before he is struck again by another plasma bolt. When he forms again from the dust, still mid-step in a running pose, he falls to the ground landing flat on his face once more. He winces and shakes in pain, but quickly picks himself up and starts to run again. He gets a little bit further this time before he is struck again by another plasma lightning blast. Again, he forms from the dust and falls to the ground. No sooner does he hit the ground when another plasma lightning blast hits him.

EXOM

THE YOUNG KING

CHAPTER NINE

-------------------------------- Come --------------------------------

The Skurj War continues to draw closer to Eluud. King Steel's search for a Zazar to select his planet as their protectorate, to protect Eluud and its people from imminent destruction, has still so far been unsuccessful. All it would take is just a single Zazar to choose Eluud as its protectorate, and then Eluud would fall under the protection of the entire Zazar Corp. Without this protection, Eluud is most certainly doomed to eventually fall victim to an ever-increasing impending Skurj attack. King Steel and Queen Aura do not give up on their petition on Aymyn.

Meanwhile, back on Eluud, deep in the forested area of the planet, something out of the ordinary has been discovered. Trill gallops back, atop of her rouk, to Chassam Castle to share news of the discovery.

While walking across the Castle gardens, towards the barracks that are built into the side of Chassam Castle, Dacos is looking at his wristband that controls his ronad. He stretches out his hand towards his ronad, still holstered to his leg. It does not move. He rolls his sleeve back down and, as he looks up, walks straight into Zippin who is playing chasey with a couple of young children. Taken by surprise, not seeing Dacos either, Zippin grabs onto his arms to save herself from falling over. Dacos also grabs hold of her. Zippin giggles as she looks up at Dacos, then smiles. *"Hey, General"*, she says to him.

Dacos looks back at her and smiles politely. *"Zippin"*, he says to her as he lets go of her.

Zippin continues to hold on to Dacos, looking at him and smiling. Feeling awkward, Dacos stares back at her curiously. *"You want to play chasey with us?"*, Zippin asks him. *"Give you are head start"*.

Again, Dacos smiles politely. *"Not now"*, he replies. *"Got a bit to do. You know. General stuff"*, he tells her. He looks over at the barracks, where he was walking to, then notices that Zippin is still holding onto him. He looks back down at her, then looks at her hands. She does not move them. He looks her in the eyes. She stares back at him, still smiling. *"Zippin?"*, he says to her.

"General", she replies, still looking him in the eyes and smiling.

"Can I have my arms back", he asks her. Zippin looks at her hands still holding onto his arms, then looks back into his eyes, still not moving her hands. *"Maybe"*, she replies very sassily, but still does not let go of him. Dacos now gives her his serious look. Her smile starts to fade. She looks disappointed at him, lets him go and steps back. Dacos smiles at her and shakes his head. *"How old are you now?"*, he asks her.

Again, she smiles at him cheekily. *"Old enough"*, she replies.

Dacos shakes his head again and scans his eyes over the gardens before looking back at her. *"Plenty of boys around here your age"*, he tells her.

Zippin stops smiling and looks away. *"The problem is I am getting older"*, she says to Dacos, then looks back at him. *"They're not"*, she adds.

Dacos smirks and nods his head. *"Give it time"*, he tells her.

One of the young children that Zippin was chasing, runs up and pushes her playfully, then runs off. Zippin spins around and looks at them. They stop running, look back at her and laugh. Zippin smiles at them and shakes her head. *"Oh, you're so....."*, she shouts out at them. Then giggling, she runs after them. They squeal and giggle as they run away from her. Dacos watches them run off, then looks back at the barracks and continues walking.

Inside the barracks, two Eluudian soldiers, having only recently showered after returning from their shift patrolling the grounds, sit on their stretcher style bed. Still half-dressed and shirtless, they are playing a type of card game when Dacos walks in.

They quickly stand to attention, their cards flying off the bed and all over the floor. *"General"*, they both say to Dacos, while standing to attention and hoping he hasn't noticed the cards laying across the floor. Dacos notices. He doesn't care.

"At ease men", he replies as he casually walks past them and heads straight to a wall safe at the end of the barracks. The soldiers pick up their cards, sit back down and continue playing their game, while Dacos places his hand on the door of the wall safe. The safe lights up, clicks and the safe door opens. Dacos reaches inside and pulls out a small box. He opens the box to reveal a number of bracelets, identical to the one that he is wearing that controls his ronad. The difference is that the built-in light on all the ones in the box are glowing blue, whereas the one he is wearing is not glowing at all as it has run out of power. He removes the one from his wrist and places it in the box. Immediately its built-in light starts to flash as it charges. He pulls out a new bracelet and clips it to his wrist.

He no sooner closes the box, and pulls his sleeve back down, when Trill comes walking into the barracks. Her pace fast and purposeful. The Soldiers jump up and stand to attention again. Again, their cards fly off the bed. *"Commander"*, they say to Trill as she walks past. Seemingly not having noticed the cards scatter on the floor, or just not caring if she has, Trill does notice the soldiers standing half undressed and does not avert her eyes as she passes them. In fact, she looks at the first one curiously, turning around and even walking backwards to keep her eyes on him, as she walks towards Dacos. Her expression half judging, half admiring. Not showing any sign of pleasure, or even displeasure. Just a simple case of "it's there so I'm going to look at it". She looks at the second soldier, more particularly his chest, then moves her gaze up from his chest to his eyes. *"Put a shirt on"*, she tells him. Both soldiers quickly reach for their shirts and start to dress themselves. *"Not you"*, Trill says looking and pointing at the first soldier. Somewhat startled, the first soldier drops his shirt on the floor and stands there, not sure what to do, as the other soldier continues to get dressed.

Dacos glares at Trill, not amused with his sister taking advantage of her position, and frowns. Trill turns around and looks at Dacos. Noticing his frown, she smiles, skips towards him, and gives him a gentle punch. *"Bro, you got to come with me"*, she tells him.

Dacos's frown dissolves, mostly out of pointlessness, and he turns to give his full attention to Trill. *"Where are we going?"*, he asks her.

Trill just winks at Dacos, not wanting to spoil the surprise. *"You'll see"*, she says. Then turns around and starts skipping towards the door. Still skipping, she turns and looks back at the soldiers. *"You two as well"*, she says to them. She skips back around and continues towards the door.

One soldier already has his shirt back on. The other soldier, the one she told not to, bends over, and picks up his shirt from the floor. *"Leave it off!"*, Trill shouts back at him just before skipping out the door. The soldier stands there, just holding his shirt, not sure what to do. He looks over at Dacos. Dacos shakes his head, then turns and puts the box of bracelets back into the safe and closes the safe door. He turns around and checks his bracelet again, stretches out his hand and his ronad flies out of his leg sheath and into his hand. He nods to himself and then looks back at the soldiers, both now just standing there, staring back at him, while looking confused. Dacos simply shrugs. *"Get dressed"*, he tells them as he walks past them and out the barrack door.

--------------------------- **Leaving So Soon** ---------------------------

All members of the Royal Alliance Council are given their own quarters within the Citadel of Light on Aymyn. They are simple, not really intended for extended stays, but large enough for a large bed, drawers, plenty of floor space and have a decent sized walk-in wardrobe. Even though Steel does not need one, preferring to stay in Aura's more spacious quarters, he has one nonetheless, which he hardly ever uses except as somewhere to store his clothes and belongings during his stay. Often preparing for anything unexpected to happen during his visits, he tends to overpack, taking with him far more clothes than he would ever wear. Which would not be such an issue except that, even when there for just a quick visit, he always unpacks everything that he brings.

Preparing to return to Eluud, Steel is in his quarters calmly throwing things into his suitcase. Nothing is folded and there does not seem to be any order to his packing. The door to his quarters opens and standing there, looking at him, is Aura. Steel looks up at her and smiles as she walks in. The door automatically closes behind her.

Noticing his suitcase, and the mess of clothes thrown in and partially overhanging the outside edges, she frowns. Trying not to get frustrated, as she is very used to Steel's messy packing style by now, though still wishing it was not the case, she walks over to his suitcase and starts taking items of clothing out, folds them up and puts them neatly back in his suitcase. *"I don't know why you bring so much. You never stay long"*, she says to him, while holding and staring at a long shirt that she has no recollection of him ever wearing.

"It's about being prepared", he tells her as he throws some more items into his suitcase on top of what she has just folded and put carefully in there.

Aura looks at what Steel has just thrown in the suitcase. She frowns again, now unable to hide her dissatisfaction, and looks over at him and glares. She shakes her head and finishes folding his shirt. Still glaring at him she drops his shirt into the suitcase and looks over towards his drawers.

Sitting on top of his drawers, she notices a holographic photo projected on a small photo stand. It is a photo of the two of them together. Arms wrapped around each other, they are looking into each other's eyes and smiling. She walks over to the drawers and reaches out to it. She picks up the base of the photo, looking at the photo more closely, and smiles. She puts it back down on the drawers and turns around to look at Steel. *"For that matter, why do we even bother giving you your own quarters here"*, she says to him. *"You are hardly ever in it"*.

Steel stops "packing" for a moment as he looks at Aura and Smiles. *"Well, yours are a lot nicer"*, he replies.

"Oh", she says to him, her smile now turning into a cheeky grin. *"So, you stay in my quarters because my quarters are nicer?"*

Steel walks over to Aura, puts his arm around her waist and pulls her close to him, matching her cheeky grin. *"Why else would I stay there?"*, he says to her. Aura smiles back, leans into him and they kiss. Aura stands there, eyes closed, as Steel lets go of her, steps back towards his suitcase and resumes throwing different items and clothing in it. *"Plus, I have to keep up appearances"*, Steel adds. *"Look respectable, in case the family come here"*.

Aura stands there and watches him "pack", this time not helping. *"You hardly ever bring them here"*, she says to him. *"And you don't really believe that they think you sleep here alone?"*.

Steel smirks and shakes his head. He grabs and looks at various items before throwing them into his suitcase. *"No"*, he replies. *"They're old enough"*. Steel looks up at Aura and smiles. *"Plus, they really like you"*, he says to her.

Aura smiles again, and again her smiles starts to change back into a cheeky grin. *"Oh, they like me"*, she says to him.

Steel walks back to her and grabs her around the waist again. *"Not as much as I do"*, he tells her.

Aura smiles, places her hands on Steel's cheeks and rests her forehead on his, gazing into his eyes. *"Lucky"*, she says to him. *"Because I kind of like you too"*.

"I'd hope so", Steel says as he pulls away again, still distracted by the amount of packing he has left to do. He looks down at his clothes overflowing from his suitcase and scratches his head. *"Why do I bring so much?"*, he asks himself out loud. Aura quietly laughs to herself as she shakes her head. Steel looks back at Aura, his face more serious and sincere. *"I'm glad I get to be with you"*, he says to her, a huge loving smile starting to take shape on his face. His words make Aura's face light up as well. *"You keep me out of trouble"*, he adds jokingly.

"Out of trouble?", Aura replies curiously.

"Oh, let me tell you", Steel starts to explain. *"There was this one night. A huge night. At least I think it was. Don't remember a great deal about it, actually. But the next morning..."*. Steel pauses as he reflects

on the memory. *"I woke up sleeping next to a large forest critter"*. Aura looks at him with surprise and confusion. *"No idea what it was"*, Steel goes on. *"I called it Maxun. It looked like something a mother would name Maxun. If it even has a mother. I don't know. Never got around to asking it. It took off the moment I got up. Never saw it again"*. Aura continues to look at Steel confused, trying to work out if he is being serious. Steel looks back at her. His eyes appearing genuine and innocent. *"Should I feel used?"*, he asks her.

Aura continues to look at Steel with confusion as she replays the story back in her head. She starts to smile at the absurdity of it. Steel smiles back at her and they start to laugh together. *"Why do I buy into your silliness"*, Aura says to Steel as she turns away from him. Steel stays watching her, still smiling, and giggling to himself.

Aura looks back down at Steel's suitcase. At the clothes and items just tossed inside. Then she looks back at Steel, thinking about how often he flies in and then flies back out. He leaves so often that he misses more Council meetings than anyone else. Then he needs to spend time catching up on the latest events. She knows he does a lot, a lot more than most. He runs a family and a kingdom full time, as well as travelling across half of Exom to represent his planet in the Royal Alliance Council. *"You do too much"*, she says to him.

With no idea what Aura is referring to at this moment, Steel gives her a confused side glance. Aura looks back at his suitcase. *"Always running around. Doing everything. Going everywhere"*, she says.

As Steel thinks about this, his expression shows that he does not agree. *"Hardly everywhere"*, he says. *"I only go here and home. Sometimes Liass. Quick trips to visit the neighbours. The occasional tours"*. Steel pauses as he reflects on the list he has just given. *"OK, maybe I go to a few places"*, he says. *"But you know me. I don't like to sit still. Remember, I'm an Arandae Sign apparently. We flight around a lot. You know more about that stuff than I do"*.

Aura is very familiar with Steel's Airy nature. Especially how they are in a direct contrast to her strong grounded Parandrae Sign traits. She has often wondered how an Arandae and Parandrae Sign ended up together, two completely different natures. Though she can not see herself with anyone else. Their contrast, at times does create issues. However, it certainly keeps their relationship interesting. And she knows that Steel needs a strong Parandrae Sign in his life to pull him in line and keep him grounded every now and then. In her opinion, anyway.

"I have always found it strange", she says to him. *"The Parkendal Signs might be hot headed and fiery. But it's the Arandae Signs that usually burn themselves out"*.

Steel shrugs as he thinks about her comment. He had never thought about that before, but then again, most Eluudians do not think about the signs as much as the Aymyn. Aura watches Steel. Able to read him, she knows he is thinking more about her words rather than realising how she is relating them to him. *"I don't want you to burn yourself out"*, she says to him. *"And I don't think I am alone on that"*.

Steel tries to comfort Aura with a smile, but it doesn't work. She just looks back at him seriously. He moves in closer to her, hoping that his smile may have a stronger affect the closer he is. *"I am not going to burn out"*, he tells her. *"I have too much energy"*.

Aura is very familiar with this fact. Energy is something Steel seems to have in abundance. *"Maybe"*, she says, looking him up and down and stopping again at his eyes. *"But what if you burn too bright?"*, she asks him.

Steel smiles to himself. He likes that thought. He looks at Aura with a smirk. *"Wont that be a blast?"*, he replies.

Aura just stares at Steel for a moment, not wavering away from her serious expression. She then looks away. She walks over to his wardrobe, opens it, and sees a jacket hanging there on its own. A jacket that she bought for him some time ago. A jacket he has never worn. *"Your jacket"*, she says to him as she reaches out and touches it.

Steel looks over at it. His expression changes, filled with a soft fondness, as though he is looking at one of his daughters. *"That goes in last"*, he tells her. *"So, it doesn't get squashed under everything else"*.

Aura runs her fingers along the sleeves of the jacket as she reflects on how she came to give it to him. An Aymyn seamstress, a plump and friendly lady, who makes a lot of the clothing and uniforms seen throughout Aymyn, designed and made it for her based-on Aura's ideas. Most of the gowns that Aura wears are original designs that this seamstress has created especially for her. *"I had this made for you so long ago and you have still never worn it"*, she says to Steel.

Steel continues to pack, trying to look too distracted to fully address the topic, while casually pretending it's not a big deal. *"Why do I have to wear it?"*, he asks Aura.

Aura is surprised by Steel's question and turns to look at him, a peculiarly confused expression on her face. *"It's a jacket"*, she replies. She starts to wonder if perhaps the reason he has never worn it is because he doesn't like it. She'd be a little upset if that was the case but would still like to know.

Steel looks up at Aura, his expression still soft, and now also very sincere. *"It's a gift from you"*, he tells her. *"It's worth more to me than just being a piece of clothing"*.

Aura feels very flattered by this statement, but still wonders if he is not telling her something. She smiles and walks over to Steel. *"Can't it be both?"*, she asks him. She looks back over at the jacket as another thought enters her head. Every time Steel has come to Aymyn he has brought the jacket with him. Never wears it, just leaves it in the wardrobe. *"You carry it everywhere but never wear it"*, she says to him. If he really doesn't like it, then why does he take it everywhere?

Steel picks up another item of clothing, about to throw it into his suitcase, when he stops and stands still. He throws the item of clothing that he is holding on the bed instead and looks over at Aura. It was not that he didn't like the jacket, in fact, he liked it a lot. It was that the jacket had so much meaning to Steel. He didn't just see it as a piece of clothing. He saw it as something more. It was something from Aura. Something that she had made. An offering from her heart. It was a piece of her. Its sentimental value made him feel warmer than wearing it ever could. But now, seeing how much it means to Aura, Steel, casually, tries to reassure her. *"I will"*, he says with a kind smile. *"Just waiting for something special to wear it to"*.

Aura sensing that Steel is still not saying everything, she tries to leave it and move on. But the thought gets stuck in her head. Not only is he a Member of the Royal Alliance Council, he is also her partner, and with both of those things come plenty of events and functions that would present an opportunity for him to wear it. *"Like we don't have enough special things here"*, she says to him as she looks away, trying hard not to make a bigger issue out of it, though the topic is significant to Aura.

"You are usually with me during all the special things", Steel says.

"I'd hope so", Aura replies giving Steel a sideways look and smirk.

"So, why do I need to wear the jacket when I have you? The real thing", he says to her. *"I promise you I'll wear it if something comes up that you can't be with me. So, that way, you will still be with me"*.

Flattered and very taken with Steel's explanation, Aura smiles to herself. She turns back to the wardrobe and picks the jacket up just as Steel finishes putting the last of his things into the suitcase. She continues to look at the jacket as she carries it to him. *"I took a great deal of time choosing this for you. Having it made"*, she says to him. *"It's strong and practical. Like you. And it also looks like the kind of thing you would wear on Eluud"*.

"The kind of thing?", Steel replies with amusement as he smiles and takes the jacket off her.

"Well, you know", Aura starts to say as she tries not to giggle at Steel's reaction. *"The fashion on Eluud is very different to that on Aymyn"*.

A fact that no one could deny. The dark style of the almost gothic and mostly black clothing worn by the Eluudians is a quite a contrast from the refined, bright white and vibrant colours worn by the Aymyn. Steel does not attempt to argue, knowing that she is right, and just smiles and carefully lays the jacket in his suitcase, smoothing it out, then closing the suitcase.

Aura is often with Steel when he arrives on Aymyn, or soon after, in his quarters, and there when he opens his suitcase to unpack it. A moment she is always excited for. Packing up and closing his suitcase is a moment that Aura never enjoys. *"When will you be back?"*, she says as she stands still just looking at him and his closed suitcase.

"I won't be long this time", he tells her. *"Just popping home to make sure it's still there"*, he says, then looks to the side and thinks, *"And no one has burnt it down"*, he adds. *"Then I'll be back"*, he tells her. Aura smiles at these words. It makes it more bearable knowing that he will not be gone long. Steel stands up and gives Aura a sly look. *"And I'll be bringing someone back with me"*, he says waiting to see her reaction.

He doesn't need to wait long. Instantly Aura is intrigued, and her excited curiosity can't be hidden. *"Who?"*, she asks.

Steel continues to smile at her, not giving anything away. *"You will have to wait and see"*, he replies.

---------------------------- **Where's Dacos** ----------------------------

Loitering around the small library near the entrance of the castle is Det. A place where she can usually be found, but as Tespa pointed out, not necessarily there to read anything despite her attempt at making it appear differently. Just as she is doing now as she peruses through the books on the shelves, something she has done hundreds of times before. By now well and truly over familiar with the location and title of every single one of them. But whether she has actually read any of them is another story. Pulled them out, and passed her eyes along every page, certainly. However, with her attention clearly somewhere else while doing this, it is anyone's guess as to if she is noticing a single word on any of the pages.

She pulls out a book, making it look as though she has specifically chosen this one, but in fact it was where her hands landed when she decided it was time to take a book in order to keep up the appearance. She opens the cover and starts turning the pages as the Queen Mother walks into the entrance from one of the few corridors that lead into the Castle entrance. She notices Det in the entrance library and stares at her for a moment. Not curiously as she knows why Det is there. Why Det is always there. Det gives the Queen Mother a side glance, trying not to draw any more attention to herself, and then continues pretending to read through the book.

The Queen Mother has no intention of making Det feel awkward about standing there pretending to read. She knows that Det is only pretending. It is obvious by Det's distracted side glances and casual flicking through the pages much faster than she could possibly read them. Occasionally even flicking over a couple of pages before she looks at them, still glancing off to the side.

The Queen Mother realises that she has not seen Dacos for a little while, not since she spoke to him regarding the concerns about the looming Skurj presence, and wonders where he is. Ironically the same person that Det is waiting to see. Only see though, Det has no intention of actually talking to him. Or even acknowledging him. The Queen Mother quickly gauges by Det's casual loitering that Dacos has not been through this way recently. She also starts to wonder how long Det will stay around waiting there. She looks away as Sergeant Mew steps out of his small office, located just off the entrance, his door almost always open. Sergeant Mew, like everyone else, knows why Det is hanging around the entrance library and leaves her alone to avoid any awkwardness, on both sides. Noticing that the Queen Mother is standing there, deliberately not approaching Det, presumably for the same reason, Mew walks towards the Queen Mother to see if there is anything that he can attend to for her.

Before he reaches her, the Queen Mother waves him over. He walks up to her, smiling welcomingly as he always does. *"Ma'am"*, he says to her.

"Have you seen Dacos?", she asks him. Not asking for herself, however. She knows that Det will never ask and is hoping that, well, knowing that Det will overhear the conversation.

Sergeant Mew knows where everyone is, if they are in the Castle, so it was a safe question to ask. Or so she thought. *"He left just a short time ago. In a hurry, with Commander Trill and some soldiers"*, Mew replies.

Though, she shouldn't be surprised, as Dacos is often patrolling outside the Castle grounds and attending to various issues on Eluud, it wasn't the answer she was expecting. Det, still pretending to be reading the book, glances sideways over at Sergeant Mew, listening in on their conversation, as the Queen Mother knew she would.

Forgetting her initial reason for asking the question, the Queen Mother now finds herself concerned at why Dacos and Trill had left in such a hurry, along with more soldiers as well. *"Was there trouble?"*, she asks Mew. Hearing the Queen Mother's question, Det stops pretending to read and turns around looking alarmed at The Queen Mother and Sergeant Mew. Neither Sergeant Mew nor the Queen Mother have noticed Det's reaction.

"I don't know what it is, Ma'am", Mew replies. *"But I believe they have taken the rouks and left the Castle grounds"*.

Remembering again that Det will be listening in, The Queen Mother tries not to appear concerned as she turns around and notices the anxious expression on Det's face. As Det stands beside the bookshelf looking at the Queen Mother, the Queen Mother stares back at Det and concludes her conversation with Sergeant Mew. *"Thanks, Sergeant"*, she says to him as she walks over to Det. Det stands there silently, watching her approach. "Time for pretending is over", the Queen Mother thinks to herself. Now it is time to reassure her granddaughter. *"Whatever it is, I am sure that Dacos can handle it"*, she says to Det, standing beside her and placing her hand in the small of Det's back.

Feigning disinterest, Det looks away and again starts pretending to read the book. *"I'm not worried about... him"*, Det replies.

The Queen Mother nods, knowing full well that Det's statement was not true, but not pressing the matter, instead choosing to add a little more reassurance. *"Plus, he has Trill with him"*, she says to her. *"You know those two always look out for each other"*. The Queen Mother then turns and looks at the main door to the Castle, *"He'll be back walking through these doors in no time"*, she adds. Det pretends to ignore the Queen Mother and continues with the illusion of reading her book. The Queen Mother smiles and moves her hand from Det's back to her shoulder before walking off and leaving her alone.

Det looks over at the main door. She picks up the book she is pretending to read, then sits herself in a chair in the corner of the room that looks directly at the doorway. Bringing her knees and legs up to rest on the chair in front of her, she stays there pretending to read and occasionally looking over the top of the book at the door.

------------------------------- **Warning** ------------------------------

Dacos, Trill and the two soldiers from the barracks, ride their rouks through the densely forested area, some distance away from Chassam Castle. Trill excitedly dashes through the trees with her rouk, ducking and dodging any low hanging branches. Dacos keeps up easily behind her, but at a distance to also keep his soldiers, traveling even further behind, in sight, ensuring not to lose them in Trill's eagerness to get to whatever it is she wants to show them.

"It's just over here", Trill yells back as she flips one leg over her rouk and rides it the rest of the way standing on just one stirrup. She rides out into a small clearing, the clearing made by R'Vian's ship, and jumps off her rouk. Her rouk travels only a few more steps before stopping as well and turning back to face her. Dacos exits through the trees into the clearing as well, soon followed by his soldiers. The first thing Dacos notices is R'Vian's Tent. The tent itself, though not looking like anything used on Eluud, would not ordinarily have been out of place. What made it look out of place was the fact that it was right in the middle of apparently recently cleared forest.

Dacos quickly dismounts his Rouk and stretches out his hand. His ronad leaves his leg holster and travels straight to his hand. He doesn't activate it but holds it tight as he walks over to the tent. He cautiously examines the outside of the tent, then carefully opens the flap door and peers inside. Nothing inside seems strange. It is very simple and mostly empty. In fact, there is not even a sleeping bag or stretcher bed inside. Dacos stops looking inside the tent, steps back out and looks into the forest, focussing particularly on the trees immediately surrounding the area. He looks back at Trill who is standing there, smiling at him, as though waiting for him to say something.

"Intriguing", Dacos says to her. *"But you did not bring me out here to look at a tent"*.

Trill shakes her head. Still smiling, she continues to stare at Dacos. Her eyes saying that there is something else to see and she is waiting for him to notice it. Dacos quickly glances around the area again before looking back at Trill. He hasn't noticed anything else.

"For someone who is meant to have this observation superpower, you are slipping, dear brother", Trill says to him as she looks at him with a friendly disappointment.

Dacos looks confused. What is he missing? Is she talking about the cleared ground? He has noticed that. That would be too obvious. Is there something about the tent that he hasn't spotted? He glances at it again. No, nothing out of the ordinary as far as he can tell. He looks back at Trill with the same confused expression as he had before. She quietly giggles to herself, feeling that finally she has one up on him, and indicates to him to go around and look behind the tent.

Dacos walks over to where Trill has directed him and can now see what it is that he was missing. A small makeshift graveyard with several tombstones, made from Dakari Rifles and armour, with a Dakari helmet placed upon each one. The soldiers dismount their rouks and walk around the tent as well. Recognising the rifle and armour instantly, they become alarmed as they look closely at one of the graves.

"Raiders", one of the soldiers turns back and says to Dacos

Trill walks around the tent, stands next to the soldiers and also looks at Dacos. Unlike the soldiers, Trill does not appear concerned, still smiling, basking in seeing something that her brother was too distracted to notice. *"Looks like we've found a Raider camp site and burial ground"*, she says to him.

Dacos is not convinced. He looks closely at the graves. Then starts looking around the area and up into the trees again, as though he is expecting an ambush. *"It's no raider camp site, and this is no Raider burial ground"*, he says to them. His tone filled with certainty and in a way that makes even Trill stop smiling as she wonders what else it could possibly be.

Dacos looks back at the makeshift graves. *"Raiders didn't make this"*, Dacos says looking back over the gravesite. *"This is a warning - to raiders - to stay away"*.

Trill looks again at the graves and tent, intrigued by Dacos's words. It is not something that she ever would have considered. Perhaps her basking in her brother's momentary omission was premature. *"So, this campsite belongs to someone who kills raiders?"*, she says to him.

Dacos looks at Trill without saying a word, not needing to, and then continues looking into the forest. Trill, seeming very impressed, looks back at the gravesite and starts to smile again. *"Done a decent job by the looks of things"*, she says. *"Must really value their tent. Wouldn't mind meeting them"*.

The soldiers, understanding now what Dacos is looking into the forest and trees for, also start looking around them. While Trill may be keen to meet them, Dacos appears to be a lot more cautious, which is making his soldiers feel all the more anxious.

"So, the owner of this tent, are they friend or foe?", one of the soldiers asks, still looking around and up into the trees. Dacos looks at the soldier and nods, validating the question without saying a word, then continues to look around again as he walks back to his Rouk.

With an overwhelming sense that they are being watched, Dacos is feeling very uneasy. A sense and feeling that is completely justified. For up high in one of the trees, seemingly camouflaged by her big green cloak, R'Vian is watching their every move through enhanced eyes that see things in the same way as electronic binoculars.

Dacos places his ronad back into his leg holster, then mounts his Rouk and waits for Trill and the soldiers to join him. All the while he never takes his attention away from the forest and looking high up into the trees. For a moment he looks directly at R'Vian, which takes her by surprise, but he doesn't see her. However, he does not need to see her to know there is someone there watching them. His gaze moves past her, onto the other trees, as Trill and the soldiers also mount their rouks and ride up beside him. With a quick flick of the reins, Dakos quickly rides back into the forest, followed closely behind by Trill and the two soldiers.

EXOM

THE YOUNG KING

CHAPTER TEN

-------------------------------- Keep Up --------------------------------

A cloud formation appears inside the outer-rim system that Eluud is situated in and starts to swirl. Travelling out through the small black void in the middle of the cloud, is Steel's Shuttle. The swirling cloud dissipates as the shuttle continues towards Eluud, which is still quite some distance away. The shuttle only manages to travel a short distance before a familiar looking shapeless Dakari vessel appears and speeds towards it. It fires two laser blasts, one of them hitting Steel's shuttle directly. The blast, not powerful enough to destroy the shuttle, but certainly enough to give it a mighty shake-up.

Senior Officer Borda has just jumped into the chair in front of the Tactical and Surveillance workstation on the bridge of Steel's Shuttle. Dressed in her all black, one piece looking uniform and ronad strapped to her leg, a half-body length cape hanging from her left shoulder stands her apart from regular soldiers and pilots on Eluud. That's because the cape she wears is the insignia of the Royal Escort, King Steel's personal guard.

Having just moved quickly from the helm controls after feeling the impact of the laser blast against the shuttle's hull, she flicks through screens at the tactical station to identify and locate the origin of the attack. Officer Linz, dressed in the same black uniform, and also wearing the cape of a royal escort, runs onto the bridge and quickly sits down at the helm control. *"What was that?"*, he exclaims as he grabs hold of the flight controls and looks at the screen directly in front of him.

"Raiders", Borda replies, now having a clear image of the attacking vessel on her screen.

Outside the shuttle, the Dakari ship is quickly approaching. It is a lot smaller and more robustly built than Steel's shuttle. It is not capable of large interstellar jumps, but in normal space is just as quick and nimble as any other small ship, and much quicker than Steel's shuttle.

It fires again as Steel's shuttle simultaneously tilts to avoid the blast. Two more Raider Ships join the first and commence firing on Steel's shuttle as well. Steel's shuttle increases speed but takes another hit from a raider blast.

Inside the shuttle, Officer Linz struggles with the helm controls. *"The ship is not responding!"*, he yells out.

"I activated the Predictive Avoidance System", Borda yells back.

Linz looks down at his screen again and shrugs. *"Could have told me that earlier"*, he says to her. Linz reaches out to deactivate the PAS and take full control of the shuttle.

"Leave it on", Borda says to him.

Linz ignores her and switches it off anyway. *"You have no confidence in my flying ability"*, he says to her. Almost immediately they are hit by another laser blast and the shuttle jolts hard. Linz reaches over and switches the PAS back on again. *"Switching the PAS back on again"*, he calls out as Borda looks over at him with a serious glare in her eyes.

Steel runs from the back of the shuttle to the bridge, alarmed by the jolting, and stands in the doorway looking at Officer Linz and Senior Officer Borda as they feverishly flick through screens and press buttons to avoid having the shuttle blown apart from the enemy attack. *"Did we hit something?"*, Steel asks them, seeming a bit disturbed by the shaking shuttle around him.

"Raiders, Your Highness", Linz replies, keeping his attention firmly focussed on the screen in front of him as he continues to struggle to control the shuttle.

Steel looks at Officer Linz, a little confused, taking his words literally. *"We hit Raiders?"*, Steel asks him.

Senior Officer Borda, still monitoring the approaching raider ships on her radar screen, does not hear Steel's second question, and adds to the statement made by Linz. *"Three of them"*, she says to Steel, also not turning around, instead staying focused on the screens in front of her.

Steel walks over and stands behind her. He looks at the radar screen, confused at being told that they have just hit three raider ships. Officer Linz, now realising what Steel has heard them say, briefly looks away from his screen to clarify. *"No, Your Highness, they are firing on us"*, Linz tells him.

"So, we didn't hit them?", Steel asks them as he briefly looks back at Linz and then returns his attention to the radar screen.

"No. They are hitting us", Linz replies.

Steel takes a step back and looks a bit more relaxed, though now a little offended. *"Well, that's rude"*, he says.

Linz returns his attention to the helm controls and continues to fly the shuttle. With the PAS active it makes piloting a little difficult. Both Linz and the computer system are fighting each other to steer the shuttle. Linz decides to let the PAS handle all the manoeuvring and only loosely holds the flight controls, increasing or decreasing the speed of the shuttle as he thinks is appropriate. Steels steps up closely behind Senior Officer Borda again and studies the radar screen more closely. *"Looks like we've flown into an ambush"*, he says to her. Borda looks up at Steel as though he has stated the obvious. Steel looks down at her and smiles. *"You were about to say that, weren't you"*, he says to her. *"I detect that you were about to say that"*. Borda looks back at her console without replying and continues to flick through screens.

The Dakari ships stay hot on the tail of Steel's shuttle, still firing away as Steel's shuttle sways and tilts to avoid being hit. So far, Steel's shuttle has been able to avoid any major damage, but as the raider ships get closer, it does not look like that can be sustained. They can't outrun them; the raider ships are faster. It can't outshoot them. Steel's shuttle is equipped with basic weapons and defence, but the shuttle is designed for short- and long-range transport, not battle. If they are to make it through this, then a different strategy is needed.

Steel stands back from the radar and watches Linz gently fiddle with the flight controls when he has a thought. *"How far are we from Eluud?"*, he asks his escorts.

"We left compression not long ago, so we are close to approach", Linz replies.

"They hit us the moment we left compressed space, Your Highness", Borda adds.

Steel quickly and excitedly turns around and looks at Borda and points to her. *"An ambush!"*, he says to her. *"See, I knew you were about to say that before, when I said it, and you like looked at me all grrrr"*.

Borda does not look back at Steel, keeping her attention focused on her screens. *"It was not grrrr, Your Highness"*.

Steel turns back around and looks over at Linz. *"Oh, it was grrrr. I know grrrr. I get grrrr a lot"*. Borda looks back up at Steel, with the same "grrrr" expression as before. Steel looks down at her, smiles, and points at her expression. Borda shakes her head and returns her attention again to her screen.

"I was about to radio the communications room", Linz says to Steel.

"We don't want to take these guys back with us, Your Highness", Borda says as she spins her chair around to face Steel and Linz.

Steel looks at both Borda and Linz and notices their panicked expression. They have trained for this in simulations, but this is their first experience in a ship battle in open space. In fact, it is Steel's first as well. However, rather than feeling panicked, Steel is finding it strangely exciting and starts to smile to himself as a plan begins to form in his head. *"Maybe we do"*, he says.

Borda looks at Steel with a very strong expression of confusion, and watches as he walks around and stands behind Linz. *"Right, this calls for some creative flying"*, Steel says as he taps Linz on the shoulder. Linz looks up at him. *"You up for some creative flying?"*, Steel asks him.

Linz shakes his head. A distinct look of fear now in his eyes. *"Not really, Your Highness"*, Linz replies. *"I'm just trying to keep us alive"*.

Steel nods at Linz and looks at him curiously. *"For how long?"*, Steel asks him.

Linz does not know how to answer that. He knows that he can not out maneuverer the Dakari, even if he turns the **PAS** off, so the little he is doing won't keep them alive for long. The look in Linz eye answer's Steel's question. Steel decides it is now time for him to take over control of the shuttle. *"May I?"*, he asks Linz as he points to the flight controls.

"Of course, Your Highness", Linz replies as he immediately stands up, giving Steel his chair.

Borda glances back at Steel with a strong look of confusion. *"Have you ever flown before, Your Highness?"*, she asks him, very concerned.

"Nope", Steel replies with a huge smile. *"Seems like a good time to learn"*, he says to her.

"Seems like a really bad time to learn", Borda replies.

Steel sits down and takes the flight controls. *"Done plenty of simulations though"*, he tells her. *"How different could it be?"*, he asks as he tries to manoeuvre the shuttle but finds it not as responsive as what he is used to with the simulators.

"You are about to find out", Borda tells him.

"I don't remember it being this sluggish", Steel remarks as he looks with some confusion at the flight controls, wondering if he has forgotten to do something.

"The PAS is on", Linz tells him.

Steel smiles and nods as if he knows what that means. *"Ah, of course it is"*, he says. He then stops nodding and looks over at Linz blankly. *"What's the PAS?"*, Steel asks him.

"Predictive Avoidance System", Linz replies.

"The only defence we have on this shuttle", Borda calls out as the ship jolts again, being hit by another Dakari weapons blast.

"We have one of those. Awesome!", Steel says as he looks over at Borda. Borda swings back around to face her console again. She does not want Steel or Linz to see how frightened she is, so flicks through

screens and touches the radar as though she is examining it all again. Steel looks back at Linz who is not trying to hide how frightened he is. *"How do I turn it off?"*, Steel asks him.

"She doesn't like it when we do that", Linz replies.

"It's what's keeping us from being hit", Borda adds, still staring directly at her screen and radar.

Another blast hits and jolts the shuttle, this one almost knocking Steel and Borda out of their chairs and makes Linz stumble forward, stopping himself only by grabbing the back of the chair that Steel is now sitting in. Steel looks back at the helm controls. *"It's doing a great job"*, Steel says sarcastically.

Linz points at the **PAS** control button on the helm display screen and Steel presses it.

Instantly the shuttle breaks hard and stops moving. Steel lunges forward and hits the piloting workstation as Borda falls off her chair and Linz flies past Steel and across the bridge.

The Dakari ships, not expecting Steel's shuttle to suddenly stop the way it does, zooms straight past it, swerving at the last second to avoid colliding into it. The shuttle sits motionless in space. Everything still functional, just not moving.

Borda picks herself up off the floor and sits back in her chair. Very ruffled and wondering what has just happened. Linz, who is lying face down on the floor at the front of the bridge, quickly flicks himself over and stands up with a fright. Both Borda and Linz look at Steel, who has just pushed himself back off the flight control console in front of him. He looks at them both guiltily. *"Sorry, my bad. That was on me"*, he says to them, with an apologetic smile. He grabs hold of the flight controls again and looks back at the helm display.

The Dakari ships spin around, fly back towards Steel's shuttle, and resume firing their weapons. Steel's shuttle launches ahead again with considerable speed, zooming through the Dakari ships and again making them have to swerve in order to avoid a collision. By the time the Dakari ships spin back around, Steel's shuttle is so far away from them that it is almost out of sight. However, the Dakari ships pursue it relentlessly.

Looking more relaxed at the helm, Steel seems to be more comfortable and familiar with the controls. Borda spins around in her chair and examines the radar and screens again. Linz walks back around and stands behind Steel once more. Steel looks up at him and smiles, again apologetically. *"Can you get Eluud's Communications room online for me, please?"*, he says to Linz, finishing his question with another big smile. Linz reaches past Steel and touches the helm control screen. Steel watches what he does and notices the screen change to a communications screen with a large white button displayed on it. Linz touches the button on the screen, and it changes from white to green. He removes his finger from the button and the button turns white again. *"Of course, it's right in front of me. You'd think I'd know that"*, Steel says to himself. He looks back at Linz. *"With this being my shuttle and all"*, Steel says to him with a smile. *"I should probably get a little more familiar with it"*, Steel adds as he turns his attention back to the helm control and the communications display on his screen.

Steel glances over at Borda. He notices that her hands are shaking as she presses buttons on her screen. It's enough to make him stop smiling. He tries to think of something positive to say to her. *"I tell you what"*, he calls out to her. *"If we survive this, we'll go out flying at least once a day. For real"*. Borda does not reply and still, with very shaky hands, continues to press buttons and flick through screens on her display. Steel turns back and looks at the helm controls again. *"Of course, if we don't survive this..."*, he says out loud to himself. Hearing this, Borda stops what she is doing and slowly turns around to look at him, no longer able to hide her fear any longer. Steel looks back over at her. *"It may only be every second day"*, he adds, with a serious look, then follows through with another smile, trying to lighten the mood. It doesn't work. Borda continues to stare at him, fear still very evident on her face.

Feeling a little awkward at her staring at him, Steel turns around and looks at Linz. *"She's giving me that Grrrr look again, isn't she?"*, Steel says to Linz. Linz glances over at Borda who looks back at him. Their expression mirroring the other. They are both very scared.

"I don't think it's a Grrrr look, Your Highness", Linz replies, still staring at Borda. They both know that Steel is just trying to distract them from thinking about their impending deaths. However, it is not working.

Borda looks back at Steel as he spins back around to face the helm controls again and starts pressing the large white button on his screen, watching it change colour. Green, white, back to green, then back to white again. Like a young child, he finds it entertaining, but then remembers that he is not a young child, but in fact a grown man, who at this moment is flying a shuttle and trying to avoid everyone on it from dying. He makes himself refrain from pressing the button again and focusses back on piloting the shuttle. He then gives in to temptation and presses the button a few more times in quick succession.

The Communications Room lies in the heart of Chassam Castle and is the main Control, Communications and Surveillance station for Eluud. It is staffed with quite a few Eluudian Communication Officers. From this room all interplanetary and ship communication, along with transit to and from Eluud, is listened to, watched and coordinated. The Eluudian and shared satellites also relay information back to this room. However, right now, and what Steel is more interested in, is the main landing hangar laser stilt cannons are also controlled from this room.

A dashboard on one of the flight controller's workstation starts to flash. Not so coincidently, also in time with Steel pressing the communications button on the helm control display screen in his shuttle. The Flight Controller examines the information on his screen and realises that the signal is coming from King Steel's shuttle. The flight controller presses a button on his workstation. *"Eluudian Flight Control"*, he says into a microphone on the desk in front of him. *"We have King Steel's shuttle on screen. Is everything alright?"*

EXOM - THE YOUNG KING

One of the Dakari ships shoots and hits Steel's shuttle, blasting off a small panel on the outer hull. Immediately air starts to pour out of the shuttle, liquefying, then freezing and streaming out into space. The small panel hurtles towards the Dakari ship. The Dakari ship dodges the panel and continues its pursuit on Steel's shuttle.

Borda watches her display light up and flash in front of her and quickly starts pressing buttons on her display. *"We have a breach. Leaking atmosphere. Sealing now"*, she says.

Outside the shuttle, air continues to pour out and shows no sign of slowing down.

Borda continues to press more buttons on her screen, even resorting to thumping it with the edge of her hand. *"Seal, dammit"*, she exclaims in frustration. Steel stands up from his chair and walks over behind Borda. She is just about to hit the screen again when Steel calmly places his hand on it. She stops and looks at Steel, who looks back down at her and smiles. He takes his hand away, flicks the display to a new screen, presses a button and slides his fingers down the screen.

Outside the shuttle, the air stops pouring out and the shuttle can be seen starting to repair itself.

Steel looks back at the screen, flicks it to another screen, then looks back down at Borda and smiles again. *"A system I do know. Go figure"*, he says to her with a smirk and shrug. He steps back and sits back down in the chair in front of the helm control.

Linz walks over to Borda and leans over pretending to press a button on her display. *"How, the heck, is he so calm?"*, he whispers in her ear. His words shaky. Borda looks up at Linz, fear still very obvious in her expression, and shakes her head. She looks over at Steel as Linz walks back and stands behind him.

"We are not going to be able to take much more", Borda says to Steel.

Steel giggles to himself, busying himself with the controls and still not seeming at all stressed about the situation. *"I hear that a lot"*, he says with a smirk. *"Mostly from Aura. And the Council"*.

With their situation appearing more perilous with each passing moment, Steel's escorts find no amusement in Steel's little inhouse joke. Even less so when the shuttle jolts again after being hit by another blast. This jolt shakes Borda more than the last. She stares at Steel, confused at how he can manage to make jokes during this time. *"Your Highness!"*, she says to him.

Steel stops giggling to himself and looks seriously at Borda. *"Sorry. Serious now"*, Steel says as he looks back at the flight controls before looking back at Borda again. *"This is my serious face, by the way"*, he tells her, hoping that may reassure her. He looks back at the flight controls again. *"Nothing but serious thoughts"*, he says out loud. Barely a second passes before he giggles to himself again. He shakes himself and straightens himself up before looking back at Borda, hoping to offer an insight that may bring her some comfort. *"If it's of any consolation"*, he says to her, *"they are not trying to kill us"*. Borda looks back at Steel a little bewildered, his words appearing to be a contradiction to what is happening.

"The Dakari are scavengers", Steel goes on to explain. *"They are only trying to disable us so that they can board this shuttle"*. Now his words do make sense and do offer a little comfort. So, this is probably where he should have ended it. *"Then they will kill us"*, he adds as he turns back and again looks seriously at the communications screen.

On land the Dakari are vicious scavengers, attacking and violently killing anyone without hesitation, then ransacking them for supplies or items they can find. Out in space, however, they need to be a bit more tactical. Shooting down a ship in space could potentially destroy it completely, leaving them with nothing to scavenge. The Dakari use a different strategy while pursuing their prey in space.

The Dakari's usual strategy is to disable targeted ships using low powered but precision laser blasts. "Precision" is of course a term used loosely when referring to anything to do with the Dakari. The Dakari are not known for their precision or delicacy. In fact, the Dakari are not known for anything other than often non-thought through vicious attacks, so these later tactical strategies most likely came about after they lent themselves to the governance of their Spectre leader, Ador.

Steel can feel his escorts looking at each other and realises that his words have not offered any kind of reassurance. *"Don't worry"*, he tells them while still studying his display screen. *"I am not about to let that happen"*. Whether this last statement would have done the trick, we'll never know, as again he proceeds to say too much. *"They'll have to destroy this ship before I'd let them anywhere near us"*, he adds.

He touches the white button on the communications screen, turning it green again. *"Comms, we are coming in fast"*, he says out loud, so that the microphone built into the helms control can pick up his voice clearly and transmit it to the Eluud Communications room. *"Going to try something a bit different here. Get ready to fire the laser stilts"*.

Steel presses the communications button on the display once more and it turns back to white again. He spins around in his chair and faces Linz who is still standing behind him, slowly freezing with fear. His body rigid, his teeth clenched and his stare wide and fixated on Steel. *"This could be very interesting"*, Steel says to him. *"Perhaps entertaining. Hopefully won't kill us"*. Steels spins back around to face the helm controls again, leaving Linz looking even more terrified than before.

Steel directs the shuttle, at speed, towards Eluud. To land the shuttle on Eluud, the laser stilts need to be fired from the Castle's Landing Bay and make direct contact with the shuttles ground supports and stilt brackets. It takes precision. If the laser stilts do not make direct contact with this specific and small area of the shuttle, then the laser stilts will be ineffective, and the shuttle will crash into the planet's surface after its power is nullified by the planet's atmosphere.

This is common knowledge on Eluud. However, with the way that Steel is tearing towards Eluud, Linz wonders if maybe he should re-explain this fact to him. *"Your Highness"*, he says. *"The Laser Stilts need to make contact with the ship's ground supports to be effective. They need to be targeted"*.

Steel is very much aware of this, and simply nods as he continues piloting the shuttle towards Eluud at rapid speed. *"Precisely why I said this could be interesting"*, he says. A faint smirk again starting to appear on his face as he focusses on the helm controls.

Linz starts to feel weak in the knees and staggers back, sitting down on one of the chairs at the rear of the bridge behind Steel. *"You also said, "Hopefully won't kill us""*, he says.

Steel pushes the flight controls forward even further, increasing the speed of the shuttle even more. *"Hasn't killed anyone yet"*, Steel replies smugly and confidently.

Linz looks a little confused, but also a little relieved as he sits forward in his chair. *"So, what you are about to do has been done before?"*, he asks Steel.

Steel continues to look intensely at the screen in front of him. *"Not to my knowledge"*, Steel replies. *"It would be suicide"*.

Linz slowly falls back into his chair, shocked by Steel's words. He looks over at Borda and she looks back at him. Again, their expressions showing the immense fear that each of them is feeling. Steel glances over at Borda and notices her expression and that she is staring at Linz, so imagines that Linz is looking at her the same way. He takes a moment to reflect on everything and remembers what his mother had said to him recently. Not everyone thrives under pressure. Some people actually feel fear. Steel had gotten so caught up with the "excitement" of the situation that he didn't stop to think that those around him may be frightened for their lives. He looks down and thinks to himself for a moment, thinking about what he can do or say to reassure his escorts. Even though what he is about to try has never been tried before. Has no history of success, and is, in all likelihood a suicidal move. However, given their situation and lack of options, it is the only thing he has left to try, so that is what he is focussing on. He spins around in his chair to face Linz again. Linz looks back at him, his fear still reflecting strongly on his face. *"Try and picture it like this"*, Steel says to him. Linz looks over at the helm controls, worrying now even more about the fact that Steel has turned his back on it and is now not even looking where he is flying.

EXOM - THE YOUNG KING

"Your Highness", Linz says to Steel. *"Don't you think you should be watching where we're going?"*.

Steel casually glances back at the helm controls behind him and shrugs before looking at Linz again. *"Oh, we're probably going to crash anyway"*, Steel says very nonchalantly. Straight away Steel hears his words leave his mouth. He shakes his head and closes his eyes, realising that what he said definitely hasn't helped what he was about to try and do.

Linz starts shaking his head as his whole body also starts to shake. Steel, noticing how terrified Linz is, turns back around to watch the screen, and hold the flight controls. *"But if it makes you feel any better"*, Steel says to him. Steel then glances over at Borda and notices that she is looking equally terrified. *"We've got this"*, he says to her and winks.

Steel again turns his full attention on to the display screen in front of him as he flies the shuttle. He glances over at Linz again. *"Have you ever walked into a punch?"*, he asks him

Linz finds Steel's question peculiar but thinks about it for a moment, then shakes his head. *"I don't think so, no sir. I mean, no, Your Highness"*, he replies.

Steel returns his attention back to the flight screen and nods. *"I don't recommend it"*, Steel says. *"I try not to. I think most people would try not to. It hurts. Nothing good ever comes from it"*. Linz looks at Steel curiously, wondering where he is going with this. Steel glances back at Linz, again a cheeky and excited smile starts to form on his face. *"Yet, ironically, that's exactly what we are about to do"*.

Linz continues to stare at Steel, still extremely terrified and feeling no more relieved after this attempt from Steel to give an analogy of what they are attempting.

Realizing that he has done a lousy job at trying to reassure anyone, Steel gives up, turns back around to the helm controls, and again presses the comms button on his screen. The button turns green. *"Comms, on my command, fire the laser stilts at the exact location they were in when we launched"*, Steel says out loud so that the microphone can pick him up. He presses the button on his screen again, watching it turn white once more. He suddenly remembers something and presses the button again. *"The end of the launch, not the start"*, he clarifies into the microphone again. *"Their final position"*, he adds.

He presses the comms button again, watching it turn white once more and places both hands on the flight controls. *"OK, Fellas. Keep up"*, he says out loud, referring to the Dakari ships that are pursuing them.

The shuttle speeds towards Eluud as the Dakari ships sit right on their tail. The Dakari have reduced the rate at which they are shooting. Being very close to the shuttle, they obviously want to avoid being hit by any more flying debris. They manoeuvre closer to the shuttle, preparing to disable and dock with it at the same time. Something that Steel is actually counting on.

Borda watches Eluud rapidly approaching on her radar, the outer atmosphere of the green and brown planet almost filling up her screen completely. Frozen in her chair, she glances over at Steel. His body poised, his eyes focussed like a beast stalking its prey, fixated on the flight screen, on Eluud, and showing no signs of slowing down. She knows that at this rate, they will have no way of pulling away before they enter the atmosphere of Eluud, and once that happens the shuttle will become non-functional and collide at the same speed with the planet's surface.

She knows what she is about to say needn't be said, however, she feels she needs to voice it anyway. *"Your Highness, you are flying us into the planet's atmosphere"*, she says, still glancing sideways at Steel and still frozen and shivering with fear in her chair. *"The Engines will cease"*, she adds.

"So will theirs", Steel replies. His words offering her no comfort.

"That is not any more reassuring", Borda says as she slowly, still shaking, turns back to look at her navigation screen.

The shuttle rocketing towards Eluud, Steel has no idea where the Dakari ships are behind him. He pans left then right, then left again, at random intervals. His hand pushing the throttle on the flight control full forward, the engines on the shuttle start to shake under the strain. He makes some fleeting glimpses over at Borda's radar. *"Are they still on us?"*, he asks her. The shuttle jolts from another small blast hitting its hull. *"I'll take that as a yes"*, Steel says to himself out loud.

Linz glances over at Borda, noticing her body frozen stiff and shivering, just like his. Her eyes firmly focussed on her navigation screen. The image of Eluud rushing up fast. Linz pulls himself out of his chair, walks over to Borda and stands behind her. He places one hand on her shoulder and looks at her radar. Borda does not respond. *"Right on our tail, Your Highness"*, Linz says to Steel.

Steel smiles hearing this answer. *"Their speed?"*, Steel asks

"Fast. Like us", Linz replies.

Steel nods, equally pleased with this response as well. Borda can only watch the navigation screen. The image of Eluud now filling it completely. *"We are going to collide with the planet"*, she says, her voice breathless, defeated, filled with horror.

"Certainly, looks like it", Steel replies. He looks over at Borda, a calm smile on his face. *"Something to tell the kids about"*, he says to her, though she can not see his smile with her back to him and frozen stiff, staring at the navigation screen. Steels smile fades as he looks back at his flight display screen. *"No, you're right. Best not tell them about this"*, he says out loud. He keeps his hand firmly pushing the throttle forward, the shuttle still shaking and now creaking from the strain of the thrusters. *"Have they realised that yet?"*, Steel asks, both his escorts now white as ghosts, which is what they feel like they are about to become very soon.

"That we are all going to collide with the planet?", Linz asks, not sure why his King is even wondering about that. *"I don't think so"*, Linz replies.

Steel's mouth parts, his tongue pressing up against his teeth as he smiles like a beast about to pounce. *"Love it"*, he says out loud. Steel presses the comms button on the screen again. The button turns green. *"Right Comms. We are coming in fast. Very fast"*, he states to the officers in the Communications Room on Eluud, then presses the comms button again, it now turning back to white.

"I think they can see that, sir", Linz says. His head lowered, body starting to slouch as he accepts that he is about to die. *"Your Highness"*, he quickly corrects himself again looking back at his King.

"Engines about to cease", Borda announces, now more matter of fact than concerned, as she leans back in her chair, defeated.

"There!", Steel says as he looks with severe intensity at his display screen. *"Count us down"*, he calls over to Borda.

Feeling like she is now counting down the seconds to her death, Borda obeys this final command. *"Engines ceasing in three, two, one"*, she says.

Steel pulls the throttle straight back as he almost punches the button on his screen, watching it turn Green again. *"Fire Stilts!"*, he yells as the shuttle suddenly decelerates, again throwing Steel and his escorts across the bridge.

On Eluud, the laser stilt cannons are focused skyward. Pointing at the last recorded position where they were when Steel's shuttle left to go to Aymyn. They fire a steady laser beam that are the stilts. The stilts converge and focus on their destination point. There is a loud boom in the sky as Steel's shuttle enters the atmosphere of Eluud and its engines shutdown. Fortunately, the moment Steel's shuttle loses power it is exactly where the laser stilts have focused. An unimaginable sight, the chances of which are less than successfully threading a needle by throwing the thread at it, from a mile away while standing in a hurricane. The end points of the stilts connect with the stilt brackets on the ground supports of Steel's shuttle, catching the shuttle and slowing its descent.

The Dakari ships tear past Steel's shuttle, entering Eluuds atmosphere. Their engines cease and they dive straight into the planet's surface. Exploding into a roaring ball of fire, dislodged land and eventually just dust.

Steel's shuttle, now safely held up by the laser stilts, is slowly lowered down to the hanger floor near Chassam Castle. The wing sections of the saucer shaped shuttle start to retract, leaving only the oblong shape of the vessel as it is brought in to land. As the landing struts contact the ground, the main door slides down creating a ramp. Both Borda and Linz run from the shuttle, down the ramp and immediately fall to their hands and knees on the hangar floor. Soon after, Steel strolls calmly down the ramp and off the shuttle. He walks past his escorts, as though nothing has happened, as they remain still crouched on all fours on the ground. Steel walks towards the Castle, quietly grinning to himself. The Flight Commander, who had been standing on the hangar the entire time and witnessed Steel's shuttle being caught by the stilts as the Dakari ships barrel past and crash into the ground, immediately runs up to greet him. *"Your Highness. Are you alright?"*, the Flight Commander asks him, seeming breathless from the urgency in his question.

Steel looks at the Flight Commander innocently and smiles. *"Fine"*, Steel replies. *"But you might want to check on my escorts"*.

The flight Commander looks past Steel and over at the escorts. Borda now appears to be frantically kissing and stroking the ground, while Linz is resting on his elbows and throwing up. The Flight Commander turns as Steel walks past him. His face filled with awe. *"I, I, don't know what to say"*, the Flight Commander stutters. *"That was some amazing flying, Your Highness"*. Steel again grins to himself as he continues towards the Castle. *"How did you remember exactly where the laser stilts would be?"*, the Flight Commander asks him.

"I guessed", Steel replies just as casually as he is strolling.

"Guessed?", the Flight Commander says, really taken back by the king's response, as he runs to catch up.

Steel stops walking, turns to face the Flight Commander as he catches up to him, then puts his hand on the Flight Commander shoulder and just smiles. *"It's alright, Lieutenant"*, Steel says to him. *"My memory has never failed me yet"*. Steel turns back around and walks off into the Castle as the Flight Commander watches on.

"It's Commander", The Flight Commander yells out after him. *"You promoted me last week"*.

The Flight Commander looks back at Steel's escorts, still kneeled on the ground. He looks past them and at Steel's shuttle, watching it repair itself from the damage caused by the Dakari weapon blasts. He stands there and shakes his head. *"Just..."*, he starts to say, before pausing speechless. He sighs, shakes his head again and turns around to face the Castle. *"Amazing"*, he concludes before also walking on into the Castle.

EXOM

THE YOUNG KING

CHAPTER ELEVEN

------------------------------ Sneak a Peak ------------------------------

The entrance to Chassam Castle is empty. Not even Det is sitting in her usual chair in the library or standing beside the bookshelf pretending to read. Solid footsteps break the silence as Sergeant Mew walks towards the main door just as several Eluudian soldiers walk in. They see Mew and nod at him. He nods back. As they walk on through and past him, Mew grabs hold of the main door and is about to secure it when it is pushed open, almost knocking him down, by someone running inside. That someone is Tespa. She is happy and smiling as usual. She sees Mew and, realising that her sudden entrance has almost collected him, she puts her hands on his arms very apologetically. *"I am so sorry"*, she says to him as she holds his arms and stares him in the eyes, making sure that he is alright.

"It's alright, Princess", Mew replies with a polite smile.

Tespa lets him go and runs off up a hallway, as was her intention when running into the Castle. She gets only a short distance when she notices Det outside the door to the Eluudian communications room, peering in and listening. Tespa quietly walks up to her and is just about to touch Det on the shoulder to startle her. Before she is able, Det, still peering into the Communications Room, intuitively grabs Tespa's wrist without looking. Tespa is quite used to this and doesn't know why she even still tries to surprise Det. Det stops peering through the doorway and looks back at Tespa, letting go of her wrist. Tespa looks past Det, through the doorway, to see what she is looking at. *"What are you doing?"*, Tespa asks her, still trying to look inside the room. *"We're not supposed to hang around here"*. Det swiftly holds her finger in front of her lips telling Tespa to shush, then turns back and continues to peer back through the doorway.

With both Det and Tespa now quietly peering through the slightly open door into the communications room, neither of them notices Dacos standing up the hallway watching them curiously. He walks up behind them, not particularly quietly, but with their attention cantered on what is happening inside the communications room, neither Det nor Tespa hear him. He stands behind them, close, just watching them. He looks down at Tespa's backpack and spots Kako staring back at him. Kako, wide eyed and excited, is just about to speak. Dacos, so slightly, raises his hand signalling to Kako to be quiet. Kako obeys. Dacos continues raising his hand and places it on Tespa's shoulder. Startled, Tespa turns around. She smiles guiltily when she sees that it is Dacos that has startled her. They lock eyes. Tespa's a bit sheepish, Dacos's more inquiring.

Dacos looks past Tespa and on to Det. Det is still peering into the Communications Room. She does not react to Dacos but is aware that he is there. Again, she holds out her finger, this time to both Tespa and Dacos, telling them to not make a sound. Dacos looks past Det and also peers into the Communications Room. He notices nothing out of the ordinary. He looks back at Det curiously and places his hand on her shoulder. Det stops looking through the doorway, then slowly turns her head to look at Dacos's hand. With his other hand Dacos gently pushes the door open. He holds it open and motions to Det and Tespa to go inside.

Det takes her eyes of Dacos's hand still on her shoulder, then looks back at Tespa before looking up at Dacos. Tespa smiles, this time excitedly at Dacos, then at Det, then immediately takes up the invitation and proceeds to march straight into the communications room. The room, still occupied by several Communication Officers who are seated at their stations, is bustling with excitement as the officers discuss amongst themselves the amazing landing of Steel's shuttle that they had just witnessed and helped make happen. Tespa has never been inside the Communications Room before, she has never been allowed.

Neither her nor Det are. She looks around the room, taking it all in, all new and exciting. Det marches in behind her, and while supposably never having been in there before either, she seems very familiar with it. She walks straight over to one of the workstations and starts to read the display screen. Her body bent over the workstation and starting to nudge the Communication Officer, who's station it is, out of the way, she touches the display and scrolls up and down reading the report.

Dacos, having just returned from other matters in the Castle, has not yet been briefed about the king's dramatic return and never-before attempted emergency landing. He looks over at Det studying the Communication Officer's screen and assumes that she is just fascinated by the equipment. However, Det had obviously heard enough during her time peering and listening in through the door to know what has happened. Though what made her go there in the first place, no one has thought to question.

Tespa notices a very large button on the wall, all on its own, positioned behind a protective screen. She runs over to it and looks back at Dacos with excitement. *"That's the button to the Great Horn"*, she says to him. The button that was only ever designed to be pressed once. And once pressed would sound the Great Horn that is on top of Chassam Castle to notify all of Eluud that they now had a Zazar and have become a Protected Planet.

"It sure is", Dacos replies as he looks back over it. The protective screen still completely intact as the button has obviously never been pressed.

"Always wondered what it would look like", Tespa says as she turns back and studies it. *"I wonder even more what it sounds like"*.

"I am sure we will hear it one day", Dacos says, looking sadly hopeful at the button. *"Your father is working hard on that"*.

Tespa nods, still excited for seeing the button and feeling confident that her father will one day make the Great Horn heard throughout Eluud. She looks around the room again. A curious expression starts to push through the smile on her face as she notices that all the officers are still looking shocked and excited, while Det is still focussed on reading the report on the screen. *"Is everyone alright?"*, she asks.

Dacos, still with no idea about what has just happened, also looks at everyone curiously. With no reason to offer for all the excitement, he decides to improvise one.

"Oh, everyone is fine", he replies. *"They all just really love their jobs. Apparently"*. Dacos does not look, or sound convinced by his own explanation. However, he decides to continue with it. *"Every single person in here is crucial to the operations and security of Eluud"*, he says as he places a hand on the shoulder of one of the Communication Officers sitting at the workstation in front of him, taking him completely by surprise. Startled, the Communication Officer almost jumps out of his seat, and looks up at Dacos, then around the room wondering why he has been singled out. *"Like this guy"*, Dacos says, completely unaware that he has startled the poor man. *"Tell them what you do"*, Dacos tells him.

Det finishes reading the report. She looks at everyone in the room as she walks back over and stands beside Tespa. The startled Communication Officer, still looking very nervous with Dacos's hand still resting on his shoulder, stutters as he tries to speak. *"Ah, er, um, what, what I do?"*, he asks Dacos

Dacos removes his hand from the officer's shoulder, then appearing very proud of all the staff in the room, smiles at him. *"Yes, tell them what you do here"*, Dacos again tells the officer.

The Startled Communication Officer looks blankly at Dacos for a moment before again stuttering as he tries to answer. *"Um, ah, I press buttons"*, he says, still looking blankly at Dacos, then looks at Det and Tespa just as blankly.

Dacos continues to smile proudly and nods as he looks at Det and Tespa. *"Press buttons. There you go"*, Dacos says. Still smiling, he looks down at the Communication Officer, waiting for him to elaborate. The Communication Officer again just looks back at him blankly. Dacos's smile starts to fade into a look of confusion. *"There must be more to it than that?"*, Dacos asks.

"No, that's pretty much it", the Communication Officer replies as he shakes his head.

Dacos tries to hide his confusion from Det and Tespa and attempts to continue with his proud and smiling demeanour. *"Ok. But they're pretty important buttons, right?"*, Dacos says to the Communication Officer before looking back at Det and Tespa, confident that the Communication Officer will back him up.

"No, not really", the Communication Officer replies. His expression still blank. He glances over at Det and Tespa again before looking back at Dacos.

Dacos continues to stand there, smiling, looking proud, for a moment anyway. Eventually he can no longer hide his confusion and looks back down at the Communication Officer with bewilderment. *"They must do something"*, Dacos says to him.

"I don't know", the Communication Officer replies. *"I've never asked. I just got told to sit here and press them"*.

"Right", Dacos says, hoping that there is more to this explanation.

"And hope nothing blows up", the Communication Officer adds.

"Right", Dacos says.

"Which hasn't yet", the Communication Officer continues.

"Good", Dacos says with a nod.

"I am not sure what will happen if I stop pressing them", the Communication Officer says as he thinks to himself. *"Probably nothing. I hope nothing. I have sometimes forgotten to press them. You know, with all the pressure of the job and all"*.

"Yep", Dacos nods. *"Lots of pressure"*, Dacos replies trying not to sound sarcastic.

"I am not even sure if they are connected to anything", the Communication Officer says as he again looks blankly up at Dacos.

Dacos looks at him silently for a moment, not sure what to say. He then looks away, straightens himself up, smiles and looks proudly again at Det and Tespa. *"Right. Well, like I said, everyone in this room has a really important job"*, Dacos tells them. He puts his hand back on the Communication Officer's shoulder again. *"Except this guy"*, he adds. *"We may need to reassign him"*.

Det looks at Dacos as Dacos sideway glances back at her and winks. Tespa notices Dacos wink at Det, excitedly smiles and starts to back away towards the door. *"Oh, look at that"*, Tespa says as she tries to sneak past them. *"I just remembered. I have to go now"*. Dacos and Det both look at Tespa, confused as to why she is trying to walk away. Tespa just smiles at Det. *"You stay"*, she tells Det. *"I need to go and, um, find Kako's boot"*.

"My boot", Kako excitedly repeats from inside her backpack.

Det grabs Tespa's shoulder and turns her slightly, looking at her backpack, and sees Kako sitting there, fully dressed in his shirt and boots. *"Um, he's wearing both his boots"*, Det says to her as she stares back at Tespa again with a disbelieving look.

Tespa just smiles and shakes her head, looking at Det as though she is being silly and not catching on. *"Yeah. That's why I need to go find it"*, Tespa says. Tespa looks up at Dacos and smiles, hoping that he has caught on. He hasn't. He looks just as sceptical. Tespa ignores their confused and suspicious looks. *"Keep showing Det stuff"*, she says to Dacos. *"Like, lots of stuff. She wants to see lots of stuff. With you"*. With that Tespa pushes Det in front of Dacos, almost into him, and then quickly leaves through the door.

Dacos stands there awkwardly looking at Det, neither of them knowing what to say to each other. Dacos forces a smile. However, Det just stares back blankly, then turns and also walks out of the room, leaving Dacos standing there looking confused.

He is not left alone for long. Looking for Dacos, Steel walks up to the communications room as Det walks out. Steel stops and smiles at Det. Det looks at her father briefly, but does not say anything, then turns and walks off down the corridor. Steel is just about to call out to her, but then stops himself and just waves at her. *"Hi. I'm home"*, Steel says quietly to himself. Steel looks at the communications room door for a moment, the question now crossing his mind as to why Det had been in there. He walks inside and sees Dacos standing there.

"Your Highness". Dacos says with a smile, pleased to see someone he can talk to

Steel stops and looks at Dacos with intrigue. *"Det was just in here"*, Steel says to him. Dacos nods. *"With you?"*, Steel asks now curiously.

"It wasn't like that", Dacos replies, knowing what his King is insinuating.

Steel's look of curiosity turns to one of disappointment. *"That's a shame"*, he says to Dacos. *"I didn't want to be interrupting anything"*. Steel turns away and looks around the room. *"The Communications Room. An interesting place for a first date"*, he says out loud to himself. Dacos looks at him confused. However, Steel continues to walk further into the communications room, all smiling and enthusiastic. *"Great work with the stilts everyone"*, he announces to the officers in the room. *"Need to put that manoeuvre in the simulator"*. He rethinks his statement. *"Or not"*, he then says. *"In fact, don't. It would be irresponsible to encourage that kind of thing. And I do not want to be known as the Irresponsible King"*.

"Pretty sure that....", Dacos starts to say before he is cut off by Steel swinging around and pointing at him. Dacos rethinks his response. *"No one would say that about you, Your Highness"*, Dacos says sarcastically. Steel detects his sarcasm and smiles it off as he turns back around and looks at the officers in the room.

"Pretty awesome though, wasn't it?", he says to them. *"Let's not let Aura find out"*, he then adds.

"Guessing I missed something?", Dacos says now looking confused.

Steel walks to the back of the room and looks at Dacos. Not wanting to alarm him, but not sure how else to describe what had happened, he thinks about how to explain it. *"I brought company back with me"*, Steel says to him. *"Raiders ambushed us in orbit"*.

Dacos eyes widen as his jaw drops. *"And I am only hearing about this now!"*, Dacos exclaims as he runs to two of the officers still sitting at their workstations and grabs them by the arm. *"Come with me"*, he says to them. The officers stand up and look at Dacos as Dacos marches towards the door, then turns back to look at Steel. *"And where are they now?"*, Dacos asks him, a sense of panic and urgency in his voice.

Casually Steel looks down at the same screen that Det had been looking at before and starts to read it. *"Dust, I'd imagine"*, Steel replies just as casually as he reads through to the end of the report. Steel smiles and looks at the officer whose workstation it is. *"Well put. I forgot about that last bit"*, he says to him.

Steel looks up and notices the confused, potentially unhappy expression on Dacos's face. He slowly and awkwardly reaches forward, switches off the screen and moves away from the workstation. He keeps his eyes on Dacos's displeased expression for a moment before awkwardly looking away and trying to look casual, but failing miserably, as he moves away from the workstation.

Now realising that this is what Det was also standing over and looking at earlier, Dacos walks over to the workstation and looks at the Communication Officer who is sitting there. *"Show me"*, Dacos says to him. The Communication Officer turns the screen back on and lets Dacos read it. Dacos bends over as he studies the report and then glances up at Steel in shock. He looks back at the report again to confirm if he has read it correctly. He has. He again looks back at Steel, the shock in his face even more expressive this time, with a strong hint of annoyance added to it. *"You..... What?"*, he says to Steel, glancing back and forth between Steel and the Screen. He shakes his head in disbelief, then looks back at Steel, before looking away, not sure what to say. He takes a moment, a breath, a sigh, then looks more calmly, but still disapprovingly at Steel. *"Don't do this again, Your Highness"*, he says to him. If it wasn't for the "Your Highness" at the end of his statement, you would think he was scolding a child.

The officer at that workstation is also reading the report, again, probably for the tenth time and is still filled with awe. *"It was amazing"*, the officer says to Steel and then looks up at Dacos standing over him.

Dacos stands up, still looking at Steel and shakes his head, not at all pleased. *"Yes. Maybe"*, Dacos says. *"Don't do this again, Your Highness"*, he repeats to Steel. *"Or anything like it. You are not exactly replaceable"*. Dacos walks away from the workstation and back towards Steel. *"I also was not expecting you back so soon"*, Dacos says to him.

"You weren't expecting me back. Aura didn't want me to leave. It's not my birthday or something, is it?", Steel replies trying to deflect the conversation. Dacos ignores Steel's attempt at redirecting and does not

respond. Steel smiles away his failed attempt. *"Just a quick trip back to pick something up"*, Steel says to him.

"Aymyn to Eluud. It's not exactly a quick trip", Dacos points out to Steel.

"I don't mind it", Steel replies with a shrug. *"Gives me time to think things through. And God knows I have a lot of that to do"*.

"Must be important whatever you are picking up", Dacos says to Steel, waiting for him to tell him what it is.

"It is", is all Steel replies, not giving anything away.

"You need help finding it?", Dacos presses further.

"No. Already found it", Steel replies, then walks around and stands directly in front of Dacos, looking up at him. *"It's standing right in front of me"*, Steel says. Dacos looks at Steel confused. This time Steel believes that Dacos is actually confused and not just pretending to be like he does when discussing Det. *"Need you to come back to Aymyn with me"*, Steel tells him. *"I need another set of eyes and ears around the place. More specifically, I need your eyes and ears"*.

"My eyes and ears?", Dacos asks, a little flattered. Steel just stares back at him, not feeling that his question requires a response. *"And since my eyes and ears come with my entire body, and not detachable"*, Dacos starts to jokingly say before Steel cuts him off.

"Don't think I didn't think of that", Steel responds equally jokingly, but keeping a straight face.

"You came all the way back here for that?", Dacos asks him as he strolls across the room towards the door. *"You could have just sent me a message"*.

"Meh", Steel replies as he shrugs and brushes Dacos's comment off.

Knowing it's pointless to persist asking his King anything else when he gets like this, Dacos simply falls back on obeying without question. *"I'll go pack then, I guess"*, Dacos says to him.

Steel starts walking towards the door. As he passes Dacos, he pats him gently on the back. *"No hurry"*, Steel tells him. *"You'll be taking your own ship"*. Dacos looks at Steel even more intrigued as Steel continues to walk out the room.

----------------------------------- Bajen -----------------------------------

The Eluudian advisor, Bajen, sits at his desk in his private and rather large office. A distinctive looking holographic projector built into the centre of his desk is active, forming the usual liquid appearance energy field hovering over his desk in front of him. What is not usual, for an Eluudian Royal Advisor anyway, is whose image is being streamed live inside the holographic field. A familiar looking silhouette of a black cloaked female fills the holographic energy field. As she moves, glimpses of her bright orange hair can be seen beneath her hood. *"It would be most unwise for you to come here at the present time"*, she says to Bajen through the holographic projection. She turns and looks at him. Her demeanour casual but no less assertive as Sabel always is.

"What I need to say is better said in person", Bajen replies. For someone who is arguing with Sabel, he appears unusually confident, if not a little arrogant.

"Better for who?", Sabel asks rhetorically.

"Well, me of course", Bajen replies, though not really needing to. A simple raise of his eyebrow would have had the same effect. But Bajen, liking the sound of his own voice and the confidence he emanates through it, even if more show than real, will answer even rhetoric questions if they are about him.

Sabel looks annoyingly at Bajen. His usefulness as a Sharlon agent is greatly becoming less than the cost to keep him. The little information they receive from him has so far not warranted the amount of times he has invited himself to a meeting with them to renegotiate his fee.

"I assume this is another attempt at renegotiating your payment?", Sabel asks him, knowing well already the answer.

"I like to see it more as an opportunity", Bajen replies, his smile still smug.

"I am sure you do", Sabel says, throwing him an astute distrusting glance. Most people like to stay well out of reach of Sabel's daggers, a fact that she knows that Bajen is aware of. So, to be arranging another dangerous conversation with her has more than aroused Sabel's

suspicions. Perhaps he has a Deathwish, Sabel wonders to herself? *"And you want this to be that time?"*, she asks him.

Either not knowing, or knowing and pretending not to, that he is treading on thin ice, and seemingly unaware of Sabel's suspicions and thoughts, Bajen again smiles smugly. *"Can think of no better time"*, he replies.

Sabel looks away and slightly shrugs. *"Very well"*, she says before disconnecting the holographic transmission. The holographic energy field floating above Bajen's desk becomes completely clear before dispersing as his projector shuts down.

Inside the dimly lit Sharlon Secret hillside Base, Sabel is still standing in front of her holographic projection table, having just disconnected from Bajen. Her holoprojector fires up again, forming the holographic energy field over the table. This time the live image of Dark comes through. Her eyes window lit and piercing. Sabel glances over at the holographic transmission for a brief moment, not surprised to see Dark's appearance, then looks away again still displeased and suspicious about Bajen. *"My Sign, I assume you were monitoring that last communication"*, Sabel says to Dark.

Dark's eyes soften for a moment as she looks aside. *"I was"*, Dark replies. She looks back at Sabel as Sabel turns back to face her. *"His greed is becoming most troublesome. Even if it is just a pretence to another motive"*, Dark says to her.

"You think there is a pretence?", Sabel asks her, her expression now more intrigued than displeased.

Dark's stare begins to sharpen again. *"It's Bajen. There is always a pretence"*, Dark replies. *"He is employed by the Eluudian Royal Family as an adviser, and they should know better than to trust him. He is also employed by the Sharlon – and we do know better"*.

Sabel turns away, again looking frustrated. *"He's becoming annoying"*, she says.

"Problematic", Dark replies.

Sabel starts to smirk as she looks aside. *"It is a problem that I feel well equipped to deal with"*, she says as she turns to face Dark again.

The confidence in her gaze showing that she knows that Dark knows what she is thinking, and suspects that Dark may also be considering the same solution.

Dark chuckles briefly. *"Of that, I have no doubt"*, Dark replies.

Still sitting behind his desk inside his office, Bajen looks across the room at two empty stools. Or at least they appear to be empty. *"Did I not tell you that this would work?"*, Bajen says out loud towards the empty stools. *"You get what you want. Then you give me what I want"*.

A shimmer moves on one of the stools. The same shimmer that the invisible being from R'Vian's ship leaves as it moves. The shimmering form appears to stand up from one of the stools, knocking it over as it moves from it. Bajen is unable to tell if the stool was knocked over deliberately or accidentally. He hopes accidentally as it was not done gently. The shimmering being moves quickly towards Bajen, throwing the desk out of the way as it does. "Okay", Bajen thinks to himself, "the stool was no accident". Bajen is lifted up, thrown against the wall and held there by the hand of the invisible being. On his forehead his skin starts to separate as though an invisible claw is slowly cutting him. Bajen is terrified. The wound reaches over an inch in length when Bajen yells out. *"You have my word!"*, he exclaims. *"It's there. You'll get it"*.

Bajen is referring to a data tablet that is located in the Sharlon hideout. A tablet containing information regarding the Valantriun. Exactly what information is unknown. A possible attack perhaps or attempt at sabotage as the Sharlon is known for. R'Vian and this invisible creature have travelled to Eluud to retrieve the tablet and find out what the Sharlon are planning. Armed with a lot of information themselves, R'Vian and the invisible creature knew that the tablet was on Eluud, inside a secret Sharlon Base. They knew that Bajen was a Sharlon Spy. They also knew that Sabel resides inside the Sharlon base – and there lies the challenge. Gaining access to the Sharlon base undetected to retrieve the tablet and escaping alive.

The plan; have Bajen lead the invisible being to the Sharlon Base. Then while Bajen is distracting Sable, the invisible being retrieves the tablet. All while R'Vian closely monitors everything, keeping their exit strategy safe and assured. Seems simple enough. But what if things don't go to plan? A well-known Valantriun saying goes, "Planning for Failure is just as important as Planning for Success". Of course, that saying is rejected by many in Exom, just like the idea of the Valantriun are. However, it is this very saying that is the reason why R'Vian is there. If things do not go to plan, then, in essence, she is there to improvise a new one.

The invisible hand clutching Bajen releases him. It then moves away and disappears completely, but not before knocking over more furniture on the way. Bajen looks momentarily relieved to still be alive. He then looks at the stools, not sure where the being has now gone, and forces himself to smile. He turns around, opens the door to his office and exits through it.

Bajen closes the door to his office and stands in the corridor, leaning against his door, relieved to be away from the invisible being. Tespa and Vessel walk casually down the corridor towards Bajen. Tespa is laughing at something Vessel has just said. Bajen notices them and makes himself smile, acting casual as though there was nothing he needed to feel relieved about. Tespa, noticing Bajen smiling at them, looks at Bajen and smiles back. She then stops walking when she notices the cut on his head and, looking concerned, turns her full attention towards him. *"Bajen?"*, She says to him.

Bajen continues to force himself to smile, though he is so good at it that it looks natural. *"Princess"*, he replies still looking very casual and pleased as always to see her.

"What have you done to yourself?", she asks him, looking straight at the cut on his head.

Faking confusion, Bajen looks at Tespa pretending not to know what she is referring to. Tespa moves closer to Bajen and touches his head. Bajen steps back, still shaken and reliving being pinned against the wall moments before. Noticing Bajen's shock, Tespa retracts her hand. *"Wasn't looking where I was walking"*, Bajen says to her, again trying to smile but this time unable to completely hide his distress.

Vessel moves in, unphased by Bajen's anguish and making herself very obvious, as she takes a closer look at Bajen's wound, before looking at Bajen suspiciously. *"What did you walk into?"*, she asks him, her tone full of cynicism. She glances over at Tespa with a sceptical look before looking back at Bajen.

"I'm not exactly sure", Bajen replies, suspecting that Vessel is not buying his story, but sticking to it anyway. *"I didn't see it"*. Well, at least there is some truth in that, he thinks to himself. Vessel looks at his wound again before looking Bajen in the eyes once more. Her expression still very dubious. Bajen smiles. *"Where are you two heading? Royal duties?"*, Bajen asks them, trying to immediately change the subject.

"I don't have any royal duties", Tespa says as she laughs. *"I just walk around, keeping everyone happy by looking pretty"*.

Vessel stops looking at Bajen and gives Tespa a playfully serious stare. *"Hello. I'm pretty sure that's my job"*, Vessel says to her.

Tespa smiles back at Vessel, then looks at Bajen again. *"Just off to get some training in"*, she tells him.

Pleased that the conversation is no longer about him, Bajen continues with it. *"Your family trains a lot"*, he says to her.

"Yeah. It's kind of our thing", Tespa replies. *"Well, mostly our thing. Well, kind of their thing. More their thing. I just do it. Occasionally. If you can call it that"*. Tespa pauses briefly. *"I don't do it that often"*, she finally confesses.

Bajen looks confused, lost in Tespa's series of statements, but decides not to try and make any sense out of it.

"She watches a lot", Vessel clarifies as she looks back at Bajen.

"I call it learning", Tespa says to him with a smile.

"You're the only one who does", Vessel replies.

Bajen now happy that the conversation has completely moved away from him, decides this is a good time to end it. *"Enjoy, princess"*, he says to Tespa, smiling contently once more.

Tespa smiles back. *"I will"*, she replies, then looks upwards as she thinks about what she just said moments before. *"I didn't make any sense before, did I?"*, she asks Bajen.

Bajen just quietly smiles back as Vessel nudges Tespa along. *"Let's go"*, Vessel says to her.

EXOM - THE YOUNG KING

Small one-inch-wide metallic balls fly across the Eluudian Training Hall with considerable speed, propelled by the catapult machines now active as the Training Hall has been placed into Advanced Mode. The machines firing up to several at a time with the briefest of intermission between. The catapult machines, positioned at the far end of the training hall, are not set to their fastest speed, but pretty close. They fire relentlessly and with purpose. Their target, The Eluudian King. He darts around the training hall, jumping from object to object and off walls just as Det had been earlier. His ronad in hand and fully deployed, he dives and dodges the metallic balls before they hit him, most only missing him by less than an inch. Those he can not move out of the way of, he deflects with his ronad, swinging and spinning it very quickly, yet also very controlled. He tilts his head slightly as a metal ball flies past his face. Before it completely passes him, he pulls his ronad in front of his face just in time for it to deflect another metal ball aimed directly at his nose. He bends back, flipping himself backwards and swings his ronad up and around his body, deflecting more metallic balls as others shoot straight past him. Balls that would have hit him had he not flipped himself out of the way. He swings his ronad, collecting and hitting about five metallic balls across the room as he falls to the ground, landing on his side. Another ball skims pass his face as he lays back quickly to avoid it. He rolls over and flips himself back to his feet, then immediately jumps towards one of the obstacles placed around the room. The catapult machine responds quickly, keeping Steel in its sight, even anticipating his moves and shooting metallic balls where he is about to land. Steel again deflects these balls with his ronad, while still in the air, before he places his foot down on his selected destination or object. He spins his ronad like a propeller in front of him as he dives to the floor again. His ronad repelling the metallic balls back at the catapult machines themselves, sometimes even colliding with other metallic balls that have just been fired. He hits the floor, summersaults, and swings his ronad back behind him deflecting more of the unrelenting targeting spheres.

Steel moves quickly through the obstacles in the training hall. Occasionally pausing, very briefly, to decide his next move. He seems to climb the walls with ease, almost running up them like an insect would, and jumping from wall to wall to obstacle and back to the wall again. The whole time he is spinning and swinging his ronad to either deflect the propelled balls or using it to launch himself even higher or further through the hall.

Sweat dripping from his head, face, and hands. Even his clothes, which are still his royal attire minus his royal cloak, seemed soaked. He has been here a while.

Tespa walks in through the main hall doors with Vessel right behind her. At first neither of them notices that Steel is inside training as they are too busy talking, laughing and even teasing each other. Vessel makes sure that the door is closed behind her as Tespa turns and watches her, walking backwards further into the hall. The expression on Vessel's face changes as she looks past Tespa and sees Steel in the training hall, still busy jumping, diving, swinging, spinning while dodging and deflecting projectiles. Tespa stops walking backwards, curious, noticing that Vessel is looking at something behind her. She turns around, and her seemingly curious expression changes into a tender smile, as she too now sees her father there. She has seen him train many times before, in fact it was he who mostly taught her and Det how to use a ronad in this very hall. However, the wonder she feels every time seeing him skilfully navigate the training hall, while being shot at by a barrage of metallic balls, always avoiding every one of them, to her feels like she is witnessing it again for the first time. She stands there, so very impressed, just watching.

She hardly even notices Vessel walk up and stand beside her. *"I forget how good he is"*, Vessel says as she too watches on in awe.

"So do I", Tespa replies, holding her smile and not taking her eyes off her father.

Not missing a step or swing, Steel sees Tespa and Vessel standing there watching him. He smiles at them. Tespa continues to smile back, a proud feeling flowing through her. Vessel continues to stare back at him with awe and wonder.

Steel throws himself into the air, spinning to avoid more metallic balls hurled at him by the catapult machine. He somersaults through the air, landing in a crouching position in the centre of the hall. He deflects two more metallic balls with his ronad before shouting *"Halt!"* at the catapult machines. Instantly the catapult machines cease firing. Steel stands up straight, deactivates his ronad and turns to face Tespa and Vessel. *"Ladies"*, he says to them with a glowing smile.

"Dad", Tespa replies, still just standing there, staring at him, and smiling.

"Are you here to train?", he asks them as he places his ronad into his leg holster and walks up to them. *"I can reset the room back to basic mode"*. He turns and looks back at the catapult machines now sitting dormant. *"Unless you want to try dodging some projectiles as well"*, he says to them. *"I warn you, those things hurt if they hit you"*, he adds turning back to smile at them both again.

Tespa shakes her head vigorously and looks at Vessel. Tespa has never tried training in the hall while it has been set to Advanced Mode. She is unsure if Vessel has. Vessel probably has. Vessel's traditional Troin upbringing has trained her to be a very skilled fighter. Still smiling, Tespa looks back at her father. *"Vessel wants to show me some Troin techniques"*, She tells him. *"To do with fighting this time"*, she adds as her smile turns into an even cheekier one.

Steel deliberately tries to ignore what Tespa has implied, while Vessel frowns momentarily at Tespa before looking back at Steel and smiling awkwardly. Tespa changes her cheeky smile back into a more comforting simple one. *"I hear you are not home for long"*, she says to her father.

Steel nods as he looks at Tespa with a kind of profound expression, as though he is only partially there and partially lost in thought. *"No. I came back for a breather"*, he tells her. *"To get my head clear about some things, but I need to get back to Aymyn"*.

"With Dacos", Tespa says, definitely as more of a statement than a question.

"With Dacos", Steel replies, thinking that news travels fast through Eluud.

"Det won't be happy", Tespa says. *"She'll have nothing to sit and watch for in the entrance library"*.

Tespa's words bring back Steel's full attention. He looks at her, trying to hold back his amused grin and expecting to see her grinning back at him. But Tespa's expression seems quite sincere. Briefly anyway. A cheeky smile starts to take shape on Tespa's face again as their smiling eyes lock in on each other's. Steel's expression becomes more serious. *"I don't expect he'll be gone too long"*, he says as his eyes move between Tespa and nowhere in particular as he thinks to himself.

Picking up on her father's words, Tespa's smile also starts to fade away, and she looks at him now with a hint of concern. *"You don't expect he'll be gone long"*, she repeats back to her father. *"You are coming back with him though?"*, she then asks.

Steel seems to hesitate before answering. *"Ah, I'll be back"*, he tells her.

Tespa noticed his hesitation and stares at him intensely. She is just about to pursue her questioning when a different question, one that she has been thinking about for a very long time but never gotten around to remembering to ask, pops into her head, making her seemingly completely forget her current conversation. *"I've been thinking about this for a while now"*, she says to her father. *"If you married Aura. Would our planets be married too and therefore Eluud extended the same protection as Aymyn?"*

A perfectly valid question, and something that Steel had also wished was the case. *"Wouldn't that be something"*, Steel replies with a smile. His smile quickly fades. *"It doesn't work that way"*, he tells her.

"Well, I don't see why not", Tespa says with a kind of pout. *"What's the point in the council only being allowed to be in a relationship with other council members if it doesn't allow for things like that?"*

Once again, a very valid question. Or seems like one anyway. Steel nods at her as he tries to think of how to answer. *"Not all council members are rulers of their planet"*, he tells her. *"Some are regents. Related but not ruling"*.

Tespa thinks about her father's explanation, the thought process leading her to change the topic once again. *"Why don't you appoint a regent instead of doing it all yourself?"*, she asks her father. *"Then you wouldn't need to travel as much"*.

"What? And stay here with you guys all the time? Are you crazy?", Steel replies jokingly while trying to look as though he is being serious. He can't hold it, and a smile breaks through his serious expression, brought on by Tespa smiling at his reply, knowing that he is only joking. In all seriousness though, this is definitely not the first time this question has been put to him. It is becoming more and more a regular occurrence by more and more people. It seems everyone close to him has at some point, at least once, asked him why he feels like he needs to do everything himself.

Steel's expression turns more serious as he tries to answer her question properly. *"I think about that a lot"*, he tells her. *"It's a tough one. Eluud is my home. I am responsible for it, for this kingdom, all its people. I need to know that being part of the Royal Alliance, whatever decisions are made that involve Eluud, that I am there to make sure that our interests are protected"*.

Tespa smiles at her father as she senses another underlying reason as well. *"And you get to be with Aura"*, she says to him.

"And I get to be with Aura", Steel replies with a little giggle.

Tespa's expression becomes more serious again. *"You could both quit the council"*, she says, not willing to leave it there. *"There is no reason why she also has to be on it as well. She could also appoint her own Regent"*.

While, what Tespa is suggesting is entirely possible, Steel seems to briefly tremble at the thought. *"You wouldn't want that. No one would"*, he replies, shaking his head. *"Except perhaps Councillor Lawn, who has his eyes firmly set on that position"*, Steel then adds as he thinks about it some more. Tespa is intrigued and, even without saying a word, her expression tells Steel so. *"Aura may seem all nice and calm"*, Steel continues to explain, *"and she most certainly is, too much maybe. But she is so incredibly strong and the reason why the council is still there and able to function. She holds it together"*. Steel looks up at Vessel, realising that he has been talking to Tespa this entire time and feeling like they have excluded her from the conversation. As Steel continues, he makes sure to look at both Vessel and Tespa as he talks to them. *"Aura is very much respected. Perhaps the most respected. By everyone"*, he says to them. *"Well, I am not sure about Lawn"*, he says as he thinks to himself again. *"I am not quite sure what he respects. Definitely no kind of change, that's for sure. If it wasn't for him being a spectre, you would think he was a Pure Light Sign"*.

Steel makes that last comment half tongue-in-cheek, but its enough to get Tespa thinking about other things again. Being Eluudian, and Eluudian's not being that big on people's signs, though some are difficult to ignore, her knowledge on them is quite limited. Her father knows a lot more about them than she does, but he spends a lot of time on Aymyn, and with Aymyns, so kind of needs to. Tespa's caring, peaceful, very friendly and bubbly nature makes it unquestionable that she is a Wendral Sign, even to those who know very little about Signs. However, also not knowing a lot about Spectres either, upon hearing her father's words about Councillor Lawn, if his traits are so strongly representative of someone of a Pure Light Sign – then perhaps he is. *"Maybe he is?"*, she says to her father. *"Why should it just be Aymyns that have a sign?"*

The thought had crossed Steel's mind before. Not specifically about other species also having a Sign. But certainly, about Councillor Lawn. However, every time he has thought about it, he has always come to the same conclusion. *"No. Not that guy"*, Steel replies. *"If you ever meet him, you will know what I am talking about. Doesn't seem intelligent enough to be a Pure Light Sign. Arrogant, definitely. But, also not at all intuitive"*.

Tired of standing, Tespa walks over towards the bench seat by the wall of the Training Hall, looking back hoping that her father will come and join her. *"Maybe he just hides it well"*, she says as she sits down on the bench seat. *"But still, someone else could represent you both on the council"*, she says returning to their conversation about her father being on the council. *"Especially us. You are not the only one here who loves Eluud. I could do it"*.

"Um, no you couldn't", Vessel exclaims, giving Tespa an intense look.

Tespa looks back at Vessel and realises what she is saying. If Tespa joined the council, then her and Vessel could not be together. *"Well, no. I couldn't"*, Tespa says to her father while smiling at Vessel. She reaches out her hand to Vessel and then places it right next to her on the bench chair. Vessel walks over and sits down as Tespa removes her hand and then rests it back down in Vessel's lap. She stares down at her hand and starts to think. She looks up at Vessel, her face curious. Vessel looks back at her, wondering what she is thinking. Tespa then looks over at her father, still standing there, staring at the both of them. She looks down at his ronad sheathed to his leg and then looks over at the dormant catapult machines before taking in the entire training hall. She looks back at her father. He can tell that she is thinking deeply about something, this is the longest she has been quiet while no one else is talking.

While her father had been telling her why he needs to be on the council, she was so pre-occupied thinking it was to be with Aura that she missed what he was saying. It's clear that her father is very much in love with Aura, and them both being on the council makes their relationship possible. Which is why she suggested that they could both leave the council and have someone replace them. However, what she failed to hear, that when she reflects back on his words were very clear, is the real reason why he has committed himself to the council. His devotion and loyalty to the Eluudian people. This was not a matter of finding someone else who could do the job for him. It's about understanding why he believes he needs to do everything himself.

She looks away, thinking, digesting her thoughts. *"You already give so much"*, she says to him while still looking away. Then she turns to him and says four very important words. Four words that she does not think he believes but needs to. *"You are not alone"*.

Steel walks over and sits down next to Tespa. He looks at Vessel, now holding Tespa's hands in her lap. A grown woman now being the one holding his little girl's hands. Something that he used to be the one to do. Only Tespa is no longer a little girl. Neither is Det. They are both actually a little older than Steel was when he became King of Eluud. He looks back down at their hands and starts to imagine his hands there, but now holding Aura's. The image in his mind changes as an older pair of hands reaches down and holds his. He looks up and, in his mind, he can see his mother, gazing into his eyes as she holds his hands firmly, comfortingly, reassuringly. He looks away, coming back out of his imagination and looks at Tespa. Her face just as calm and reassuring as his mothers. He takes a breath, lets it out and nods. *"I know that"*, he says to Tespa, his words sincere but not entirely convincing.

"Do you?", Tespa asks, her eyes almost staring right into his soul.

Steel looks away. *"Yeah....I..."*, he says, struggling to speak. *"It's just that...."*. He stops speaking as he can not find the words he wants to say. Perhaps he doesn't know what he wants to say. Tespa does. Seeing, feeling, hearing his words in her head as though they were her own. She takes one of her hands out of Vessel's lap and reaches up and places it on her father's cheek, turning his face to look at her. She smiles at him and nods. *"I know. Say it"*, she tells him. Not because she wants to hear him say it, but because she knows that he needs to hear himself say it. Again, Steel looks back softly at Tespa, the words still seeming so hard to find, so he stays silent. Her gaze still looking deep into his soul, Tespa nods. *"Let me help you"*, she says to him. She takes her hand off his cheek and holds his hand and starts to speak the words that he couldn't find. *"Tespa. The weight that I feel resting on my shoulders at times feels so incredibly heavy"*, she says for him. Steel looks at Tespa in awe and wonder, always amazed at how she finds the words that other people can't. *"And could someone else do it and help take some of that weight off me?"*, Tespa continues to say for him. *"Yes, probably. But who I am is someone who could never ask someone else to do that"*.

Her words resound in his head. He hears her speaking but knows that the words are his. So true and stating his feeling and thoughts precisely. All he can do is look at her and nod. *"My love for our home"*, she continues to say for him. *"For our people, for every single soul, the responsibility I feel for them, for me, means that I can not burden them with anything. I want to unburden them. I would do anything for them. I hope they know that".*

Steel gazes at his daughter, still speechless but now not feeling the need to speak as she has spoken for him with such precision. Tespa takes her other hand from Vessel's lap and holds both of her father's hands with both of hers. She stares back at him, not as deeply as she was, no longer looking into his soul, just looking into his eyes, looking at him. *"They do"*, she tells him as she smiles warmly again at him like she always does. *"And they would do anything for you too"*. She leans back but does not let go of his hands. *"You are loved, dad"*, she tells him. *"Very loved. And you are not alone. I hope one day you realize that. Before it's too late"*.

Steel and Tespa remain looking at each other for a while, still holding each other's hands, as Vessel watches both of them. *"I hate the way she does that"*, Vessel says to Steel rather despondently.

-------------------------------- **The Lockbox** --------------------------------

Det is standing in her bedroom in front of a large bookshelf. Her room only lit by the light coming through the windows of her outside facing wall. As it is not very light outside, with Eluud being in one of its Twilight periods which it spends a significant part of each day, her room is very dimly lit, but still light enough to see everything clearly. Other than her wardrobe, bed and side tables, her room is mostly empty and simple. In her hands she is holding a small box about the size of both her hands. A metallic silver in colour. The lid, hinged to the main part of the box, simple, slightly ornamental design around the edges with a small lock built into the centre. She has only just closed it. She locks the box with a small key that is attached to a thin delicate chain. A single, small, blue crystal dangles from the chain about halfway down. At the other end of the chain is a small fastening clip.

Det puts the box in the corner of one of the shoulder high shelves on the bookshelf and places some books next to it. Not to hide the box, but to keep it enough out of view that it does not draw attention. She then puts the keychain in her pocket, clipping the end of the chain to her belt, and walks out of the room.

EXOM

THE YOUNG KING

CHAPTER TWELVE

-------------------------- It Only Takes One --------------------------

Steel's shuttle, now fully repaired, retracts its side wings, having just landed on the rooftop hangar of the Citadel on Aymyn. Aura stands on the hangar, waiting eagerly for the main door to Steel's shuttle to open. She waits. The doors have not opened. She is curious to know who Steel has brought back with him. Her foot starts tapping on the ground, unable to hide her anticipation. She looks frustratedly at Steel's shuttle as if to say, "come on!". Finally, the door opens, sliding down creating a ramp. Aura smiles, this time with excitement as she steps forward towards the shuttle, eager to see Steel. A figure appears, but not the figure Aura is wanting. Senior Officer Borda steps onto the ramp and walks down off the shuttle, closely followed by Officer Linz. They notice Aura standing there and smile at her politely as they take their positions at either side of the shuttle ramp. Aura looks past them and peers into the shuttle as Borda and Linz glance up into the air. A second Eluudian shuttle approaches the hangar. Its side wings starting to retract as it prepares to land. Aura looks at the second shuttle with intrigue. It lands and takes no time to open its door. The door lowers down converting into a ramp and, though again not what she was expecting to see, a familiar figure strolls down the ramp and off the shuttle. Aura's eyes widen in excitement as she sees Dacos. Having spotted her immediately, he smiles and walks directly towards her. With such long legs, taking naturally large steps, he reaches her quickly. Without speaking he leans forward and hugs her. She hugs him back as he leans back, lifting her off the ground. Taken a little by surprise, Aura squeals slightly then laughs. Dacos places Aura back down on the ground and steps back to look at her, or more specifically, lets her look at him. Aura can't hold back her smile, such happiness at seeing Dacos again. *"Oh, it's so good to see you, Dacos"*, she says to him.

"And you, Your Highness", Dacos replies.

Aura gives Dacos a dubious look. *"Please"*, she says to him. *"Are you still calling me that?"*

Dacos looks behind Aura, at Steel, who has just walked off his shuttle while Aura was distracted with Dacos and is now walking towards her. *"I still call him that"*, Dacos says to Aura.

Aura's smile grows even wider, even happier to again see the man she loves. *"You kind of have to"*, Steel says to Dacos. *"I'm your king"*. Without slowing down, Steel casually puts his arm around Aura, swinging her around, though willingly, kisses her, then leads her back towards the building entrance. Dacos follows closely behind them as Borda and Linz stand guard outside Steel's shuttle.

Seeming more usual than not whenever Steel arrives on Aymyn, he is not there long before another Royal Council meeting is convened. Dacos is left to wonder the Citadel on his own, undertaking a very specific mission bestowed on him by Steel just before they left Eluud.

Aura and Steel take their seats at the Council Table. Already seated there is Regent Bassal, Monarch Dllm, Princess Illyana, King Yord, Regent Pfyne, Prince Niyan, Queen Klatanaria and Councillor Orcom. Councillor Lawn's chair sits vacant.

No one can remember the last time a Council meeting has ever gone smoothly. Always someone throwing a disgruntled argument, tragedy, or confusion into the itinerary. This particular meeting being no exception.

Regent Bassal, usually forever the calm one, sometimes sinisterly so, smirking and grinning at everyone else's chaos, even when he is the subject of their accusations, this time is the one that seems agitated and making a bit of noise. *"It is not exactly the Aymyn's strongest trait"*, Bassal states to the councillors at the table.

"The council is not only made up of Aymyn", Steel says as he looks at Bassal curiously.

"And yet an acceptance of diversity is very much unrepresented", Bassal replies.

Monarch Dllm, definitely no Aymyn, stares at Bassal. He then looks at the likes of King Yord, a dwarven species, and Princess Illyana, a Troin, and is confused by Bassal's accusation. *"I would not agree with that"*, Dllm says, his voice sounding like he has two voice boxes speaking at once. He looks across the table at Queen Aura who is sitting there quietly. It is Aura who should be most offended by Bassal's words. She has worked very hard, and against great resistance, to bring about greater diversity on the council. Many, like Dllm look over at Aura, waiting for her to respond to Bassal's words. Instead, she sits there not reacting at all or saying a word, as she wonders about the intention behind Bassal's statement and if by responding will she simply be aiding his agenda.

"I think that this council, under Queen Aura, is very accepting of difference", Dllm states, frustrated that Aura is not speaking up, so deciding to speak up for her.

"As do I", Princess Illyana states, looking at Bassal as she jumps in to also support Aura. *"I will point out that it was not so long ago that the Troin were also not accepted on this Council"*.

Dllm nods at Illyana, appreciative and acknowledging her support. *"Again, a change that we can thank Queen Aura for"*, he says.

"Not an easily accepted one", Illyana adds, knowing only too well how difficult that battle was for Aura given the history between the Aymyn and the Troin.

"But needed", Aura says as she puts her hands together, resting them on the table in front of her, as she smiles at Princess Illyana.

Illyana looks at Aura and smiles back. *"And you will forever have our respect and support"*, she says to her.

Aura nods humbly with gratitude at Illyana before addressing the entire table. *"Something that we should all have for each other"*, she says.

Bassal seems to be completely disregarding what Aura is saying, along also with everyone else's objection to his remark, and continues with his rant. *"And then there's the mighty Pizians"*, he adds. *"Uniters of us all. Their race has no hierarchy. They have no kingdom. Yet, they have a seat on this council"*.

Bassal is right about this. The Pizian do not exactly fit into the criteria required to be a member of the Royal Alliance. However, since it was the Pizians that made such an entity even possible, this is one exception that is made for them. Though probably needlessly so, as the Pizian's have never attended a single Royal Alliance Meeting and seem to have no interest in ever doing so.

"A seat they never occupy", Councillor Orcom says.

"Not even the council of seven is interested in what is discussed here", Queen Klatanaria adds. The Council of Seven, the Pizian's own High Council which consists of, as the name would suggest, seven members, all Pizian. One of them being The Watcher. The Council of Seven is only interested in scientific discovery, which is something that is hardly ever discussed at any Royal Alliance Meeting.

"Concessions are made for them, yet they still do not indulge us", Bassal vents to the council.

"The Pizian are the reason we can all be here", Aura finally states sternly to Bassal. *"Their veracity is not in question"*.

"It is not this council's place to issue demands or expectations upon the Pizian", Illyana steps in to say to support Aura.

All at the council table nod in agreement of what both Aura and Illyana are saying. All, that is, except for Bassal who seems to ignore everyone's response. *"Shirking us like they are more superior"*, he says huffily as he dismissively looks away from the table.

Aura continues to stare at Bassal, again not responding to his remark. Steel, who is seated between Aura and Bassal, turns to look at Bassal, a little shocked and taken back by his remark. *"They are"*, Steel says to Bassal. *"In many ways"*. Bassal hears Steel's words but does not respond. Instead, he just shakes his head in frustration. Steel remains looking at Bassal. His confusion growing. He has never seen the Regent speak out in this way, wondering what it is that has riled him.

"Something's worked you up", Steel says to him with a hint of a smile, but more feeling a little concerned. Steel then thinks again. Bassal is a very intelligent man, and perhaps he is not actually speaking out of frustration. He may be speaking out on this for another reason. Perhaps to direct the conversation, redirect it from something else, or just to spur people into thinking about something in particular. *"Or is there a reason behind this discussion?"*, Steel asks him.

Bassal's expression changes. Looking less frustrated now, he looks back at Steel as though he knows that Steel is working him out. *"No reason. An observation"*, Bassal replies.

Steel looks at Bassal with intrigue. Still at least semi convinced that he was working towards something, but what? And now to just stop and not pursue the conversation? Bassal should know better than to think that will stop people thinking about what he was saying. Perhaps that is his intention. It has certainly got Steel thinking. What has Bassal observed about the Pizians that is making him bring their attention to the Council? Knowing that Bassal is an expert at not divulging anything he does not wish to, if he has not told them yet then there is every chance that he won't. Instead, perhaps just leaving everyone to think about it. Steel looks around at the other councillors, all still looking at Bassal. The difference is that their expressions do not appear to be filled with much curiosity, but rather an angry distrust. Perhaps Steel is the only one thinking about what Bassal was saying, or not saying, and everyone else is caught up in their suspicions about Bassal. For at least one councillor that is particularly true.

"We could all be equally curious about you, Bassal", King Yord says. A strong tone of cynicism in his voice.

Bassal looks at King Yord, his stare showing a glimpse of annoyance. *"I thought we had all moved beyond rumours"*, Bassal says to him.

"Not all of us", Yord replies glaring defiantly at Bassal.

Steel looks back and forth between Yord and Bassal. Yord's distrust of Bassal is obvious. However, Bassal's annoyance has Steel intrigued. It can't be the continual accusations about him being a Sharlon Spy that has him annoyed. Surely, he is very used to this by now. Perhaps it is that no one else has stopped to think about what he was saying earlier?

Not finding any of the conversations that the council are currently having to be constructive, Aura decides that she needs to regain control. *"Rumours aside. Let's deal with what we know"*, she says as she looks at all the councillors seated around the table.

"Or what we don't know", Steel jumps in and adds as he turns around and looks at Aura.

Aura is completely taken by surprise with Steel's comment and change of direction. *"King Steel?"*, she says to him curiously and more noticeably formally.

Steel pauses in silence for a moment as he wonders; has Aura just called him by his full title to be proper in this council setting - or is he in trouble for interjecting? He looks at her curiously for a moment, then decides to continue anyway and explain himself. *"Which for me, I'll agree is a lot"*, he goes on to say. *"But what I would like to point out, and I can't be the only one who thinks about this, despite the constant attacks, espionage, and our own spies, we are no closer to discovering who the actual identity is of this woman they call Dark. All that we know is that her people refer to her as "Sovereign""*.

Steel is correct. He is not the only one who thinks about this. It is thought about by many people, not just in the council but even all throughout Exom. They know very little about the leader of the Sharlon other than what people call her, "Sovereign", or by her name "Dark", which may not even be her name. It may be a reference to her Sign - which, if it is the case, would itself be a very scary thought for a lot of people. Particularly the traditional Aymyn.

"They may call her Dark, but how do we know she really is", Queen Klatanaria says. *"She may be something less"*.

"Or something more", Bassal adds, his familiar ominous stare once again returning as if he knows something no one else does.

Something more than a Pure Dark Sign? The only thing "more" than Pure Light or Dark Signs is someone of the Lightning Sign. A seer. There has not been one of those, none that anyone has ever known about anyway, in all of Exom for many millennia.

"There has not been anything more for thousands of years", Orcom says. *"Not since Theorone"*.

Bassal nods as he turns and looks at Orcom and then at the rest of the council. *"Theorone himself predicted that there would be one that would come that was the same as him"*, he says. *"And that they would bring about great change"*.

"I believe that was Great Destruction", Klatanaria interjects.

"You can believe that if you want", Bassal turns and says to her. *"I believe the Church of Light redefined his wording to "Destruction". We all know they don't like change"*.

"The Aymyn see Change and Destruction to be the same thing", Princess Illyana says, very familiar with this fact from her own planet's history. Aura turns and looks at Illyana confused. Not confused about what she is saying but confused as to why she is supporting Bassal. Illyana looks back at Aura, noticing her stare, and shrugs as if to say, *"well, it's true"*.

Bassal could very well be right. Since the Church of Light opposes change and considers it dangerous to their ways, it is very likely that they did in fact, over time, alter the wording of Theorone's messages to one that would better suit their philosophy.

Bassal looks at Aura. Being the Guardian of the Church of Light, he is expecting some kind of argument or reaction from her. He does not get one. Aura may have been tasked with the position to protect the ways of the Light, but that doesn't mean that she must completely ignore things that she knows herself to be true, or suspects. Instead, she finds herself looking back at Bassal and nods, very slightly, almost validating his comment, then looks away.

With this validation, Bassal continues. *"It could be equally interpreted that someone of the Lightning Sign will save all Exom. Perhaps from the Skurj"*.

"Not exactly something we can wait around for", Aura says, now finding something that she can speak up against to Bassal.

Bassal continues to stare at Aura. *"But isn't that what we are doing?"*, he says to her, again a slight knowing grin takes shape on one side of his face.

"Dark's actions do not appear to be those of any saviour of Exom", Steel says, breaking the tension between Aura and Bassal as they both

turn and look at him. *"Her actions are destructive. Leaving planets and entire systems unaware and unprepared of impending attacks. Interfering with support and evacuation attempts. If she is something more than a Dark Sign, then changing Theorone's wording from Change to Destruction may be more accurate"*.

Bassal is just about to speak, but Orcom speaks up before he has a chance to. *"Who and whatever she is, by all accounts she seems very powerful and has a very big following"*, Orcom says.

"There is talk that she may even be royalty", Yord adds casually. His words being news to Steel. Steel looks around the council table. Judging by the lack of reactions from the others it appears that Steel is the only one there that had not heard of this theory. The notion actually alarms him, and he looks over at Aura. *"If that's so, then it's not improbable that one of us knows her"*, Steel says.

Bassal's expression does not change. Still that hint of a smirk like he knows something. But now he is looking at Steel and seeming quite impressed with Steel's reasoning. *"Or maybe - even is her"*, Bassal says. Bassal then immediately moves his gaze from Steel and over to Aura. Aura looks curiously back at him as everyone on the council starts looking at all the Female Aymyn council members, including the female Aymyn Council Members themselves.

Feeling a little uncomfortable, as well as sensing the discomfort of others at the table as well, Aura again speaks up as she tries to regain control of the conversation. *"I am not so convinced that uncovering Dark's identity should be on top of our list of priorities"*. Steel turns and looks at Aura with a strong confused expression. How can this not be a priority he thinks to himself. The thoughts showing through his expression as Aura looks back at him. *"We are not even certain that she is the one in charge"*, Aura adds.

"She most definitely appears to be", Orcom says. A sentiment shared by everyone else at the council table. Something that makes Steel even more confused as he looks at Aura. Dark's leadership of the Sharlon was something no one had ever questioned. Not even by Aura with all the conversations that Steel has had with her. It seems very

strange for Aura to now say "We" are not certain. As far as Steel and the other councillors are concerned, "We" are pretty certain.

"No one has ever mentioned anyone else", Queen Klatanaria says.

"What about the other one?", Dllm speaks up and asks. *"The Lieutenant. The one they call Sabel"*.

While Dark's identity and history is a mystery, Sabel's is not.

"More is known about her", King Yord answers. *"A renegade assassin from the Lorina Guild"*.

"Quite a lethal piece of work", Prince Niyan adds. Something else that is well known.

"She seems to hold a lot of power and influence", Illyana says.

"As you would expect for Dark's right hand", Dllm replies.

Aura and Steel still find themselves staring at each other. Steel's confused expression not wavering. Aura looks away, feeling like she needs to explain herself, and her previous remark, so that she can close this topic and move on. *"Granted. But Both Sabel and even Dark could be just a mouthpiece for someone higher"*, Aura says to the councillors at the table. *"The Sharlon have infiltrated us, the alliance, the community, maybe even this council"*. And on those words, most of the council, with the distinct and deliberate exception of both Steel and Aura, instantly look at Bassal. Bassal feels their stares but does not react or stare back, instead keeping his attention focussed on Aura. *"We have less than a handful of Sharlon operatives which we are aware of and keeping under surveillance"*, Aura continues. *"The rest we have no idea of. Putting our efforts into uncovering the identity of one particular individual seems superfluous"*.

The council sit quietly and finally Aura feels like she has put this topic to bed. However, after mulling over Aura's words, Steel speaks up. *"I disagree"*, he says. With a combination of frustration, and also feeling a little insulted, Aura gives Steel an unfriendly look. As Steel looks back at Aura, he knows that he is in trouble with her, but feels compelled to continue. *"It could mean cutting the head off this beast"*, he adds.

"We have no evidence to say that she is the head of this beast", Aura says quite assertively.

"We have no evidence to say that she's not", Steel replies equally assertively. *"And all indications…"*.

"Are only indications", Aura interjects.

Steel and Aura stare uncomfortably at each other as neither of them continues to speak. The rest of the council are also not used to seeing Steel and Aura quarrel or take a contradictory view, at least publicly, and also sit there uncomfortably and not sure what to say. The only one seeming unaffected by the awkwardness is Regent Bassal, who seems more intrigued by the conversation and as though he is waiting for it to continue. Aware now that it is not going to, Bassal himself decides to break the awkward silence that this event has caused, by changing the topic completely.

"Instead of us quarrelling over what is and what isn't", Bassal says, *"I believe we had tabled for discussion the issue of extending the Zazar protectorate influence"*.

Aura and Steel take a moment to continue staring at each other, then both turn their attention to Bassal, feeling relieved to be pulled away. The topic of extending the Zazar Protectorate Influence was one that Steel himself had tabled. *"Yes, thank you, Regent"*, Steel says. Steel sits forward in his chair, leaning his arms on the table as he addresses the council. *"I can't be the only one here who believes that there should be some kind of extension to allow for fewer unprotected planets"*, Steel states to the Council. *"This one Zazar, one planet leaves too many without protection"*.

This is something that many have thought about before. Particularly those on unprotected planets.

"King Steel, what is it that you suggest?", Bassal asks with intrigue and an unusual appearance of openness. *"This law was put into place by consensus due to resources within the Corp"*.

"A single Zazar needs to be able to defend, at least mostly, their protectorate on their own if need be", Niyan says to Steel as though it may be something that Steel was unaware of. *"They have the backing of the entire Zazar Corp but in an all-out mass war scenario each Zazar may need to fight as an individual without any backing from the Corp"*.

However, Steel is very aware of this fact. The "One Zazar – One Planet" law was established to safeguard the protected planets in the event of an All-Out War. This meaning the Skurj attacking every planet at once. In such an event it would be necessary for all individual Zazars to be able to independently defend their protectorate. In such an event a single Zazar would not be able to protect multiple planets at once, so any change to the law would make the Zazar Protectorate Principle meaningless. However, there is another fact regarding this that has failed to be addressed.

"We have never had an all-out mass war scenario – ever", Steel states. *"The Skurj just pick us off. Planet by planet"*.

"This is true", Niyan agrees. *"However...."*, he adds as he also leans forward, his arms resting on the table, matching Steel's pose. *"Once they attack, they don't stop. On a protected planet the Zazars may defeat them. But they will be back. They always come back. The Zazar's kill a few. More come and take their place later. We may not have an all-out war scenario yet. But it's coming"*.

Bassal sits back in his chair and grins reproachfully. *"And until then we just sit and wait for it"*. Aura glares at Bassal, knowing that his remark is aimed at her. *"You may despise what the Sharlon is doing"*, Bassal adds. *"But they are doing something. And while they are, and you aren't, you will never defeat them"*. Aura continues to glare at Bassal, now seeing the pride he feels in his words, and it starts to worry her. He sits smugly in his chair, staring back at her, confidently, arrogantly. An intimidating smirk now matching his piercing stare.

Hardly anyone else notices the interaction between Aura and Bassal. *"There are many Skurj battles taking place on many planets as we speak"*, Dllm says as he too leans forward, resting his arms on the council table. His long grey skinned hands and fingers moving in to clasp and overlap each other as they rest against the surface of the tabletop.

"I know that only too well", Steel says. *"Some are very close to my own planet. It's common knowledge that the outer rim planets are the most vulnerable and will be the first to be attacked. Yet we have Zazars*

undeployed, doing nothing, waiting for a battle on a planet that may or may not ever happen".

Regent Pfyne, who until this moment has remained completely silent and just listening to everyone on the Council, looks up at Steel. Feeling that she is about to say something, just this simple movement of turning her full and undivided attention towards Steel is enough to make everyone look at her, waiting to hear her speak. *"I think we all agree that it will happen"*, she says. *"It is only a matter of time".*

Steel looks at Pfyne, wanting to say more, but also not wanting to interrupt her, even though she appears to have finished speaking. The words building up in his head as he sits there, looking at her and biting his lip. An unlikely ally to Steel's argument actually comes in the form of Regent Bassal. *"Even here on Aymyn, a planet in the mid system, could not be any further away from the Skurj War, yet has its own Zazar"*, Bassal says.

Steel is surprised to hear Bassal speaking out in support, but tries his best not to look surprised, or even look at Bassal. He fails at both. However, he turns his attention back to the entire council to continue. *"I understand that the Zazar law is put in place to safeguard a worst-case scenario. I do"*, Steel says. *"But until such a scenario becomes actuality, we have an opportunity to do something....."*, Steel hesitates to finish his sentence. *"Else"*, he finally says.

Bassal smiles at Steel. *"You were going to say "different", weren't you?"*, Bassal asks Steel, knowing and not requiring an answer. Steel looks back at Bassal, innocently, as though he has been found out, but now doesn't care. In Steel's mind, what he is asking for is for the Zazar Laws to be made flexible. A concept very unfamiliar to the Royal Alliance Council.

"Our laws have always been black and white", Niyan says to Steel, out loud as if making a council-wide statement.

"Black and White", Bassal replies, looking over at Niyan. *"And by that we really only mean white, don't we?".*

Niyan looks back at Bassal silently, not sure what he means or how to respond. Aura knows exactly what Bassal is referring to. The undeniable Light influence on the Council and that being the reason their laws are never changed or made flexible. However, Aura wants to believe that it is not just a Light influence that has made things this way, but also, hopefully more so, an intellectual and wise investigation into where to draw boundaries by those that made them. *"We understand that real life contains many grey areas that our laws do not seem to account for"*, Aura says. *"But if we were to be flexible within these grey areas, then when and how would we know where to draw the line when it is needed and was originally set there for in the first place?"*

Steel hears Aura's words, and understands what she is saying, but still believes her thoughts are heavily influenced. *"Spoken like a true Light"*, he says. His words unintentionally cutting and hurting Aura as she looks at him appearing both confused and annoyed. *"How about Common Sense?"*, Steel adds.

"An antiquated ideal", Bassal replies.

Aura is still firmly focused on Steel. So focused that she forgets that there is anyone else in the room. *"It is not about Light"*, she snaps back at him. *"I was appointed as head of this council, and with that position comes the responsibility of upholding and supporting our laws. Whether I agree with them or not"*. Her look starts to soften, become saddened as she hopes that Steel can grab onto that last sentence – "whether she agrees with them or not". *"Even as this council's head"*, Aura continues, *"my personal opinion has no more weight than any other member here. It is frustrating, as I see so many valid arguments for change"*. A tear escapes her eye and runs down her cheek. Steel notices it, along with the hurt on Aura's face and feels his heart sink into his stomach as his expression changes into one of sadness and shock. *"Would your "True Light" speak of the validity of change?"*, Aura asks him, a real upset anger in her voice.

Steel really begins to regret his words and wishes he could go back and swallow them. She is sitting here, as the Queen of Aymyn, and Guardian of the Church of Light, while talking about agreeing with the soundness in reason to change. His expression softens greatly, becoming remorseful and apologetic. He has so very unfairly and publicly judged her.

Aura takes a breath as her focus starts to widen and she awakes again to the fact that she is still sitting with more than just Steel in the room. *"But any change needs to be done by process"*, she says as she wipes away her tear and composes herself once more, as she addresses the rest of the council, and not just Steel. *"A process that took a very long time to refine. As Prince Niyan stated, our laws are black and white, and none of them that the decision on where to put the line came easy and without a lot of debate and even contention. If flexible, our laws would be open to persuasion and emotional attachment that would potentially undermine the very reason the laws were put there for in the first place. Our laws seem fixated, tough, and unemotional, perhaps even uncompassionate. But they are that way so that they are not compromised when the day comes for which those laws were created for"*.

These are not just words to Aura. This is what she strongly believes. Steel was absolutely right with the way he described Aura to Tespa back on Eluud. Yes, she is very nice and calm, but she is also so incredibly strong. Strong enough to hold the council together and, when needed, able to stand up to any and every member in it - even Steel if she has to.

"You think you are asking for things to be flexible", she says as she turns back to look directly at Steel. *"You're not. You're asking for things to bend. Being flexible means that they can flex back when they need to. There is no flexing back from what you are proposing. If a Zazar is the protector of multiple planets, and they all require protecting at the same time, which one do they choose? Their decision will mean that the other planets, their other protectorates, are unprotected. A complete contradiction to having a planet be protected. The Protectorate Code would mean nothing. The safety and security that comes from being a protected planet would cease to exist. You think that what you are suggesting will result in there being more protected planets. It will result in none of the protected planets being truly protected"*.

Steel looks down. Not only feeling like he has been put back in his place, but now also feeling defeated. He finds himself only able to say one last thing, *"Then we need more Zazars"*.

There is not a single person in Exom who would disagree with that statement. *"No one will argue with you there"*, King Yord replies. *"But the Zazar test is most complicated"*.

"It needs to be", Prince Niyan adds.

"If it was easy, it would defeat its purpose", Councillor Orcom says.

"A test so difficult that only the Morn can complete", Dllm says. *"And not even many of them"*.

Queen Klatanaria thinks about that as she is sure that she has heard of other species passing the test. *"There have been non-morn Zazars"*, she says. The council looks at her confused as she thinks to herself, "maybe it was a rumour".

"Name one", King Yord says to her, challenging her statement. She can't. No one can. People only know of Morn passing the Zazar Test.

Bassal looks up, as though about to add to what everyone is saying, but really only looking at and addressing Queen Aura. *"If it were easy"*, he says to her, *"then every planet could put forward a champion to become a Zazar"*. Aura looks back at him, a little confused with what he is suggesting. Bassal looks over at Steel then back at Aura. Aura starts to feel herself sink into her chair as she realises what Bassal is suggesting. She feels the blood race from her face and her skin goes cold and pale. She shakes her head at Bassal. Bassal sits quietly just staring back at her.

"Many planets do. And fail", King Yord replies. A sad but true fact. People from a lot of different planets have attempted the Zazar test. None other than the Morn succeeding as far as anyone knows.

"Most planets are occupied by Aymyn", Niyan says. *"The test is nothing but suicide to them. The feebler species would stand no chance. Even those species more physically superior to Aymyn have not been able to make it through the gauntlet"*.

"The Gauntlet is designed to kill", Dllm comments. *"A test that could kill even Zazars"*.

"They'd encounter no less from the Skurj", Niyan replies. *"To defeat the Skurj the Zazars need to be better than the Skurj. Death defying"*.

"Our Zazars are not death defying", Pfyne stepping in to say. Again, her words make everyone else go quiet as they turn and give her their entire attention. *"As we have all sadly experienced"*, she adds as she looks back down remorsefully.

"Maybe the test can be made easier", Bassal says, still looking at Aura. Aura continues to stare back at Bassal and still just shakes her head.

"The Zazar test will never be simplified", Niyan says defiantly. *"It can't be. It would negate the reason for a test and undermine the Zazar Corp. A Zazar needs to be a Zazar, and all that the position comprises. The mightiest of them all, able to fight and defeat, single-handedly if required, the Skurj"*.

"The Zazar test is not of Council design", Aura says still staring at Bassal then turns and looks at Niyan then the rest of the council. *"It was designed by the Pizian for the reason that Prince Niyan has already mentioned. The Pizian's have known the Skurj for much longer than we have. No one on this council is anywhere near qualified to suggest an altering or easing of the test. If anyone, perhaps the Zazars themselves. But I have spoken to Zargah, and he has never once voiced an opinion that the test should be eased"*.

"Zargah has an opinion", Steel retorts jokingly, a smile forming on his face as he looks back at Aura.

"He has an opinion about you", Aura hits back.

Illyana smiles at Steel affectionately. *"You took the hand of his princess, King Steel"*.

"You mean his Queen", Steel tries to correct her.

"She was his princess long before she became his Queen", Illyana replies. Steel looks away and nods.

Not paying any attention to the conversation between Steel, Aura and Illyana, King Yord places his hands firmly on the Council Table. *"Let me tell you"*, he says. *"We either find a way to grow our Zazar numbers or the demise of Exom is inevitable"*.

EXOM - THE YOUNG KING

"Well, let me tell you", Prince Niyan replies. *"The current process is all, and the best, we have"*.

"Well, let me tell you!", Steel jumps in, not wanting to miss out on being part of this conversation. Then pauses as he realizes his jumping in was purely impulsive and he actually has nothing to add. *"Nah, I got nothing. Sorry"*, he says.

Aura looks back at Bassal and notices that he has not stopped staring at her this whole time. She stares back, this time not giving him any reaction at all. Being in the middle, between them, Steel now notices them staring at each other. Out of the corner of his eye, Bassal notices Steel looking at them, so now makes it more obvious that he is speaking to Aura directly. *"It's a test"*, Bassal says to her. *"A difficult one, yes, but still just a test. And one that has obviously not been designed to be completely failed or we wouldn't have any Zazars at all"*. Again, Aura's head starts to shake as she glares back at Bassal. *"It's not designed to fail"*, Bassal continues. *"It is designed to find those that are worthy. Even just statistically there must be worthy people on every planet. At least one"*. Aura's head continues to shake, her glare undeniably willing Bassal to shut up. Steel notices Aura's glare and looks confused. He turns and looks at Bassal, trying to work out what is going on. Bassal continues to stare directly at Aura and, defying her glare, does not shut up. *"Every planet, especially an unprotected one, must have someone who is not only strong and skilled, because it's more than just being strong and skilled, isn't it? One who is determined. Who will not give up. Who can't give up"*. Bassal slowly moves his gaze from Aura and onto Steel. *"It would only take one"*, Bassal says to him.

Steel looks at Bassal, a little confused, still trying to work out where he is going. Slowly his words start to line up and make sense. Steel continues to look at Bassal with intrigue. *"Once one passes the test"*, Bassal says to him, *"they could nominate their own planet as their protectorate, and they would have the backing of the entire Zazar Corp"*. Steels expression starts to change as he thinks about what Bassal is saying. Suggesting. He doesn't notice Aura staring at him, knowing what he is now thinking about, and filled with concern. Beyond concern. Actually, filling up with panic, though trying not to show it.

Steel's eyes start to wonder the room as he sits there quietly, lost in his thoughts. *"You can't tell me that there is no one"*, Bassal continues to say, again getting Steel's full attention. *"Who is trained, committed, determined, passionately so, with their every fibre, who will not back down, who could pass the test"*. Steel's eyes begin to wonder again, again lost in his thoughts. *"No one?"*, Bassal again says to him, regaining Steel's full attention once more. *"Surely"*, Bassal then says to him, and encouraging smirk taking form on his face.

Unable to stay silent any longer, Aura finally speaks up. *"Regent Bassal"*, she says to Bassal sternly but trying to make it appear friendly. *"Do not put such ideas in King Steel's head. As you can see, he is likely to entertain them"*.

Some of the council also start to catch on to what Bassal is suggesting to Steel. King Yord smirks, thinking about how ridiculous it is, but still finding the way Steel is considering it very amusing. *"Feeling that fighting spirit are you, King Steel?"*, Yord says to Steel, a low grumble of a jolly laugh quietly in his voice.

Bassal, feels Aura's gaze on him. Though it looks friendly, he knows it is not. He smiles as he seems to relax his intensity and looks back at Aura as if to agree with her. However, he knows full well that his suggestion has already been received by Steel. *"No, you are right, Your Highness"*, Bassal says to her as he smiles back. *"It's a stupid idea. No Aymyn has even survived the Zazar test, never lone passed it"*.

Even while deep in thought, Steel hears Bassal's last statement. No Aymyn has even survived the Zazar test, never lone passed it. A fact that may very well be true and may very well remain true. However, Steel can only think of one response to that. Something that his family and the people of his planet have been saying since it was first colonized. *"I am not Aymyn"*, Steel says as he looks back at Bassal. *"I'm Eluudian"*.

Aura can no longer hold her friendly expression as she looks at Bassal. Her face now expressing fear, she looks at Steel, just as Bassal also turns and looks at Steel, smiles, and nods. *"Yes. That you are"*, Bassal replies.

------------------------------- Running? -------------------------------

The footpath that travels around Chassam Castle's Gardens is a popular walking track for Eluudians who enjoy a pleasant stroll, especially during the time of day when there is plenty of sunlight. The path is wide enough for many to walk along, side-by-side, or even roomy enough to share it with those wanting to use it for a casual run, which is what Tespa is doing right now. For once she is not wearing her backpack that carries Kako. A rare occasion, but probably a good thing as the bouncing around would have done very little for his wellbeing.

A father holding the hands of his two small children walks up to the footpath about to cross her path. Tespa stops jogging any further along the path, and instead jogs on the spot and lets them cross the path. She smiles at them and waves at the children as they pass. The father and both children smile back at her. One child turns around and waves back at her. This makes Tespa smile even more, and as she jogs on the spot, she turns around to watch them walk away and waves even more enthusiastically back at the child. As soon as they are clear she takes off again and jogs even faster down the path.

As she passes a large hedge, someone's arm reaches out, grabbing her, and pulls her into the hedge. Taken completely by surprise, her face fills with fear and she instinctively readies herself to scream. A second hand reaches out and covers her mouth, then both hands, working together, pull her through the hedge.

The hedge is not very wide or dense, so luckily it does not hurt her as she is pulled through it to the other side. She struggles, managing to break free from whoever has grabbed her. She continues to struggle, trying to turn around to face her abductor as the strangers' arms and hands continue to try and grab and cover her mouth. She thrusts her body back, pushing them backwards and off her, then as she spins around, she reaches down, pulling her ronad out of her leg sheath and quickly activates it. She grips it with both hands, swinging it back ready to thrust it into whoever has grabbed her. The strangers' hands still waving around in front of her face, the stranger lowers his arms and stands still. It's her uncle Orlow. Tespa looks even more startled and confused. She lowers her ronad as Orlow looks at her, while also looking all around as though he is fleeing from someone. He puts his hand back over her mouth. Tespa now lets him, as she looks at Orlow concerned, now no longer feeling frightened by him, but wondering what he is hiding from that is so bad that he has had to also rescue her and pull her through the hedge. Orlow looks at Tespa again. His look appears to be more concerned for her than himself. He slowly removes his hand from her mouth, puts his cheek up against hers, as if to have the same perspective and vision of whatever she is looking at, and continues to look around as if scouting for danger. *"What's wrong? What's happening?"*, he asks her, concern and panic in his voice.

Tespa, now even more confused by her uncle's words and actions, is not sure where to look. Her face pressed up tightly against his, she has no idea what he is talking about. She tries to look sideways at him. *"What? Why?"*, she asks him. She also starts to look around, feeling concerned, as though something is going on that she is unaware of. It wouldn't be the first time.

Orlow, realising Tespa's confusion with him, makes him equally confused about her and what is going on. He pulls his face away from hers, but still holding onto her, he stares into her eyes with a very questioning look. *"What were you doing?"*, he asks her.

Confusion continues to mount in both of them as they both stop looking around and just stare at each other, wondering if each other is alright. *"When? Just now? Just running"*, Tespa replies.

Orlow does not let go of her. It was as he thought. He knew she was running. What he didn't know was – running from what? He resumes glancing around again before looking back at her bizarrely. *"Why?"*, he asks her.

Tespa stops looking concerned, now realising that there is nothing wrong or anything to be worried about. Trying not to laugh, instead showing her amusement through a smile, she looks back at her uncle and puts her hand gently on his arm. *"Fun"*, she replies calmly, a true look of care in her eyes as she looks into his.

Orlow starts to calm down as his expression now turns into one of extreme confusion. What she is saying does not make sense. Who runs for fun? He is not sure he has heard her correctly or has perhaps just not understood completely. *"Fun?"*, he repeats back questioningly. *"There's nothing chasing you?"*, he asks.

"No", Tespa replies with a smile and shakes her head, still amused at her uncle's innocent confusion.

Orlow lets go of Tespa and shrugs. He guesses he has heard her correctly, and though accepting it, finds it all a little bit.... *"Strange"*, he says to her. He then turns and walks away casually, not thinking any more of it or what he has just done. Tespa watches him walk off, thinking to herself that was a very "interesting" moment.

Vessel, who herself was just walking casually in the garden on that side of the hedge, and having seen the whole thing, continues to nonchalantly walk past Tespa. *"He's your uncle"*, Vessel comments to her and continues to stroll off. Tespa stops watching her uncle, shakes off the strange experience, looks over to Vessel and runs to catch up with her.

---------------------------- I Don't Get That ----------------------------

Walking through the corridors of the Citadel of Light, Dacos is trying his hardest to not look conspicuous. However, with his height combined with the fact that he does not seem to be going anywhere in particular, instead stopping outside doorways and listening in on people's conversations, blending in and avoiding standing out he is not.

The door at the end of the corridor, leading to the Council chambers, opens. Dacos quickly moves away from another random doorway that he happens to be standing next to and trying to listen through. He watches as Regent Bassal walks out through the open council doors. As the door closes behind the regent, Bassal looks up the corridor at Dacos, who is now awkwardly just standing there, not sure where to look. Dacos starts faking a cough as he looks around, looking even more guilty, and pretending not to see Bassal. Bassal walks up to him, appearing very friendly but in reality, very curious. *"Lost something, General?"*, Bassal asks him.

C.C.DAVISON

Dacos pretends to only have just noticed Bassal and struggles to find his words. *"Oh! No. Yes, yes, um. No, not really. Um, sort of. My um"*, Dacos says as he puts his hand in his pocket and pulls it out again, empty, and looks at it. *"Oh, there it is"*, Dacos remarks then quickly puts his empty hand back into his pocket and smiles at Bassal.

Bassal just looks at him strangely and nods reassuringly. *"Good save"*, he says to Dacos, a slight smirk starting to appear on Bassal's face as he struggles to conceal his amusement. He is not sure what Dacos is doing there. However, at the same time, does not want to put much time and effort into finding out when he doesn't need to and has other things to do. *"I'll leave you to it"*, Bassal says to Dacos. *"Whatever that is"*.

Bassal starts to walk off when Dacos runs up and walks with him. *"You've been around for a while"*, Dacos says to him, somewhat innocently, but very strange opening words. Bassal wonders to himself, is Dacos referring to his age, or to his time on Aymyn with the Council? *"Around?"*, he asks Dacos, not stopping his walk down the corridor, nor showing any discomfort with Dacos walking with him.

"The Citadel. The Council", Dacos replies. *"You know - around"*.

Now that Bassal knows what Dacos means by "around", the next question is, how long does he define as "a while". He has been there longer than King Steel has, so can assume that if Dacos is using that as any kind of benchmark then yes, he has been "around for a while". *"Yes, I guess so"*, he replies.

Without pausing to think of how to word it, Dacos just comes straight out with another seemingly nonsensical statement, *"You have no doubt seen things"*.

Bassal thinks to himself, he has seen many things, was there something in particular that Dacos was referring to? *"Seen things?"*, he asks, again continuing his pace down the corridor.

"You know. Things", Dacos replies.

"Things?", Bassal again repeats.

"Like out of place things", Dacos clarifies. *"People doing strange things"*.

Strange things? So far today the strangest thing Bassal has seen is Dacos. *"Like someone hanging around in corridors, looking for air in their pockets?"*, Bassal asks him.

Dacos sighs. *"Yeah"*, he says looking down regretfully at the ground. *"Like that"*.

Bassal has not seen Dacos on Aymyn for quite some time and knows that Steel would not bring him here unless he had a reason, preferring to keep Dacos back on Eluud to keep an eye on his family and kingdom. From the moment Bassal saw Dacos standing suspiciously in the corridor, he has worked out what Dacos is really doing there and looking for. *"If you are looking for a spy, General, then I am probably the last person you want to be seeking advice from"*, Bassal says to him.

Dacos looks curiously and innocently at Bassal. *"Not really looking for a spy"*, Dacos replies. *"Well kind of, I guess so. But, why's that?"*, Dacos stops stuttering to ask.

Bassal smiles, almost letting out a silent laugh. *"Haven't you heard?"*, he says to Dacos. *"Many think that I am the spy here"*.

Dacos's look of innocence and curiosity now turns to confusion and almost shock. *"You?"*, he asks Bassal curiously. Bassal does not respond or react to Dacos's question. Instead, just keeps walking and allowing Dacos to walk along beside him. *"Strange. I don't get that"*, Dacos says. *"And I am not here often enough to know what people are saying"*.

Bassal seems a little taken that Dacos was not aware of this fact. But not just that, also, unlike everyone else it seems, Dacos sensing something different in him makes him smile. *"You don't get that?"*, he asks Dacos.

"No, I don't", Dacos replies. *"I am told I do miss a lot of obvious things. But I make up for it by not missing less obvious things"*.

This intrigues Bassal, making him now actually look up at Dacos for the first time since walking down the corridor together. *"Less obvious?"*, Bassal asks, hoping that Dacos picks up that he would like him to explain that statement.

Dacos doesn't. *"Yes"*, is all Dacos replies. Perhaps it was too obvious.

Bassal smiles again, looking away once more and straight ahead to where he is walking. *"So then, on a less obvious level, what do you make of me?"*, he asks Dacos.

Dacos looks at Bassal, briefly, as if to acknowledge that he is still aware that Bassal is there, and that he is talking to him, and not lost in his own thoughts. *"That's hard to say"*, Dacos replies. *"You seem as reserved, guarded, and secretive as is everyone else I have met from the council. Not any more so, though. I know more secretive and guarded people who are not even on the council".*

With no idea who Dacos is talking about, and no real interest in enquiring, Bassal attempts to sum up Dacos's conclusion about him. *"So, I'm not a spy then?"*, Bassal says to him.

"Well, if you are, then you are a very good one", Dacos replies.

Bassal is very pleased, if not a little amused with this assessment. *"A double-edged compliment"*, he says to Dacos. *"Perhaps you trust too easy".*

Bassal's words make Dacos stop in his tracks as he thinks to himself. No one has ever said that to him before. Innocent, perhaps. Oblivious, always. Trust easily, never. *"Now, that is not something that I have ever been accused of"*, he says out loud to himself.

Bassal continues walking off alone. By the time Dacos stops thinking about what Bassal has said, Bassal has already walked some distance away from him. Instead of following him, Dacos turns around, a little clumsily, and accidentally knocks the button beside another door. The door opens to reveal a young lady, standing side on, completely naked except for a long dress that she is casually clutching to her body as she looks into a full-length mirror. As he door opens, she seems completely unstartled, something very peculiar on its own, and casually looks at Dacos standing in the doorway. Dacos feels the embarrassment running through his body as he stares at her in shock. Immediately he makes himself look away and he fumbles to try and find the door button again. He taps around the wall, nowhere near it, not willing to look up. The young lady just stands there. Dress still casually held to her body. Dacos stops fumbling, takes a breath, then looks back at the young lady and smiles. The first thing he notices is her long black hair flowing over her back and far shoulder. Her eyes just staring at him. Her expression blank as though casually watching a stranger in the street. She does not move or react in anyway. He recognises that look and quickly realises who he is looking at. It is Queen Aura's handmaiden. He has seen her a number of times. Always with Aura but has never spoken to her. He is not even sure if she does speak.

Looking down Dacos can not help but notice the tattoos running down the side of her body. A kind of tribal design. All over her shoulder, down her arm, forearm, side and thigh. At least on the side that is exposed to him. Dacos looks away again, this time looking at the door button on the wall and presses it. The door closes again and Dacos sighs a breath of relief. He turns back around and again, almost clumsily walks straight into another female Aymyn citizen walking down the corridor. Startling her, she stops and looks at him wordlessly. Dacos feels apologetic and almost stumbles over his own height as he quickly tries to move out of her way. *"Ma'am"*, he says to her, and he lets her pass and continue on her way. He turns around again, this time being careful to not bump into anyone else as he does so. Success.

Standing further up the corridor, watching Dacos stumble around and just generally looking awkward, is Steel. He watches Dacos and laughs quietly to himself. He has never seen Dacos looking so awkward before. Always very comfortable and confident with his height. Dacos definitely seems more at home at - well - home than he does here on Aymyn. Perhaps thinking that Dacos can sneak around looking for anything out of place was too big an ask, especially considering Dacos is the one that looks out of place in this environment. Still, Steel is curious to know what Dacos has found out.

Dacos notices Steel standing there watching him and smiles, relieved to see a friendly face. Steel walks towards Dacos, then walks past him and motions for Dacos to walk with him. Dacos does. *"Anything?"*, Steel asks.

"No, I didn't see anything", Dacos replies, the image of Aura's handmaiden still being strong in his mind and subconsciously thinking that's what Steel is asking about. *"Tattoos"*, he adds. *"She has tattoos. Lots of tattoos. Right down her...."*, Dacos waves his hand down his

side. Steel looks up at him, very confused, wondering what he is talking about. Dacos looks back at Steel and quickly works out that he was not asking about Aura's handmaiden at all. *"Ah, right. Not what you meant"*, Dacos says. *"You meant...."*

"What I brought you here for", Steel interrupts.

"Yes. That", Dacos nods, a little relieved in the shift of topic. *"Well, I haven't been here very long"*, Dacos says. *"People have really boring conversations here"*.

Steel again laughs to himself. That was something he didn't know. He starts thinking about his own conversations that take place on in the Citadel. *"Most of my conversations take place in the Council Chambers where they are anything but boring"*, Steel tells Dacos. *"Well, sometimes they are. I have been known to drift off occasionally and not hear a word that has been said. I try not to do that too often. To my defence I have only ever fallen asleep once. Twice if you count that night after the ball, but I don't think we should count that. I did snore once though. Surprised a few on the council. Including me. I wasn't even asleep"*. Steel looks up and notices Dacos blankly staring back at him and realizes that he has distracted himself, again. Then remembers that he wants to hear what Dacos has found out. *"Anyway"*, he says to Dacos. *"I brought you here because of your uncanny ability of reading and seeing things and situations – that don't involve you and Det"*.

Dacos completely tunes out the last part of Steel's sentence and proceeds with his report. *"I was just speaking to that old Councillor before you got here"*, he says to Steel.

"Old Councillor". Steel knew exactly who Dacos was referring to. *"Probably shouldn't refer to him as that"*, he tells Dacos. *"Not to his face anyway, he might take offense. That would be Regent Bassal. Now, he is a spy"*.

So, calling someone "old" is offensive, but it is alright to call them a "spy", Dacos thinks to himself curiously. *"You are the second person to tell me that about him"*, Dacos tells Steel.

"Who was the first?", Steel asks.

"He was", Dacos replies.

Steel stops and takes a double take on this comment. *"What? He told you he was a spy?"*, he asks Dacos, a little blown away.

Dacos stops and looks back at Steel. *"No. He said that people think he is a spy"*, Dacos replies.

Steel shrugs at that clarity. *"And what do you think?"*, Steel asks.

Dacos reiterates exactly what he told Bassal. *"I don't get that"*, he tells Steel.

Steel looks suspiciously at Dacos. He thought, out of anyone, that Dacos would definitely have detected that about Bassal. *"Perhaps I should take back what I just said about your ability"*, Steel says to him and starts walking again down the corridor. Once again, Dacos speeds up to walk alongside him.

"I get the feeling that there are a lot of people here hiding many things", Dacos says to him. *"Are they spies? They could be, and really good at hiding it. Purely basing it on people who are hiding secrets, I probably wouldn't trust anyone on the council"*.

"I hope that doesn't include me", Steel asks.

"Not you, Your Highness", Dacos replies. *"I know all your secrets"*.

Steel gives Dacos a smirking sideways glance as Councillor Lawn walks around a corner in front of them. Both Steel and Dacos stop when they see him, which makes Councillor Lawn look more intensely curious at them both. Dacos immediately gets a bad feeling about Lawn. Both Lawn and Steel nod at each other, though both completely expressionless and without any sense of happiness to see each other. *"King Steel"*, Lawn says coldly.

"Councillor Lawn", Steel replies with an equally cold tone.

Councillor Lawn looks at Dacos and Dacos stares back at him. A strange feeling falls over Dacos that he can not quite put his finger on. Steel looks up at Dacos and notices Dacos's penetrating gaze at Councillor Lawn. *"This is my General. Dacos"*, Steel says to Lawn while still looking at Dacos. Councillor Lawn continues to look at Dacos and gives him a slight nod without taking his eyes off him. Dacos stands there just looking back at him and does not say a word. Steel looks back at Lawn, feeling the awkward exchange between Lawn and Dacos. *"We missed you at the last meeting"*, Steel says to Lawn.

Lawn looks back at Steel. *"Yes"*, he replies, still cold and expressionless.

Steel remains silent, staring back at Lawn, aware that he is not entitled to any explanation from Lawn, yet still waits to see if Lawn is going to say anything else. He doesn't. As Steel and Dacos both stand there uncomfortably looking at Councillor Lawn, Lawn seems to show no discomfort at all in this uncomfortable situation. *"Good chat"*, Steel says to Lawn, then looks up at Dacos. *"Come Dacos"*, he says to him. Steel guides Dacos around Councillor Lawn and they continue walking down the corridor. To anyone else leaving this way could be seen as rude. However, Steel knows that Councillor Lawn, being a Spectre, does not distinguish rudeness from any other behaviour. In fact, most people would consider a lot of the ways that Spectres behave to be quite rude. And, since Steel simply did not want to speak to Lawn anymore, just walking away seemed the most effective course of action.

Dacos is still left with a bad feeling about Councillor Lawn. *"Now him, I get a bad feeling about"*, Dacos says to Steel.

"He's a spectre", Steel tells him.

"Noticed that", Dacos replies. *"Still get a bad feeling"*.

Steel starts to wonder if Dacos means that he gets a feeling that Lawn could be a spy. *"Spectres make terrible spies"*, he tells Dacos. *"They are too direct. Arrogantly so. If you ask them what they are really up to, they are likely to tell you and think nothing of it"*.

Dacos was not getting the feeling that Lawn was a spy. He wasn't sure what he was sensing, only that he didn't like it. *"Still gives me a bad feeling"*, he says.

"You and me both", Steel says, knowing exactly what Dacos means. Steel places his hand on Dacos's back. *"Come, let's get you among the rest of the council members"*, Steel says to him as he guides him around the corridor corner.

------------------------- **Don't Mess with Sabel** -------------------------

Bajen has made his way to the Sharlon Hillside Base, alone. Inside the base, the holoprojector at the centre of Sabel's Table has created the floating pool of energy. Dark's live image can be clearly seen inside. Bajen stands next to Sabel, looking completely relaxed and not at all uncomfortable. An unusual sight for anyone standing within daggers reach of Sabel. *"This is not what we agreed, Bajen"*, Dark says to him, her voice calm but her words stating a frustration. *"You should not even be there"*.

Sabel's face and body are directly facing Dark's projection. However, her gaze is fixated sideways firmly on Bajen. Bajen notices her staring at him but brushes it off dismissively. *"Things change, my Sovereign"*, he says to Dark. *"You more than anyone know that"*.

Bajen's words have no effect on Dark. She doesn't so much as blink. She does not trust his motives for being there. She does not trust him. If anything, she trusts in the fact that Bajen is a deceptive character and believes that this is another one of his deceptions. *"And some things don't"*, Dark replies. Dark closes her eyes, then opens them again, looking directly at Sabel as though Bajen is not even there. *"Sabel"*, She says.

Sabel moves her gaze from Bajen to Dark, without moving her body or head. *"Yes, my sign"*, Sabel replies. Bajen looks over at the long table with the many object scattered on it. He stares at one in particular. An electronic tablet.

Dark continues to speak to Sabel as though Bajen is no longer there, giving her one final instruction. *"Please refrain from killing him inside the base"*, Dark tells her. *"I am sure that the clean-up must be starting to become bothersome"*.

Sabel smiles at Dark, both pleased and amused by her words. *"Yes, my Sign"*, she says. *"No more killing inside the base"*. Sabel turns and looks at Bajen. Bajen now starts to look a little uncomfortable. *"I'll take him outside and do it"*, Sabel says to Dark while staring directly at Bajen. Sabel's smile slowly changes into a more serious expression. One that fills Bajen with fear.

Outside the Sharlon Hillside Base, the shimmer of the invisible being can barely be seen moving along the face of the hillside and towards the large metal door. The door starts to open by itself. As it does, the Guardian, who is standing unseen in the shadows outside the base, steps out of the shadows. He looks to see who has opened the doors and is leaving the base. The invisible being also stops moving, blending in with the rocky walls of the base exterior.

Bajen is forced outside through the door, held in a very painful restraining hold by Sabel. Despite his efforts to resist, and though Bajen is a larger build than she is, Sabel seems to be holding and moving him around with considerable ease. Sabel throws Bajen towards the Guardian. The Guardian holds out his hand and steadies Bajen as Bajen bounces off him. The invisible shimmering being starts moving again, making its way towards the open door.

Straightening himself up and readjusting his shirt, Bajen looks at Sabel as she turns around to walk back inside. He starts running his hands down his chest and body, as though looking for something. He is, signs of injuries, lethal injuries, possibly with Sabel's daggers still sticking out of them. He stops when he finds none and is surprised to be alive. His look turns to one of confusion, surprised at why Sabel is walking away, and he is still standing. Perhaps he misunderstood Dark's words. Perhaps Dark meant that Sabel was not to kill him? Perhaps Sabel was only joking when she said that she would "take him outside to do it"? There are just too many perhaps's for Bajen to make any sense out of this. So, he stops and is just relieved to be alive. So, with that contentment, Bajen once again adopts his confident and cocky demeanour, now glaring at Sabel. *"It did not have to be this way"*, he yells out to her. Sabel ignores him and continues walking back towards the hideout entrance. *"I make a much better ally. Believe me, I am cheaper as a friend"*, Bajen adds.

Sabel stops and looks to her side as she thinks. Anticipating her thoughts, the Guardian steps back and readies his giant axe to strike Bajen. Hearing, feeling what the Guardian is doing behind him, Bajen starts to realize that he did not misunderstand Dark's words. Sabel has left his execution to the Guardian.

The invisible being silently sneaks past Sabel, making its way inside the base through the open door. Terrified, Bajen looks at the Guardian and pulls out a handle-shaped device from his coat pocket that instantly extends into a small sword. He holds the sword with both hands, swings it back as he readies himself to take on the Guardian. However, it was not the Guardian he should have feared. With a very brief glance over at him, and with an even quicker flick of her wrist, Sabel pulls out and throws a small dagger directly into Bajen's throat. Bajen drops his sword, stumbles back and falls to his knees clenching his throat with his hands. The Guardian watches him for a moment as Sabel, emotionless, continues walking into the hillside hideout. The giant door starts to close behind her. The Guardian draws back his giant axe ready to finish the job that Sabel has started. He swings it down as the sound of the giant entrance door closing masks the sound of the Guardians giant axe separating Bajen's head from his body.

Sable walks back into the large hall area of the hillside base and past the long table, still with various objects and electronic devices scattered on top of it. The invisible being moves along the wall behind her, blending in with its background and completely unnoticed by Sabel. Sabel stops and picks up one of the devices on the table. A kind of handheld tablet. She studies it closely, briefly, before putting it back down again. She then walks away from the table and out of the room.

The invisible being makes its way over to the table and starts moving different items around, seemingly looking for something in particular. Its hand, shimmering and blending in with the table as well as the objects on it, seems to be very large and almost clumsy due to its size. It finally comes to rest on one of the objects on the table. The same electronic tablet that Sabel had just examined and which Bajen had stared at earlier. The invisible being attempts to grab it. However, before it can do so, Sabel appears, almost out of nowhere, and stabs a large dagger through the invisible being's hand, pinning it to the table. Instantly the being's invisibility camouflage disappears revealing the being to be an Alrorgan, a large upright lizard-like creature with a large tail, long claws and long razor-sharp teeth. It throws its arm up, the table with its hand pinned to it by Sabel's dagger flying up with it, throwing everything into the air. As it quickly swoops its arm back down again. Sabel's dagger dislodges from the Alrorgan's hand and, along with everything that was on top of the table, comes crashing to the ground.

The Alrorgan turns to face Sabel and snarls viciously as it lunges towards her.

Sabel does not move, nor does she show any fear. Instead, she pulls out another couple of daggers, one in each hand, and very quickly slices the Alrorgan many times across the face, throat and torso as it lunges at her. The Alrorgan stops charging and slightly backs away in pain. However, Sabel does not retreat, and instead she now lunges at the Alrorgan, pushing it to the wall and launching her dagger up through its underjaw and into its head. Sabel's face, not even an inch away from the Alrorgan's long razor-sharp teeth, shows no emotion as she stares it in the eyes and watches it die.

She pulls her dagger out of the Alrorgan's head, stands back and lets the Alrorgan drop to the floor. As she stares at it, laying there dead and completely visible on the floor, a thought makes her turn her attention to the inactive holoprojector on the mezzanine overlooking the hall. She remembers her commitment to Dark not to kill anything else inside the hideout. A commitment she has just broken. She looks back again at the dead and bleeding Alrorgan on the ground and sighs. *"Dam"*, she exclaims to herself.

-------------------------------- **Bedtime** --------------------------------

Through the window of Det's bedroom, the night sky can be seen. The sun has set and even the long twilight has passed. Det sits on her bed, ready to lay down and go to sleep. She is wearing only an open, short, sleeveless white shirt that ends at her waist and nothing else. She twists and reaches over to grab the covers, ready to pull them back when she stops still, lets go of the covers, turns back and looks at her bedroom door. At that moment her door opens as Tespa lets herself in.

"I've just got to share this with you", Tespa says smiling excitedly. *"I have been thinking about this all day"*. Det stares at her and does not say anything. *"All these rules on the Aymyn Council"*, Tespa says.

"The Royal Council", Det corrects her.

"I don't know why I didn't think of this earlier", Tespa continues ignoring Det's correction. *"Well, what if...."*, Tespa starts to say, then

looks down and notices that Det is only wearing a short shirt. *"And you're not wearing any pants".*

Det just continues to sit there and stare at Tespa. *"I was about to go to bed"*, Det tells her.

"Then this can wait", Tespa replies and turns back towards the door. She quickly turns back to look at Det and stares down at her leg. Still strapped to Det's leg is her ronad. Tespa looks at it a little surprised. *" You sleep with that strapped to your leg"*, she says to Det. *"Wait, you sleep with it?"*, she then asks. Det does not respond and just sits there staring back at her. *" What, actually sleep with it?"*, Tespa asks again. Still Det does not reply. Tespa gives Det a big smile. *"Night Det"*, She says as she turns and walks out the room. Det sits there quietly and watches her leave.

EXOM

THE YOUNG KING

CHAPTER THIRTEEN

----------------------------- Training Hall -----------------------------

Back on Aymyn, standing in the middle of one of the many corridors within the Citadel of Light, Dacos is deep in conversation with Regent Pfyne. The hood of her cloak still pulled up over her head, she looks shyly up at Dacos whenever he speaks to her, or her to him. When neither are speaking Pfyne will often look away shyly again, choosing to look down at the ground instead. Ironically, so does Dacos. Both seeming socially awkward in each other's presence as the other.

Very polite and quietly spoken, Pfyne in no way tries to evade or avoid Dacos's questions. Questions that Dacos is still struggling to find the right words with which to ask. They both stop talking again and once again return their attention to the ground. Pfyne looks up at Dacos, his gaze still looking away. She smiles, but tries to conceal it, then stops trying and lets it shine through as a kind of flirtatious confidence fills her. Dacos looks back at her and they lock eyes. Dacos looks at her with intrigue, wondering what she is thinking. If only he knew. She sweeps her hand back along her face, pulling back her hood slightly and letting her long brown hair flow along her hand as she moves her hand through it. *"I hope you find what you are looking for, General"*, she says to him.

Dacos pretends to look confused. *"What makes you think I am looking for anything?"*, he asks her. Pfyne smiles again. Her smile innocent but seems to piercingly see straight through him. Dacos, blushes, no longer able to pretend. *"Am I that obvious?"*, he then asks.

Pfyne holds her smile. *"You stand out"*, she replies. *"In a nice way"*. She looks away again, bashfully, embarrassed by her words. *"A good way"*, she says to correct herself. She peers back up at Dacos. *"In a good way"*, she tells him. Taking a moment to watch him awkwardly and randomly look around the corridor, she smiles again. *"If you have any more questions?"*, she says to him.

Dacos looks back at her, smiles and shakes his head. *"No. I don't really go on questions"*, he tells her. *"Mine is more a feeling. And you feel alright"*. Once again Regent Pfyne looks away bashfully, not sure where to look, but smiling at Dacos's comment. Quickly realising that his comment has made the conversation awkward, Dacos says, *"For a councillor"*, adding for clarification. Regent Pfyne gives a sideways glance up at Dacos, amused at his clarification. *"I mean, you're younger than all the other councillors"*, Dacos then says, feeling that he still needs to explain himself. Regent Pfyne's amusement, along with her smile, starts to grow. *"Not that age should make a difference"*, he tries to explain, feeling himself digging himself into a hole. *"I am sure you're old on the inside"*, he adds, then immediately thinks to himself, *"Oh boy, that didn't come out right"*. He shakes his head and says, *"No, that sounded even worse coming out"*, as Pfyne can no longer hold back her amused smile at Dacos's words. *"What I am trying to say is, that I am sure under all this"*, he starts to explain as he points to her long dark red cloak, *"You look just as old as everyone else"*. Regent Pfyne tries to hold back her laugh, but a small snigger escapes, as she covers her mouth trying to hide it. She gives Dacos an obviously fake disappointing stare. Dacos feels himself shrink inside himself as he realises he has not said anything that he was trying to say. *"I am just going to stop now"*, he says as he turns and looks away, peering sideways to look back at her again.

"That sounds very wise", Pfyne replies still smiling with amusement.

Dacos recomposes himself and smiles at Regent Pfyne politely. *"It has been really nice talking to you"*, he says to her. *"I am sure we will do it again"*.

Regent Pfyne turns to walk away, but before she does, she gives Dacos one last sideways glance, ever so slightly pulls back the hood of her cloak to reveal her long brown flowing hair, smiles at him and says, *"I hope so, General"*. Regent Pfyne turns away again and walks off as Dacos innocently looks around the corridor, still embarrassed by his choice of words, but trying to move past it by working out where else he can go to continue with his investigation. As he turns around, he notices that this whole time behind him is a very large double door. He had probably noticed it before but paid it no mind. However, now that he is looking for something else to focus on, or at least give the appearance of, he fixates on it and studies the doorway as though seeing it for the very first time. He presses the panel button beside the doors and the doors open, revealing the large Aymyn Training Hall inside. The size of the Hall is almost overwhelming. Way larger and more sophisticated than the one they have on Eluud. In fact, "way larger and more sophisticated" is something of an understatement. You could fit perhaps at least a hundred Eluud training halls inside this one. In the distance he can see the far end of the training hall. However, looking upwards the ceiling is very far away. The hall is many stories high, possibly the height of the entire Citadel.

Training inside the hall is a number of Aymyn soldiers. Wearing a kind of minimalistic Virtual Reality headgear and armed with imitation weapons, they appear to be involved in an intense combat simulation. They show no signs of holding back and their reactions appear aggressive and very real.

On the other side of the training hall is a couple of Morn Zazars. They have their Tription Weapons activated, forming long glowing red whips that hover, not touching the ground. They swing their tription whips at various objects and targets around them, the whips slicing through the objects just as easily as cutting through the air. The Zazars move through several formations, often with their backs to each other as though perfecting a combat routine where they are surrounded by multiple adversaries. The Morn are focused, their expression fierce, they swing their tription whips incessantly and with purpose.

Standing in front of them, observing and scrutinizing their every move, is an attractive lady with short black hair and dressed in a long flowing, yet revealing dress which exposes her long legs from her hips down to her short red boots. The top of her dress clips around the neck, but leaves her arms and shoulders naked, revealing a symbolic tattoo on her left shoulder that stretches from her shoulder blade to the top of her chest. Her dress is completely red, the colour worn by teachers and instructors, of which she most certainly is one. For this is Kalrain, the Tription weapons teacher. And since it is only Zazars that use Tription Weapons, this makes her the Teacher of the Zazars.

On her left arm she is wearing a Tal, which would explain why her dress is very scant. In her other hand she is holding a long metallic staff, the same colour as the Morn Zazar's Tription Handles, and is using it to push the Zazar's hands higher or lower as they move through their routines. Her movement so fluid and elegant, she dodges and weaves past their swinging tription whips with ease, showing no fear of being touched by the tription Flame of their weapons as she corrects their technique. Likewise, the Zazars do not seem to be worried about hitting her, having complete faith in their instructor's ability, swinging and flicking their tription whips around and at objects as though she is not there, all the while being careful not to hit each other.

While holding his tription handle firmly, one of the Zazars swings his arm down, the tription whip whizzing and spinning as it drops. Before it touches the ground, Kalrain snares his arm with her staff and, in a single, quick movement, redirects his arm back up again. The tription Flame whip instantly changes direction and starts spiralling upwards. Kalrain continues raising the Morn's arm with her staff. The Morn does not appear to mind and appears very comfortable with her correcting him.

Dacos stands in the doorway, watching in awe, not sure what has impressed him the most; the Zazars, Kalrain, the soldiers training with their Virtual Reality equipment, or the sheer size and layout of the training hall.

Having been searching all over the Citadel for Dacos, Steel spots him still standing in the doorway, peering into the Training Hall. He walks up and stands beside him. Dacos, still appearing so encaptivated by what he is watching inside the Training Hall, Steel believes he has not even noticed him walk up and stand beside him. That is until

Dacos, still staring into the Training Hall, speaks. *"Have you seen this place?"*, he says to Steel, still not taking his eyes off what is happening inside the hall.

Steel looks past Dacos and peers inside as well. *"Seen it. Never had reason to come here"*, he replies. *"Thought about it though"*, he adds as he also watches the Zazars training at the other end of the hall. Just like Dacos, Steel is spellbound by the Tription whips being flung around by the Morn Zazars, and the way their instructor so effortlessly weaves and slides past them, occasionally placing the end of her staff on the Morn's arms and manoeuvring them how she likes. It is almost like watching a dance routine. As he stares at Kalrain, Kalrain stops moving around and turns her head slightly to the side and stares back at him. Her stare calm but intense, it instantly makes Steel look away and start looking around the rest of the hall instead. *"Quite humbling, isn't it"*, Steel says to Dacos referring to the sheer size and layout of the hall.

"A little", Dacos replies with a nod. "A little" being something of an intentional understatement.

Steel gently guides Dacos back into the corridor and closes the Training Hall Doors in front of them. Dacos seems disappointed to no longer be able to watch the show. He steps back and reflects on what he has just witnessed as he turns and looks at Steel. *"So, a Troin Woman with a staff taking on two Morn Zazars"*, Dacos says. Dacos shakes his head at how preposterous that sounds. *"Now, I've seen everything"*, he adds.

Steel places his hand on Dacos's arm as he walks off. *"Walk with me, Dacos"*, he says to him. *"Fill me in on what you've learnt"*. Dacos looks back at the closed Training Hall doors one last time, momentarily wanting to open them again and continue watching, before walking off with Steel.

-------------------------------- Stockpile --------------------------------

Aura runs to her chair in the Council Chambers, sits down and quickly places her hand on the table. An electronic tablet rises out of the table in front of her as the doors to the council chambers open and King Yord hurriedly marches in. *"We need to talk"*, he barks at her. His voice angry and with a real sense of urgency. However, he is not angry at Aura, but rather about some alarming news that has just been brought to their attention. The same news that has made Aura run to her chair and activate her tablet.

Aura looks up at him briefly but remains more focused on trying to quickly type on her tablet. *"I just heard"*, she says to Yord. *"Has Orcom left yet?"*, she asks him.

King Yord walks over to his usual place at the council table and his chair rises up in front of him. *"I don't know, Your Highness"*, he says as he sits down in his chair. *"Not long gone if he has"*, he adds.

A pool of rippling holographic energy starts to form above the centre of the council table. Inside the rippling holographic energy pool, the live image of Councillor Orcom can be clearly seen sitting inside his shuttle. He turns to look at Aura through the holographic projection. *"Your Highness"*, he says to her. *"I have only just been told myself. I had no idea that this was going to happen. Or that it was even being considered"*, his voice shaky and sincere, appearing just as alarmed as Aura and Yord.

On Mesto, Councillor Orcom's home planet, lies the only refining plant for Sygra Steel in Exom. With Crom, the only source of Sygra Steel now fallen victim to the Skurj, the government of Mesto have decided to cease distribution of the last remaining stockpile of Sygra Steel. Being such a widely used resource all throughout Exom, the current situation has made it now a very rare one. One that the government of Mesto intends to hold on to. *"Councillor, I do not need to tell you what this will do to trade and diplomatic relationships throughout Exom"*, Aura says to Orcom. *"This will create wars and put your planet right at the centre"*.

"You most certainly do not need to tell me that, Your Highness", Orcom replies. *"I am only too aware of what this could mean. I am hoping I can talk some sense into them and stop all of this"*.

"Every civilized planet uses Sygra Steel", Yord says. *"Structures, foundations, weaponry, defence. What is your planet playing at, holding for ransom the last remaining stock that we have in Exom?"*

Councillor Orcom, appearing very flustered, honestly having no idea that his government were planning on doing this, does not know what to say and simply shakes his head as he continues to pilot his shuttle. Orcom is a mere representative, an advisory councillor of Mesto. He may represent his planet on the council, casting a vote on behalf of his planet and act as a go between with regards to any information. However, he is not a ruling official of Mesto. He has no power to make these kinds of decisions, and it appears that the ruling powers of Mesto have made them without consulting him. Orcom hopes that this is a spontaneous, brash and changeable decision. Made in haste and panic after the fall of Crom and not something that had been planned for longer. He turns and looks back at Yord through the holographic energy field. *"I am hoping, Your Highness, that is not what is happening"*, Orcom says to him. *"I am currently heading back to my system, but not directly. I need to make a number of stops on the way that can not be avoided. However, I have managed to just cut that in half"*. He looks down at his shuttle controls for a moment, presses a couple of buttons to get information on his course and systems. He turns and looks back at both Aura and Yord again through the holoprojection energy field. He sighs, still unable to accept what his government is doing. *"I will have a better idea about what is going on once I reach Mesto and can speak to the Prime Minister"*, he tells them. *"As soon as I know more, you will know more"*.

"I hope so", Yord replies as he huffs in his seat, seeming to reluctantly accept Councillor Orcom's position.

Aura, despite her anxiety over what is happening, keeps herself calm, at least in appearance. If they are to have any luck in turning this situation around, it will involve the strong cooperation of Councillor Orcom and his persuasion with his planet's government. *"Councillor, I trust you to find out what you can and do what you can"*, she says to him. *"We have quite a job ahead of us trying to avoid a panicked reaction from the other planets and systems"*.

"Hopefully I can help with that, Your Highness", Orcom replies. *"But first let me find out exactly what is going on. I believe a peaceful, collaborative outcome is in everyone's best interest here".*

Aura smiles at Orcom. *"Agreed"*, she says and looks over at Yord. Yord looks back at her and nods, also in agreement of Orcom's statement. *"Thank you, Councillor"*, Aura says as she looks back at Orcom. Orcom turns back to look at his shuttle controls and Aura presses a button on her tablet. The holographic energy pool disappears, and Aura pushes her tablet back into the table. She looks at King Yord again. Yord looks back at her, his expression still very displeased and troubled.

-------------------------- The Heavy Case --------------------------

A warm ambient light fills Tespa's bedroom as Tespa throws herself onto her bed. Not to rest or even relax, but in an effort to try and catch Kako who is happily jumping around the place. He bounces from her bed to her pillow, and then back all along her bed again. As Tespa reaches out to grab him he jumps over her arms. He makes a kind of excited chirping sound, looking very amused and entertained with his actions. Tespa, not so much. *"Kako! I have to sleep in this"*, she yells at him in an agitated but not aggressive or even loud tone. *"You are going to get it all lumpy".*

The door to Tespa's bedroom barges open, as Det walks in backwards, dragging a large, weird, shaped case. It looks heavy and Det is struggling as she pulls it into Tespa's bedroom. She looks exhausted as though she has been dragging this thing all over the castle. Which is not far from the truth. She has dragged it from the music room, which is at the other end of the castle, all by herself.

Tespa looks up at Det and smiles. She makes no attempt to get off her bed and help, seeming content to watch Det drag the heavy case in all by herself. Kako also stops and watches Det as well, then starts to look even happier.

Tespa looks over at the spare space by her wall and points to it. *"Can you put it over by the wall?"*, she says to Det with a polite smile. Det stops dragging the case and turns to face Tespa, looking tired and frustrated. Det doesn't even look at where Tespa is pointing, instead focussing all her glaring directly at Tespa.

"Why don't YOU put it over by the wall?", Det says to her in not so quite a polite tone. *"I don't know why I am even dragging this thing across the castle. It belongs in the music room"*.

"It relaxes Kako", Tespa replies as she rolls over on her bed and sits up. *"And I'd much prefer to practice it in here in my room"*.

Still frustrated at Tespa, but not wanting to talk anymore, Det turns around and starts pulling the large heavy case into the room again. She moves it in through the door, stops again, turns around, leaning her back against it, and looks at Tespa again. *"You could help me you know"*, Det says to her. *"It's yours"*.

"It is too heavy for me", Tespa replies as she smiles all innocently. *"Plus, it's all dusty"*.

Det frowns at Tespa and shakes her head. *"Don't be such a princess!"*, she says to her.

Tespa looks at Det oddly. *"Um. Hello?"*, she replies pointing at herself with both hands, shrugs, and then also points at Det with both hands. Pointing out the obvious – they are both princesses. Det continues to just shake her head, closes her eyes, takes a breath, and then turns back around to face the large case and resumes dragging it in.

The case stops wanting to be moved, appearing caught on something. So, Det walks around to the other side of the case and starts pushing it instead. The case moves again, further into the room, slamming into Tespa's bookshelves. Det thinks nothing of it, still frustrated with Tespa not helping her. *"Be gentle! You're going to break it"*, Tespa exclaims, now looking at the case with a little concern.

Det stops pushing, throws her hands up in the air and looks angrily at Tespa. *"I am being gentle!"*, Det growls back. She takes a deep breath and lets it out, steps back and realises that her belt has got caught on the latches on the case. She manages to get her belt free, but then notices that her delicate key chain with the blue gem attached to it, which she has attached to her belt, has also got tangled on the latch. She tries to untangle it as well, unclipping the keychain from her belt. She successfully untangles it and places it on Tespa's bookshelf, then goes back to pushing the case again.

Kako jumps off Tespa's bed and onto the large case. He climbs up, stands on top of it and looks at Det. *"Allo. I'm Kako"*, he says to her with his usual giant happy smile. Det looks up at Kako, looking even more frustrated. She looks over at Tespa who is still just sitting on her bed watching her. Det shakes her head, throws her hands into the air again and walks out of the room. Kako looks at Tespa confused, not knowing why Det has walked away. Tespa, disappointed that Det has left and now has to move this large thing herself, just looks back at Kako and shrugs.

------------------------- In Good Hands -------------------------

Two small vessels land on the Hangar on top of the Citadel of Light as another takes off, launching itself into a high altitude before jetting off out of sight. Aymyn guards patrol the hangar as part of their routine as a technician appears to be making minor repairs to an electronic chassis panel near the landing gear of a medium-sized cargo vessel.

Standing beside his shuttle, Dacos appears a little despondent as Steel bids him farewell, sending him back to Eluud. *"I'm sorry I didn't find anything useful out"*, Dacos says to him. *"Seems this was a wasted trip"*.

Steel looks back at Dacos, at first with a little concern but then smiles reassuringly. *"You did exactly what I asked of you, Dacos"*, Steel tells him. *"You have helped more than you give yourself credit for"*.

"I don't think that's true", Dacos replies, looking disbelievingly at Steel. *"You wanted me to see if I could work out if there was any Sharlon on the Council"*.

"Specifically Dark", Steel replies and nods, *"as we have no idea who she is"*.

"I didn't do that", Dacos says, looking Steel directly in the eyes while still holding his glum expression.

"But you did", Steel replies, still smiling, while glancing up at Dacos. He knows that Dacos sees everything as either complete or incomplete, often selling himself short on a lot of good work that he does as he doesn't feel it has reached the desired conclusion. *"I have learnt to trust your instincts from since you were a small boy"*, Steel tells him. *"You have spoken to all the council members that are here today and confirmed that none of them are Dark. Something that I could not have been certain about before. Now I am"*. Dacos looks down as he reluctantly accepts Steel's praise. Steel turns and places his hand firmly on Dacos's shoulder. *"Not a waisted trip"*, Steel adds.

Dacos looks over at his shuttle and then looks back at Steel. *"I don't feel right about leaving you alone here"*, Dacos says to him. *"Especially given what you suspect"*.

Steel giggles to himself. *"Oh, I don't suspect anything"*, he replies. *"That's one of my flaws. I'm too carefree. Just ask – well, anyone"*.

Dacos smirks at Steel. *"Arandae through and through"*, Dacos tells him.

"You calling your King Airey?", Steel jokingly asks him.

"To his face", Dacos replies with a smile.

Steel shrugs and looks away. *"Well. Don't tell the girls"*, Steel says to him.

Dacos just looks at Steel and nods. *"I'm pretty sure they know"*.

Steel looks back up at Dacos with a guilty smirk and places his hand firmly on his shoulder again. *"I've kept you away from Eluud too long already"*, Steel says to him. *"I'll be alright here. I always am"*.

Dacos stares at Steel for a moment. *"And you'll be...."*, Dacos hesitates to finish his sentence. Takes a moment and then rephrases. *"I can tell the girls that you'll be home soon?"*, he states as a question.

"Soon-ish", Steel replies hesitantly with a nod. *"Not sure how soon just yet. I have some conversations of my own that still need to be had"*. Steel looks down at the ground as though thinking about these conversations and not looking forward to them.

Dacos knows better than to ask what conversation and with whom, so instead thinks about Det and Tespa back on Eluud. *"The girls won't be happy"*, he says. *"You know they worry about you"*.

"And I about them", Steel replies. *"Which is why you are going back now. They'll be in good hands"*.

Dacos grins, knowing that this conversation has been completely turned around in Steel's favour and there is not much point pushing it any further. *"Yes, Your Highness"*, he says as he turns and walks towards his ship. He walks up the ramp, not stopping to look back at Steel, and enters his ship. The ramp slides up to seal the entrance. Seconds later the wings of the ship extend out, completing the ship's saucer shape, then starts to lift off the hangar floor. Steel watches Dacos's shuttle launch off the hangar, through the busy skyways and into orbit, then turns and walks back into the Citadel.

EXOM

THE YOUNG KING

CHAPTER FOURTEEN

-------------------------------- The Cave --------------------------------

An entrance of a cave, naturally formed high up into the side of large hill, overlooks the forest of Eluud. A single hand reaches up from outside and grabs hold of the ledge. The hand is wearing Troin combat armour. Another man inside the cave, wearing simple Eluudian style clothing, the kind worn traditionally by the farmers and villagers on Eluud, frantically reaches out and grabs hold of the armoured Troin hand and pulls his friend up and into the cave. The Eluudian is looking very dishevelled, his clothes torn as a result of a combination of running through the forest, up into the cave, and also from whatever it is that he was running from. Since his Troin friend found the need to wear full Troin combat armour, it would not be a stretch to assume that whatever they are running from is both aggressive and formidable. On Eluud that can really only mean one thing. Dakari raiders.

Attacks on farms and villages from the Dakari has always been a common occurrence on Eluud, dating back to not long after the first colony settled on Eluud. Since the Dakari only inhabit this region of Exom, often targeting small settlements and ships from which to pillage, with Eluud considered by many as a "backward" planet due to the atmosphere restricting a lot of technology, Eluud is considered the perfect picking ground for the Dakari as, with the exception of the Chassam Castle, most of Eluud is populated with farms and small villages.

It was just such a farm, in the forested outskirts of an Eluudian Village, that this dishevelled Eluudian, Rien, now huddled up in this cave, was earlier hard at work on with his Troin partner Pree. Along with a few other villagers, they were ambushed by a Dakari Raiding party inside the farm barn. Only Rien and Pree were able to flee, and barely at that, with Pree sustaining life-threatening injuries. Though fleeing from Dakari is neither common nor, in most cases, achievable. The Dakari are vicious, relentless, and more noticeably not very bright. They tend to pursue their target, unyieldingly, to the end, even if there is very little, or nothing, to be gained from it. It used to be believed that the Dakari hunted and killed for food and resources, something that the Eluudians would be more than happy to negotiate, share and trade with them if this had been approached. However, negotiation, sharing and trade is not the Dakari way, instead resorting to raiding, killing, plundering, and taking everything. Fierce enough with their sharp claws and long daggers, the Dakari prefer to use their long rifles in battle. Something that is not possible on Eluud due to the environment – though, sometimes the Dakari forget about this and then suffer the consequences when their rifles explode in their hands.

Scarcely conscious, Pree is barely able to move by himself and is dragged into the cave by Rien. Pree's Troin armour starts to fluctuate, disassembling back into nanoparticles and starting to return back to his Tal, before stopping and forming his Troin Armour again as he he goes in and out of consciousness. Pree falls unconscious again, his Troin armour completely disassembles, returning to his Tall, and Rien is able to see the horrific injuries that Pree has sustained to his body. *"Come on!"*, Rien yells at him as he rolls Pree over onto his back and frantically tries to wake him up.

Rien leaves Pree's side only for a moment to take a look over the edge of the cave. He can see the Dakari in the distance, starting their climb up the hill-face towards the cave. He returns to Pree again, desperately trying to wake him. Pree's Troin armour has now completely disassembled and returned to his Tal, though his Tal is still in a lattice armband formation on his arm revealing that he is still alive, just unable, due to being unconscious, to form any external clothing or equipment.

Rien sits down beside Pree, pulling his partners naked and unconscious body into him. Holding him tight, rubbing Pree's arms to keep in warm. Even in these moments, before their imminent death, Rien's thoughts are of comforting Pree. Pree starts to wake up, seeming very dazed, in a lot of pain and not sure where he is or what is going on. Rien sits him up, drags him further into the cave and leans him up against a rock wall as Pree continues to wince in pain. Still not with it and very weak, Pree looks down at his own naked body. He looks at Rien, confused, cringing and grimacing in pain with every movement. *"Come on, Pree"*, Rien says to him, his voice a mixture of desperation and futility. *"You need to arm up"*. Rien wraps his arms around Pree again.

Pree looks down at his Tal, clenches his hand into a fist and the nanoparticles start to pour out of his Tal again, coating his arm and solidifying into armour. The process continues up his arm, cutting through Rien's shirt as it lays rested against Pree's naked skin. Rien lets go of Pree before the nanoparticles cut through Rien as easily as his clothing. The Troin Armour covers Pree's body completely, including the Troin helmet covering his head. As soon as it is formed, Rien stands up and tries to help Pree to his feet. It is no easy task, Pree is still very weak and unable to assist. No sooner does Rien stand Pree up when Pree falls back down again, collapsing completely on the ground. His Troin armour again reverting into nanoparticles and returning to his Tal. *"No no no. Come on"*, Rien exclaims as he drops to his knees and rolls Pree over onto his back again. Pree's armour returns to his Tal at a faster rate than before. Rien tries desperately to sit him back up again as Pree's Tal armband reverts into a simple bracelet. *"No no no no no"*, Rien cries, tears pouring out of his eyes as he pulls Pree closer to him. He brushes his hand through Pree's hair and looks down at his face, no longer showing any pain.

Two Dakari climb up into the cave and stand at the entrance. *"Go Away!!"*, Rien screams at them, his arm wrapped around Pree's body as he holds Pree's left arm with his other hand and points it at the Dakari, futilely hoping that Pree's Tal may do something. The Dakari stare back at him, their eyes completely black and pupilless. There is no response from Pree's Tal bracelet, but Rien continues to point Pree's arm at the Dakari. *"Why?!"*, Rien screams at the Dakari. *"We don't have anything!"*. Focussed on Rien, the Dakari hold firmly onto their large daggers, then pounce on him.

Outside the Cave, all is silent. No movement. It stays that way for a short while until the two Dakari exit the cave alone and start to climb back down the hillside.

------------------------------ Time Alone ------------------------------

The giant laser stilt cannons shut down as Dacos's ship, now resting on the hangar floor adjoining Chassam Castle on Eluud, retracts it side wings. The main door to the ship lowers, forming an exit ramp and Dacos casually walks out of the ship and down the ramp. He is about to head straight inside the Castle when he notices Tespa running across the Castle gardens out of the corner of his eye. He walks over to the end of the hangar and looks down over the side, overlooking the gardens, just as Tespa disappears inside one of the Rouk Stables. She looks like she is running after someone. Perhaps Vessel, he wonders, though Vessel has never shown any interest in rouk's before. Tespa is also not wearing her backpack, so she could again be chasing after Kako, a very regular occurrence. Dacos remains standing there, just watching and thinking to himself.

Inside the Rouk Stable, Det is saddling up a Rouk when Tespa walks in. It was Det that Tespa had followed. *"Where are you going"*, Tespa asks her, standing a bit back so as to not get in her way, or within her reach in case she was angry at something.

"I just need to be alone for a while", Det replies grumpily as she continues saddling the rouk and deliberately not looking at Tespa.

"Alone from who?", Tespa coyly asks as she slowly makes her way around to the front of the rouk and pats its forehead.

"Alone from everyone", Det replies as she swings the reins over the rouks head, almost hitting Tespa in the process.

Tespa steps back, a little taken back at Det's seemingly careless, though she suspects deliberate actions. *"Alone from me?"*, she asks Det, as she continues to stare at Det and watches what she is doing.

"Yep", is all Det replies, still not looking at Tespa, and placing her body between Tespa and the Rouk as she tightens the reins gently. Firmly holding the reigns, she swings her leg up, placing her foot in the stirrup, then throws herself onto the rouk and into the saddle. She positions herself properly, both feet in the stirrups, then reaches down to make sure that she can easily reach her ronad. She can. The rouk saddles and stirrups are arranged so that a rider can always reach their ronad easily. In fact, this is the reason the ronads are worn in holsters on the leg in the first place, as they are designed to be easily reached and used while riding in battle.

"You don't need to go riding off out into who knows where just to get away from me you know?", Tespa says to her.

"I do", Det replies as she grabs her ronad, activates it and uses it to push open the gates.

"So, you are going through all this just to get away from me?", Tespa then asks her.

Det deactivates her ronad, returning it to its much smaller and shorter handle shape in her hand, then returns it to her leg holster. *"Yep"*, Det once again replies.

Tespa looks aside as she thinks to herself. *"I should feel insulted by that"*, she says out loud. She then looks back at Det and smiles. *"But I don't"*, she adds. *"Can I come with you?"*, Tespa surprisingly asks as she walks around and stands next to Det. Det looks at Tespa confused. What part of needing to be alone and getting away from Tespa didn't Tespa understand? Tespa looks up at Det and Smiles innocently. Det looks away, just wanting to ignore her, but then gives in, looks back at Tespa and with a frustrated and disbelieving expression holds out her hand. Tespa grabs Det's hand and Det pulls her up onto the Rouk. Tespa wriggles and comforts herself, sitting behind Det, and puts her arms around Det's waist as they ride off.

EXOM - THE YOUNG KING

Savonq, like Eluud, is a planet located in an outer-rim system of Exom, though Savonq is well over the other side of Exom to Eluud. The planet spends half its year underwater, not very deep but certainly land covering. The rest of the year it is a desert. During its desert season the planet appears lifeless. However, the life is simply dormant in the dirt and sand of the planet waiting for the flooding season. As soon as the waters start to rise the planet is teaming with marine life of all shapes and sizes.

A large city built, surrounded by an equally large, extremely high, strongly reinforced barrier wall, used to keep the water out during its flooding season, has been built on Savonq and over the centuries has become heavily populated. Predominantly Aymyn, however Sarvonq is home to many species found throughout Exom. All of which are at this very moment running in a mass-panic all throughout the city. Running in droves to get away from a Skurj that is darting around, at considerable speed, amongst them. Stopping only momentarily to devour a citizen, or group of, here and there before charging again.

The streets are filled with people running mostly in the same direction. Trampling over anyone and anything in their way. In many ways their disregard for those they trample on and leave behind makes them hardly any better than the Skurj that they are trying to get away from.

Atop of the roof of a very tall building, a Morn Zazar is battling a single Skurj. The Skurj speeds towards him as the Zazar dives and slides underneath it. As they pass each other, the Zazar pulls out his Tription handle and slides on past towards the centre of the roof. The Skurj, now at the outer end of the building, turns back around, its tail smashing through the wall surrounding the roof, and again swiftly charges at the Zazar. The Zazar stands up and immediately moves to the side, dodging the Skurj's attack. As he does so, he throws the Tription handle from one hand to one of his others and activates a Tription Flame blade. The Zazar spins around, and holding out the Tription sword, slices the Skurj across the head, taking a decent slice out of it. The Skurj spins around again, this time almost taking out the Zazar with its tail, but the Zazar dives and slides underneath it then flips himself up to his feet when clear. The Zazar jumps towards the Skurj and stabs his tription Flame sword through the Skurj's head. The Skurj falls dead on the ground as the Tription Flame sword continues to slice through it.

The Zazar runs to the outer edge of the building roof, right where the wall has been smashed by the Skurj he just killed. Looking into the distance, he can see the second Skurj still speeding through the city streets, stopping only to eat people and spew mazzie into the air. The Zazar turns and jumps backwards off the roof, through the smashed wall, and scales down the side of the building. Using a combination of his hands, feet and Tription weapon to cut through the building walls, he quickly reaches the ground and charges towards the Skurj as people run past him in the opposite direction.

The Zazar reaches the Skurj during one of its short snack stops. He swings his Tription sword and slices the Skurj across the shoulder. Unfortunately, this was only enough to wound it, and not even that significantly, as the Skurj looks briefly at its shoulder, then at the tription Flame sword that injured it, before quickly turning and racing away, back down the city street. The Zazar chases after it, tossing vehicles, and anything else in its way, aside like toys.

Outside the city walls, the ground is completely desert. Only dry sand and scattered rock formations litter the landscape. Unlike the noisy chaos that fills the city inside the walls, outside is completely silent. From the outside you would never even know that the city was under attack. You would never know that, on the other side of those walls, thousands of people are crowded together searching for a way to break through. The walls were designed to hold back oceans, they will not succumb to a frantic charging crowd of civilians.

A single battle aircraft, flying at speed, darts out from behind and over the large city walls. It dives down again, turning around to face back towards the walls. It is soon joined by several more aircrafts, all of which spin back around to face the wall. They prepare to blast through the wall, giving the people somewhere to run and hopefully buy some time to conduct an evacuation, loading as many of them into shuttles as they can. They aim their laser cannons ready to blast away, but before they can fire, something bursts through the wall from the inside, with such force as to create an incredible dust storm and send bricks, rubble and Sygra steel shooting through the air. Some of this rubble and steel colliding with a couple of the battle aircrafts, damaging one, and sending the other hurtling into the ground. As the dust clears, the cause of the destruction can be clearly seen. A single Skurj, the same injured one that the Zazar was pursuing, now stands outside the walls below the aircrafts.

Immediately the battle aircrafts change direction and dive towards it, rapidly firing on the Skurj with everything they have. Nothing has any effect. The Skurj propels itself into the air directly at one of the aircrafts, the aircraft tries to manoeuvre out of the way by quickly gaining altitude, but inadvertently ends up colliding with a second aircraft that was right above it. The first aircraft, seriously damaged in the collision, falls towards the ground, hitting, and collecting the Skurj still in the air charging towards it. Both the Skurj and the aircraft hit the ground with considerable force, the aircraft landing right on top of the Skurj and immediately exploding. The second aircraft, badly damaged and in trouble, is out of control and also falling towards the ground. Out of the Flames from the first aircraft the Skurj emerges, completely intact. It sees the second aircraft a split second before it too collides with it. Just like the first aircraft, this one too also explodes, the Flames tearing past the Skurj. Again, with no effect. The Skurj looks at the destroyed aircrafts, just as the Morn Zazar that was chasing it comes running through the hole made by the Skurj in the city wall. The Zazar spots the Skurj and charges at it, diving through the air, Tription sword held ahead of him, and straight into the Skurj's neck. The Zazar's weapon penetrates straight through the Skurj. The Zazar rolls down off the Skurj, his Tription Flame sword still held firmly in his hand, slicing through the Skurj as he lands feet first on the ground. The Skurj's now lifeless body falls to the ground. Through the destroyed section of the wall, people are gathered and peering through. The Zazar looks back at them, then with his tription sword still flaming, runs back towards them. They all move aside as he pushes through them and back into the city.

The remaining battle aircrafts land and open their doors. The citizens all surge forward again, towards the aircraft and are quickly ushered inside by the aircraft personnel.

------------------------------ The Barn ------------------------------

Dense Eluudian forest trees stand still and motionless as the sun dwells down on them. Twilight is soon approaching but is not here yet. A rustling sound emanating from within the forest gets louder, closer, finally parting the branches and bush between the trees as Det and Tespa, still mounted on the rouk, push through the forest and out into a clearing. Tespa is covering her face with one hand while hiding behind Det and holding her tight with the other. Det seems completely uninterested in shielding herself from anything, her gaze determined and firmly looking forward. She rides out into the clearing, when she suddenly pulls back the reins on the rouk, bringing it to a stop. The sudden stop pushes Tespa further into Det, smothering her face in Det's back. She pushes herself back, looking a little stunned and then looks at Det curiously. She notices that Det is just sitting there, staring over into the distance at something. Tespa looks over in the direction that Det is staring. It's a barn. Just a perfectly normal looking barn. Normal with the exception that it has one of its doors torn down and barn animals are wandering around outside.

Tespa looks at Det and can tell by Det's expression that she is either concerned or incredibly curious. Probably both, but knowing Det, most likely suspecting danger and wanting to walk on into it. Det is no stranger to this area, she has ridden through this way many times before, even recently. The last time she was here the barn was intact. There was also people around, something that there does not appear to be any sign of right now.

Tespa looks over at the wondering farm animals and then back at the broken barn door. *"What happened here"*, she asks Det, but Det does not reply, still just sitting there and staring at the barn. *"There is no one here"*, Tespa adds. *"That's strange, right? There's no one here. Animals running loose. Barn door - like that. It's strange, yeah?"*. Again, Det does not answer. *"Yeah, it's strange"*, Tespa says answering her own question. Tespa reaches up and holds onto the top of Det's arms. *"We should go back"*, Tespa says to Det. *"I think we should go back now. Tell the soldiers back at the Castle. Get them to come here and investigate. Yeah. We should go back?"*. Det still does not reply. Instead, without even listening to her sister's words, or maybe she did and just chose to completely ignore them, Det jumps down off the rouk and starts walking towards the barn, much to Tespa's surprise. *"Or we do the complete opposite to that"*, Tespa adds, watching Det with disbelief before yelling, *"Det, come back here"*, in a loud whisper, as though she only wants Det to hear it.

Det continues towards the Barn, completely ignoring Tespa's words. Now a little frustrated, as well as concern for Det and whatever she may find in the barn, Tespa also dismounts the Rouk and goes after her sister. *"I swear one of these days you are going to get us both killed with your racing off"*, Tespa huffs away at Det. *"And when that happens, I will be most unhappy about it"*.

The inside of the barn looks like nothing special. Some hay bales and barrels up against the walls. Also scattered throughout the interior of the barn as though there has been some sort of skirmish. Large shoulder height windows, built into the external barn walls, appear as though they open and remain intact. The barn doors open inwards and, as Det enters the barn, she notices that only one of them is damaged. The other is simply pushed back almost all the way up against the wall.

Det runs her hand along the barn door as she walks past it and towards some large barrels laying scattered along the middle of the barn floor. An intrigued expression on her face as though she is expecting to find something interesting there. She looks at the barrels and can see nothing of interest at first. She then pushes one slightly aside with her foot. Her stare starts to intensify as she starts to see what it was that she was expecting to find. An outstretched Eluudian farmer's arm now visible and poking out from behind the barrel. Det pushes the barrel further away with her foot to reveal it is more than just an arm. It is the entire Eluudian farmer. His throat and chest have been cut open. Not by some animal looking for something to eat. No, this was done by something that took real pleasure in killing. A Dakari.

Cautiously, suspiciously and feeling very uneasy, Det stands there and looks around the barn as Tespa walks inside. Tespa notices Det standing in the centre of the barn looking around. She takes a few steps inside, about to walk up to Det, but stops in shock, just inside the barn entrance, as she sees the dead farmer's body by Det's feet. *"Please tell me he was dead before you came in here?"*, Tespa asks Det. Again, Det ignores her question and continues to survey the barn, looking thoroughly at every wall, high and low, and even the ceiling above her.

As Tespa stands there just watching Det, wondering what she is looking for, she also starts looking above her, feeling a little paranoid now on top of everything else. The undamaged barn door behind Tespa starts to slowly swing away from the wall. Feeling it move behind her, Tespa slowly turns to look at it as it moves closer to her. She steps out of the way just as it swings shut. Another dead body that had been propped up behind the barn door falls to the ground. Another farmer, female, no visible injuries, from behind at least as she now lays, face down, on the barn floor.

Tespa squeals, startled and now completely freaked out. She runs towards Det, reaching her and grabbing onto her for support, as Det quickly turns to look at what Tespa is running from. *"Can we go now? I'd really like to go now"*, Tespa says to Det, holding her firmly and refusing to look anywhere else but into Det's eyes. Det pulls away from Tespa, still focussing on the dead woman's body and walks over to it, leaving Tespa standing in the centre of the barn.

Seeing no visible injuries on the woman's body, Det crouches down next to her and places a hand on the back of the woman's head. The body is still warm. Det tilts the woman aside and can see the start of another torn throat. *"Raiders"*, Det says out loud to herself, but loud enough for Tespa to hear.

Two dead bodies are quite bad enough. Now Det is also talking about Dakari raiders as well. Tespa did not want or need to hear this. *"I don't want to be here"*, Tespa says, her fear increasing.

Det, still crouching down next to the dead woman's body, again moves her gaze all around the barn. If what she just said frightened Tespa, then what she is about to say next will make her feel worse. *"They're still here"*, Det announces.

It made her feel worse alright. Not knowing where to go, not wanting to head back towards the door where the dead woman is, and certainly not wanting to stay where she is next to the dead man, Tespa starts to walk backwards towards the barn wall at the other side of the barn. *"I really don't want to be here"*, Tespa says as she reaches the back of the barn and leans her back against the wall beside a large window.

Det continues to turn around, taking in everything around her, as Tespa stands there staring at Det. With Det's back turned, something starts to crawl through the window beside Tespa. Tespa catches the movement in the corner of her eye and, terrified, she slowly turns around. She screams as she watches a Dakari climb through the window, pull out a long dagger and charges straight at her.

Det spins around quickly. Seeing the Dakari, she instantly pulls out her ronad, activates it and throws it like a spear, spearing the Dakari straight through the chest and pinning it to the wall next to Tespa. Tespa stands frozen, terrified, and watching the Dakari die while pinned to the wall next to her. It drops its heavy dagger, which lands point first into the ground narrowly missing Tespa's foot.

Tespa looks down at the dagger, millimetres away from her foot, and then, equally freaked out about that too, looks at Det. Det looks briefly at Tespa, then down at the Dakari dagger next to Tespa's foot and slightly shrugs. Tespa looks back down at the dagger and also starts to shrug.

As they both focus on the Dakari dagger beside Tespa, neither of them notices a second Dakari emerge from behind the damaged barn door and creep towards Det. It grabs Det by the neck, its long sharp claws piercing into her throat, lifts her up and pins her up against the wall. Startled but refusing to show any fear, Det starts laying punches, in very rapid progression, into the Dakari. She sweeps its arm with hers, knocking away its grip from around her throat, and drops to her feet. She grabs the Dakari and tries to push it away, but her strength is no match for such a powerfully built adversary. The Dakari pins her up against the wall again as Det reaches out and wraps her hands around its throat. Still no match for the Dakari's strength, Det starts kicking the Dakari with both legs. Kicking it quickly, rapidly and anywhere her feet and shins will land. The Dakari seems completely unphased.

Without thinking, Tespa instinctively reaches down and picks up the Dakari dagger by her foot, then goes to throw it at the Dakari that has her sister pinned up against the wall. Det continues to struggle and fight the Dakari, still refusing to show any fear. That is until she looks at Tespa and sees her about to throw the dagger. Det's expression completely changes, having no faith in her sister's ability to accurately throw a large dagger across the barn, she looks at Tespa, shock and fear now apparent, and shakes her head. Tespa throws the dagger anyway. It completely misses the Dakari and imbed itself into the barn wall, right next to Det's head, only very narrowly missing her as Det moves her head out of the way in the last split second.

Det looks with shock at the dagger that has almost killed her, then, still shaking her head, looks back at Tespa. Tespa looks back at Det, equally shocked, but only shrugs.

Not wasting another second, Det grabs the dagger, pulling it out of the wall, and thrusts it into the head of the Dakari. The Dakari releases its grip from around Det's throat and steps back holding its head with the dagger still deeply imbedded in it. Det pushes it back, away from her. It staggers back and pulls the dagger out of its head as it falls to its knees. Almost casually, Det marches over to the dead Dakari still pinned to the wall beside Tespa and pulls her ronad out from its chest. As the dead Dakari falls to the ground, Det walks back over to the kneeling and dying Dakari and thrusts her ronad straight through its back and out its chest. The Dakari stops holding its head as its arms and hands drop lifelessly to its side. Det deactivates her ronad, the long spear ends returning inside the small handle, and the Dakari faceplants itself into the ground, where it lays dead and motionless.

Tespa runs up to Det and again holds onto her arm as Det continues to look around the barn. *"Can we go now?"*, Tespa says to Det, still expecting Det to completely ignore her again. This time Det looks at Tespa and nods.

Cautiously, still very much looking around them, they start to walk towards the barn doors. They only manage a few steps before more Dakari, a lot more, walk into the barn through the open, broken barn door. The Dakari stop in front of Det and Tespa, looking at them, then look over at their dead comrades. They look back at Det and Tespa. Tespa looks scared. Det just shrugs at them before activating her ronad again. Det stands on guard, ready to engage the Dakari. Tespa, still looking terrified, quickly grabs her ronad from her leg holster, activates it and stands ready next to Det. Det reaches out and grabs Tespa, slowly and cautiously pulling Tespa behind her. She then pushes Tespa back towards the back of the barn as more and more Dakari enter through the barn doors. Holding her ronad in one hand, while holding onto Det with the other as Det guides her back towards the back of the barn, Tespa can feel Det's uncertainty. She has never known Det to retreat, so the fact that she is keeping Tespa behind her and walking backwards with her is enough to tell Tespa that Det does not feel sure about this situation at all. She is correct. Det is looking at the large number of Dakari now walking towards them, knowing that she is well and truly outnumbered and out matched.

The last Dakari to walk into the barn closes the barn doors behind them, then turns back and starts walking towards Det and Tespa. It draws its long daggers from out of its belt and grips them tightly in each hand. Some of the other Dakari do the same, as other seem more content to raise out their long claws. Their black pupilless eyes fixed on Det and Tespa, they prepare to pounce.

Suddenly both barn doors are kicked open with tremendous force. The Dakari quickly turn around to find Dacos standing there, in the doorway, with his ronad fully extended. He marches in, looking at the Dakari as well as all around him, assessing the situation. He throws his ronad at the Dakari, spearing two of them at once, and then using his bracelet summons his ronad back to his hand. The Dakari instantly charge at Dacos as Dacos swiftly, calmly, and seemingly effortlessly, starts taking them out with his ronad. One at a time, sometimes two or three at a time.

"Stay here!", Det says to Tespa, pushing her up against the wall, then running over to join in the fight with Dacos. Standing back-to-back, Det and Dacos fight against the Dakari as a very effective team. They look like they are about to easily defeat the Dakari when two Dakari grab Det, one on each of her arms, and throw her to the ground. They each pin one of her arms to the ground, holding her down as she struggles against them. Det tries frantically to swing her ronad but is unable to move her arms. Dacos swings around then, putting his ronad under both Dakari, he throws them off Det. He spins his ronad, hitting one Dakari across the head, then thrusts the end of his ronad through the chest of the other one.

Watching both Dakari fall dead on the ground, and feeling very pleased with this act of heroism, Dacos smiles to himself and then looks at Det to see if she is equally impressed. She does not seem to be and has already jumped to her feet, apparently not noticing, or not caring what Dacos has just done, and continues to fight the remaining Dakari. Dacos looks disappointed, before swinging back around and taking out more Dakari with his ronad as he does so.

Back-to-back Det and Dacos fight the Dakari. Blocking the Dakari daggers with their ronads, then swinging their ronads to trip, sweep or club the Dakari, followed by sending their ronads straight through the neck or chests of the Dakari.

Det spins her ronad, hitting a Dakari across the head. The Dakari flinches but does not fall. It lunges at Det with its daggers. Dacos grabs Det, pulling her out of the way and face first right into his chest. With his other hand he reaches out and spears the Dakari straight through the head with his ronad. Another very impressive move, and again another one that Det seems to have missed. Only this time the reason she has missed it is because she still has her face pressed against Dacos's chest. She pulls her head back and looks at his chest for a moment. Momentarily forgetting where she is, her only thought now is Dacos, his smell, his body. Unconsciously she reaches up and lays her hand on his chest as she bites her lower lip, and slowly looks up at Dacos.

Dacos looks back down at her. The moment their eyes meet, Det again quickly turns away, spins around and lunges her ronad into another Dakari. Dacos stays looking down at her as a hint of a smile starts to take shape on his face.

A single Dakari starts to back away from Det and Dacos as they fight the few Dakari that are left. It backs right up to Tespa who whacks it over the head with her Ronad. Evidently not hard enough and it turns around to face her. She gives it a frightened smile as it prepares itself to lunge at her. Before it manages to pounce, a ronad comes shooting out through its chest. Both the Dakari and Tespa look down at the Ronad, then look back at each other. The ronad disappears back into the Dakari's chest and the Dakari collapses in front of Tespa, revealing Det standing behind it, ronad in hand. Tespa looks at Det, then at Dacos who is standing with his back to Det and looking at the pile of dead Dakari laying scattered on the ground around him. Det looks down and to her side, also observing the pile of dead Dakari and deactivates her ronad.

"Can we please go now?", Tespa again asks Det, a scared but hopeful grin on her face as she also deactivates her ronad. Det looks back at Dacos as Dacos marches towards the barn doors, not deactivating his ronad but rather tucking it under his arm. Det turns back to Tespa, smiles, grabs her hand, and then runs again to join Dacos, pulling Tespa along with her.

EXOM

THE YOUNG KING

CHAPTER FIFTEEN

-------------------------- The Discussion --------------------------

The Council chambers in the Citadel of Light are empty, with the exception of Steel who is pacing around aimlessly, lost in thought. The main doors to the chamber open and Aura walks on in. She sees Steel there, as she knew she would, pacing, not having noticed her. She stands still and watches him for a moment before finally interrupting. *"I thought I'd find you here"*, she says to him.

Steel snaps out of his thoughts and looks up. Seeing Aura, he smiles. *"Am I that predictable?"*, he asks her.

"Yeah", Aura replies with a cheeky smile and nod, as she continues to walk into the council chambers, the doors now closing behind her. *"You do that a lot"*, she adds.

Steel looks curiously at her. *"Do?"*, he asks.

"When you get a thought in your head, you go back to the place where you first got it to think it through", Aura replies.

"Do I?", Steel asks. Aura smiles and nods. *"Wow"*, Steel says as he looks back at her and smiles, *"I really am that predictable"*. Then, just as quickly as he snapped out of his thoughts, Steel returns to them, and again continues to pace. Aura walks up behind him and puts her arms around him. Steel instantly stops pacing and snaps back out of his thoughts again. Aura knows what he is thinking about. After the intense discussion and idea that Bassal has put in Steel's head, it is also something that she has been thinking about. Not for the same reasons as Steel, however. She knows Steel well enough to know that once he

gets an idea in his head, he does not let go. Though, this time, she was really hoping he would.

"Are you seriously still thinking about it?", she asks him, secretly hoping that he will deny it, move on and forget about it.

"Becoming a Zazar?", Steel replies. *"More than just thinking about it"*.

Aura lets go of Steel and steps around in front of him, looking anxious and upset. *"Seriously?"*, she asks, looking directly into his eyes.

"Very", Steel replies. He can see her concern but sees no point in lying to her about this. Having exhausted everything else, it is now all he can think about.

Aura shakes her head in disbelief. Beyond disbelief, she is starting to feel distraught. He can not consider attempting the Zazar test. No Aymyn has ever survived it. What he is considering is the same as suicide. She tries to put all her thoughts into words, but only one word comes out, *"No"*.

Steel feels Aura's pain but feels helpless. *"I've tried everything else"*, he tells her.

Aura desperately searches for a reason for him to change his mind and stutters on her words. She struggles to find one, with only one thing coming to mind, *"Don't you think you should talk about this with the people you love?"*, she asks him.

Strangely, not something Steel was considering, as he slightly giggles to himself trying to make her comment light-hearted. *"Everyone I love is standing in front of me"*, he replies.

Aura looks at Steel, knowing he is only joking, but still very unimpressed. *"Your family? Your daughters?"*, she says to him.

Mockingly, Steel smiles and shakes his head. *"Nah, never really liked them. They all chew funny"*.

"Steel!", Aura shouts at him, frustrated with him making jokes while she is trying to be serious.

Seeing that his attempt at humour is not working, Steel shakes his head, stops smiling and returns to being serious. *"They'd only try to talk me out of it"*, Steel tells her.

"As they should", Aura replies, even more determined now, by his response, that this course is the right one. *"I'm going to call them"*, she tells him as she walks over to her chair, sits down, raises an electronic tablet out of the council table and starts pressing buttons on the screen.

Steel walks over and puts his hand on Aura's hand, stopping her from typing, then holds her hand as he looks at her. Aura looks up at Steel and into his eyes, not wanting him to stop her from contacting his family on Eluud but also not wanting to fight with him. Sadness is starting to overwhelm her, and her arms feel weak as Steel holds her hand. Steel knows that her intentions are good and pure. And also that she has his and his families, not just hers, interests at heart. However, this decision to try out and become a Zazar, his last hope to save his planet, he feels was an inevitability. With no other Zazars willing to select Eluud, there was no one else left. If someone from Eluud had to attempt the Zazar test, then it had to be him. He could not even consider asking it of anyone else. The odds are seriously against any kind of success. No, he is the king, it is his planet, this is for his people, his family, the decision to do this is his, must be his, and be his alone. *"It's a decision that no one can make. So, I have to"*, he tells Aura.

Aura still refuses to accept it. *"To become a Zazar?"*, she says. *"It's absurd. Its suicide. No, it's not happening"*. Still holding her hand, Steel looks deep into Aura's eyes. He feels her sadness, it echoes his own. Aura shakes her head, fighting her own logic, feeling her heart burst from what her brain is telling her is going to happen. *"No"*, she says again. She looks away, desperately trying to think of something, anything, that could make him see reason. She knows how stubborn he is, but perhaps, just perhaps, there is something that he has not thought of.

There may be. Something occurs to her. Had she been arguing this all wrong with him? Steel, solely focussed on attempting the Zazar test, passing it and becoming a Zazar, but has he thought of what else that would mean? *"Let's say you do this"*, Aura says to him. *"Which you're not"*, she quickly adds. Steel raises his eyebrow at Aura, a slight smirk starting to take shape, amused by the way she puts her foot down. Like that is going to work. *"What's the Zazar motto?"*, Aura then asks him.

Steel thinks about the Morn Zazars that he has seen. He smiles as one thing comes to mind. *"Look at me, I'm a big grumpy galoof"*, he replies while pulling a face and smiling.

"Stop it", Aura scolds at him as she gently hits his chest. She knows that Steel is just trying to make her laugh, but she is not amused. *"I'm being serious"*, she says.

Steel stops smiling and looks seriously at Aura. He knows what she is talking about. He knows the Zazar motto well. Everyone does. *"Only and Always"*, he says to her.

He may know the words, Aura thinks to herself, but does he realize what they mean? *"Only"*, she recites back to him, pausing for a moment on that word. *"And Always"*, she continues. *"Always a Zazar. And Only a Zazar. Forfeiting all other titles and positions. You'd no longer be King. You'd be renouncing your throne. You'd be renouncing your position on the council"*. Aura takes a long, deep, heart-wrenching breath. A tear spilling from her eye as she struggles to say the next words. What it would mean if Steel was no longer on the council. *"You'd be renouncing us"*, she says, her voice shaky as more tears flow down her cheek.

Steel looks blankly down at the ground for a moment and takes a deep breath. *"I know"*, he replies. His voice soft and filled with sadness. He had thought about this. Giving up his title as King of Eluud was easier than giving up being able to be with Aura. The thought of losing her killed him inside. It was not what he wanted. Ever. Yes, he had most certainly, and painfully, thought about it. Still painfully thinking about it.

He sits down in his chair next to Aura. Knowing that after he goes ahead with the test, pass or fail, this will be the last time that he will sit there. He gazes up at Aura, looking miserable. *"But is there any other way?"*, he asks her. Another way to save his planet. She knows there isn't. Her mind still reaches for answers. She finds herself venturing into very dark thoughts. Bring everyone from Eluud onto Aymyn. It's not the same thing. It's not their home. She wonders, could she really contemplate the destruction of an entire planet, the home of so many, just to hold onto the man that she loves. For a moment she believes she can. But that moment quickly passes. She looks away shaking her head, then looks back at Steel still shaking her head. She wants him to see that she is not shaking her head because she is agreeing with him. She is shaking her head because she still does not want him to do it.

"I may not even pass the Zazar test", Steel says with a sadistic grin. *"With everything that I am hearing, I may not even survive it"*, he adds still trying to make light of things and make her smile. He fails.

"Oh, that makes me feel so much better", Aura replies, looking at him disdainfully.

Steel refuses to stop smiling, still intent on trying to lighten the mood, even though he is filled with as much fear and sadness as Aura. *"Hey, if Zargah can pass it, how difficult can it be?"*, he says to her jokingly.

Aura looks at Steel with disbelief. Is he really comparing himself to Zargah? The General of the Zazars. Someone who Steel himself only recently described as "the biggest goddamn morn to ever walk". *"Um, hello"*, she replies. *"There is a bit of a size difference between you two"*.

"Only on the outside", Steel remarks, again jokingly.

"That's kind of the point", Aura says, not allowing her emotions to be lifted by his humour.

Steel may call himself an Eluudian as though that makes him different to regular Aymyn. But physically it does not. His body is Aymyn and in every single way inferior to that of a Morn. There is simply no comparison. He is weaker, smaller, and more fragile. But....

"I have two things that he doesn't", Steel says to her. Aura looks at Steel waiting to hear what these are. *"I'm out of options - and I'm desperate"*.

Not exactly what Aura wanted to hear, but again reaffirms what she knows; Steel's mind is made up. Her heart breaking, all she can do is look at him in silence. Her face, her body, every part of her conveying what she is feeling. Steel feels it too, but like he said, he is out of options, and he is desperate. *"I have to try"*, he tells her. Aura does not know what to say. She can see every point that he is making, but everything about this path fills her with pain.

She knows the answer to this next question, but she has to ask. *"Is there no one else that could do this instead?"*

The answer is not that simple. There may be, but no one believes so, which is why no one has ever stepped forward and volunteered. And everyone may well and truly be right, which is why Steel would never expect anyone else to do so. *"I could not ask anyone else to do this"*, Steel replies. *"Right now, I am still King. The responsibility is mine"*.

Steel smiles at Aura again. *"Hey, you always said that I should try new things"*, he again says jokingly to her. It as the opposite reaction to what he was expecting. Aura turns her body to him, tears flowing even faster down her cheeks, she closes her eyes and starts hammering her fists into his chest. *"Stop it! Stop it! Stop it!"*, she yells at him. Steel grabs her hands and holds them to his chest. She looks deep into his eyes, barely able to see through her tears. *"You're breaking my heart"*, she cries.

Steel holds her hands firmly and raises them to his lips as he stares back into her eyes. Tears now flowing from his eyes as well. *"I'm breaking mine too"*.

They both sit silently, staring into each other's eyes, feeling completely helpless. Worse than just feeling like they are breaking up. Feeling like they are both having to offer Steel up as a sacrifice. Aura can not move. Her strength is all gone. All she has left is enough to hold herself up in her seat and stare back at the man she loves, the man she is about to lose.

Steel can feel her, her very soul. He knows that she can not move. She can not do what is needed to make this decision happen. So, Steel reaches over and touches the screen on the tablet in front of her. He changes the screen and starts typing with one hand while still holding onto hers firmly with his other. He finishes typing, stops, and stays looking at the screen. Aura does not look at it. She does not want to. She continues to just look at him. Steel has done as much as he can on Aura's tablet. As only a council member he does not have the authority to go any further. The next step needs to be completed by the Head of the Royal Alliance for this to proceed any further. Aura needs to complete it. Aura needs to approve his application.

Steel takes a moment to just stare at the screen. Looking like he is having doubts, but he isn't. He is just feeling extremely sad by the decision that needs to be made. His sadness still very apparent in his eyes as he looks back at Aura. *"You need to authorize it"*, he tells her. Aura does not look at the tablet. She remains sitting there just staring back at Steel. Steel nods, letting her know that it's alright. She shakes her head, tears still spilling from her eyes, letting him know that it isn't. Steel takes a moment to smile at her through sad eyes and then nods again.

Aura remains looking at Steel then looks at the tablet. She covers her eyes with both hands to hide away her tears. Steel stands up and walks around beside her and puts his arms around her. Hold her. Aura looks up at Steel through her tears, then looks back at the tablet and places her hand on it. Steel looks at the tablet and can see the screen change and his name and picture come up on it under the heading "Zazar Selection Test". Underneath his name is a highlighted button with the word "Accept" written on it. Aura stares at the tablet, unable to press that final button. She looks back up at Steel, unable to go any further, unable to do any more. Wishing with all her heart that this was not happening. It's not too late. They could still not press the "Accept" button. She could close down her tablet and stop this from going any further, but she does not even have the strength to do that. She feels her heart falling to pieces, even breathing is painful. Steel feels the same thing. He looks at the screen one more time, then reaches out and presses the "Accept" button for her. The screen changes again, this time showing a location. A location that he knows and had been to just recently. The Large Training Hall.

Aura looks at the screen, knowing what it says, she does not read it and instead pushes the tablet away. The tablet slides across the table, coming to a stop near the centre and then retracts into the table. Aura folds her arms, resting them on the table. Her shoulders and body drop as she lowers her face into her arms. Steel, still standing beside her with his hand on her back, sits down slowly in his chair. He looks over the table then back at Aura, unable to take his hand off her.

-------------------------------- **Goodnight**--------------------------------

Tespa lays on her back in bed. Hovering above her is a shimmering pool of energy created by a holoprojector in the ceiling above her bed. The live image of Det can be seen in it. Det is also laying in her bed in her own room, though she is laying on her side and not looking at Tespa through an identical energy holographic energy field floating over her.

"Do you ever think about them", Tespa asks Det.

"No", Det quickly replies, still not looking at Tespa through the holographic energy field. Her eyes are open as she just stares at her wall.

"How can you say no?", Tespa asks her. *"I haven't even said who I am talking about yet"*.

"Go on", Det says to her, still not moving.

"Your birth parents", Tespa says.

"No", Det again replies.

"You knew I was going to say that, didn't you?", Tespa says as she giggles. Det does not answer. *"It's a little spooky how you do that"*, Tespa says to her. Det still remains quiet. Tespa gently throws her head back, looking at the wall above her head and sighs. *"I think about them"*, Tespa tells Det. *"Not wanting anything to change or anything. I kind of feel bad about that too. Our father is the only father I have known. The only one I want to know. But I do often wonder if our birth parents would be just as happy with how things turned out for us. You know what I mean?"*. Det still remains quiet. Tespa waits for Det to reply, then realising that she isn't going to, she continues. *"I'm sure they would"*, Tespa says. *"I feel like we are so blessed. I guess what I am trying to say is..."*

"You are glad that our father is our father", Det cuts in.

Tespa smiles and looks up at the ceiling. *"I am"*, Tespa replies. *"He loves everything so much. And he chose us. Or maybe we chose him"*, Tespa smirks as she looks back at Det through the holographic energy field. *"I know you feel that way too"*, she says to Det. Again, Det does not say anything. This time her silence makes Tespa smile. *"Don't worry"*, Tespa says to her. *"Your secret is safe with me"*.

Det continues to just lay on her side, staring at the wall. Then closes her eyes and tries to go to sleep.

A naked Vessel, lying beside Tespa, reaches over and waves her hand through the holographic energy field floating above Tespa. The Energy field starts to dissipate, then disappears completely as the holoprojector shuts down. Tespa smiles at Vessel and leans up into her and gives her a kiss.

As Det lays asleep in her bed, the door to her bedroom opens. Hearing it, Det opens her eyes, but does not move, pretending to still be asleep. Someone quietly walks into her room. It's Dacos. Still laying on her side, with her back to him, Det can tell by his footsteps that it's him. She still does not move and remains, eyes open, staring at the wall.

Dacos walks over to her bed behind her. He gently pulls back her covers, completely, exposing her laying there in just her short shirt. He lays down on the bed behind her, slides closer and puts his arm around her. He runs his hand down her arm that she has resting on the bed in front of her. Det feels Dacos's body press against hers. His hand slowly stroking her arm. She closes her eyes and reaches up to touch his hand, but it is only her arm that she feels. She opens her eyes and looks down at her arm, his hand is not there. He is not there. She feels the covers still pulled up over her. She sighs, pulls the covers even closer to her, shuts her eyes and goes back to sleep.

-------------------------------- **Clean Up** --------------------------------

Five Dakari stand outside the barn that Det, Tespa and Dacos had been inside of not that long ago. Three more Dakari are inside the barn, looking at all the dead Dakari laying around the place. Two of them walk outside the barn, gather with the rest of their group, and stand there looking around. There is no sign of what or who has defeated their brethren. Just some faint rouk hoof tracks in the ground leading back into the forest.

EXOM - THE YOUNG KING

As they study the tracks and stare into the forest, R'Vian calmly walks out from the trees, right up to the Dakari and stares at them. Not used to anyone approaching them so confidently, she takes the Dakari by surprise. It takes them a moment before two of them instinctively grab their rifles and fire at her. The Rifles blow up in the Dakari's hands, seriously injuring but not killing them, as R'Vian watches on with amusement.

She pulls two very large weapons of her own out from under her large cloak. Though very large and heavy looking, she raises them easily and casually shoots the two Dakari that just shot at her. Surprisingly her weapons do not blow up. Each blast blowing the Dakari into ashes. The remaining Dakari charge at her as she calmly keeps walking towards them and shoots them. When they have all been blown to ash, R'Vian watches the ash float around the air and fall to the ground. She returns one of her weapons back to under her cloak, then removes a small box shaped device from her other weapon and looks at it closely. It's flashing faintly, indicating that it is running out of power.

She returns the other weapon to under her cloak as well, then remains looking at the flashing box shaped device. The remaining Dakari, still in the barn, having heard the weapons fire, slowly exits the barn behind R'Vian, sneaking up behind her. R'Vian can hear it behind her, but still just stares at the box-shaped device in her hand. Not moving her head, she glances sideways with her eyes as she listens to the Dakari approach. She presses a button on the box-shaped device, it clicks, and she casually throws it over her shoulder towards the Dakari sneaking up on her. Instinctively the Dakari catches it, looking at it for a second, right before it activates, sending a lethal electric shock through the Dakari's body, killing it instantly. R'Vian turns around and walks over to the Dakari, as its dead body falls to the ground, and she gives it a nudge with her foot. The body of the Dakari rolls over and the device it was holding falls out of its hand and onto the ground. R'Vian walks over to the device, kicks it up into the air with her foot, catches it with one hand, puts it in her pocket and walks off back into the trees leaving a new pile of dead Dakari in her wake.

EXOM

THE YOUNG KING

CHAPTER SIXTEEN

The sunlight from the morning twilight shines through Det's bedroom window, starting to fill the room. Still in bed, Det starts to wake. Laying on her side, she brushes her hair off her face and looks around the room, well as far as she can without actually moving her head. She pulls her covers off her. Still only wearing a waste length, open, white shirt, she sits up, reaches over, and grabs her skirt from her side draws. She slides it on, stands up and walks over to her window. She looks out at the castle grounds and takes a moment to wake up.

Standing facing the window, she lets her shirt slip off, then still looking out the window, reaches down to her draws again and picks up her usual top. She puts it on, then straps up her belt.

The solid wall to the side of Det's Bedroom actually adjoins an area of the barracks. More specifically, it adjoins Dacos's bedroom, though there is no direct path between the two without going outside of the castle and through the gardens.

Dacos has also just recently woken up, still sitting on his bed wearing only long pants. He places his face into his hands and rubs it as he wakes himself up. Then stands up, walks over to his window, and also looks out over the palace gardens.

Det continues to watch out over the gardens, her hand reaching up as she runs her fingers down the inner edge and opening of her top. She casually turns around and looks around her room, then starts to slowly walk over to the wall that divides her and Dacos. She stands and stares at the wall, then places her hand on it, dragging it gently down the wall and letting her hand fall back to her side.

Dacos, still staring out his window, turns and looks at his wall as well. He walks over to it and also places his hand on it. He turns around and leans his back on it.

Likewise, Det also turns around, leaning her back into the wall.

At the same time, they both slowly slide down the wall and sit on the floor, their backs still pressed up against the wall. There is only now that wall between them. Det pulls up her knees and wraps her arms around her legs. Dacos raises one knee and rests his hand on it.

-------------------------------- Bullies ----------------------------------

As the sun starts to shine over the castle gardens, a couple of children run towards one of the garden hedges, appearing as though they are looking for something. They creep quietly alongside the hedge. There is a rustle. The children hear it and turn around. They hear the rustle again, and this time also see some movement in the hedge. They look at each other, smiling, trying to hold in their giggling as they place their hands over their mouth. They creep up slowly and quietly towards the rustling hedge. They get close. Very close. When Zipping jumps out of the hedge, throwing her hands up into the air. *"Raaar!"*, she roars at them. They squeal, giggle, and quickly run off. She gives them a little head start as she smiles, watching them run off, then runs off after them.

She passes the hedge, almost catching up to them, when something collides with her, knocking her straight into the ground. Surprised, she looks up and finds three boys, the same age as her, standing there. Seeing her running their way, one of the boys has pushed his friend straight into her as she passed them. All three boys look down at her, laughing, as she looks back scoldingly at them. She jumps to her feet and immediately starts pushing the boy that collided with her. *"You think that's funny?!"*, she yells at him. The boy she is pushing, Fray, looks a little worried as his friends continue to laugh. He points back at his friend that pushed him, Mayne. *"He pushed me"*, Fray tells her. Zippin stares at Mayne, her chest heaving as her eyes glare into him.

She takes a step towards him, ready to push him as well, when the children she was chasing call out to her. She stops and looks over at them. The children have now stopped running and are standing in the middle of the gardens watching Zippin and the boys. Zippin's face softens as she takes a breath. She looks back at the boys, her expression turning stern again as she takes another breath. She stares at Mayne. He stares back, still smiling, seeming very amused by what they have done. Zippin shakes her head at him. Takes another deep breath, then looks away still shaking her head. She looks back at the children and smiles. *"Raaar!"*, she roars at them, throwing her arms up again, and recommences chasing again. Again, the children squeal and giggle as they run away from her.

---------------------------- Watcha Doin? ----------------------------

The Training Hall on Eluud has been set to Advanced Mode. Dacos, with his ronad fully extended, spins it like a propeller, deflecting the shiny metallic balls as they are rapidly fired out of the slingshot machines. He stops spinning his ronad around and swings it around his back and over his arms and shoulders, still deflecting the metallic balls with considerable ease. Unlike how Steel was training, jumping and diving all over the training hall, Dacos stands in the one spot. Focussing on his precision and accuracy, each ball that he hits back going exactly where Dacos has intended, keeping them tightly grouped together, near the machines that are propelling them.

The doors to the training hall open and Trill walks in from outside. She walks through the entrance area, then quickly stops before walking out onto the training hall when she realizes that the hall is set into advanced mode. Noticing Trill standing there, Dacos yells out, *"Halt!"*. His voice command deactivating the slingshot machines, they immediately stop firing. Dacos lowers his ronad and looks over at Trill. Trill gives the hall a quick look-over from where she is standing. The slingshot machines now quiet and inactive, she feels safe enough to walk out into the hall towards Dacos.

Trill smiles as she almost reaches him, about to say something with the usual Trill excitement, when one of the slingshot machines, appearing to malfunction, starts propelling balls again at both her and Dacos. Dacos grabs Trill as they both quickly move out of the way. Dacos dives to the floor, rolls, then throws his ronad like a spear at the malfunctioning machine. His ronad penetrates deep into the slingshot machine and it instantly stops firing again. Dacos takes a moment before standing up, watching the machine intensely as Trill crawls across the training hall floor back into the entrance area. With the machine again appearing inactive, Dacos stands up, reaching out his hand in front of him. His ronad flies out of the slingshot machine and back towards him. He catches it, retracts it back into itself and places it in his leg holster, all the while keeping a sharp eye on the slingshot machine.

Trill stands up behind the entrance area wall and peers around the corner at Dacos. She looks over at the slingshot machine curiously, then looks back at Dacos. Dacos turns around and looks at Trill. Confused as to why the machine malfunctioned in the first place, he just shrugs. *"I guess it wasn't finished with us"*, he says to Trill, trying to make light of the situation. His attempts at humour always work at making Trill feel at ease. Just as hers makes him feel like she is up to something. Trill smiles and giggles slightly as she skips back over to Dacos and hands him a message stick. Dacos takes it curiously, thinking it must be something important for Trill to interrupt his training session to bring it to him. He activates it, the small screen projects from it and in front of him, and he starts reading

Trill stands next to him, not looking at the screen that is being projected, as she knows what it says, but instead just stares at Dacos. Dacos glances at her out of the corner of his eye, wondering what she is up to. Trill notices Dacos glancing at her, and it makes her giggle even more, though she tries to hold it back.

Now Dacos knows that she is up to something. But what? He continues to read the screen from the message stick. It is a report about the Dakari attack at the barn with himself, Det and Tespa. A report that he wrote.

He lowers the message stick and stares at Trill. Surely, she did not interrupt his training to show him a report that he himself wrote? *"This couldn't have waited?"*, he asks her. Trill shakes her head as she tries to hold in her smile and giggle. It's not working, Dacos can still see it. *"Yes, it could"*, he tells her.

No longer able to hold back her smile, Trill nods her head. She doesn't say a word, still just staring at Dacos. He stares back at her, trying to work out what is behind that smile. Is she being cheeky? Is there something that he is missing? What is she really up to? Whatever it is, it can not be about the report on the message stick.

"This is my report", he tells her. *"You know I know about this, right? I wrote it"*.

Dacos closes down the message stick and puts it in his pocket as Trill just stands there still smiling at him. Dacos continues to look at her wondering what she is really up to. Knowing that if he asks her straight out, being the playful sister that she is, she will not give him a straight answer, or likely not even an answer at all and just start giggling again. Though curiosity is getting the better of him, he decides not to play her game. She will tell him soon enough, in her own way, if he ignores it long enough.

"Is that everything", he asks her. Trill still does not say anything, still just smiling at Dacos as though he should know why she is there. It quickly becomes apparent to her that her innocent brother has no clue what she is smiling and giggling at. She stops smiling. Looks down at the ground then looks back up at him with a very innocent and coy expression. *"So, um, whatcha doin?"*, she asks him.

Dacos, knowing that this is all still part of her game, shakes his head and turns away to ignore her. Trill skips around in front of him and looks up at him again. *"Time to give him a clue"*, she thinks to herself. *"So, um, you and Det, fighting those Dakari - together"*, she says to him, her cheeky smile returning.

Dacos frowns at her, now realizing what Trill is getting at. *"Tespa was there as well"*, he tells her.

Trill ignores his comments and keeps the conversation focused on him and Det, paraphrasing words from his report. *"The two of you. Working as a perfect team, together like one"*, she says to him.

Dacos starts to feel a little defensive. *"It wasn't like that"*, he replies.

Trill continues to smile at him, completely disbelieving his defence. *"Really?"*, she says to him.

Dacos takes a moment to think. *"Well, OK, it was like that"*, he says as he remembers that it was words to that effect that he wrote in his report. He starts to reflect on the whole Dakari encounter at the barn and begins to smile. *"She can really fight"*, Dacos says to her. *"It was impressive to watch. I think it would amaze her father"*.

Hearing her brother finally starting to talk this way about Det gives Trill a warm, happy feeling inside and her face shows it. But this time it is not just his words, as he has often commented on Det's skill in the past. It's that glowing smile that Trill is also well and truly observing right now.

Looking back at Trill and noticing her expression, Dacos starts to feel uncomfortable, knowing exactly what message she is taking away from all this and the way he is speaking about Det. *"I was quite impressive as well"*, he says to Trill with a cheeky smile. His smile soon fades as he remembers how he saved Det, and she completely dismissed it. *"Not that anyone noticed"*, he adds.

Trill continues to smile and tilts her head, wanting and hoping that there is more to this story. *"So, after the heat of the battle"*, she says to him, *"when you were both basking in your teamwork...."*

"We were not basking", Dacos buts in to correct her. Again, Trill just ignores his comment.

"Did you ask her out?", she asks him.

Dacos gives Trill a discerning look, only mildly frustrated by her question, as he has long come to expect this kind of thing from her. Not just her either, but by many people lately it would seem. Dacos simply shakes his head in silence. Trill is disappointed. If ever there was an opportunity, surely this was it. Why can't her brother just acknowledge things and get a move on?

"Bro! Come on already!", she says to him. *"I want nephews and nieces. I'm not getting any younger and living vicariously through you is starting to get boring"*.

"Stop living through me then", Dacos tells her.

"Nah. Too much invested already", Trill replies.

Dacos just wants this conversation to end, so ignores his sister and walks over to the Slingshot machine that he destroyed with his ronad. He pushes a button on it, and it retracts down into the floor before raising up again, looking completely restored. *"You want to train?"*, he asks Trill, turning back to look at her.

Realizing that she is not going to get anything else out of her brother, Trill looks around at all the equipment that is out for the advanced mode setup of the training hall. *"Nah. I'm good"*, she replies. Though she has, and sometimes does, also train with the hall in advanced mode, training is not the reason she came here.

The doors to the training hall open again and Det walks in carrying her workout bag. Expecting to find the place empty, Det steps out straight into the training hall and stops when she sees Dacos and Trill standing there, now looking at her.

Trill smiles at Det then looks back at Dacos with the same smile. *"But you continue"*, Trill says to Dacos, her smile now taking its usual cheeky form.

Trying not to draw attention to herself, though a bit late, Det turns around, crouches down, putting her bag on the ground and starts to rummage through it. Knowing exactly what Trill is suggesting through her comment and cheeky smile, Dacos shakes his head and turns his attention back to the slingshot machine. Still wearing a huge smile, Trill skips over to Det. *"You here to practice?"*, Trill asks her, staring at her with an intense curiosity.

Det glances up at Trill briefly, and just as briefly looks over at Dacos before looking back into her bag. *"I was going to"*, Det replies. *"But I'll come back later"*.

Worried that this could turn into a missed opportunity for both Det and Dacos, Trill stops smiling and looks sincerely at Det. *"No, you should stay"*, Trill tells her. *"I was just about to leave anyway, and I know my brother could do with a good sparring partner"*. Trill looks back cheekily at Dacos, *"He still has so much that he could learn"*, she adds. Trill looks back at Det again, Det still searching through her bag, in her own world and not showing any reaction to Trill's words. *"I'm sure you could both teach each other some things"*, Trill says to her, a little more quietly, as though she is just saying it out loud to herself. Again, there is no response from Det.

Dacos, trying hard to ignore the one-sided conversation between Trill and Det, activates the Slingshot Machine. As he does so, he grunts under his breath, stamps his ronad into the ground, trying to get Trill's attention and get her to shut up. This action makes the Slingshot Machine malfunction again and it shoots a single metallic ball directly at Trill. Trill hears the shot and turns around just as the ball is about to hit her in the face. Unable to get out of the way quick enough, Trill cringes, closing her eyes and awaits the impact. She waits. And waits. There is no impact. Maybe it missed? She slowly opens one eye into a squint, then surprise and filled with disbelief with what she sees she opens the other and stares at the metallic ball, which has stopped in the air only inches away from her face.

Stunned, both eyes now wide open, she looks straight ahead, past the ball and sees Dacos standing there, looking at her equally shocked and surprised. Trill focuses again on the ball in front of her face and notices that the reason it has stopped is because something has stopped it. The ball has been speared by a ronad, the end of the ronad having penetrated straight through the metallic ball. Trill follows the ronad down and sees that it is Det that is holding it, still crouched down and looking in her bag, seemingly having grabbed her ronad from her leg holster, activated it and speared the ball all in a single instant before it hits Trill – all while never even turning around to look at it.

Still paying no attention to what is going on or what she has just done, Det deactivates and retracts her ronad. The speed of the spear ends retracting into the ronad handle seem to leave the metallic ball suspended in the air for a moment before dropping to the ground in front of Trill. Det places her ronad back into her leg holster, completely aware of what she has just done, but paying it no attention.

Trill and Dacos look at each other, still in total bewilderment of what has just occurred. Trill looks over at the Slingshot Machine, which seems to have only fired that single ball and is not shooting anything else. *"Wow, that thing really has it in for me"*, Trill says.

Still rummaging through her bag, Det stops and leans back, looking frustrated. Trill looks back at Det and, trying to get passed the awe of the event they just witnessed, notices Det's frustration. *"Everything alright?"*, Trill asks her curiously, with a little concern but still in shock over what happened.

Det remains glaring at her bag. *"I can't find it"*, Det replies, a combination of frustration and worry in her voice.

Trill moves in closer to Det to help her. After the way that Det has just saved her face from being smashed, it is the least she can do. *"Whatcha lost?"*, Trill asks her. Det stands up and looks at Trill, not saying a word. She then looks away, picks up her bag, looks back at Trill again briefly, before turning and walking out of the training hall.

Trill watches Det leave, then turns back to look at Dacos, who is still just standing there quietly not saying anything. Both of them still amazed and in shock at what they had just witnessed. *"She's a strange one"*, Trill says to him. *"But you saw that right? That whole "Psshhhhh", stabbing the ball before it hit my face while not looking, thing?"*, she asks Dacos.

Dacos saw it alright. He is still not quite sure what he just saw, but he saw it. *"Yep"*, Dacos replies.

The whole event just flashes back through Trill's head as she turns back and looks at the main doors that Det has just exited through. Her stare filled with curiosity and intrigue, Trill can only find one word to describe what she is feeling and thinking, *"Wow"*.

------------------------------- **Where is it?**-------------------------------

Tespa sits on her bed. Her Carmadile, a large eight-stringed Eluudian musical instrument that was originally in the large heavy box that Det dragged in earlier, now resting on the floor between her legs. With one hand strumming the combination of the four long thin strings that run the entire length of the instrument, and another four much shorter and thicker strings which are only half as long, she uses her other hand to create the notes along the neck of the instrument which stretches well above her head. The Carmadile makes a very beautiful sound and Tespa plays it very well. Changing from a soft classical piece, into a more upbeat rock rift and back again to a sombre classical melody.

Her curtain drawn, letting in only a small amount of sunlight to illuminate the room, her room has a relaxed serene feel. Kako lays back on Tespa's pillow, his eyes closed and being soothed by the music. Suddenly startled, his eyes open wide as Det barges into the room. Looking angrier than normal, she stares at Tespa with great intensity. Tespa looks up at Det, quite used to her just barging into her room, does not even break her rhythm and continues playing.

Det marches over and stands in front of Tespa. *"Where is it?"*, she scolds at Tespa in an angry and accusing tone. Unruffled by Det's bursting in and tone, Tespa looks back down at her instrument as she continues playing and relaxes into its soothing sounds.

Det starts hastily looking around Tespa's room. Under the bed, under the covers, even under the pillow throwing Kako off in the process. Tespa changes the music she is playing into a very slow, soft and relaxing piece, as though trying to create a balance in the room counteracting Det's impetuousness.

Tespa knows what Det is looking for. *"It is where you left it"*, Tespa tells her. *"Where it has been since you left it there"*. Det stands in the middle of the room looking around. No clue where it is that Tespa is talking about. Tespa looks at Kako and nods her head towards the bookshelves. Kako stands up and walks along the bed to the bookshelves. He climbs up them, stopping halfway up, and ambles along one of the middle shelves. He stops and picks up Det's delicate looking key chain that has the special crystal and key hanging from it. He holds it out to Det and smiles. Det does not smile back. Instead, she just walks over and snatches it from Kako's hand. *"I'm Kako"*, Kako says to her.

"I don't care", Det replies as she turns and just as quickly leaves Tespa's bedroom. Tespa continues playing her Carmadile, not even watching Det leave. *"You're welcome!"*, Tespa calls out to her.

"Welcome!", Kako also calls out, still smiling while standing on the shelf.

Tespa looks up at Kako and smiles at him. *"Must be important"*, she says to him. *"I don't even know what that is"*.

Kako looks innocently back at Tespa. *"I'm Kako"*, he says still smiling.

Looking very happy and relaxed in her music, Tespa returns her attention back to her Carmadile. *"Yes, you are"*, she says to Kako.

Kako climbs back down off the bookshelves, onto the bed, lays down on the pillow, closes his eyes again and enjoys Tespa's playing. *"I'm Kako"*, he mumbles to himself as he drifts off to the music.

EXOM

THE YOUNG KING

CHAPTER SEVENTEEN

-------------------------------- Surprise --------------------------------

Making full use of the daylight on Eluud, well outside Chassam Castle's walls, some villagers are going about their business, farming, and carrying supplies to their huts, when a group of Dakari come out from the forest and start viciously attacking them. Some villagers try to run while others stay to fight. Neither is of any use. The Dakari quickly kill all the villagers and then start gathering up the villager's supplies.

They hear something in the trees of the forest near them and stop what they are doing, all staring in the direction that the sound is coming from. A couple of them draw out their long daggers and take a couple of steps towards the forest, when a small cylinder object is thrown out from the trees and lands on the ground near them. The Dakari all look at it curiously, but do not approach. Suddenly the cylinder shoots out a devastating pulse from all sides that makes the ground ripple. The ripple shoots up the bodies of all the Dakari. They scream in pain before dropping dead on the ground.

-------------------------------- The Call --------------------------------

A little later that day, the sunlight has given way to the usual twilight that dominates Eluud. Inside the meeting hall, a holoprojector is active, creating a rippling pool of energy near the shelves along the wall. Gathered around it is Orlow and the Queen Mother. Within the holoprojectors energy field, the live image of Steel can be clearly seen. He is sitting down, perhaps on his bed, in what appears to be his quarters in the Citadel of Light. He is smiling at his mother and uncle, though the smile hides a more serious expression.

Tespa walks into the room, wearing her backpack carrying Kako, and closes the door behind her. The Queen Mother reaches her hand out to her, beckoning her to come close. Tespa smiles when she sees her father in the holoprojection energy field and walks over to join her grandmother and great-uncle. *"Hey. How's Aymyn"*, she asks her father.

"Still here", Steel replies. *"I haven't destroyed it yet"*.

"Oh, you're just not trying hard enough", Tespa says with a laugh.

The door to the meeting hall starts to open again. Everyone turns around to look at it and sees Det standing there peering in. Like she did with Tespa, the Queen Mother reaches out her hand and beckons Det. Tespa motions with her head for Det to come in. Det opens the door wider and starts to slowly walk inside the room. Steel looks over at Det through the Holoprojection energy field. *"Nice of you to join us, Det"*, he says to her with a smile. Det does not smile back, nor does she say anything. She walks over and joins her family in front of the holoprojection field and stares at her father curiously. It is not unusual for him to speak to his family while he is away, as you would expect. However, he has never gathered them all together in one room like this before.

Orlow walks back towards the large table and picks out a piece of fruit from the bowl in the centre. As he walks back to join the family, he notices Kako sitting in Tespa's backpack. He looks at Kako curiously as though he has never seen him before. Strangely, Kako is not saying anything. Instead, he is looking at Orlow with a fearful confusion as though he thinks Orlow is a ghost. They both silently stare at each other, wondering if each one exists. Orlow is pretty sure Kako doesn't, being just a figment of his imagination.

The rest of the family stare at Steel through the holoprojection energy field. As Steel smiles at them, happy to see them all, they all stare back at him wondering why he has gathered them all together, though it is a question that no one seems to ask.

"Have you found a Zazar yet willing to select us?", Tespa asks her father.

"Not yet", Steel replies casually. Casually due to it being the answer he has unfortunately given so many times before to the same question.

"The horn remains silent", Orlow comments looking a little disheartened.

"Hopefully not for too much longer, uncle", Steel replies as the Queen Mother nudges Orlow harshly with her shoulder. She looks curiously at Steel after hearing his words. She has heard Steel say those words before. In fact, he tells them all the time, always being hopeful and determined. However, this time, she detects something different about the way Steel says it.

"Has something happened, son?", she asks Steel as Orlow looks at her wondering why she just nudged him with her shoulder.

Steel kind of nods while not giving too much away. As yet, nothing has happened. Only his hopes that he will be successful. *"Stay tuned"*, he replies.

Tespa turns and looks at Det, wondering what her father is not saying and wanting to see if Det may be wondering the same thing. Det does not look back at her. Instead, she just stands there watching her father in the holoprojection field, showing no expression at all. Now Tespa is more curious about Det and her lack of reaction. Tespa looks around, noticing everyone else in the room, including herself, giving each other that look of "what is going on?". Everyone except Det. Does Det know, she wonders? How could she know any more than anyone else? Tespa looks back at her father.

"The Zazars are stubborn", Steel tells them. *"I'm beating my head against a wall with them. It's time to try something new"*.

"New?", the Queen Mother asks, even more curious about what Steel is hinting at.

Steel momentarily gets lost in his thoughts and speaks without thinking. *"I have made it my life goal to sound the horn"*, he says. *"It has to happen. Now this is all or nothing"*.

"All or Nothing", the Queen Mother thinks to herself? *"Not sure I like the sound of that"*, she says to Steel.

"What do you mean?", Tespa asks, also alarmed by those words.

Steel snaps himself back out of his thoughts and realizes that his words have caused the others to be concerned. He quickly tries to regain the calmness of this family conversation. *"It is nothing I want you to worry about"*, he tells them.

It's a bit too late for that. They were already a little concerned the moment he asked them all to come together. Tespa again glances at Det who is still just staring blankly at her father. Orlow looks over at Tespa and sees Kako in her backpack still staring, wide-eyed, at him. Orlow looks equally wide-eyed back at Kako. Orlow then looks at the Queen Mother and tries to get her attention to see if she can see the same thing that he is looking at. The Queen Mother looks back at Orlow but thinks that he is looking at her out of concern for what Steel is saying.

Steel notices everyone looking at each other, except for Det, who is just staring at him, which actually concerns him even more. Det usually withdraws more and reacts less the more something troubles her. Which is what she appears to be doing right now. *"It's nothing to worry about"*, he tells everyone. *"It's fine. It's just something that I haven't tried before. I'm hoping it works"*. Nothing Steel is saying is helping the family worry less.

"You're hoping what works?", Tespa asks him.

Before giving her father a chance to answer, Det chooses this moment to ask exactly what everyone else is thinking. But when she asks, it's almost like she knows the answer and just wants to hear how her father answers it. *"Is it dangerous?"*, she asks.

Steel looks at her, then at the rest of his family, not saying a word for a moment, trying to choose his words carefully. *"Nah"*, he finally replies. *"Dangerous is dealing with you guys. I've been doing that for long enough. I can take on anything"*, he adds jokingly with a wink, hoping his attempt at humour has distracted them from their concern. It hasn't.

Again, Det asks a question that everyone else is wondering. But is she asking it to have an answer, or to corner her father into revealing what he is not being forthright in saying? *"So, you will be home soon?"*, she asks him.

Steel takes a moment to answer, now starting to realize that there is a precision about Det's questions. *"That's the plan"*, he replies. Steel nods and makes himself smile. *"Yes. I'll be home soon"*, he tells them.

The family still all look uncertain at Steel, not fully convinced by his words. If his vague answers were not enough to make them concerned, there is still that elephant in the room that no one has address yet. That is until now. *"Why did you call us?"*, Det asks him.

"Det!", Tespa says, turning to Det, looking annoyed at her question. Not annoyed at what Det asked, but rather how she asked it. Though really, like everyone else, she is relieved that someone has.

"You don't usually gather us all together for a call when you are away", Det tells her father. Staring directly at him. Her expression still not changing.

Finally, someone has said it. The whole family look at Steel eagerly awaiting his answer. Steel looks at Det, at first wishing she hadn't asked, but then noticing her expressionless stare become more intense. Looking straight into him as though he was actually in the room and not a trillion miles away. *"Like I said, Det"*, he starts to explain. *"I'm trying new things. You guys are my family. You are what gives me strength"*.

"You need strength?", Det asks him. A strange question and again so precise. It hits his heart hard, almost taking his breath away. It's obvious now that they know something is up. He is sure they don't know what, but their concern for him he can feel halfway across Exom.

"Always", Steel replies, making himself smile again. *"And besides, while I'm away, I need to know that you are taking good care of my kingdom. And each other"*.

The Queen Mother looks at Det, knowing that although she is still not showing anything, she is thinking and feeling the same as her. Det may not speak a lot, not like Tespa, but when Det speaks she speaks true. Sometimes speaking true is not what people want to hear – and therefore Det will often choose not to speak. She knows that Det will not respond to Steel's last comment. Steel is wanting reassurance that his family and kingdom will be alright and take care of each other while he is "away" – and the Queen Mother is well aware what he means by "away".

"Always", the Queen Mother replies, looking back at Steel. *"You don't need to worry about that. We always will"*. The words feeling heavy on her chest.

Steel and the Queen Mother look at each other in silence for a moment, an unspoken sense of knowing. The Queen Mother's eyes trying to look strong, just like she did when his father, her husband, was killed by raiders years ago and she was left to console a much younger Steel. Steel knows and understands that look. The Queen Mother also knows that Steel knows that look. He has asked his question, the real reason why he called, and he has got an answer. Whether that answer is true or said only because it is what he wanted and needed to hear, well, he has to believe with all his heart that they are one in the same. Steel forces himself to smile again.

"Good. Very good. Well, ah", he says as he starts to stutter, feeling a little agitated but trying his hardest not to show it. *"I've got to go now – and – um, do this – thing"*, he adds. He takes a deep breath as he recomposes himself and looks straight at them all. He tries to make himself smile again, but unsuccessfully this time. His grimace now barely hiding an overwhelming sadness. His teeth grind together, then bite down on his lip, as he takes another deep breath. Feeling this may be the last time that he sees his family and, more importantly, they see him. His lips start to quiver. He needs to end this conversation before he loses his composure completely. He reaches forward to touch his holoprojector. *"I love you all"*, he says, then switches it off.

As the holoprojector in the Meeting Hall also shuts down, the floating energy dispersing in front of the family, the Queen Mother and Orlow look at each other, then walk over to the large table. Still holding the piece of fruit that he picked out before, Orlow looks back at the fruit bowl and picks out another as the Queen Mother pours herself a glass of water.

Det remains standing, staring at where the holoprojection energy field was. Tespa turns around and looks a little confused, still not sure what she has heard, and still unsure why her father called in the first place. *"That was a strange call"*, Tespa says to everyone. *"Det's right. He doesn't usually gather us all together like this to say hello"*.

"He wasn't saying hello", Orlow casually replies, tactlessly speaking without thinking, as he is known to do. *"He was saying goodbye"*.

The Queen Mother quickly slaps Orlow over the head, infuriated at his insensitivity, as Tespa looks at them confused. Det continues to just stare blankly at where the holoprojection field was, not moving. Orlow looks at the Queen Mother startled at her reaction, but then dismisses it and moves on and takes a bite out of his piece of fruit. The Queen Mother looks over at Tespa to make sure that she is alright after Orlow's careless response. Tespa still appears confused but is now starting to think it all over and put it all together. She turns and looks at Det and, like everyone else, notices that Det is still standing there and not moving.

Orlow looks back over at Tespa, her back now turned to him as she looks at Det, he is again looking straight at Kako. Kako stares back at him from Tespa's backpack, still wide eyed, and does not say anything. Again, Orlow looks curiously at the Queen Mother. *"Does anyone else see that thing?"*, he asks her. The Queen Mother looks at Kako, then looks back at Orlow, and just shakes her head before walking over to Tespa and Det.

---------------------------- **Not That Day** ----------------------------

Meanwhile, making their way onto Chassam Castle's hanger, A large army of Dakari sneak towards the Castle, slowly and cautiously passing stationary ships and shuttles. The Flight Commander is crouched down, looking under a large freighter ship, as the Dakari approach closer to him. Seeing their reflection in the freighter's hull at the last moment, the Flight Commander dives under the freighter just as a Dakari swings its large dagger at him. It only narrowly misses as the Flight Commander scurries under the freighter and makes his way to the other side. He stands up and runs away from the freighter a few steps, turns back and sees a number of Dakari also scurrying underneath the freighter towards him. He turns again and starts running towards the castle. The first Dakari that makes it out from under the freighter dives at him with its long dagger in its hand. The Flight Commander leaps sideways, diving to the ground, dodging it, summersaults and pulls out his ronad from his leg holster. He stands up, when suddenly a hand grabs him from behind and pulls him back towards the castle wall. It is Sergeant Mew. Mew presses a button inside a protected console and an alarm immediately starts sounding. Mew and The Flight Commander lean shoulder to shoulder into each other. Turning to face the Dakari, they activate their ronads and prepare to fight.

The alarm alerts everyone in the Castle and surrounds, including Det, Tespa, Orlow and the Queen Mother in the Meeting Room. They all look at each other wondering what has happened. Curious, scared, are they safe? Det then looks at the Queen Mother, as though she has a different kind of thought, before turning and walking towards the door. Knowing Det's thoughts have something to do with at least investigating the alarm, and very likely taking an active part in confronting whatever has created the need for it, the Queen Mother puts her hand on Det's chest to stop her. Det stops and looks at the Queen Mother with a perplexed expression. Not confused about what is going on like everyone else, but confused about why the Queen Mother is stopping her from finding out.

The Queen Mother hurries over to the door and leans against it, trying to listen through it. Det walks up and stands behind her, just wishing that she would move out of the way. Det then turns to look at Tespa, who also knows what Det wants to do. Tespa looks back at Det and shakes her head, looking really concerned about what is happening. Whatever it is, she is sure that Dacos, Trill and the soldiers will sort it out, but she'd feel a lot better if her father was there as well. Det, shakes her head and shrugs at Tespa dismissively then turns back to looking impatiently at her grandmother. She puts her arm on her grandmother's shoulder, hoping that she will move out of the way. She doesn't. The Queen Mother gently brushes Det's hand away and motions for her to go back to the other end of the room. Det ignores her.

The Dakari stop on the flight deck as soon as they hear the alarm, and momentarily look confused, not knowing whether to continue charging or run away. A large battalion of soldiers run out of the Castle; Trill is amongst them. As the soldiers stop and stand with Mew and the Flight Commander, Trill pushes on through them, sliding along the ground on her knees. She pulls her ronad from her leg holster and activates it. Her ronad extends into a spear. She twists the handle of her ronad and it quickly retracts again, then extends once more, this time not as a pole spear but as a long bow. Trill pulls a thin, about one inch long, bar from her belt and squeezes it. Like her ronad, it instantly extends into a full-length arrow. She quickly knocks the arrow to the bow, pulls back the bow string and fires the arrow into the chest of the closest Dakari. The Dakari spins around from the impact and falls to the ground clutching its chest. Trill pulls out another small bar from her belt and likewise extend that into a full-length arrow, knocking it to her bow ready to fire again.

Several more soldiers step forward and stand next to Trill, pulling out their ronads and, like Trill, activating it into a long bow. They too pull out small bars from their belts, activating them into arrows and fire at the Dakari. Some arrows hit their target, others do not. The Dakari again charge forward towards the soldiers. The rest of the soldiers activate their ronads into pole spears and charge forward to meet them, joined by Mew and the Flight Commander.

More Dakari climb up onto the flight deck, more than any Eluudian has ever seen, and run to join their comrades. Now greatly out numbering the Eluudian soldiers, the Dakari engage the soldiers, fighting viciously, swinging their long daggers as others lash out with their razor-sharp claws. The Eluudian soldiers do not retreat, fighting back strongly. The Eluudian soldiers fighting as a team, back-to-back with their colleagues, as others with Trill continue firing arrow after arrow into the Dakari.

Despite all this, the sheer number and berserk viciousness of the Dakari is not placing this battle in the Eluudians favour.

"There's too many of them", one of the archers says to Trill.

"We'll be slaughtered", another one says to her.

Trill stays focussed, firing arrow after arrow successfully into the Dakari. *"Slaughtered?"*, she replies. *"Maybe. One day"*. She looks over at her archers and smiles. *"But today is not that day"*, she adds, firing one more arrow directly into the head of a Dakari.

She gives her ronad long bow a quick flick and it retracts back into itself, then extends again into a pole spear. Jumping to her feet, Trill then charges at the Dakari.

The Dakari fight like fierce armed animals, slashing and diving at the soldiers. The soldiers do their best to fight back, and put up a very good fight, but are also taking heavy casualties. They give back as good as they get however, with many Dakari also falling as well.

Taking the lead, Trill fights spectacularly, spinning and swinging her ronad like no tomorrow, and often taking out more than one Dakari at a time. The fight continues and intensifies. The Dakari still having the upper hand with their larger numbers. Trill knocks one Dakari to the ground and thrusts her ronad into its throat. She spins around just as two Dakari swing their long daggers at her. With no time to react, Trill crouches to the ground and shields her face with her arm. The Dakari daggers stop just before striking her, blocked by another ronad. A very different looking ronad. The ronad belonging to Dacos.

Trill looks up and sees her brother standing there. The two Dakari daggers still held back by his ronad. He smiles at her, quickly but calmly, then swings his ronad at the Dakari, taking both of them out at once. He looks back at Trill and extends his hand to her. She smiles, grabs his hand and he quickly pulls her up. Trill jumps back into the fight.

Ever so calm, Dacos smiles at her again. Then, with a quick flick of his wrist, he throws his ronad at a Dakari approaching him from the side. It spears the Dakari through its torso. Dacos reaches out his arm towards the speared Dakari and his ronad flies back to his hand, letting the Dakari fall to the ground. Dacos launches himself into the fight. Standing beside his sister, they fight the still very large group of remaining Dakari.

EXOM - THE YOUNG KING

Five Dakari line up in front of Dacos and Trill, standing prepared to charge at them. Dacos and Trill ready their ronads to fight. However, before the Dakari can charge, they are blown over by a number of laser blasts. As the Dakari fall down, Trill and Dacos can see Vessel marching towards them, her hands already holding Troin blasters created from her Tal. She continues firing at the Dakari as Troin Battle Armour starts to form on her body.

Two Dakari, one from each side, charge at her. She holds her Troin blasters out to her side and shoots them both at the same time. The blast spins them around and as they die, they fall into her before she can move out of the way. Two more Dakari take their place and charge at her from each side. Vessel forms her giant Troin wings and, holding them stretched out, she spins around and knocks the charging Dakari to the ground. Trill and Dacos pounce on the same Dakari and finish them off.

The Dakari break off into two groups as Trill, Dacos and Vessel look back at them. One group stays and fights the Eluudians on the hangar while the other runs inside the castle. Thinking immediately of Tespa, Vessel runs straight into the castle after them, without any hesitation. Dacos looks worriedly at Trill. His thoughts predominantly on the royal family, but also on everyone else who happens to be inside the castle. Very capable of reading her brother, Trill turns her back to him and faces the remaining Dakari group still on the hangar. *"I got this!"*, she yells at Dacos. *"Go!"*. Straight away Dacos runs into the Castle in pursuit of the Dakari.

Vessel charges into the castle entrance and watches the Dakari run down a corridor. The Castle has many corridors, and the one the Dakari have chosen to run down, fortunately as far as Vessel is concerned, does not lead to the Meeting Hall where the Royal family are gathered. Instead of pursuing the Dakari, Vessel runs directly down the corridor leading to the Meeting Hall.

Dacos enters the castle entrance seconds later. He cannot see any Dakari. He catches the final flash of Vessel running down the corridor towards the Meeting Hall. He is just about to follow her, then stops. He looks down the corridor the Dakari have actually run down, and detecting something, he starts marching down that one instead.

The Queen Mother still has her ear to the door, trying to listen through it. She hears someone running and steps back, holding onto Det and moving her back with her. The door opens quickly. Its Vessel. She stands in the doorway and looks at the family. She focusses on Tespa, then quickly enters the room, and closes the door behind her. Everyone else in the room is alarmed that whatever is happening out there, it is enough for Vessel to wear full Troin Armour.

"What is it?", the Queen Mother asks in a panic, reaching out to hold on to Vessel. Vessel pushes past her and runs directly to Tespa.

"Everyone, get back, away from the door", Vessel tells them as she pushes Tespa behind her and then aims her Troin blasters at the door. The Queen Mother grabs Det's arm and tries to lead her to the back of the room with everyone else. However, Det breaks free and instead walks up to the door, then tries to listen through it.

"Det! Get back here", The Queen Mother yells at her as she stands behind Vessel. Orlow moves around and stands behind Tespa. He looks at her backpack and notices Kako still staring, wide eyed, at him. Orlow takes a few steps to his side and stands behind the Queen Mother instead, trying his hardest to not look at Kako.

Det ignores her grandmother and still stands by the door, her ear pressed up against it and her hand reaching for the handle. As the rest of the family look very much frightened and concerned, huddled together at the back of the room with Vessel standing in front of them as a shield, Det does not seem scared at all. In fact, Det curiously wants to leave the room and join in with whatever is happening outside.

Very casually and calmly, Dacos walks down the Castle corridor. Several Dakari jump out at him from an open room, their daggers and claws slashing down at him. Dacos quickly and effortlessly blocks their attack. He dispatches them just as quickly, hitting and spearing them with his ronad. As they fall to the floor, Dacos continues walking calmly down the corridor.

Another Dakari jumps out at him from the shadows. Dacos spears it through the neck with his ronad just as a second Dakari lunges at him from his other side. Dacos weaves out the way and the Dakari hits the wall opposite him. As the Dakari bounces off the wall, Dacos grabs its head and slams it back into the wall again, knocking it unconscious. He then pulls his ronad out from the first Dakari, spears it straight down into the second Dakari laying on the floor, then again continues to calmly make his way down the corridor.

As Dacos reaches the end of the first corridor and turns down another, Dakari continue to jump out at him from every corner and room. Dacos quickly takes them out, sometimes spectacularly, but always seemingly effortlessly. He turns and starts to walk down a long corridor. At the end of the corridor is a single closed door. A door that leads to the Meeting Hall.

As Dacos walks towards the Meeting Hall, more and more Dakari jump out at him. He again drops them quickly, then continues walking calmly towards the Meeting Hall door.

On the other side of the door, Det can no longer hold herself back, not that she was really trying to in the first place. She turns the handle and opens it slightly. *"Det. Don't!"*, the Queen Mother yells at her.

"Det, get back here!", Tespa tells her. *"It's not safe"*. Vessel shakes her arm, now getting tired from pointing at the door with her Troin blasters, then aims again at the door. Det holds her hand up to the family, motioning to them to be quiet. The family complies but with considerable trepidation. Det opens the door wider and quickly slips out of the room. Tespa looks up with alarm at Vessel. Vessel looks back at Tespa, but has no intention of leaving her to go after Det.

Still quite some way up the corridor, Dacos makes his way towards the meeting hall. He sees Det come out. She does not see him as she turns back to face the door, carefully and quietly closing it behind her. A Dakari walks out from an adjoining hallway right next to Det and swings at her with its large dagger. She does not see it, her attention still focused on closing the door. Seemingly intuitively, Det moves slightly, dodging the Dakari's attack. It quickly swings at her again. Again, Det moves out the way while still focussed on closing the door.

The door now closed, Det turns around and sees the Dakari. As it prepares to swing at her again, Det looks up the corridor and sees

Dacos now running towards her, his calm demeanour now gone. He throws his ronad at the Dakari, spearing it through the back and pinning it to the wall next to Det.

Looking completely calm and unruffled by the speared Dakari next to her, Det's eyes are fixated on Dacos. Dacos runs right up and stands in front of her. Their eyes lock. Still looking at Det, Dacos grabs his ronad and pulls it out of the Dakari. The Dakari falls to the ground. Det looks down beside her as the dead Dakari lands on the ground next to her feet. She looks up at Dacos curiously, then looks past him at all the dead Dakari that lay littered along the floor up the corridor. Her expression one of intrigue and fascination, she looks back at Dacos. *"Is there anymore?"*, she asks him.

Dacos smiles, his mind thinking back to their teamwork back at the barn. *"Maybe"*, he replies. *"Did you want to come help me look?"*.

Det looks back up the corridor as she thinks for a moment. Then looks back at Dacos and nods.

-------------------------------- **Kalrain** --------------------------------

Dressed a lot more casually, but still wearing his royal coat, Steel returns to the large double doors, leading into the Training Hall, that he was standing at with Dacos while Dacos was at the Citadel. As he had said to Dacos, he had seen this place before but never had any reason to go there. Now he does. This is where the Zazar tests are also conducted. Before opening them, Steel stands there looking at the doors, seeing them as almost symbolic. Once he steps through, he passes from one life to another. From one path to another. He looks back down the corridor, like he is taking one last look at this corridor, these walls, these doors. Depending on how this goes, it could well be. Once he steps inside these doors, his life is either about to change - or end. He will no longer be the King of Eluud. He will no longer be a Member of the Royal Alliance Council. He will no longer be with Aura. He is either going to lose so many things that have ever meant anything to him, or he is going to lose everything entirely. "Is this really worth it?", he looks down and wonders. He sighs, takes a deep breath, then reaches up and presses a console on the wall. The doors open, he walks inside, and the doors close behind him.

Being so large, the Training Hall in the Citadel of Light is also very versatile. Able to change according to its needs and what it is intended for. When Steel and Dacos were standing there, looking in, the last time they were here, there was nothing overly special about it. Very big, yes, which is what impressed Dacos. Some soldiers training with VR equipment, and a couple of Zazars with their instructor standing in the open hall. This time the Training Hall is very different. This time, in the centre of the hall is a very large and very complicated obstacle and challenge course. In fact, to call it very large and very complicated is a gross understatement. The course is absolutely huge, layer upon layer, level upon level, reaching as far up as Steel can see. And the complexity, in many ways defies words. Walls of all different kinds, shapes, sizes and at a variety of angles. Ledges of various widths, ropes, chains, scaffolding, and platforms. All of which are moving with no apparent sequence or any specific direction. The whole thing entangled and arranged into a multilevel gauntlet. Adding to its complexity, some of the obstacles appear to be made of pure fire or lasers. Some appearing only intermittently and then disappearing just as fast as they appeared. When they appear again, they are often, but not always, in the same place.

Making the gauntlet even more complicated is the random firing of laser blast cannons, shooting in all kinds of directions with again no apparent pattern. Some located on the walls around the hall, others on the gauntlet itself. The blasts however are only aimed within the gauntlet, an area marked on the floor by a different colour tiling. Where Steel is standing, outside the gauntlet area, is perfectly safe from the laser cannons.

Steel looks up into the gauntlet and sees someone zipping through it. A woman, Kalrain, still dressed in her long and quite revealing flowing red gown. She is holding her 5-foot-long staff, which she occasionally uses to propel herself on and off walls and ledges. Sometimes even to snare ropes and chains, using them to swing herself to lower or higher levels of the gauntlet. She dodges the numerous and rapidly firing laser cannon blasts, occasionally deflecting them with her staff.

The way she moves through the gauntlet with such ease absolutely amazes Steel and, wide eyed, he can't look away. Completely encaptivated in the skill and acrobatics this woman is using; Steel does not realise that he is walking forward to get a closer look. That is until he steps past the safety area and onto the different colour flooring that represents the gauntlet area. One of the blast cannons instantly turns and aims at him. While still deeply involved in performing her amazing gymnastics skills, Kalrain notices the cannon turn towards Steel and dives off the gauntlet. She somersaults across the floor, then pushes Steel out of the way with the end of her staff just as the cannon fires at him. Steel flies back from the impact of Kalrain's staff and stumbles to the floor. Kalrain raises her hand in the air and yells, *"Halt!"*.

Instantly the cannons stop firing. All the laser and fire obstacles disappear, and the walls and ledges stop moving. Still on the floor, Steel sits up and looks around, only now realising what he did. He looks over at Kalrain, his face expressing his shock and embarrassment. Kalrain, still standing inside the gauntlet marked area with her back to the gauntlet, stares back at Steel. Steel tries to work out if her gaze is one of confusion or frustration. It is both.

Kalrain is fully aware of why Steel is there. To attempt the Zazar test. A test that almost killed him before he even started it. However, like everyone else who now knows about his intention, she does still wonder why he is there. She looks down at Steel feeling strongly, like so many others, that he should not be here. Not because he is not allowed to be, but because it is extremely foolish for him to be.

Steel looks up at the gauntlet again. It's now looking a lot less dangerous than when he first saw it while walking in. *"Looks like I'm in the right place"*, he says.

Kalrain turns away from looking at Steel, walks over to the wall beside the large doors and presses a button, activating an intercom. *"Guards to the Training Hall"*, she says into the intercom. *"I have someone here who should not be"*.

Hearing her words and believing that she does not realise who he is or why he is there, Steel jumps to his feet and runs over to her. *"Wait!"*, he yells, as Kalrain turns and stares at him. A stare so intense that it makes him stop in his tracks, freeze, and dare not approach her. As he stands there frozen, speechless, Kalrain's stare starts to soften, and she looks at him with more of a curious expression. Feeling a little more at ease to move again, Steel stands up straight and straightens up his royal coat. *"I'm King Steel of Eluud"*, he tells her. *"I'm here for the Zazar test"*, he adds with a smile. Kalrain continues to stare at him curiously, while showing at least a hint of frustration. Steel starts walking towards her again, holding out his hand, waiting to see her expression change as she realizes that he is actually meant to be there. It doesn't. She still looks at him and thinks that he shouldn't be.

"I know who you are and what you are here for", Kalrain replies. *"You failed"*, she adds, her expression or stare not changing. She turns and presses the intercom button again. *"Guards, I'm still waiting"*, she says into it.

The two large doors to the training hall open and three Aymyn guards march in. They look at both Steel and Kalrain, then at each other, a little confused, as they know who Steel is. Also, like everyone else within the Citadel now, as word has gotten around quickly, they know what he is there for.

Steel only looks briefly at the guards as they walk in. However, he is more interested in what Kalrain has just said. He's failed? Now, his expression is also one of confusion and frustration. *"Wait, that's hardly fair"*, he says to her, now standing a little more confidently and a little defiantly. *"I was told to come here. I was not told I was going to be shot at the moment I got here"*. He has not gone through all this pain and mental anguish for it to all end before it has even begun.

Kalrain turns away from Steel and walks back towards the gauntlet. *"You were told to come here and be tested"*, she says to him while not looking at him. *"You failed"*. She stops walking only to glance sideways at the guards. *"Take him"*, she tells them. Then continues walking towards the gauntlet.

The Guards are still confused about arresting Steel, a member of the Royal Alliance who does not appear to have committed any crimes or broken any rules, other than somehow annoy Kalrain. The Dilemma is that Kalrain's position as the Tription Weapon's Teacher also falls under the area of Aymyn Security, and her position outranks that of the guards. She has given them an order and, whether they agree with or understand it or not, it is not for them to disobey it. The guards move in to apprehend Steel. Steel dodges the guards as they reach for him. *"I wouldn't do that if I was you"*, he tells them as he steps back and holds his hands out in front of him.

Hearing Steel's defiance, Kalrain stops walking and looks at Steel out of the corner of her eye. One of the guards pulls out a firearm and points it at Steel. Kalrain turns around quickly and looks at the Guards, then at Steel. She does not appear to be concerned but rather intrigued with what is about to play out. Steel looks at the guard firmly, his body tensing up as though preparing to fight. *"This is about to get messy"*, he says out loud to himself. The other two guards also pull out their firearms as well. *"Very messy"*, Steel adds.

All three guards now have their weapons pointed at Steel, as Steel stands in a fighting pose as though ready to take them on, unarmed. He looks a little anxious, as you would expect, but not scared. *"It doesn't need to be this way"*, Steel tells the guards. *"It's not too late for you to stop and just leave peacefully"*. The guards look confused. They look at each other, each with weapons aimed directly at Steel, as Steel stands there with his unarmed hands held out in front of him. They are not sure who Steel is referring to about stopping and leaving peacefully.

"Who are you talking to? Us, or yourself?", one of the guards asks him curiously.

Steel realises how this looks, three armed guards against one unarmed man, which is exactly how it is. *"I'm not sure yet"*, Steel replies.

Kalrain, now becoming annoyed by the standoff, which should not even be happening, walks back and stands next to one of the guards. *"Shoot him already"*, she tells the guards as she rests her staff against the wall. Before the guards even have time to follow her order, she spins back around, quickly taking the gun from one of the guards, points it at Steel and fires. Steel dives towards the wall, the shot narrowly missing him. He somersaults along the floor and quickly stands up near Kalrain's staff as Kalrain turns to shoot at him again. Steel grabs hold of her staff as she fires at him a second time. He deflects the weapon's blast with her staff, then looks at her staff, really impressed by it. *"Nice"*, he says out loud as he takes a moment to admire it

Still aiming the gun at him, Kalrain seems almost amused by his interest in her staff. *"You damage that and you're paying for it"*, she tells him as she prepares to shoot again.

Steel dives again, this time landing behind one of the guards. As he stands up, he quickly snatches the guard's firearm from the guard's hand. Flipping around to within reaching distance of Kalrain, holding her staff in one hand, he points the firearm at her head with the other. Just like Steel, Kalrain too has the firearm that she is holding aimed straight at Steel's head. Steel's eyes dart between Kalrain and the barrel of the firearm she has pointed at him. *"I said messy, didn't I?"*, Steel says to her. *"I said this is about to get messy. Very messy. Not quite the mess I meant"*. His eyes look back and forth between Kalrain, the firearm he has aimed at her head and the firearm that she has aimed at his. *"I'd hate to be on clean-up duty in this place after this"*, Steel adds.

Kalrain's expression does not change. She still looks at Steel with the same intrigue and frustration, not even looking at or caring about the weapon that he has pointed at her. Steel, on the other hand, is now starting to look flustered. He uses the firearm that he is holding to gently push aside the firearm that she has pointed at him. Kalrain does not resist, still staring at him with intrigue. Steel lowers his firearm and huffs, staring at her, still flustered. *"This is crazy"*, Steel exclaims. *"I am here to do the Zazar test. You can kill me, but I am not leaving until I do it"*, he tells her.

Kalrain looks confused at Steel as she wonders if he realises what he just said. He does. *"Unless you kill me"*, he adds. *"So please don't. Or at least not before the test. Preferably not after either. Because that would also suck"*.

Kalrain is amused and for the first time actually smiles. Then, with a quick swipe of her hand, snatches her staff back from Steel. At the same time, and in the same action, she also uses her staff to take his firearm from him. Now holding her staff and both firearms, she casually walks back over to the guards and throws their weapons at them.

The guards catch their weapons as Kalrain turns around and again walks back towards the gauntlet. *"Leave now"*, she says, not looking back at any of them.

The guards all turn and leave the room through the two giant doors. Kalrain continues to the gauntlet and places her staff at rest against one of the platforms. Steel watches the guards leave and then looks over at Kalrain, her back still turned to him. His mind quickly reflects on what just happened, and he is relieved to still be alive, but confused about what is happening now. Any standoff that just happened between him and Kalrain was, at best, an illusion. It is obvious to him now that at any point Kalrain could have ended it - and him. She didn't even need to call for the guards, as she proved she was far more capable than they were anyway. In fact, if he is to be completely honest with himself, Kalrain was far superior to everyone in the hall at that moment, combined.

He looks back and watches the last of the guards disappear out the Training Hall and the doors close behind them, then looks at Kalrain again, still wondering what he should do. Was her order to leave also directed at him?

"Do I...", Steel starts to say before he is interrupted by Kalrain.

"Not you", she cuts him off by saying. *"I thought you came here to be tested"*.

Now, Steel is really confused. First, she tells him to go, calls the guards on him, shoots at him, tells everyone to leave and now she is telling him to stay? *"Yeahhhh, but I, ok, I'm confused"*, he says, not able to make complete sentences.

"You sure are", Kalrain replies, still not looking at him as she starts walking around inspecting the gauntlet. *"No Aymyn has ever passed the Zazar Test"*, she says to him. She stops and looks back at him. *"Or survived it"*, she adds.

"I'm Eluudian", Steel replies confidently, meeting her gaze.

"Same thing", she says to him, not impressed with his confidence, and shows no reaction to his words at all, as she continues to inspect the gauntlet. *"You're still Aymyn. All started from the same place"*, she tells him.

Steel watches Kalrain inspecting the gauntlet. He again looks over the gauntlet in awe of its extraordinary size and complexity. He thinks back to when he was watching Kalrain zipping through it. Her herself also still just an Aymyn. *"Well, so are you"*, he says to her. Her back still facing Steel, Kalrain holds her arm up showing off her Tal. Steel had noticed it before. She is Troin, but even the Troin started out originally as Aymyn, so he throws her words right back at her. *"Still - started from the same place"*, he tells her.

The two large doors to the training hall open once again. This time Zargah and two more Morn Zazars walk in. Steel looks at all three Morn, surprised to see them, though not sure why as the Zazars are often found in the Training Hall. He wonders if Kalrain had secretly summoned them, instead of the guards, to remove Steel, and her talking to him this whole time has just been a distraction. *"Reinforcements?"*, he says looking back at Kalrain.

Kalrain casually turns around and looks at the Morn Zazars, then looks at Steel. *"Your examiners"*, she replies as she picks up her staff and walks towards the doorway and Morn.

Steel watches her head towards the exit and is now even more confused. She was the one he saw zipping through the gauntlet. She was the one that knew he was coming. And she was the one that told him to leave and that he had failed. *"Wait"*, he says, shaking his head with confusion. *"I thought you were the examiner?"*, he says to her.

Kalrain stops and looks at Steel with novelty. Fully aware of why he is confused and finding it amusing. *"No"*, she replies. *"It's the Zazar test. You are to be tested by Zazars"*, she tells him.

Steel still doesn't get it. He thought this whole gauntlet was the Zazar test and he just saw her zipping through it like it was nothing. So, isn't she also a Zazar? He looks again at the gauntlet to take it all in. *"But isn't all this part of the Zazar Test?"*, he asks her.

"It is", she replies, staring back at him and revelling in his confusion.

"So, you are a Zazar?", he says looking back at her, convinced that his theory is correct.

Her expression does not change. She continues to just stare at him. *"No"*, she replies. *"I have never submitted myself for testing and have no plan to do so"*. Watching the confusion on Steel's face, and predicting his next question she adds, *"I have enough responsibility already. I don't need to add being a Zazar to it"*.

Looking at Kalrain fills Steel with more confidence. The only reason she is not a Zazar is because she has never applied to actually be tested. However, evidently, she could easily pass it if she wished. Meaning, that it is possible for an Aymyn to pass the Zazar Test! Not that Steel considers himself in the same league as Kalrain. But still, it gives him hope.

Kalrain begins to turn around again towards the door but pauses to point down at Steel's leg. *"You won't be able to take that in with you"*, she says.

"My boots?", Steel asks looking at her curiously.

"What's strapped to it", Kalrain replies. Steel pulls the bottom of his coat back to reveal his ronad still strapped to his leg. *"I'm surprised you didn't pull your little stick out when the guards came in"*, she says to him, then continues on walking towards the doorway.

Steel looks at her staff. *"I liked yours better"*, he yells out to her. *"It's shiny"*. Kalrain ignores him and continues walking, she looks up at the morn Zazars briefly standing inside the doorway as she walks past them. *"It's Tription, isn't it?"*, Steel yells out to her. Kalrain stops walking. She stands still in the doorway but does not look back. *"Your staff. It's made of Tription"*, Steel says to her.

"Yes. It is", Kalrain replies, still not turning back to look at him, then continues walking out of the Training Hall. The morn Zazars step forward further into the hall as the doors close behind them.

Steel looks up at the Morn. *"Now, she's just confusing"*, he says to them, wondering if they have the same thoughts about Kalrain as he does. They don't. They don't seem to show any care or interest in anything that is going on. They just stand there looking at Steel, the next victim about to sacrifice himself on the almost impossible test. They look at Steel as though them being there to conduct this test is just a waste of time. Zargah sizes Steel up and shakes his head. *"Pitiful"*, Zargah says out loud, referring to Steel and not caring that he heard it.

-------------------------------- Happy Det --------------------------------

Det is sitting up in her bed in her bedroom. She has a blanket draped over her, covering her body and arms. Her eyes are closed, her head is tilted back, and her expression is difficult to read. Is it feeling at peace, is it just feeling calm or is it something more? Maybe bliss? Sitting open on her bedside table beside her is her lockbox. It is empty. Whatever was in it, it's not there now and is likely under the blanket with her. She opens her eyes as if sensing something or someone approaching. Her door swings open and Tespa walks straight into her room. Standing right in the middle of Det's bedroom, not even closing the door behind her, Tespa appears to be bursting with something to say.

Not moving from her bed, or showing any surprise to see Tespa, Det just looks up at her. Again, her look is peaceful. Definitely not a typical Det look. Tespa hardly notices the difference in Det, as she is preoccupied with the news that she has come running into Det's room to share. *"There are dead raiders all throughout the Castle!"*, Tespa excitedly tells Det

Det's only reaction to Tespa's excitement is a smile. Again, very unlike Det. *"I know"*, Det replies. *"I helped Dacos find the last of them"*.

Tespa now notices the difference in Det. A softer more pleasant Det. A softness, she wonders, that perhaps may have been brought about by Det hanging out with Dacos. *"Did you now?"*, Tespa says to Det, her eyes smiling as she stares intently at Det with intrigue. Det stays under her blanket and just nods, not giving anything else away.

Tespa looks at Det curiously, waiting for something else, anything else, just a little tidbit of information that she can then go and blurt out to everyone in the kingdom. Det gives her nothing.

Tespa notices that Det's lockbox is open on the bedside table beside Det. Her curiosity overrules her thinking. *"Your box is open"*, she says as she heads straight for it to take a look. *"I always wondered what was in..."*.

"Don't!", Det shouts at her before she can finish her sentence. Det's interruption startling Tespa. Tespa stops walking before she gets near it. Tespa looks back at Det, who is now looking like her typical cold hard self again, though she still has not moved from underneath her blanket. Tespa looks down at the blanket covering Det and notices that Det's hands are underneath.

"What are you doing under there?", she asks Det. Det just looks back at Tespa, as again as glimmer of a smile starts to appear. Tespa looks confused at Det and then, with a sudden realisation as she thinks she has just worked it out, an embarrassed and shocked look falls upon her face. *"Oh god. Oh. Um"*, Tespa says as she shields her eyes and looks away. Her mind starts racing. Det laying on her bed, blankets pulled up, her secret lock box open beside her and her hands nowhere to be seen. *"Oh God"*, Tespa exclaims again. *"I do not want to know"*, she adds as she makes her way back to Det's door, with her arm still shielding her eyes. Her embarrassment amuses Det and even starts to make her smile. Tespa reaches the doorway, lowers her arm and looks straight into the hallway, deliberately not looking back. *"I'm, ah, just going to leave you, ah, to, um"*. Tespa steps out into the hallway, grabbing the doorhandle as she passes it. *"See ya!"*, She says as she darts out, quickly closing Det's door behind her. Det looks content at the closed door and still does not move from her bed or from under the blanket.

THE YOUNG KING

CHAPTER EIGHTEEN

-------------------------------- Listening In --------------------------------

Aura is standing outside the closed large double doors to the Training Hall. Her ear pressed up against it as though she is trying to listen in or get any indication about what is happening inside. A futile attempt as the walls and doors in the Citadel are incredibly solid – and soundproof.

Not noticing her there, the Aymyn General walks down the corridor towards her, with a group of Aymyn Soldiers. *"No. Four men posted at all times"*, the General tells his soldiers.

"Yes, General", one replies.

"They have been there a while", another solider tells the General. *"They are getting tired"*.

"We are all getting tired", the General replies. *"I am tired"*. The General looks up the corridor, towards the Training Hall, and notices Aura standing there. He stops walking and does not take his eyes off her. The Soldiers also stop walking as well, however, they have not noticed what the General is looking at, still focusing on their conversation with him. The General continues talking to them while standing there and watching Aura. *"Replace those currently there now"*, he tells his soldiers.

"Yes, General", one replies and marches off. As the soldier passes Aura, he startles her. *"Your Highness"*, he says to her with a nod as he keeps walking. Aura quickly steps away from the Training Hall doors and pretends like she wasn't listening in, but rather just standing in the corridor looking around. She spots the General down the corridor,

standing there with his soldiers, staring back at her. She smiles at him and awkwardly looks away. The General continues to stare at her and then starts walking again towards her. He stops in front of her as Aura, still awkwardly, tries not to look at him. Eventually she does, out of the corner of her eye, and gives him a guilty smile.

"Your Highness", the General says to her.

Aura turns to face him. *"General"*, she replies, now smiling properly.

The General looks at Aura, looks at the doors to the Training Hall, then looks back at Aura. Aura knows that the General knew what she was doing but tries to keep her composure. The General shows no reaction. The other soldiers walk up and stand beside the General and nod at Aura. *"Your Highness"*, they all say to her. She looks at them all, smiles and nods back.

"Dismissed", the General says to his soldiers, looking at them briefly to give the order, before looking back at Aura.

"Yes, General", one says, as they all nod at him and then walk off. Aura continues to look at the General, feeling a little bit embarrassed with what he has seen her doing.

"Anything I can do for you, Your Highness?", he asks her, his expression and stare not changing.

"No. I'm just...", Aura starts to say, before stopping herself from saying something that isn't true. She looks back at the doors to the training hall and then again at the General. *"Well, you know what I'm just"*, she says to him.

The General continues staring at Aura for a moment, then looks past her at the Training Hall doors, knowing exactly why she is standing outside them and trying to listen in. News of Steel attempting the Zazar Test was no secret now. Not within the Citadel anyway. However, unless you were actually inside the Training Hall, there is no way to hear anything that is going on in there. *"These doors are soundproof, Your Highness"*, the General tells her. *"Like all the doors and walls throughout here"*.

Aura knew that. Of course, she knew that. She starts to feel foolish. *"Yes"*, she replies.

The Generals next words do not make her feel any better. *"These ones for good reason"*, he tells her. *"You would not want to hear what comes out of there"*. He looks back at Aura. *"Particularly during moments like this"*, he says to her. Aura looks at the General with a mixture of anger and sadness. The General looks back at her unapologetically. She was trying to listen in and find out what was going on inside after all. It seemed right that he should give her a hint as to why she shouldn't.

Aura looks down, now lost in unpleasant thoughts. The General takes this as his queue to leave her alone. *"If you need anything, Your Highness"*.

Aura looks back up at the General, still caught in her thoughts, and nods. *"Thank you, General"*, she says to him

The General starts to walk off, but only gets a few steps before Aura speaks to him again. *"Do you think..."*, She says, but stops herself, as the General also stops walking away but does not turn back. He waits for her to ask her question. *"Like, the chances of..."*, she starts to say, again stopping herself from finishing her question. Though she can not get the words out, the General knows what she is trying to ask. She wants to know if the General thinks Steel has any chance of surviving the Zazar Test. Right now, she doesn't even care if Steel does not pass it, she just wants him to come out alive and alright.

The General turns around and looks at Aura. His expression showing that he is again about to speak truthfully, and not necessarily what she wants to hear. *"Not good, Your Highness"*, he replies. *"Not something I would have advised be done. No Aymyn has ever..."*

Aura cuts off the General before he finishes saying what she already knows. *"Yes, I know"*, Aura says. *"Thanks, General"*, she says as she stares back at him. The General does not try to continue with what he was saying. Instead, he just nods at his Queen. *"Your Highness"*, he says as he turns back around, then continues on his way again.

Aura stands there, watching the General walk away. She looks down again, visibly upset. She leans back, leaning her back against the training hall doors. She turns her head and looks at the doors, then can't help herself from placing her ear against the door again, trying to listen in, though she knows its futile.

Two more Aymyn soldiers walk down the corridor towards her. Before they see her, Aura immediately stops trying to listen through the doors and turns to face them. They notice her, smile and nod. She smiles and nods back, then walks off past them.

-------------------------------- Gauntlet --------------------------------

The inside of the Training Hall is literally flaming with activity. Large cannons on the walls and Gauntlet throwing large, fierce streams of fire into the gauntlet in random directions and at random intervals. Other cannons, also mounted on the walls and throughout the gauntlet, blasting away at a more specific target. That target being Steel, as he makes his way through the multitude of levels, obstacles, moving platforms, swinging walls and scaffolding.

Steel is currently the equivalent of several stories above the ground, running along platforms that will drop randomly underneath him. He needs to move quickly. If he is on a platform when it drops, he will fall to his death. Unless, that is, he can somehow catch onto something along the way. Which he does several times, making use of the scaffolding or pushing himself off walls as he falls past them, and throwing himself onto other platforms or walls.

Other more dangerous walls and platforms move past him quickly, occasionally spinning around like a fan, chopping up anything in their way. Steel keeps running, jumping, diving, climbing, occasionally reaching impenetrable dead ends, and having to turn back around. Laser cannons shooting at him relentlessly. These cannons are not there to hurt or stun him. They are set to kill, as is every part of the gauntlet.

The course is very large and very high off the ground. From all appearances, this was not made for someone of average Aymyn height or build. Ropes hang from some obstacles, but even these are not to be trusted as they will also break away randomly. Steel is climbing such a rope and jumps off just as it breaks. He lands on a ledge, and it too starts to crumble beneath him. He jumps at walls, pushing himself off them and onto other walls, floors, scaffolding or ledges. All the while dodging laser cannon blasts, fire streams and a multitude of other walls and platforms, some very large, moving and spinning at him with speed.

Steel starts to climb up a rope as it breaks. The drop beneath him is great. He grabs for some scaffolding but misses. He reaches for more scaffolding as he falls past it and manages to catch a railing. He throws himself onto another ledge, managing to get to his feet just as an entire wall is thrown at him. He jumps at the wall, flipping himself over it, as it smashes into another wall at the other side of the ledge. The vibration shakes everything beneath him so fiercely that his legs give way, toppling him to the ground.

This is an obstacle course where any wrong move, or move in the wrong direction, can be fatal. The problem is, it seems every move is a wrong move. Even not moving and staying in the one place too long will have the same outcome. So too not dodging, ducking, or weaving fast enough. There is no surprise why almost no-one survives this test. This gauntlet was not designed to be passed. It was designed to kill.

The objective may seem to be staying alive long enough to complete this lethal maze, as you make your way from the start to the finish. However, the difficulty was knowing where the finish was. With all the jumping, diving, falling and being spun around, Steel did not know if he was even heading in the right direction. For all he knew, he could have made it halfway and is now heading straight back towards the start again. The entire course was constantly changing. With everything he is relying on, holding onto, or standing on, falling out from under him. Lasers constantly shooting at him. He didn't even know where abouts in the course he was anymore. Nor did he have time to try and work it out. He had to keep moving. Not just moving but also dodging, ducking, weaving, and flipping himself over the variety of structures that were being propelled at him. All the while also avoiding getting hit by the lethal Flame-throwing and blast cannons.

A laser from a cannon flashes past, grazing Steel's arm. Steel cringes in pain, but only briefly before quickly dodging, at the last second, another laser blast that narrowly misses his head. There is no holding back of anything on this course. This gauntlet means business. It has a fantastic success rate at defeating all those that attempt it, and it doesn't look like it intends to break that record at any point. Steel takes a moment to try and get his bearings, work out where he is, as he dodges and ducks even more laser cannon fire.

Watching everything from a control tower overlooking the gauntlet, is Zargah and the other two morn examiners. None of them believe that Steel has any chance of passing this test, just like every other Aymyn that has gone before him. However, Steel has now lasted longer than any other Aymyn before him. The two Morn Zazars watch casually, waiting for Steel to make a wrong move. Zargah, however, appears a lot more captivated, watching it with great intensity. As Steel stands there, getting his bearings, Zargah knows that it's only a matter of time, mere moments, before the platform that Steel is standing on will fall away like every other platform he has stood on. Especially if he does not move.

For a moment Zargah forgets that he is meant to be silently assessing Steel, getting swept up in the excitement of Steel's progress, and feeling more like a fan at a sports game. *"Keep moving!"*, he yells out. The other two Morn Zazars look at Zargah, wondering what he is doing. Zargah realizes the inappropriateness of his outburst, but only looks at the other Zazars and shrugs. All three Zazars return to watching and assessing Steel's progress.

Steel launches himself at another wall, again pushing himself up onto another platform. Like so many before, this platform starts to crumble beneath him and Steel falls to the platform beneath it. Another laser blast narrowly misses his head as he falls. Had the platform above not crumbled beneath him, causing him to fall, the blast would not have missed. Partially kneeling on the ground, Steel looks up at where he fell from and at the laser cannon that just missed him. *"That was lucky"*, he says out loud to himself.

Steel looks over at another laser cannon attached to the Training Hall wall. This one seems to have it in for him. No matter where Steel goes, and how much he ducks and weaves, this cannon finds him, targets him and shoots at him. Never relenting. Steel has decided that this particular canon is his nemesis.

Steel feels like he has been running this course for hours. This is because he has. He is exhausted, injured, disorientated, and still not sure if he is closer to the end or still near the beginning. He launches himself onto another platform. No sooner does he land when the platform buckles and falls away beneath him. He catches onto a dangling chain for a moment before it also breaks. As he falls, he reaches out, catching onto some scaffolding and using it to launch himself onto another platform. A Flame-throwing cannon on the wall by that platform fires at him. Steel falls to his back as the Flame jets over him, mere inches from his face. As soon as the Flames stop, Steel notices something he was starting to think he'd never see. The platform high above him is actually the end of the course. He can hardly believe his eyes. He has almost made it. If only he can make it to that platform.

Knowing that he can't stay laying down on the platform he is on, suspecting that it too will eventually fall out from underneath him, Steel jumps to his feet. He spots a swinging rope at the end of the platform he is on and runs towards it. If he can make it to this rope, climb it, providing it holds long enough, he should be able to make it to the finish line.

He runs along a platform towards the swinging rope, jumping over and ducking beneath laser cannon fire and jets of Flames. Before he can reach the rope, a wall shoots up in front of him, blocking his path. This wall is very tall and wide, with no way over or around it. Steel tries to stop before running into the wall but is running so fast that he is not able to pull himself back in time. He collides into the wall and bounces backwards, falling down on the platform. He quickly picks himself up, knowing he can't stop moving with the cannons aiming at him. He looks at the large wall in front of him. He is not even thinking about any pain he felt from colliding with it, only that this wall is preventing him from reaching the finish line. *"Oh, that's not fair"*, he says, as he places his hands behind his head and looks around, desperate to find another way around.

He looks up and can still see the ledge high above him. He can see the finish line. He is so close, but with no way past this wall and nothing to climb, he has no way to reach it. He stands there thinking as his nemesis laser canon continues to take shots at him. One hits Steel in the shoulder and throws him against the wall. His wound not insignificant. It would probably stop most people. Ordinarily, Steel is just like most people. But not today. Not right now. Right now, he needs to be more. Extremely exhausted, clothes torn and deep penetrating wounds on his arm and shoulder, Steel looks at the Cannon. He then looks at the wall and ledge high above him, then runs back away from the wall. The Zazar examiners watch this, then one looks at the other and shakes his head. So close, but now he is running the wrong way. Steel's nemesis cannon starts to increase its firing rate, with shots grazing Steel multiple times, no matter how much he ducks and weaves. One blast hits Steel in his side, spinning him around in pain. The two Morn Zazars look at each other and nod. It's almost over. Steel is almost done. Soon he will have the same outcome and join the same ranks as all the Aymyn that have gone before him. Zargah, on the other hand, still watches on, intently. One could almost say, excitedly, hopeful. If he wasn't a Morn, anyway. Unlike, his Zazar colleagues, Zargah has not written Steel off yet.

Suddenly, surprising even Zargah, Steel turns back around, then runs full steam towards the large wall blocking his path to the rope that will lead him to the finish line. The Zazars look confused, thinking that Steel has lost his bearings again. As Steel approaches the wall, he leaps straight at it, landing high up the wall, then pushes himself off it and up towards the ledge above him. It is a huge jump. He just reaches the ledge and rolls onto it, avoiding blasts from another cannon that is situated on that ledge. A cannon that is also exactly at the finish line, right where Steel needs to be. Steel runs towards the cannon, jumping over and dodging laser fire. He reaches the cannon, grabs it, rips it off the ledge, while it is still firing, then aims it at his nemesis cannon that has not stopped tormenting him. The laser blast from the cannon that he is holding completely destroys his nemesis cannon.

The Zazar examiners look at each other, amazed that Steel has completed the course. However, Steel does not end there. He continues to point the laser cannon that he is holding at other canons and obstacles within the gauntlet, blasting them to pieces as well. He yells out with a berserker style roar as he turns around shooting at every part of the course around him. Walls, floors, and scaffolding fall down around him. No longer due to it being part of the test, but now a result of Steel blasting away at it with the laser cannon. In a very short time, Steel has destroyed almost the entire gauntlet.

Zargah raises his hand and yells out, "Halt!". The Gauntlet shuts down. The laser cannons stop firing. The walls and floors all stop moving and the lights come on. Walls and scaffolding that Steel has blasted continue to fall down around him. Steel throws the cannon that he is holding on the ground, smashing it, then straightens himself up as Zargah enters the hall. Puffing and panting, calming himself down from his berserker rage, Steel stands there, still high up on the finish line platform, looking down at Zargah. Zargah looks at the gauntlet and all the damage that Steel has done with the laser canon. Some ledges and scaffolding hitting the ground around him.

Zargah shakes his head, then looks up at Steel. Steel stops panting, takes a deep breath and then smiles at Zargah innocently. *"Pitiful"*, Zargah says to him, shaking his head again, then turns and walks away towards the main doors. The doors open and Zargah walks through, stopping in the doorway. He does not look back. His shoulders heave as he takes a deep breath. *"But pass"*, Zargah says before walking out of the training hall, the doors closing behind him.

Steel stares blankly at the doors. The exhaustion from the test is taking its toll, and it takes him a moment to realize what Zargah means. *"Wait. What?"*, Steel shouts out. *"Pass? He said pass!"*. Steel starts looking around the training hall, then up at the two morn Zazars in the control tower. *"I passed?"*, he asks them. *"I passed!"*, he now exclaims.

The two Morn Zazars look at each other, then shrug, before leaving the room, appearing disappointed. Steel starts to make his way down the gauntlet, climbing down and flipping himself over the remaining scaffolding that he has not destroyed. He reaches the floor, looks around and notices that he is alone. *"So...... What now?"*, he yells out, hoping that someone is still around somewhere to hear him. There is no reply.

Steel is not particularly worried about the lack of response. He heard the word that he was longing to hear. He starts to do a little excited dance. Looking at the floor, while still dancing, he notices one of the destroyed laser cannons by his feet. It is his nemesis laser cannon. Not even the sight of that is going to bring him down. He kicks it across the hall, then pumps his fist in the air. *"Passed!"*, he yells out again.

An announcement comes over the Training Hall Speaker. A computerized voice. *"Stage one of Zazar Testing Complete"*, it says. Hearing these words, Steel stops dancing and looks disappointedly confused. *"Wait, what?"*, he says, looking around for someone, anyone, again. *"Stage One? There are more stages?"*, he asks out loud.

-------------------------------- **That Time** --------------------------------

Orlow strolls down one of the corridors of Chassam Castle, reaching into his pocket, searching for a piece of fruit. His pocket is empty, which seems to take him by surprise. As he searches his other pockets, he realises that he has found himself in the unusual position of being fruitless. Luckily for him, he is standing right outside the Meeting Hall, which always has a bowl of fruit on the table.

He opens the door to the Meeting Hall. The lights are switched off, filling the room only with the ambient twilight through the windows. Orlow sees no reason to turn the lights on, the ambient twilight is more than enough to see in the room. He only intends to be there a few seconds anyway. Long enough to refill his pockets with fruit and leave.

Not expecting to find anyone else in the room, Orlow walks on in, then stops suddenly in the doorway when he notices the Queen Mother sitting at the table, all alone. Orlow quickly abandons his mission to restock on fruit, instantly pivots 180 degrees around, and starts to walk back out, not even caring if she notices him or not. The Queen Mother has noticed him and, as she sits there quietly, decides to not let him make his exit so easily. *"Do I scare you that much, Orlow?"*, she says to him casually.

Orlow stops walking, takes a moment, then turns back to look at the Queen Mother. *"You don't scare me at all"*, he replies. *"Never have. There is nothing scary about you"*.

The Queen Mother smiles, not entirely sure she believes him, and looks away appearing to be deep in thought. *"Solso always said that I could be very scary when I wanted to be"*, she says.

Orlow looks intensely at the Queen Mother, then nods. *"Oh, it's that time"*, he says out loud. He is used to this now. Every so often the Queen Mother reflects on her past. Reflecting back on her time with Solso, and needing to talk. For some reason she always seems to choose Orlow to be the one to speak to. Perhaps because Solso was his brother. Perhaps because there is no one else old enough in Chassam Castle to really remember King Solso. She could talk to Steel, but he has enough on his plate to worry about; he does not need to also add to it with the sad memories of others. He has enough sad memories of his own.

For someone who seems to have no interest in the Queen Mother or her thoughts, Orlow still knows at these moments the thing to do is be there to listen. So that is what he does. He walks up to the table, pulls out a chair and sits down facing the Queen Mother. The Queen Mother looks over at Orlow, not smiling, but glad that he is there.

"You know what he's doing, don't you?", she says to him

Orlow thinks this is a stupid question. Solso has been dead and buried for many years now. *"Laying peacefully in his grave, I would imagine"*, he replies.

The Queen Mother looks at Orlow, appearing frustrated with him. She wasn't talking about Solso. She had moved on. Why can't he keep up? *"Steel"*, she says to Orlow.

Orlow looks confused. He was sure she was just talking about Solso. *"Oh, did we change topics?"*, he says to her. *"I missed that"*. He starts to wonder if he really should have come back and sat at the table.

The Queen Mother shakes her head, still frustrated that Orlow is not keeping up with her random, non-informing, change of topics. She continues. *"You know what he's up to?"*, she says to Orlow again.

Orlow knows what the Queen Mother is getting at. She knows that Steel is going to undertake the Zazar Test. While the news is all over the Citadel of Light, it has not left Aymyn yet and it certainly has not reached Eluud. But she doesn't need to hear the words. Or even for Steel to tell her. She just knows. Orlow knows too. *"I have a good idea"*, Orlow replies.

The Queen Mother looks down and shakes her head, already starting to feel the grief of losing another loved one. *"You imagine yourself getting old"*, she says. *"Surrounded by the ones you love. Also having them get old around you"*. She looks back over at Orlow, a sadness in her eyes. *"You never imagine that it will just be you, old, sitting alone"*.

Orlow looks at her, stands up and takes a few steps closer to her. Looking as if he is moving closer to comfort her, but instead just picks up a piece of fruit from the bowl in the middle of the table. *"I'm still here"*, he says to her.

The Queen Mother watches Orlow take a piece of fruit and put it in his pocket. She tries to smile, wanting to say something nice, but still lost in her sadness. *"You'll leave me too"*, she says to him.

"She's right", Orlow thinks to himself. If he could have, he would have left the room the moment he saw her. *"In a heartbeat"*, he replies, then turns around and walks out the room.

------------------------- Calm Your Mind -------------------------

Steel is strapped down to a chair inside another, much smaller room within the Citadel. He is wearing a helmet that covers his entire face and has no visible opening to look through. Attached to the helmet are numerous wires and sensors. One can only imagine what is happening inside that helmet as Steel appears to be screaming out in pain, as though he is being electrocuted. His cries seeming to concern a Morn Zazar that is watching him through a large view window in the next room.

In front of the Morn Zazar is a large control panel with many buttons and dials on it. The Morn presses one of the buttons activating a microphone built into the panel. *"Calm your mind!"*, the Morn says into the microphone. His words echoing through speakers in the small room that Steel is in. *"You need to calm your mind"*, the Morn explains.

Steel continues to scream in pain as the Morn Zazar looks at the control panel with frustration. The door to the control room slides open and Kalrain walks on in, where she stops the moment she hears the screams. Looking confused, she walks over to the viewing window and stares through it at Steel. She looks back curiously at the Morn, then walks over next to him and examines the control panel. Screaming is not uncommon during this process, the second part of the Zazar Test. The first part of the Zazar test, the Gauntlet, is to test the candidate's physical ability. This device that Steel now finds himself hooked up to is to test his mental ability. More specifically, to see if he can maintain a particular mental state, that is required to produce the Tription Flame, while basically being tortured. Not only do Zazars need the strength of mind to be able to focus on producing the Flame, but they also need the mental acuity to be able to do that while under great stress and with other, sometimes painful, distractions. There is not much point in a Zazar being able to summon the Flame of a Tription Weapon if they are not able to maintain it while actually in battle.

Not many even make it to this stage, certainly no Aymyn, and the Morn Zazar stares, puzzled, at the console wondering if there is anything else he should be doing. *"What setting do you have it on?"*, Kalrain asks the morn, also trying to make sense of what she is seeing.

The Morn Zazar looks at Kalrain and shakes his head. *"I have not switched it on yet"*, the Morn replies.

Kalrain looks confused. If it is not switched on, then why is Steel screaming? She looks at the Morn, who just shrugs at her. She walks back to the viewing window, staring back through it at Steel. Suddenly Steel stops screaming, seeming perfectly fine and sits calmly as though nothing is happening, which it isn't. He raises his hand and waves, though he can not see who he is waving to. *"All good now"*, he calls out. *"Just practicing. I'm ready whenever you are"*, he tells them.

Kalrain continues staring at Steel and shakes her head. She is not amused. She looks back at the Morn. *"Set it to full power"*, she instructs him. Without any hesitation, the Morn looks back down at the control panel and dials the power right up.

Steel sits calmly and looking happy in the next room. *"Yep, all psyched up and ready to..."*, Steel starts to say, as Kalrain walks over past the Morn on her way be to the door, pressing a large button on the control panel on her way. Steel's body immediately goes rigid and starts pulsating like his head is being electrocuted for real, which this time it actually is. *"Holy.....mother of....Ahhhhhhhhhhhh!"*, are the last words Kalrain hears from Steel as she leaves the room, the door sliding shut behind her.

----------------------------- **Impressive** -----------------------------

Four Dakari Raiders walk out from behind trees and into the clearing made by R'Vian's ship. The Raider's Spectre leader, Ador, the same elderly Aymyn looking man that had before led the attack on the Laden camp on Prono-4, walks out closely behind them. The Dakari stand guard as Ador walks past and stands in front of them. He is standing next to the Raider Gravesite near R'Vian's tent. He stands straight, a little rigid, and doesn't move in too close. Seeming cautious, he studies the graves from a distance.

He looks over at the tent. Then looks to the side, not really appearing to be looking at anything in particular. *"I know you're here, watching us"*, he says out loud. *"Let us see you"*.

Standing guard, the Dakari look around, trying to see who Ador is talking to. They don't have to wait long. R'Vian walks out from the trees to their flank. The Dakari quickly turn and aim their rifles at her. R'Vian looks completely at ease and smiles a cheeky smile at them. Ador turns around and looks at R'Vian, also appearing very calm, then looks back at the graves. *"You've been busy"*, he says to her.

"You guys keep me busy", she replies. She taps her leg, revealing that her hand is positioned on her firearm ready to draw, and then motions towards the Dakari. Ador looks down at R'Vian's weapon,

then looks at the Dakari and motions to them to lower their rifles. The Dakari obey.

"They are quite ferocious", Ador says, still looking at the Dakari. *"They make great soldiers".* He looks back at R'Vian. *"They are more effective on planets where their weapons don't explode"*, he says to her. *"They do not appear to have worked that out yet".* Ador looks back at the Dakari as they stare blankly at him. He returns his attention to R'Vian and her weapon. *"How do I know that yours are any more effective here?"*, he asks her. R'Vian smiles at Ador and waves her hand towards the gravesite. Ador does not show any reaction, remaining completely focused on R'Vian. *"The rumours of your existence had me intrigued"*, Ador says to her. *"I had to see for myself".*

"See anything you like?", R'Vian asks him.

"Not really", Ador replies as he looks over at the graves then back at R'Vian.

R'Vian calmly walks up towards Ador, staring him directly into the eyes as she approaches. He does not move and simply stares back at her. *"I'll give you a choice I didn't give them"*, she says to him. *"Leave now or become a monument".*

Ador looks piercingly at R'Vian, as though trying to work her out. Something is not adding up. She has been going around killing raiders, sometimes groups at a time, why is she giving him a warning? Is it perhaps because he is there and not just the Dakari? Is there something about him being a spectre that is making this encounter different for her? No one likes Spectres, so that is most unlikely. He suspects she is hiding something. Something more than just her Valantriun weaponry. But what? *"It is clear you do not like us"*, he says to her. *"Why are you giving me any choice at all?"*

R'Vian smiles at Ador as though she knows something that he doesn't. In fact, she knows a lot of things that he doesn't. But isn't about to give any of them away unless it suits her. So, she just matches his piercing stare, raising it with a smile, and waits to see if he flinches, like two gunslingers about to shoot it out. R'Vian almost seems amused by the perceived stand-off that appears to be happening.

Ador just stands there, not appearing at all intimidated, as he looks around the area before returning his attention back to R'Vian. *"There is only one of you"*, he tells her. He opens his arms indicating his Dakari soldiers. *"There is more of us"*, he adds.

"True", R'Vian replies as she walks over to the gravesite. She looks at all the Dakari graves, then turns back around and faces Ador again. *"But I can make room"*, she says to him with a smile.

Ador looks at R'Vian, not saying a word, as he thinks for a moment. He looks her up and down, before again focussing on staring her directly in the eyes as he tries to work her out. *"You are clearly no ordinary citizen of Eluud"*, he says to her. *"An ex-soldier perhaps? No regular soldier either"*, he adds.

He looks over at her tent, noticing that other than that, and the graves, there is nothing else around. She is living very simply, if not rough. *"You don't need to live like this"*, he tells her.

R'Vian is amused. These raiders and their spectre leader have no idea. But she will play along. *"Something better in mind, have you?"*, she asks him.

"I do", Ador replies.

R'Vian laughs as she walks towards her tent. She thinks to herself that she now doesn't even want to hear their proposal. *"You rob and kill the poor and helpless"*, she says to him. *"There is something wrong with that"*.

"They are not all poor", Ador says to her.

R'Vian looks back at Ador with disbelief. *"You don't see too many rich people around this sector"*, R'Vian replies. *"Certainly not on this planet. They are farmers and soldiers. Even the Castle is modest compared to anywhere else. They seem to share everything they have. You seem to just want to take it and kill everyone"*.

"What we do, we do to survive", Ador tells her. *"Are we so different?"*

R'Vian feels almost insulted by that question. There is no way that one could compare how she lives to how the Raider's live. *"Well, for a start, I don't kill anyone I don't have to"*, R'Vian replies. Ador does not entirely believe that and points towards the graveyard. RVian knows where he is pointing but looks at it anyway, then looks back at him, her stance not changing. *"Like I said, if I don't have to"*, she tells him. *"Those I had to"*.

R'Vian stands in front of her tent, next to the part of the ground where one of the anchoring poles is. She steps back and the pole raises up from the ground in front of her. Ador watches on curiously. R'Vian presses the side of the pole, and it opens up revealing the Valantriun technology and weapons inside. Ador's expression now changes. He had definitely underestimated her. He has never encountered a Valantriun before, but he knew enough about them to know that he was looking at one right now.

R'Vian reaches for her firearm under her coat and pulls it out, alarming the Dakari. They instantly raise their rifles and point them at her again. Amused, R'Vian looks at them, then gives Ador a "really?" stare. Ador stares back at R'Vian and motions to his Dakari soldiers to lower their rifles again. Reluctantly they do so.

R'Vian reaches inside the pole and pulls out a small device. It looks identical to the one that she used to electrocute the Dakari back at the barn. She attaches it to her firearm and immediately her weapon starts to light up. Ador works out what this means. Her firearm is now charged. Meaning that it wasn't before when she flashed it at him. He actually admires her bluff. *"Impressive"*, he says to her.

If it even was a bluff. She is Valantriun after all. He doesn't know what other technology and weapons she may be carrying. R'Vian puts her firearm back into its holster. Closes the door on the pole, then watches it as it sinks back down into the ground. Ador remains staring at where the pole has just gone into the ground. His thoughts wondering how easy it would be to dig it up and just take everything inside. R'Vian looks at him and smiles, knowing exactly what he is thinking. *"Good luck trying to open it"*, she tells him. Ador returns his stare back to R'Vian.

R'Vian walks over to the Dakari, their towering height standing over her, but she is not at all intimidated. She looks at the large claws on one of the Dakari and runs her fingers along one of them. The Dakari she is touching does not know what to do. It looks at Ador. Ador just looks back at it but remains still and gives no direction to the Dakari. The Dakari looks back at R'Vian as she finishes tracing its claw with her finger, then looks at and touches its rifle. *"You guys make it too easy though. Using these on Eluud"*, she says. She turns her back to the Dakari and starts to walk towards Ador. *"More often than not they blow up in your hands and do the job for me"*, she says to him. Ador points at her firearm. R'Vian smirks back at him. *"Mine are different"*, she says to him.

She walks up to Ador and touches the lapel of his clothing, feeling it. He does not react and just keeps looking at her. She then turns to walk off but pauses and looks back at him. *"You still have your two choices"*, she says to him. *" You should probably decide. Before I get antsy"*.

She removes her hand from his clothing and continues walking towards the forest. Ador does not turn around to watch her. Still remaining exactly how he is and just listening to her walk off behind him.

"How long do you think you can continue to live here? Alone", he calls out to her. *"You obviously outmatch the likes of us. But there is worse than us. How do you plan to beat the Skurj when they come?"*

The question strikes R'Vian to her core. However, she does not stop, but instead continues to walk towards the forest. *"You can't beat the Skurj"*, she replies. *"At best, you can avoid them"*.

Ador remains expressionless, still just standing there listening to her behind him. *"The Skurj are an inevitability"*, he tells her. *"There is no avoiding them. They don't leave behind graveyards of their victims"*.

"The Skurj don't leave behind anything", R'Vian replies.

Ador now turns around to look at R'Vian, but instead notices that she is nowhere to be seen. He stands there, looking into the forest and through the trees, and can not see her anywhere. Again, he is filled with admiration. *"Impressive"*, he says out loud to himself.

EXOM

THE YOUNG KING

CHAPTER NINETEEN

------------------------------ Small Hands ------------------------------

Just as news travelled quickly throughout the citadel about an Aymyn attempting the Zazar Test, news has travelled just as quickly that the same Aymyn has passed the Zazar Test. Though it is believed by many to be only rumour, and an impossible one at that. It is only due to the same guards that were summoned by Kalrain to remove Steel from the training hall originally, that have since seen Steel alive and well walking around the Citadel, that this story got out in the first place. Though, still many soldiers will only believe this story if they see Steel for themselves.

This shouldn't be so hard, for right now Steel is very casually, and somewhat excitedly, walking through the citadel corridors. He walks down the same corridor that leads to the training hall, though that is not where he is headed.

Four Aymyn guards pass Steel in the corridor, two of them instantly recognising him and excitedly stopping and nudging the other two. The guards all look at Steel a bit starstruck. They wonder if it's appropriate to go up and shake his hand. It's not, but one does anyway as the other three just stare at him. Steel is happy to take all the positive attention that he can get. It's common knowledge that in general the Zazars, up to now really only Morn, are not particularly liked. Feared, respected, and seen as necessary, but best always to stay clear of. Steel is not sure how him, being an Aymyn, will fit with all that. However, right now he doesn't much care. He is elated.

He continues on his way, passing another two guards. Like the previous guards, they immediately recognise him and almost trip over each other as they watch him. Neither of them sure what to say, or if they should say anything. Do they congratulate him? Do they act professional and pretend that everything is just normal with nothing to see? The moment passes just as quickly as Steel does, with all of them only managing to look dazed as Steel walks past, smiling at them equally awkwardly.

As Steel walks further down the corridor, he is greeted by Queen Aura's Handmaiden who is walking towards him. She looks as though she has been looking for him, and although not showing any expression of happiness or even being pleased, she does look at him a little more softly than usual. *"Congratulations, Your Highness"*, she says to him. *"The Citadel echoes with the voices of people saying your name"*.

Steel smiles at the Handmaiden, thinking that it is nice to be congratulated, but also that this is probably the most that she has ever said to him the entire time he has known her. Already, so much is changing. He is just going to go with it. *"Word travels fast around here"*, he says to her. He waits for her reply. However, now something that he is more familiar with, she does not speak, but instead just looks at him blankly. Her stare almost forcing him to think about Aura. If everyone is talking about him, then Aura will already have heard the news. News, that he himself has not had a chance to tell her personally. *"Aura?"*, he asks her Handmaiden.

She nods. *"Aware"*, she replies.

Though the Handmaiden's expression is still blank, Steel knows that the news has not brought Aura the same kind of joy and excitement that the other "voices" within the Citadel are expressing. *"I had hoped to tell her myself"*, he tells the Handmaiden. She continues to look at Steel and nods. Though her expression, still blank, and not giving anything away, Steel is feeling a connection is being made. For once he can relate to her feeling that there is no need for words. *"Apparently, I have one more thing to do"*, he tells her, as he looks down the corridor, then around him, and finally at the door that he just happens to be standing in front of. *"Here actually"*, he adds, a little surprised. He looks past the Handmaiden and further up at the other doors and entrances that line the corridor. *"I think, anyway. I hope"*, he says as he looks back at the Handmaiden and smiles awkwardly. *"It is so easy to get lost in this place. Everything looks the same"*.

Again, the Handmaiden just looks at Steel, expressionless, and nods. She looks up the hallway, the way that she was heading when she ran into Steel, then starts to walk off. No goodbye. Just as if she had never stopped and had a conversation.

Steel looks back at the door, then the button on the wall that opens it. He turns and looks back at the Handmaiden. *"Can you let her know that I will see her soon?"*, he calls out to her. The Handmaiden stops walking but does not look back. She does give a sideways nod, so that Steel can see her acknowledgment, before continuing on her way.

Steel looks again at the closed door as he wonders what lays on the other side. It is a room that he has never been in before. He has never had reason to, though he has no doubt walked past it many times. It is an office, or meeting room, for Zazars and their instructor. It has never even crossed his mind what the inside of this room will look like, but now as he stands in front of its door, anticipation grows. He imagines boards filled with illustrations of fighting techniques and battle strategies. Chairs, many chairs, large chairs since the Zazars are Morn and will need large chairs.

He presses the door button. The door opens and he walks inside. It is not what he imagined. In fact, nothing like what he imagined. No boards or illustrations anywhere. Not even a single chair. The room is completely empty. Steel walks in, wondering if he is in the right room. The door closes behind him. Steel looks the room over wondering if he has missed something. At the opposite end of the room, a single desk-like table, along with an official looking office chair behind it, start to rise and form out of the floor.

Steel smiles as the desk and chair appear in front of him. He realizes that the empty room is due to the way a lot of the rooms within the Citadel are not furnished until needed, and then the furniture is constructed according to requirements. *"Of course"*, Steel says to himself. *"Why have unused furniture laying around"*. Much like the Counsellors own chairs in the Council Chambers. However, even the Council Chambers always has the large Council Table and a few chairs always there. The furniture in Steel's quarters never changes or disappears. He has also spent a great deal of time inside Aura's quarters and the furniture in hers, like his, are always there no matter if the room is occupied or empty. So, while this building technology is widely used within the Citadel, it is not so wide that Steel expects to see it everywhere that he goes. So, like now, he is still taken by surprise when he walks into an empty room.

The chair behind the desk is not that large. Certainly not made for a Morn to sit on. It would disappear under the large tush of a Morn. In fact, the Morn could not even sit on the desk. The desk and chair are obviously built for someone the size of an Aymyn. Steel wonders if the chair was built for him to sit in. He is the only one in the room after all, and it is the perfect size for him.

He walks towards the desk, and as he gets closer, another chair, this one simpler and not so official looking, forms in front of the desk. This chair is very similar to his own in the Council Chambers, though slightly smaller and doesn't look quite as comfortable. However, perhaps this is where he is to sit? Yet, he is still the only one in the room, so this is confusing. Steel again looks around wondering what he is missing.

"Hello?", he calls out. There is no answer. Just silence. Though Steel does start to feel as though someone is watching him. He looks at the smaller chair again. *"Um, do I just sit down?"*, he calls out as he looks around the room. *"I'll just sit down"*, he announces.

Steel sits down on the smaller chair and makes himself comfortable. He is not sure which way he should be facing. He swings his chair to face the desk and sits there waiting. Then he leans over the desk, resting his arms on it, clasping his hands together, and waits before sitting back and readjusting himself in his chair. He feels silly sitting in an empty room staring at an empty desk and office chair, so swings his chair around to face the door. He waits. He folds one leg over on top of his lap as he tries to get more comfortable in his chair. That doesn't work. So, he sits in the chair properly and waits. Finally, the door he entered through opens. A Pizian enters the room carrying a box. The Pizian looks at Steel but does not react, as though he was expecting to see Steel sitting looking at him. The Pizian remains expressionless but not unfriendly looking.

Steel notices the interesting looking box it is carrying as it moves over to the table and stands beside the larger, more official looking chair. Steel spins around in his chair, now facing the desk again, and smiles at the Pizian. The Pizian still does not respond to him, or even look at him, as though accepting Steel as just part of the furniture. It opens the box to reveal several Tription handles positioned inside. Each one slightly larger than the one next to it. The Pizian starts carefully pulling out the handles, then lines them up on the table in front of the box.

Being that this is an important meeting and moment, passing the selection stage of the Zazar Test and moving onto the training section, Steel is not surprised to see that this stage is being conducted by a Pizian. Though he was never aware of the Pizians having anything to do with the Zazars, always thinking that it was facilitated, coordinated, and controlled entirely by the Royal Alliance Council. Something that the Pizian are part of, but also something that they have shown no interest in. Thinking about it, this is probably the closest he has ever come to actually interacting with a Pizian. Seen them around, sure. Passed and nodded to them a few times, with no response back from them. However, to actually sit across the table in a room alone with one is a unique experience.

Not one to stay silent, especially when there is someone to talk to, Steel tries to strike up a conversation with the Pizian. Knowing that the Pizian's are not big on talking, or getting involved in anything remotely social, Steel is aware that he is going to have to do most of the talking. *"I'm actually really excited to be doing this"*, he says to the Pizian. *"Wasn't sure I'd make it this far. Actually, pretty sure I wouldn't. But hoping I would of course. Glad I did. Relieved. So relieved. Am I talking too much? I often talk too much. Sometimes. When I'm excited. Or Nervous. Or hungry. Think I'm hungry. It's been a long day. They don't provide snacks during these tests, it appears. But then again, they probably didn't expect me to be around to eat anything"*. Steel giggles and looks at the Pizian for a reaction.

The Pizian looks up at Steel and blinks. This surprises Steel and he is actually taken aback. This is the biggest response he has ever received from a Pizian. A Pizian actually acknowledging him. At least he thinks it's an acknowledgment. He wonders how many others can say that a Pizian blinked at them? He starts to feel the excitement build inside him. Just as quickly as it builds, it fades away when the Pizian looks away again, moves away from the table and back towards the door. The door opens and, without any hesitation or a word of "Goodbye", the Pizian leaves. Second person in a row that has just done that to him.

Steel spins around on his chair again and watches the door close behind the Pizian. Now he is even more confused. If it wasn't the Pizian he was waiting to see, then who is it? Perhaps Zargah. That would make sense if the chair was bigger, he thinks as he spins back around to face the table. He looks at the Tription handles placed on the desk. Curious, he stands up and walks around the desk to the other side, then sits down on the larger office chair. He looks intensely at the Tription handles, wondering if he is allowed to touch them. He tries to resist the temptation, but his body has other ideas as his hand moves slowly towards them. He watches his hand, as though it is out of his control, move towards the Tription handles and tries to convince his body to obey his mind. *"Don't touch. Shouldn't touch"*, he says to himself. His body does not listen, and he ends up picking up one of the Tription handles and examines it.

Engrossed in what he is looking at, Steel doesn't notice anyone else enter the room, and definitely does not notice them walk through the room and stand in front of the desk. *"I believe you are in my seat"*, he hears a female's voice say to him.

Startled, Steel drops the handle and looks up to see Kalrain standing there, still dressed in her long revealing and flowing red dress. Also still holding her staff. *"You again"*, he says to her, then thinks, "That sounded a lot ruder than was intended", as he quickly stands up and moves away from the office chair.

Kalrain's expression is similar to the Pizian. Mostly expressionless as though she was expecting Steel to be there, and not entirely unfriendly.

Well, maybe a little unfriendly. *"Believe me. I am even more surprised to see you"*, she replies.

It starts to make sense now. Kalrain is the Tription Weapon's Teacher. Steel is here to learn how to fight like a Zazar. That involves Tription Weapons, if not entirely. It's only logical that he is here to see Kalrain. He is not sure why he did not put that together earlier. But then again, this is all new to him and he has never had that much to do with Zazars before. And, before his encounter with Kalrain in the Training Hall, he has also had very little interaction with her. A casual acknowledging nod as they pass each other in a room or corridor. He had never actually spoken to her before meeting her in the training hall. Or even really looked at her for that matter. He always felt a little awkward around her if he was to be honest. The way she was always looking at him. Never unfriendly, but with an intense curiosity. Much like how she was looking at him in the training hall. An encounter where she basically told him that he would never pass the Zazar Test. Well, he showed her. Time to rub it in.

"Oh, The Zazar Test?", he says to her. *"That was a piece of..."*.

"Please take a seat", she says, cutting him off. This time pointing to the smaller seat at the other side of the desk, making it clear to Steel which seat he is to be sitting in.

Steel walks over to the smaller seat again and sits down. Kalrain rests her staff against the wall and sits in the larger official looking chair. She picks up the box left by the Pizian and moves it out of the way, leaving the Tription handles still lined up on the table.

Steel sits in his chair, just looking at Kalrain, as he remembers the last test when his head was inside the electrocuting helmet. *"I thought I heard your voice at the start of that last test"*, he says to her.

"I'm surprised, over all your screaming", she replies, peering up at Steel.

Steel concedes to himself, he did scream a lot. *"That was a lot more painful than I imagined"*, he tells her. *"Not that I really imagined anything. Or knew what to imagine. Certainly, didn't imagine that. Which makes everything I have just said make no sense. Hearing myself speak now, I should probably have stopped earlier. But I didn't.*

And I appear to still be talking. But I really didn't know what to expect. As you know". As his mouth runs away saying everything that enters his head, Steel's main thoughts are of the pain he felt during that last test. *"But that, is it always that painful?",* he asks her.

Kalrain just stares at Steel, showing no emotion, knowing it was her decision and instruction to raise the intensity that added to Steel's pain. *"Can be",* she replies.

As Steel just said, he had no idea what to expect with the Zazar Test. The Gauntlet made some sense. He can understand its purpose in testing and training elite soldiers. He can also understand why hardly anyone ever passes it. But he has no idea what that last, electrocution helmet, test was about. *"What was its purpose?",* he asks her.

Kalrain's expression softens as she looks at Steel. Knowing that he has no familiarity with Tription weaponry, or the kind of mental state and focus one needs to be able to use them, she acknowledges that his question is reasonable. *"To prepare your mind",* she tells him.

"Mind conditioning?", Steel asks.

Kalrain nods. *"We need to see if you can still stay focussed and maintain a calm mind when under severe stresses",* she replies.

"Severe, is an understatement", Steel tells her, still remembering the pain.

"Maybe", Kalrain replies as she continues to look at Steel, still softly, but also still showing no emotion.

Even though he reflects on the painful experience and sits there under the non-emotional gaze of Kalrain, Steel starts to relax. *"It was torturous. Have you tried it yourself?",* he asks her, expecting that she has. She seems to be competent at everything.

"No", she replies, her answer taking Steel by surprise. So many questions run through his head. They all mix together, and he can't put any of them into words. If he opened his mouth to speak only garbled stuttering would come out. So, he looks away and clears his mind of all his questions regarding Kalrain, conceding to himself that she is just a mystery that he will never work out.

He thinks back to the last test and its purpose to teach him to maintain a calm mind under severe stress. *"What would have happened if I couldn't have kept my mind calm during all that?"*, Steel asks her.

"It would have killed you", Kalrain answers. Again, showing no emotion in her answer as she remains looking at Steel. Steel thought that was the purpose of the first test. Didn't realize it would also be a possible outcome for this last test as well. *"Sounds extreme"*, he says to her.

Kalrain hides her amusement in Steel's comment, surprised that he even said it. *"Is there any part of this test that has suggested to you that it wouldn't be?"*, she asks him. Steel thinks about that, then realizes how silly his comment was. The Gauntlet tried to kill him in about a hundred different ways, and that was only the first test. *"You got me there"*, he replies.

Steel wonders about the electrocution test, and how Kalrain said that is to condition his mind. Condition his mind for what? What do Zazars need mind conditioning for? They are an army used to fight against a physically unstoppable beast. The first test, a physical challenge, made sense. But mind conditioning? Being able to stay calm under stress, that also makes sense. Fighting the Skurj would be extremely stressful. But this test was not about putting him in a stressful situation and just remaining calm. This test was specifically about causing him pain while still needing him to still maintain a calm mind. A calm mind for what? As he looks at the Tription handles laying on the table, remembering that he is talking to the Tription Weapons teacher, all the pieces start to come together. *"So, this mind conditioning"*, he says. He motions his head towards the Tription handles on the table in front of Kalrain. *"Is it to condition my mind for that"*, he asks her. Kalrain does not look at where Steel is motioning to. Noticing that she is not looking where he wants her to look, Steel makes his movements even bigger and more obvious. Kalrain ignores them while continuing to just stare at him.

"Hand", she says to him. Steel looks at her confused. She should really look at where he is trying to get her to look with his vigorous head movements. It is definitely not towards either of their hands. *"Your hand"*, she says to him a little more sternly.

Alright, he thinks to himself, he is just going to have to say it. *"No, those Tription ha..."*. He stops himself from finishing that sentence as he realizes what Kalrain is telling him. *"Oh, you want my hand?"*, he says to her.

Kalrain remains looking at Steel and nods towards the desk. Steel places his hand, palm down, on the desk in front of Kalrain. Kalrain grabs his hand and, not so gently, turns it over so that his palm is facing up. She picks up the Tription Handle in the centre of the row of handles, then looks at Steel's hand, comparing the size of each. She then puts down the handle and picks up another slightly smaller one. She places the Tription handle that she is holding into Steel's hand and then closes his fingers around it. She let's go of Steel's hand, looks at it and nods. *"Hmmm"*, she says to herself.

Steel looks at his hand holding the Tription handle. He opens his hand up and looks at it sitting in his palm, then closes his fingers around it again. He likes the feel of it, and the shape of it is sure intriguing. He has seen the Tription handles that the Morn Zazars carry. Of course, theirs are a lot larger than the one he is holding. In fact, the ones the Zazars carry are larger than any of the ones on the table in front of him.

"This looks a lot smaller than the one Zargah carries", Steel says to Kalrain. Kalrain looks at Steel, now as though he is just being stupid. The Tription handle that Steel is holding is smaller than one of Zargah's fingers, not just his Tription handle. It would probably take both of Steel's hands to hold the one that Zargah carries. Kalrain reluctantly feels like she needs to state the obvious. *"Small Hand. Small handle"*, she tells Steel.

Steel looks at Kalrain and nods. It makes sense. Though he is not sure he likes being told that he has small hands. If she is suggesting that his hands are small, what else could she be insinuating? *"I have been told my hands are a pretty good size"*, he says a little defensively. *"Never had any complaints in the, um, hand department. Aura has always liked them. They seem to do the trick. Sometimes lots of tricks. Repeatedly. Like, I may need to take a quick break now and then, but they keep going. You know, doing - hand stuff. Like a hand should do"*. Kalrain just ignores him.

Steel looks back down at his hand holding the Tription Handle and realizes that his hands really are small. Especially when he thinks about the other Tription Handles he has seen. He looks back at Kalrain to ask what he believes is a valid question. *"Does size really matter?"*, he asks her. Kalrain looks up at Steel, seemingly unimpressed with his question. Steel looks past her and at her staff resting against the wall, noticing how long it is. He looks again at the Tription handle that he is holding, then back at her staff. Kalrain notices him looking past her and turns to look at her own staff, realizing that he is comparing sizes. She turns back to face him, waiting for him to move on from the topic. He doesn't. *"So, then what would happen if I had a bigger one?"*, Steel asks her. *"Not that there's anything wrong with this one. But, you know, what if it was a little bigger. Like..."*. Steel holds out his other hand and mimics holding a larger, thicker, Tription handle. Kalrain briefly gazes down at his hand shaking and pretending to hold a larger Tription handle, then stares back at him. *"You'd drop it"*, she replies.

Steel looks at Kalrain curiously but seriously, not sure if he should feel amused by her statement or insulted. *"Do you really think so?"*, he asks her. Kalrain quickly flicks Steel's hand with her fingers and Steel flinches in pain. He instantly drops the handle on the desk as he pulls his hand back and shakes it. He looks at the handle now rolling across the desk, then looks back at Kalrain who is still just staring at him. Realizing that she has just proved her point, Steel nods. *"OK, you made your point"*, he says to her.

Steel picks up the handle again and looks at it. Kalrain looks away and starts putting the rest of the handles back into the box. There is an empty space inside the box that had the handle that Steel is now holding. Kalrain looks back at Steel and watches him holding his Tription Handle. Again, her look softens. She is now looking at him with a hint of admiration, though trying very hard not to show it. She never thought she'd be in this situation, sizing up a Tription handle for an Aymyn Zazar. *"You have made it further than any other Aymyn"*, she says to him.

Steel looks at Kalrain and smiles. Is this a compliment that she is giving him? *"I'm..."*, he starts to say before Kalrain interrupts him.

"I know. You're Eluudian", she says to him. Steel watches Kalrain's expression, waiting for the sarcasm. It doesn't come. He now feels the sincerity in her words, and it surprises him. Actually, relaxes him. Something he has never before felt around her. *"From what I have heard"*, Kalrain says to him, *"Eluud was settled not that long ago"*.

"Wow" Steel thinks to himself. "She is talking to me about Eluud". How things have turned around. Finally, a subject that he is more familiar with than she is. *"Still, well before my time"*, Steel replies. *"My Great Grandfather was the Commander of Chassam, the ship that first landed on Eluud. Well, I say landed..."*. Steel pauses for a moment. Kalrain knows what he means. Ships don't land on Eluud. Unless they have help from stilts. It's pretty safe to assume that being the first ship on the planet, there were not any stilts there yet. *"My Great Grandfather, the first King of Eluud"*, Steel continues. *"Had the Castle built. Named it after the ship that brought everyone there, Chassam Castle. My father was still a baby at the time. My Grandfather was the next King. Then my father. Now me"*. Steel looks away as he thinks about his words. *"Well, was me"*, he corrects himself, looking a little saddened.

Kalrain looks at Steel with intrigue, wanting him to continue. Steel looks back at Kalrain and, noticing that she is still intrigued, he feels proud to continue. *"So, we are a young planet, sure"*, he says. *"But still in every way one worth protecting"*.

Kalrain can see the passion in Steel's eyes, as he talks about his home, and feels herself agreeing with him. *"I see nothing wrong with wanting to protect your home"*, she tells him. *"It would be a sentiment that you are not alone in"*, she adds. Steel imagines that would be true. *"But are you the person to do it?"*, Kalrain asks him.

And there it is. That change of look again. This time from intrigue back to her usual stare. It's like every question Kalrain throws at him is a test. *"I have been doing it"*, Steel replies.

"You think that by becoming a Zazar you will be better equipped to protect your planet?", Kalrain asks him.

EXOM - THE YOUNG KING

"By becoming a Zazar, I will then have the support of the Zazar Corp fighting beside me", Steel replies. *"So, better equipped? Yes, I'd say so"*, he answers.

"Interesting", Kalrain says to him. Her expression still not changing. *"The Corp would be hoping that you should be an addition to them. Not the other way around"*.

Steel is finding Kalrain's statement really one sided. Does she have a strong view on what she is saying, or is this another test? Either way, Steel is going to say what he believes. *"No reason it can't work both ways"*, Steel replies.

Kalrain's look changes again. Still looking like there is some kind of judgment going on, but this time like the judgment may be in Steel's favour. *"Such wayward thinking"*, she says to him. *"That is very unlike Council mentality"*.

Kalrain draws on a point that Steel is all too familiar with, and a point that has been made to him before. The way he sees, thinks about and approaches things are not exactly the way most on the council would. A fact perfectly highlighted by his choice to try out and become a Zazar. *"Well, if I make it through all this, I am not exactly eligible for that position anymore"*, Steel replies.

A realization falls over Kalrain, one that makes her start to see Steel in a very different light. All this time, from the moment she saw him in the Training Hall, she has judged him. An Aymyn, or Eluudian, or whatever he wants to call himself, wanting to be a Zazar. Many want to be Zazars. Give their life to try out. Wanting the respect, the honour, the teamwork and achievement that comes with being a Zazar. But that is not what Steel is doing this for. He is not doing this for honour, respect, title or prestige. He already had all of that and more before. A member of the Royal Alliance Council. A King of a planet. In fact, he is throwing away all those things to be only one thing. One thing that can save his planet. None of the reasons that Steel has chosen to do this are about him at all. There has never been a king, politician or any kind of leader or nobility that has attempted the Zazar test. All the previous candidates have been either commoners or soldiers. These people have sacrificed their lives while trying to become a Zazar. However,

Steel sacrificed his the moment he made the decision to try. Every person that attempted these trials before, went in believing they had what it took to make it through. But not Steel. Steel went in believing he had to make it through even if it took everything he had. And it pretty much has. Some will say that he got through on his skill. But Kalrain can see that it was his selflessness, devotion, determination, and resolution that got him through.

Kalrain is a weapons teacher. Skill is what she teaches. She can teach Steel to be skilful. The qualities that Steel has, qualities that have enabled him to get this far, is something that can not be taught. No, this is new. Not even the Morn possess these qualities. They, well some, those that pass, do get through the test based purely on their physical ability. As far as Zazars go, Steel is not just the first Aymyn Zazar, Steel is a new breed of Zazar in every way. And this realization actually moves Kalrain.

Completely unaware of what is going through Kalrain's head right now, Steel stares down at the Tription handle that he is holding again. He plays with it in his hand, still thinking about how small it is, yet holds such power. *"Strange, how such a little thing can make such a big difference in battle"*, he says. Kalrain looks down briefly at the Tription handle being played with in Steel's hand before, returning her gaze to Steel. *"A battle perhaps"*, she says to him. Steel stops playing with the Tription Handle, intrigued by Kalrain's choice of words. *"A battle?"*, he asks her.

"There are more battles than just the Skurj that are being fought", Kalrain replies. *"The better the Zazars get at defeating the Skurj, the more the unprotected planets can not understand why the Zazar Protectorate Code is not expanded"*.

Steel laughs to himself. This is the argument that he has been having this entire time. With Aura. With the Council. *"Don't get me started on that"*, he says to Kalrain. *"It's why I ended up here"*. Kalrain remains looking at Steel for a moment, then looks away. She feels like this is a conversation that she could really throw herself into. But now is probably not the most appropriate time.

"What would you have them do if you could?", Steel asks her.

Still looking away, Kalrain stands up and picks up her staff. *"In my position here, I have the luxury of not having to make those decisions"*, Kalrain replies, as she walks out from behind the desk and heads towards the exit. She glances over at Steel and gives him a "come on" motion with her head and eyes. *"Follow me"*, she says to him. *"Let's see if we can make something of you"*.

The door opens and Kalrain walks out of the room. Steel stands up and is about to follow when he stops and goes back to the table. He looks inside the box of Tription Handles. He pulls out another handle and compares it to his own. This new one is slightly bigger. He puts it back in the box then pulls out another one, comparing that one to his as well. This one is even bigger than the one he just put back. Steel looks at the Tription Handle that Kalrain gave him, then the larger one that he has just taken out of the box. He likes the size, and the way the larger one looks in his hand. He puts his original handle back in the box and holds onto the larger one, feeling it in his hand. He smiles, very content with his choice, then walks towards the door and exits the room.

Despite Steel's best attempts at destroying the Training Hall, with his berserker take-out of the Zazar course and canons, the training hall is completely back to normal. No sign of damage, no destroyed walls or scaffolding laying around. More importantly, no sign of the gauntlet. Again, that good ol' rebuilding technology. Now all that stands there is a number of smaller makeshift walls and partitions.

Steel stands between them, holding his Tription handle as Kalrain stands next to him, watching him closely. Holding his Tription handle out in front of him, while closing his eyes and focussing his mind, Steel tries to summon a Tription Flame. *"Keep your eyes open"*, Kalrain instructs him. *"If you can not summon the Flame with your eyes open, you will be no good in battle"*. Steel opens his eyes and focuses again on his Tription handle. As he does so, a small Tription Flame starts to appear. Only a very small one, but enough to make Steel smile with excitement. Amazed at what he is seeing, what he is doing, amazed with himself, he looks over at Kalrain. Kalrain nods and motions for him to keep going. Excited to see what he can do; Steel looks back at the handle and continues to focus. The Flame grows larger and larger. *"Now, make it take form"*, Kalrain tells him.

Steel continues to stare at the Tription handle, but nothing happens. The Flame does not change. He intensifies his stare but still nothing happens. *"It's not going to change form just because you look at it strangely"*, Kalrain tells him. *"Form it with your mind. Have the image in your head and see that image appear in your hand"*.

Steel smirks and the tription Flame goes out. *"Oh, if I could do that, I wouldn't be standing here holding this thing"*, he jokingly replies.

"Concentrate!", Kalrain tells him, not amused by is joke.

Steel looks back at his Tription handle, focusses on it again, this time with a more relaxed expression and intensity. He envisions a flaming sword in his mind. He watches his Tription handle as the Flame starts to appear again. The Flame gets larger, then starts to form into a small blade. Again, Steel struggles to contain his excitement, as he watches the Flame sword coming out of the Tription handle in his hand. It doesn't last long before the sword sags into a floppy whip. In whip form, the Tription Flame seems to float around, not touching the floor. An impressive feature of the Tription Whip, but still not what Steel has intended to do, nor what Kalrain has instructed him to do.

Kalrain slightly shakes her head, her disappointment showing clearly. Steel remains focused on the Flame whip. It starts to stiffen up and looks like it is about to form a blade again, but then sags back into a whip. Steel now also looks disappointed as he watches the end of the Flame whip hover above the floor. *"Do you need a hand?"*, Kalrain asks him, staring at him again with her usual disapproving expression.

Steel looks frustrated at Kalrain, then turns his back to her. *"Don't look at me"*, he tells her. *"I can't perform when I am being stared at"*.

Kalrain smirks and shakes her head. *"It's ok. It happens"*, she tells him.

"Not to me, it doesn't", Steel replies. Kalrain wonders if they are talking entirely about the same thing. *"It's cold"*, Steel tells her. *"Maybe if I just warm my hands up a bit. You know what it's like when it's cold"*. Kalrain doesn't really. Being Troin, the cold is not exactly something

that she has to contend with a lot. *"Just give me a moment"*, Steel tells her.

Steel continues to concentrate on his Tription handle, forming the image again in his mind. He turns back around, and the Flame sword is once again standing strong. Steel smiles, feeling proud once more to show what he has produced. Then the Flame droops into a floppy whip again. Steel's smile disappears. *"Bugger!"*, Steel exclaims.

As time passes, Steel continues to practice with his Tription handle under the ever-watching eye and guiding words of Kalrain. Steel has mastered keeping the Tription Flame formed as a sword. He uses it, swinging it around and slashing with it, as he goes through various fighting routines. Still standing between the makeshift walls, Steel is trying hard to make sure that he does not actually hit anything with his Tription sword, fully aware that the Flame will cut through anything.

A number of large objects are now also scattered throughout the hall. Steel is swings his Tription sword while dancing around them. Dancing, because that is what it looks like. He is supposed to be walking, and staying in formation, as he moves strategically around the obstacles. However, Steel appears to be having too much fun, really loving being able to make a Tription sword.

Kalrain is now standing by the wall, next to the large sliding doors of the Training Hall. Next to her are two Morn Zazars. They all remain expressionless, as Kalrain shakes her head with disappointment as they all watch Steel dance around. None of them feel the need to say anything, as Steel seems to be doing alright maintaining the Flame sword as he goes through his fighting routines.

Steel is now feeling very impressed with himself. He looks over at Kalrain and the Morn, then gives them a wink. He starts to speed up his routine but underestimates his distance between himself and one of the makeshift walls, accidently cutting straight through the wall with his Tription sword. He quickly pulls his Tription sword out of the wall with such haste that he accidently thrusts it back cutting through another wall behind him. Kalrain and the morn Zazar shake their heads, as Steel looks at them and smiles guiltily.

Kalrain turns and walks towards the large doors. They open as she approaches them, and she steps out into the corridor. She stops and looks back at the Morn Zazars. *"Put him through the gauntlet again"*, she tells them. *"Let's make sure he can still maintain the Flame in battle"*.

Both Morn Zazars look at Kalrain. *"He may not survive a second round"*, one of them says to her. Kalrain turns and looks back at Steel, a slight smirk taking shape on her face. *"Oh, I think he will"*, she replies. She turns back, then continues walking out into the corridor, as the large Training Hall doors close behind her. The morn Zazars resume watching Steel.

Steel looks at his Tription sword and it changes form into a whip again. This time it was intentional. He starts swinging it around. He likes the way the Tription Whip can hang there, floating, without going completely down, touching, and slicing up the floor. He doesn't seem to be as competent with a whip as he was with the sword, and accidently hits one of the large objects scattered around the hall, slicing it in half. His eyes light up, as his face expresses his excitement once again. *"Sweet"*, he says out loud.

He swings the whip around, trying not to actually hit anything this time. The Morn Zazars, a little concerned for their own safety, take some steps back and away from each other. Steel gets more and more carried away, swinging the whip in all kinds of directions as he practices his routines. The whip cuts through many obstacles and, at one point, even flies towards one of the Morn. The Morn quickly dodges it, then looks at Steel very unimpressed.

Steel stops swinging his Tription whip, recalls the Flame back into the handle and stands there smiling at the Morn. The Morn look at all the destroyed obstacles around the place and, reflecting back on Steel's destruction of the Gauntlet, are starting to see a common pattern. Steel looks at all the destroyed objects laid scattered around the hall, then looks back at the Zazars and shrugs. *"At least the walls are intact"*, he tells them. The makeshift walls fall down behind him. Steel doesn't turn to look at them, instead just remains smiling at the Zazars. *"I might stick with the sword version"*, he tells them.

-------------------------------- Change --------------------------------

Sabel paces slowly beside the Viewing Table inside the Hillside Hideout, as a live hologram of Dark is projected inside the floating energy field above it. *"You appear happy about this, my Sign"*, Sabel says to her. *"Whereas I can't help but have a bad feeling"*.

"It's a change", Dark replies. *"I expect many will have a bad feeling about it. At first, anyway"*, Dark adds.

Sabel still looks uncertain. *"I'd have thought that given your..."*, Sabel searches for the right words, *"Connection, with this particular Aymyn"*. Sabel stops talking when she notices the frown coming from Dark.

"Don't call him that", Dark says sternly to Sabel. *"He's Eluudian. If nothing else, he is showing people how that is different"*.

Sabel takes a moment to get her thoughts in order, staring back at Dark, still appearing displeased, as she continues to pace by the table. *"Given your connection to him"*, Sabel says to Dark, *"I'd have thought you'd want him as far away from this as possible"*.

"He did not share his intentions with his family", Dark replies. *"Had he of, there would most definitely have been opposition. Not enough to sway him though, I suspect"*. Sabel stops pacing and turns to face the table while still looking at Dark. *"I expect he will encounter some tension when he returns home"*, Dark adds with a slight smirk.

Sabel briefly remains unresponsive, before taking a moment to think as she looks down at the table. *"Well"*, she says, then pauses for a moment. *"It is definitely an interesting development, my sign"*, she says looking back up at Dark.

"It is", Dark replies. *"And it's one that is done. I am sure that there will be much that we can learn from this"*.

Sable shrugs. *"Well, we know now that an"*, she pauses for a moment to get her words correct, *"Eluudian can pass the Zazar test"*. Dark nods, appreciating Sabel's acknowledgment of *"Eluudian"*. Sabel stares intensely at Dark. *"Others may start thinking about it as well"*, Sable goes on to say to her. Dark responds with a quick raise of her eyebrow, knowing exactly what Sabel is hinting at. *"Are you sure you are prepared for that?"*, Sabel asks Dark. *"I may never see you again"*, Sabel adds.

Dark acknowledges Sabel's concern with a simple slow blink. Sabel turns away from the table again. *"If that is your only concern...."*, Dark says to her, before Sable quickly turns back around to face her.

"You know it is", Sabel snaps back at Dark, cutting her off. Sabel again stares intensely at Dark, an anger in her eyes. She takes a deep breath and starts to soften her expression, before looking away again.

Dark remains looking back at her. A familiar intensity in Dark's eyes, but her face showing more concern. A softness. She puts aside Sabel's comment and moves on. *"I believe this situation is one that can benefit us"*, Dark tells her. Sabel is still not so sure, but is intrigued to hear Dark's reasoning. She looks back at Dark, silently, waiting for her to continue. So, Dark does. *"It is a situation the Council has never encountered before"*, Dark explains. *"A council that likes to believe they have plans in place for every scenario. This may be enough to realize they don't"*. Sabel seems even more intrigued now. *"A member of their own Council"*, Dark continues, *"willing to sacrifice everything they have for the change they need. A Council forced to watch change - from within. This change could very well have a cascading effect. That could work for us. Having an Aymyn Zazar could work for us"*.

Sabel smirks and lets out a little giggle. *"You said Aymyn"*, she says to Dark. Dark smiles back at Sabel.

EXOM

THE YOUNG KING

CHAPTER TWENTY

------------------------- Only and Always -------------------------

Aura is in her quarters, pacing. Waiting. She has not seen Steel since he left her in the council chambers to go and do the Zazar Test. Now nearly everyone in the citadel is talking about the Aymyn that has passed it. An Aymyn that is to be sworn in immediately as a Zazar. Even her Handmaiden has seen him more recently than she has. Delivering to her a message from Steel, saying that he will see her soon. So, she has been waiting and pacing in her quarters for the hours since she received that message. Just as she was the hours before she received that message.

She did manage to find time to put on a new gown after being told of the ceremony that she is to attend. A ceremony that officially makes Steel a Zazar. A ceremony that officially means that they can no longer be together. The gown that she has chosen is one that Steel has never seen before. She had it made to surprise him on a future date. It contains the traditional aqua and gold colours of Aymyn, interwoven with strong black highlights to signify Eluud. She loved how it looked, and she had always hoped that Steel would love how it looked on her. She knows that the date this gown was intended for will never happen now. She still wants him to see it. She still wants him to see it on her. She still wants to look nice for him.

As time passes, and she continues pacing, she starts to wonder if she is actually going to see him before the ceremony. More thoughts cross her mind. What will she do if she sees him? When she sees him? If he was to walk into her quarters right now? Would she hug him, kiss him, or would that be too painful? If she saw him before the ceremony, it would literally be to break up. She is happy, and very relieved, that he amazingly and surprisingly passed the Zazar Test. However, she has still lost him either way.

The door to her quarters opens. It makes her jump. Even though she has been waiting for it, it still startles her. She turns and looks towards the doorway. Steel is standing there. Aura stops pacing and stands facing him, looking at him with a blank expression. It is blank because she is filled with so many different emotions right now, now that she is looking at him. Love, sadness, relief, her face does not know which one to express. Steel enters her room and starts walking towards her as the door closes behind him. Aura stands still, watching him walk towards her. Steel can see the uncertainty in Aura, the confusion, the sadness and stops in front of her. The same emotions that consume Aura, he also finds himself drowning in. He wants to hug her, hold her, but not sure if he should, if he is allowed to. She wants him too as well but can not get herself to move.

"You passed", She says to him.

Steel nods. *"Yes. I passed"*, he replies. For the first time, as Steel says those words, they are filled with sadness instead of joy. With those words, also seeing Steel standing in front of her to say them, comes the realization to Aura that everything she is upset about is really happening. It is not just playing out in her mind; it is standing right in front of her. They stand looking at each other for a while. Then Steel walks up to Aura, to hug her, but Aura walks away and turns her back to him. Not out of anger or to hurt him. Not even to reject or discourage him. She just feels herself shrinking into herself and does not know what to do. She stares blankly at the wall, tears building up in her eyes.

Steel stops and does not try to approach her. He stands there looking at her, not sure what to do. He looks back at the door, wondering if he should just leave. He doesn't want to leave. He looks back at Aura, the back of her, and feels like he should not stay. He wants to stay. He looks at the door one more time then, taking a deep breath, walks up to Aura, puts his arms around her and buries his face into her neck. Aura instinctively goes to put her hands on Steel's arms but stops herself just before making contact with him. Her hand hovers about an inch over his arm. She stares at her hand. Steel stands there holding her. His eyes closed and his face pressed against her head and neck. He does not see her struggling, wanting to touch him and hold him as well. He pulls himself away and walks straight to her door. It opens and he walks out. Aura does not move. She listens as she hears him leave and the door close behind him. The tears finally escape her eyes and run down her face.

Steel marches quickly down the corridors of the Citadel towards his own quarters. He passes many Aymyn citizens and soldiers. They stop and look at him, but Steel does not look at any of them and just keeps marching straight ahead. His gaze showing that he is lost in his own thoughts - and they are not happy ones.

Aura remains standing in her quarters. Tears still rolling down her cheek. She tries to straighten herself up, wipes her tears away, but they keep flowing. She is also lost in her own thoughts. Even breathing seems difficult as she takes the occasional gasp.

Steel marches right up to his quarters. The door opens, he walks straight inside, and the door closes behind him.

Aura wipes her tears away again and turns to look at her door. Only moments before, the love of her life was standing there. She knew he wasn't any longer, but something inside her was still hoping, maybe, but no. The tears again start to flow.

Steel stands in his quarters, dressing himself in preparation for the ceremony. He has everything on except for his royal coat. He looks over at his drawers and stares at his holographic photo of both him and Aura together. Next to the photo is his Tription handle. Steel walks over to pick up his Tription handle, however, as he reaches for it, he stops and looks at the photo. His hand starts moving towards the photo. He goes to touch the photo, but it is only a hologram, there is nothing there to touch, and his hand passes right through it. He takes a moment, standing there, still holding his hand through the hologram. He moves his hand back, picks up the Tription handle and attaches it to his belt.

He picks up his royal coat and is about to put it on, when he suddenly stops. He turns around and notices the jacket that Aura bought for him hanging in his wardrobe. He lets go of his royal coat, letting it drop to the floor. Then walks over to his wardrobe, grabbing the jacket that Aura bought for him instead and walks out of his quarters.

Steel walks through a large double doorway that leads outside to the Grand Stage in the Citadel Gardens. He has just finished putting on his new jacket and there are already many people on stage waiting for him to appear, including Zargah and several Morn Zazars who are all lined up. In front of Zargah and the other Morn is Kalrain, still dressed in the same flowing red dress and holding her staff. Standing beside her, chosen to preside over today's ceremony, is Princess Illyana. Lastly, standing off the side of the stage, is regent Bassal, King Yord, as well as the Aymyn General and an escort of Aymyn soldiers.

Hundreds, if not thousands, of Aymyn citizens and Citadel staff, including some guards, crowd together on the ground to the front of the stage, eager to get a glimpse of this Aymyn that is about to become a Zazar. Princess Illyana smiles, and gives a little wave, to some children right at the front of the stage, who are jumping up and down to get a better look.

As Steel walks out onto the stage, the crowd starts to clap. Steel smiles at them, though it seems pained and forced. He looks over at Regent Bassal and King Yord, expecting to also see Aura. She is not there. He looks at the General and his soldiers. She is not with them either. Steel's smile quickly fades as he turns and looks at Kalrain. Kalrain looks back at him, then motions with her head for him to stand at the front of the stage by Princess Illyana. Steel looks over at Illyana. She is still smiling and waving at the children in front of the stage. He walks over to her, as Aura walks out onto the stage from a side door. She is accompanied by her handmaiden and four Aymyn soldier escorts. She takes her position at the side of the stage with the other Councillors and General.

Not having seen Aura come out, Steel takes his place in front of the line of Zazars, then faces Kalrain and the Troin Princess. Illyana smiles at him. Not just a courteous hospitable smile, but a real one, she is very happy to see him. Aura notices that Steel is wearing the jacket she bought for him and can no longer hold herself together. She turns around and cries into her hands. Immediately she is comforted by her handmaiden. Aura is distraught and struggling to breathe.

Steel glances over and sees Aura. Sees her crying. Feels his heart stop beating. Kalrain also looks over and sees her too. Steel is about to run to Aura, but Kalrain looks back at Steel, holds out her staff and stops him. Steel looks at Kalrain as she shakes her head. Steel knows that running to Aura right now would show everyone that, not only is he unable to make the commitment to the Zazar Corp over Aura, but it would also put a question over Aura's head about whether she can stay committed to the Royal Council law. Specifically, the one regarding relationships with those outside of the Council. Steel is finding this extremely difficult. As he stands there watching Aura, his heart breaking, just wanting to run to her. Hug her, comfort her, and make everything alright. But he knows he can't.

Aura recomposes herself and turns back around to face the stage, face Steel, but still looking extremely sad with tears still rolling down her cheek.

Zargah walks up and stands right behind Steel. Illyana places her hand on Steels head and then Kalrain places hers on top of Illyana's. Steel looks back at both Illyana and Kalrain, then bows his head. Zargah places his hand on top of both Illyana and Kalrain's. Zargah's hand almost covering Steel's head. Illyana starts to say a few words, but though Aura watches on she is unable to hear them. Her sadness has deafened her. Zargah, Kalrain and Illyana raise their hands. Kalrain then turns to face the audience and produces a large Tription Flame sword from her staff. Steel looks at Kalrain's staff, amazed. He knew her staff was made from Tription, but this is the first time he has seen her summon a Flame from it. Zargah then raises his Tription handle up and also produces a Tription sword, holding it up high. *"Only and Always!"*, Zargah yells. The rest of the Zazars then raise their Tription handles, and, like Zargah, they produce Tription Swords, holding them up high and yell out, *"Only and Always!"*

Steel smiles, his sadness distracted now by his excitement. He pulls out his Tription handle, summons the Flame sword and holds it high.

"Only and Always!", Steel also yells out. He then stops smiling and looks back at Aura who is just staring at him with tears still flowing. *"Only and always"*, she softly and sadly says to herself.

Again, Aura can no longer hold her composure. She breaks down. Crying, she quickly turns around, walks off the stage and back inside the citadel, escorted by her handmaiden. Steel watches her leave and lowers his Flame sword. The Flame disappears back into the handle.

Princess Illyana stands in front of Steel again and smiles at him, having not noticed any of what was happening with Aura. *"Zazar Steel"*, she says to him. Steel makes himself look back at Illyana and forces himself to smile. Her words resound in his head. "Zazar Steel". This is the first time he has been called that. It's official now. He is now a Zazar. *"A duty bestowed upon all Zazars of the Zazar Corp, is to select a planet to be their protectorate"*, Illyana tells Steel loudly for all those in attendance to hear. *"This planet will be afforded the full protection of the Zazar Corp and, from nomination, will be referred to as a "Protected Planet". A Zazar may only select one unique and unselected planet to be their protectorate and, once selected, that decision is final until either the Zazar or planet are no more. You do not need to make that decision now. It can be made at any time of your choosing"*. Illyana pauses and again smiles at Steel. She is about to ask a question that she already knows the answer to. *"Zazar Steel, do you have a planet that you wish to name as your protectorate?"*, she asks him. Illyana continues to smile at Steel, awaiting his answer. Steel looks back over at the doorway that Aura just left through, staring blankly at it. Illyana's smile is slowly replaced with a look of confusion. She looks at Steel wondering why he does not answer. It is the moment he has been waiting for. The reason he has done all of this. She thought he'd be screaming his planet's name even before she finishes asking the question. However, going by his blank look, she wonders if he even heard the question. *"Zazar Steel?"*, she says to him, hoping to get his attention.

Kalrain nudges Steel with her hip. It is a gentle-ish nudge but catches him by surprise, almost knocking him over. He shakes himself present, looks at Illyana, and again smiles. She is right, this is the moment that he has been working towards. The whole reason that all of this, all that he has endured and given away, has been for. Everything he has ever wanted, his people have ever wanted, has all come to this moment. The moment when a Zazar selects Eluud as a protected planet. It is now about to happen, and he is that Zazar. The question echoes in his head, *"do you have a planet that you wish to name as your protectorate?"* and he can hardly contain his excitement. But he tries to. He stops smiling and looks at Illyana with a serious stare. *"Oh gosh. I don't know"*, he replies. *"This has all happened so fast. Do you have like a list or anything?"*, he asks her. Princess Illyana looks at Steel confused. Even Kalrain is taken by surprise and looks at Steel with confusion. Steel just smiles at Illyana with a cheeky grin. *"Just kidding"*, he says to her.

-------------------------------- **The Horn** --------------------------------

Det is back sitting on her chair in the Entrance Library. She has a book in her lap which she is pretending to read. Dacos is standing in the Entrance with Trill, speaking to Sergeant Mew, when a Communication Officer comes running down from the corridor and stops in front of Dacos. He is breathless, as though he has been running all over the castle. *"General!"*, the Communication Officer says fervently, his eyes wide and filled with excitement. He looks at Trill, *"Commander"*, he says with equal excitement. He looks back at Dacos. *"General"*, he says again. *"Everyone"*, he then adds. Dacos, Trill and Mew all look at the Communication Officer with interest. He appears to have something to say, and by his expression it does not appear to be anything bad. *"Come with me"*, the Communication Officer says to them.

Trill looks at Dacos, confused. Not only having no idea what the Communication Officer wants with them, but also confused that the Communication Officer has just given the General an order. Dacos knows why Trill is giving him that look. However, more intrigued with what the Communication Officer wants, he waves Trills look off and nod at the Officer. *"Okay"*, Dacos replies, looking at the Communication Officer curiously.

The Communication Officer starts walking excitedly back up the corridor, as both Dacos and Trill follow him. Det peers over the book she is pretending to read. At first, she looks curious, but then her expression changes, and it is almost like she knows what they have rushed off to see. She does not move from her chair, but watches Trill and Dacos leave with the Communication Officer. Sergeant Mew looks over at Det. He is curious to know what is happening. Det notices him looking at her, so raises the book up in front of her face, going back to pretending to read.

The Communication Officer enters the Communications Room and holds the door open for Dacos. Dacos walks in followed by his sister. Still neither of them knowing what is going on, a second Communication Officer hands Dacos a message stick. The Second Communication Officer looks as excited as the one that brought Dacos and Trill into the room. Dacos takes the message stick, activates it, and the small projection screen displays in front of him. He reads it. As he reads it, he puts his hand on Trill's shoulder. Not to get her attention, but for support as he feels his legs go weak beneath him. His expression first one of shock, then amazement. Trill feels Dacos's weight on her shoulder and looks up at him, wondering what is going on. *"What is it?"*, she asks him.

Dacos hands Trill the message stick. She quickly takes it, then starts to read it as Dacos stands there looking at all the officers in the room. They all look back at him, everyone now with sheer excitement on their faces. Trill finishes reading the message stick, then looks up at Dacos, stunned. Dacos looks down at Trill. They both smile at each other. They then look over at the giant shielded button on the wall that activates the horn. The Officers all move out of the way as Dacos and Trill run straight for it. Dacos throws the button's protective shield up and it stays open. He looks back down at Trill and nods. They both reach up, putting their hands on the button, and press it together.

Outside in the Castle gardens, the sun is set high in the sky. It seems like any other ordinary sunny day. The Eluudians are carrying on with their usual business. Children are playing together, as adults sit and soak in the calm atmosphere. Soldiers march casually along the footpath towards the barracks, smiling at Eluudian civilians as they pass them, the civilians smiling back. A very young girl child runs up to a soldier and grabs onto his leg, as another young boy child runs up and tags her. She doesn't think it's fair, as she believes touching the soldier's leg should protect her from being tagged in this game, and she starts to argue with the young boy. The Soldier crouches down and tries to mediate. Over at a simple hut on the outskirts of the gardens, a husband is carrying in some firewood as his wife holds the door open for him. He is carrying in more than what will fit through the door. As he tries to squeeze through with the firewood, his wife stands by removing wood from the pile he is carrying and throws it on another pile just outside the door.

Suddenly, the giant horn on top of Chassam Castle begins to sound. It is loud and piercing. Loud enough to be heard for hundreds of miles, as the treble rumbles and vibrates through the ground. It is something that no Eluudian has ever heard before, so no one is quite sure what it is that they are hearing or what is going on. Some look concerned, worried that it may be an alarm of some kind. Everyone stops what they are doing, including the young children, the soldier mediating, the husband carrying wood, and parents relaxing in the gardens. They all look up at the castle, towards where the loud sound is coming from. The giant horn on the roof of the castle. Eluudians come out of their homes, some concerned, some confused, but all interested to know what the sound is about. The husband carrying the wood realizes what it is and what it means. While still staring up at the horn, he drops the pile of wood that he is carrying. His wife looks at him confused. He looks back at her, a smile growing larger on his face as his expression turns to one of sheer excitement. Seeing his face, his smile, his excitement, the wife also works out what is happening and her expression changes to match his. They grab hold of each other and start jumping up and down. The mediating soldier stands up, still confused, looking at the horn as his comrade pats him on the back, having himself worked out what has happened. The soldiers both look at each other, now both knowing what this means. The children still stand by the soldiers' legs, having no idea what is going on.

Orlow is standing in the middle of a corridor within the Castle. He was about to take a bite out of the piece of fruit that he is holding, until he heard the Horn sound. He now stands frozen, mouth still open and his hand still holding the piece of fruit in front of him.

The Queen Mother is just outside the Castle Main Doors with the Albearian Twins. The Twins start looking around the grounds as the Queen Mother looks up at the Horn, instantly working out what is happening. She pats her chest, as her jaw drops, and a look of excited relief falls over her.

Tespa is sitting on her bed. She has been trying to dress Kako but has now stopped, and he has stopped trying to fight her. They are both now just sitting there, wide-eyed, as Tespa is trying to work out if she is hearing what she thinks she is hearing. The door to her bedroom bursts open. Vessel stands in the doorway, looking at her and bursting with excitement. Her expression confirms Tespa's suspicion and Tespa starts to smile with excitement as tears well up in her eyes. Vessel just stands in the doorway, silent, and nods.

Inside a simple small hut, Zippin is sitting down on a small stool in front of six young children, who are all sitting on the floor in front of her. Zippin has her mouth dropped open, appearing a bit shocked as she looks towards a window. She stands up and looks out the window at the many Eluudians gathering in the gardens, staring up at the horn, smiling with excitement and hugging each other. She turns back and looks at the children, her jaw still dropped, tears of joy start to run down her cheek.

As the Eluudians work out what is happening, some taking a little longer than others, but catch on quickly when observing the reactions of everyone else around them, the Castle gardens is filled with revelling. Many are jumping, cheering, and hugging each other. Some are even crying, overwhelmed with emotions. Eluudians are walking up to each other, patting each other on the back and shaking their hands. One Eluudian is even laying on the grass, flapping out his arms and legs as if to make a grass angel.

Det is still sitting in the Entrance Library. The book still on her lap. She has stopped pretending to read and just sits there listening to the

Horn. She knows what it means but does not seem to be excited. If anything, she seems a little concerned by the reactions of the people both inside and outside of the Castle. She repositions herself on the chair, crosses her legs and returns to pretending to read the book.

High up in a tree, in the forest miles away from Chassam Castle, the celebration is being watched closely by R'Vian. She shows no excitement, nor disappointment. She shows no reaction at all. If anything, her interest has been sparked, since not being an Eluudian, or even having been on Eluud all that long, she does not know what the horn means. She doesn't know that Eluud has just become a protected planet. However, watching the reactions of the Eluudian people in the distance, she knows that whatever that horn means, it is a good thing.

www.ingramcontent.com/pod-product-compliance
Lightning Source LLC
Chambersburg PA
CBHW031142050726
47495CB00018B/433